D1615825

**THE BRUTAL
SHOCK-WAVE NOVEL
THAT WILL CHANGE
YOUR VIEW
OF WORLD WAR II.**

DEATH DEALERS

The SS soldiers were no more than twenty paces away, with their arms raised in surrender. Kessler lowered the machine gun and opened fire. When he was finished, the three soldiers were lying on the ground like butchered cattle. Beccione was stunned.

"O.K. So they were SS murderers. They kill old men and women and children. But where does this put us, Kessler? We're no better than they are."

THE
WAR GOD

Frederick E. Smith

THE WAR GOD
A Bantam Book / May 1981

First published in Great Britain in 1980

ISBN 0-553-13663-1

Published simultaneously in the United States and Canada

Bantam Books are published by Bantam Books, Inc. Its trade-
mark, consisting of the words "Bantam Books" and the por-
trayal of a Bantam, is Registered in U.S. Patent and Trademark
Office and in other countries. Marca Registrada. Bantam
Books, Inc., 666 Fifth Avenue, New York, New York 10103.

PRINTED IN THE UNITED STATES OF AMERICA

0 9 8 7 6 5 4 3 2 1

To my old and dear friend
David Doig
who shared the long and sometimes
exciting journey through Italy with me.

The author wishes to acknowledge his debt to the following books and works of reference:

War in Val D'Orcia   by Iris Origo.
Love and War in the Apennines   by Eric Newby.
Popski's Private Army   by Vladimir Peniakoff.
History of the Second World War   by Purnell.
Pebbles in My Skull   by Stuart Hood.

Part I

Part I

1

The tanks and their transporters were parked in a wide clearing on one side of the pass. Steep slopes covered with shrubs and dwarf trees rose on three sides. In the gathering dusk glimpses of snow-covered peaks could be seen. Although Basilicata and Calabria in the south were said to be enjoying a freak heatwave, it was still winter in the Marche and the wind that was sweeping down the pass had the cutting edge of a knife.

As darkness crept down, the glow of braziers and fires brightened against the uniforms of the German and Italian troops huddled around them. The men were talking quietly, their spirits subdued by the bitter cold. The German soldiers in this tank division had been brought over the Brenner Pass into Italy the previous September when Badoglio had made his armistice with the Allies. As a result of the Allied threat at Anzio, they had been ordered to move south immediately. A platoon of Italian fascist militia was dispatched to guide them through the maze of narrow roads and steep mountains that made up the Marche.

Few of the Germans shared their fires and food with the fascist militia. Since Badoglio's capitulation and the defection of some Italian units, the Germans' distrust of their allies extended even to the zealous Italian Black Shirts. The German

3

tank crews accepted the wine the Italians offered them, but offered little back in friendship.

A group of German officers was huddled around a brazier at the back of the clearing. The tank commander, a veteran of the Russian front, could have enjoyed his meal in his tent, but to his officers' secret dismay he insisted on sharing his men's discomforts. His face was visible in the glow of the brazier, lined and thoughtful with iron-grey hair.

A junior officer excused himself, set aside his plate and rose. All day his stomach had been upset—he blamed Italian food—and a need to defecate had suddenly become urgent. He began climbing the steep slope at the back of the clearing. Here the shadows were dense and he searched for a place to squat. As he paused behind a clump of rocks and began to unfasten his belt, a shadowy figure appeared behind him and thrust a knife expertly through his ribs to his heart. With no more than a gasp, he sagged forward. His attacker lowered his body to the ground and sank down beside it. A moment later a second shadowy figure dropped down behind the rocks. When the first man nodded at his question, he pulled a Very pistol out of his belt. Five seconds later a star shell burst high above the clearing.

The effect was startling. The tanks and the upturned faces of the crews seemed to leap upwards in the icy light. For a long moment time was petrified. Then the spell was shattered like glass as a machine gun began chattering from the northern side of the clearing. It was followed by a dozen more, the din reverberating across the clearing and from the mountains.

Some men were killed before they could drop their mess tins. Others, who managed to scramble to their feet, toppled into braziers. In the stark light of the flare their shadows looked like wolves dragging them down by the heels. Thin screaming could be heard through the rattle of the guns.

The tank commander, who had survived more than one partisan ambush in Russia, was yelling orders to check the panic. If his men could reach their tanks they could turn the table on their attackers.

But their attackers were as aware of this as anyone. As the tank commander and a young lieutenant ran towards the nearest tank, something streaked past them with a paralyzing roar and the vehicle disappeared in a cloud of smoke and flame. The young lieutenant, his voice shrill with fear, caught the commander's arm. "That was a panzerfaust, sir. Who the hell are these people?"

More rockets were spearing out from the hillsides, adding their hideous din to the gunfire, the shouts and the screams. Tanks had their tracks blown off, transporters burst into flames. Nothing in the clearing—Germans, Italians, tanks and transports—was spared.

The tank commander found himself lying alongside a wounded Italian as a second star shell rose. It was clearly meant as a signal because by this time the slaughter was fully illuminated by the blazing vehicles. The Italian lifted his head, gave a cry and pointed at the hillside above. Following his gaze, the tank commander saw a tall gaunt figure in German uniform standing in full view of the clearing. Bathed in blood-red light, the man was staring down at the slaughter with a look that was at once triumphant and tormented.

The Italian gave a moan and tried to cross himself. The German commander, an imaginative man, wondered if it might be some image created by the fear, agony and death all around him. It was a question that did not haunt him for long. A burst of machine gun fire, sweeping across the clearing, hurled him over and left him staring sightlessly at the crimson sky.

"Hey, Joe. Sergeant Stanton wants to see you."

Joe Beccione turned. The bright sunlight in the doorway made him narrow his eyes. "Who says?"

"Corporal Watson says." The silhouette in the doorway moved forward. "You want me to take your hand until you get back?"

"The hell I do. Stanton can wait." Beccione turned back to the makeshift table littered with cards and money. Four other men were seated around on ammunition boxes. Until Baker Company had moved into Castelmonte, the stone building had been a stable. Now it was an armory with three racks of rifles and a bench complete with a sizer, vice, and tools. Ammunition and grenade boxes were stacked round the walls. There was an odor of manure beneath the smell of gun oil and sweat that no amount of scrubbing and whitewash had been able to dispel.

Because of the freak heatwave, all five card players were stripped to the waist. Attracted by their sweat, insects were buzzing around the table and a man cursed as he slapped a horsefly from his neck. Baker Company had been in residence in Castelmonte for eight weeks and nerves were beginning to fray. Combat soldiers from the U.S. 6th Corps, they had been sent into the mountains after fighting at Salerno and the Volturno. They were divided among three villages that lay along supply routes to the 5th and 8th armies. Officially on rest, their task was to provide escorts for convoys whose route lay through the mountain sector. With the Front already miles to the north, the men had greeted their role with derision. But, since it provided a rest from the desperate fighting along the Garigliano, no one had voiced any real objection at the time.

As spring drew nearer, however, the men's moods had changed. The escort duty was spasmodic, irksome and worst of all seemed pointless. With no outlet for the aggression their combat training had instilled in them, they had become bored and irritable. Extra Military Police had been brought in to keep order in the sector.

Beccione, determined to ignore the messenger, turned to the soldier on his right, a skinny man with a face like a sad spaniel. "What's your move, Koslo? You seeing me or throwing in?"

The man's face remained mournful but there was excitement in his voice. "I ain't doin' neither, Joe. I'm doublin'."

A murmur ran round the table as Koslo pushed a wad of lire into the pot. This was the second time that Koslo had doubled that afternoon. A powerfully-built soldier with tattooed forearms gave a grunt of disappointment and tossed in his cards. "You think I'm crazy?"

Beccione grinned. "He could be bluffin', Fisher."

"Yeah. And pigs could fly."

Beccione's eyes moved on to a dark-skinned soldier whose small-boned face and liquid brown eyes made him look little more than a schoolboy. "What about you, Nunez?"

The Puerto Rican shrugged and let his cards fall gently on the table. "Too good for me, Joe. *Finito*."

The fifth soldier at the table was a few years older than the others, a man of Jewish origin with a crumpled face and thatch of untidy black hair. As he pondered over his cards, Wilkinson, the messenger, moved nearer to Beccione. He was a tall bespectacled youth with a crew cut. "You'd better move your ass, Joe. Watson said it was important and Stanton's only waiting to jump on you."

Beccione's eyes stayed on Rosenberg. "I said to hell with

Stanton. What're you doing, Rocky? Seeing Koslo or raising?"

Rosenberg was known for his sense of humor. "What're you tryin' to do, Joe? Ruin me?"

"I'm not trying anything except to remind you it'll be Christmas in ten months."

Rosenberg grinned. "Maybe that's what I need. Santa Claus." He pushed forward a wad of notes. "I always was a sucker. I'm seeing Koslo."

All eyes turned back to Beccione. With curly black hair and a square rugged face, he was a handsome man whose features were marred only by heavy scar tissue over both his eyes. The scars gave him a withdrawn and slightly menacing expression. Beccione picked up a fistful of notes and laid a pile on the table. His voice was a flat monotone. "And I'm doubling him."

The players stirred expectantly. Wilkinson whistled and tried to move behind Beccione. "What've you got there, Joe? Four aces?"

Without warning, Beccione swung round and shoved Wilkinson away. Then he turned back to Koslo. The man was trying to control his expression, but there was a faint twitching of the small muscles around his eyes and mouth. Beccione was figuring him for a flush or full house. He'd bought one card and was too yellow to bluff this high.

Koslo was stalling for time. "How much to see you?"

Beccione pushed his bid towards him. "Count it!"

Koslo obeyed, then pushed the money into the center of the table. "You bought one card, didn't you?"

"He called his buy," Rosenberg told him. "You should keep your flaps open." He threw in his cards. "I'm runnin'."

Koslo turned and appealed to Fisher. "A guy's entitled to ask the dealer what he's bought, isn't he?"

"I bought one," Beccione said before Fisher could answer. "And so did you." He grinned. "Your flush against my full house. You calling me or quitting?"

There were beads of sweat on Koslo's forehead now. A cautious man and a bad loser, he had enjoyed an almost lustful feeling when he had bought the fifth card to an ace high flush. Now the excitement was gone, replaced by the familiar sensation of being trapped. With a curse he hurled his cards down on the table. "Sonofabitch, I didn't make it."

It was clear nobody believed him. Beccione shrugged, laid his cards face down and drew in the pile of notes. As he began straightening them, Fisher gave a loud laugh and snatched the cards up. "Let's take a look what you had." His laugh choked between surprise and anger. "Two pairs—five high? Christ, I had better cards than that."

A second later Fisher felt the makeshift table drive brutally against his legs and throw him off the ammunition box. Coming round the table fast, Beccione grabbed him under the arms, lifted him bodily and slammed him against a rack of rifles. He pushed his face, black with anger, right up next to Fisher's. "Don't you ever do that again! You hear me? Never again."

Before Fisher could find his breath, he was swung round and thrown against the workbench. Beccione's expression killed any lingering thought he had of retaliation. Beccione snatched up his cap and shirt and turned to Rosenberg. "Sort out my winnings, will you, Rocky? I'll go see what Stanton wants."

For a moment his massive frame dimmed the sunlight in the doorway, then he was gone. Fisher cursed as he pushed himself away from the bench. "The sonofabitch! What the hell did he do that for? It's only a chickenshit game, isn't it?"

Rosenberg shrugged. "Some guys play harder than others. When ya gonna learn that?"

"He's mean," Fisher said. Across the armory Wilkinson nodded his agreement. Lighting a cigarette, Fisher discovered his fingers were trembling and his resentment flared again. "That sonofabitch is vicious and mean. I hope Stanton fixes him good."

2

A narrow cobbled street radiated from the center of the small mountain town. Bleached cottages flanked it on one side, a row of dusty gum trees on the other. Behind the gums was a steep and dried-up river bed that served as a sewer. Scrawny chickens pecked along its banks and a mangy dog lay asleep beneath a bush. An old woman in a black shawl dumped a can of garbage into it and shuffled back to her cottage. The hazy peaks of mountains rose and dipped in the blue sky.

An old man sitting on a doorstep bared his teeth in a grin

as Beccione passed by. Two women gossiping in the road turned. The younger of the two smiled approvingly. Beccione had shrugged on his shirt after leaving the armory but it could not hide his teak-tough body. The older woman turned away. In Italy in 1944 both emotions and allegiances were confused. Today it was the Americans but tomorrow it might be the *Tedeschi* again. The bold declared their preference; the cautious hedged their bets.

Thirty yards down the road two boys were fighting. As a man on a bicycle approached the bigger boy ran off. The smaller boy, his shirt half torn off his back, ran into a cottage opposite. A moment later a woman's scolding voice jarred the still air. The American's face tightened. For him, it was a sound only too reminiscent of his own childhood.

The son of an immigrant Italian family, Joe Beccione had been born in the decaying tenements of New York's Hell's Kitchen three years after World War I. The analogy of a cub born of two wild tigers into a jungle would not have been an exaggeration. From the moment he could identify sight and sound, the infant Joe had been assaulted by the hostility and endless quarreling of his parents. Because he had been the handcuff that had chained the hating couple together, the child had suffered the resentment of both.

As he listened now to this Italian mother punish her child, he thought of another small boy ripping his clothes in a fight he could not avoid. His apprehensive return home up the dingy tenement steps, the sound of voices raised in argument before he opened the door, two hate-filled faces turning to stare at him. Then his father's yell of rage, the thwack of his belt, the cries of pain the boy sought to suppress, the burning shame when he failed.

The Italian boy was crying bitterly as Beccione passed by the cottage and the American felt a strong desire to slap the face of the woman who was punishing him. The aggression did not subside as he approached the large MP tent that was Stanton's HQ. It stood just inside a fenced enclosure that surrounded the transport pool on the outskirts of the town. Although Beccione was a good combat soldier, he could never see Germans in the same light that his NCOs and officers did. As far as he was concerned, you killed them because they were trying to kill you—but when the fighting was over they were not worth the trouble of hating. You kept your hatred for the Army that had screwed up your life and for sons-ofbitches like Stanton.

Ducking under the tent flap, Beccione found Stanton seated behind the desk. As always the NCO was immaculately turned out—his slacks tucked into white gaiters and his MP helmet resting on the table alongside him. Strapped around his waist was a .38 Smith and Wesson revolver. A big man with shoulders like an all-in wrestler, Stanton had a large roll of fat above his belt; but Joe knew there would be muscle beneath it. With his round, close-cropped head, fleshy cheeks and loud laughter, Stanton could seem almost avuncular until you noticed his small eyes. A top sergeant in the provost unit that policed Baker Company, he was a man who enjoyed his work. And Beccione—renowned for his dislike of the Army and its authoritarian structure—would be an especially challenging horse for Stanton to break.

Stanton was talking to a fair-headed corporal when Beccione entered the tent. "I got a message from Watson you want to see me. That right?"

Stanton eyed the GI for a moment, then reached out a hairy arm and picked up a truncheon. Weighing it carefully, he laid it alongside his helmet before answering. The evenness of his voice emphasized its menace. "Next time you're ordered to come here, Beccione, you'll stand outside and ask permission to enter. You got that, Beccione?"

Face expressionless, Beccione nodded.

"Another thing—who's Watson? Corporal Watson?"

"Who else?"

"Then call him Corporal Watson. Say it, Beccione."

Beccione looked at him with loathing. "Corporal Watson."

"That's better. You'd better start showing some respect for your NCOs, soldier, or your ass is going to fry."

The fair-haired corporal laughed. Beccione glanced at him and the man's laughter died. Stanton jabbed a tobacco-stained forefinger at his gold watch. "What took you so long to get here?"

"Nothing. I had to walk."

Stanton picked up the heavy truncheon, grinned and pressed his legs in readiness against the ground. "Where from? Carlotta's brothel or your girl friend's bedroom?"

Beccione's powerful body stiffened. "You haven't said why you wanted to see me yet."

"That's right, I haven't. You're on duty tonight. In my squad."

"Your squad?"

"Yeah. A couple of my guys are down with stomach trouble, so Corporal Watson's helping me out."

"But I've got a pass for tonight."

"You mean you *had* a pass, Beccione."

"What do you want me in your squad for? I'm not a cop."

Stanton grinned. "If we wanted you to be a cop, Beccione, we'd soon make you one. Your job tonight is riding shotgun on a convoy coming up from Ariano. You're to relieve the guys in the first jeep when it pulls in. Corporal Jackson here will be in overall charge."

Beccione's scarred eyes moved to the fair-haired NCO. "You mean he's riding with me?"

"Naw. He'll take over the second jeep. Rosenberg's riding with you."

"Rosenberg?"

"Yeah. Tell him when you get back. What's the matter? You and he are buddies, aren't you?"

"Who're we guarding against? I thought the nearest Heinies were thirty odd miles away."

Stanton leaned forward. "You're forgetting our friends the Wops. You have to keep an eye on those bastards, Beccione. They're so treacherous they'd steal the panties off your old mother." Seeing a muscle flex in Beccione's cheek, Stanton grinned and leaned back again. "What's your problem? I was sure you'd enjoy a run outta this one-horse town. Were you taking your girl to the dance tonight?"

"What time do we report here?" Beccione ignored his digs.

"After chow. 19.00 hours sharp. You'll have to wait for a return convoy so you might be away a coupla days."

"Is that all?"

Stanton eyed the big GI reflectively. "Yeah, that's all for the moment. Only make sure you're here at 19.00 hours. If you're late again I'll run you right into the stockade."

Without another word Beccione turned and ducked beneath the tent flap. The corporal listened to the thud of his footsteps dying away. "How do you explain it—a guy as mean as that?"

Stanton grinned. "Beccione? I got him all figured out. Authority problem. A guy in Records told me he spent eight years in a kid's home in Brooklyn. It appears his mother dumped him there before running off with a car salesman. The home was run by a gang of Evangelists and you know how those hell and brimstone guys handle tough kids. He ran off when he was around thirteen and got himself into a reformatory a couple of years later. They say there wasn't a racket in New York he hadn't been in."

"I sure thought he was going to kick his slats when you talked about his girl friend," Jackson reflected.

Stanton shook his head as he lit a cigarette. "Naw: he's not that dumb. In fact he ain't dumb at all. But one of these days he's gonna make a slip and then I'll have him."

Curiosity gave the corporal a rare courage. "He gets under your hide, don't he? I ain't seen anyone do this to you before."

Prepared for a rebuff he relaxed as Stanton exhaled smoke before turning towards him. "You want to know why, Jackson? I like this man's army. I've been in it since I was a kid and it's kinda like family to me. So I hate sonsofbitches like Beccione who try to screw it up."

The corporal nodded doubtfully. "Just the same, they say he's a good soldier. He got mentioned in dispatches at Salerno."

Stanton spat down on the earthen floor. "Any guy fights when someone chases his ass with a bayonet, Jackson. There's a hell of a sight more to being a good soldier than that, like being properly dressed and obeying orders and having pride in one's outfit. Guys like Beccione are like rotten apples: if you leave 'em alone, in no time at all the whole barrel's gone sour. You ever stopped to think what we'd do if our armies went sour on us, Jackson?"

Jackson tried but the effort was too great. "I guess I'd never thought about it that way, sergeant."

"Sure you haven't. Not many people have. But it's still a fact, ain't it? Guys like Beccione screw the Army up; that's why I'm gunning for the sonofabitch."

3

The Via Medici that led towards the piazza was filling rapidly as Beccione turned into it. It was market day in Castelmonte and the stalls that ran down both sides of the street were attracting the crowds as the afternoon grew cooler and the offices closed for the day. Women, elderly men, and American soldiers made up the bulk of the customers. Most of the young male civilians, fearing they would be conscripted to fight against the Allies, had fled into the mountains when the new Fascist government had been formed. Now, with the Americans in possession of Castelmonte, they were beginning to return, but only in dribs and drabs. Allied intentions were still vague to most Italians at this time of the war, and rumors they might still be conscripted, only this time to fight the Germans, were keeping many young men still hiding in remote farms and villages.

For the female population this shortage of young males was not as serious as it sounded. The resident American soldiers were doing their considerable best to redress the balance. As they prowled around the stalls, the young girls eyed them covertly in spite of their chaperones' scoldings. Older women tossed their heads or returned their stares boldly according to their temperaments or their needs. Louder than the hum of voices was the normal buzz of city life: the raucous shouts of the vendors, the humorous remarks of sceptical onlookers, the blare of bands and radios. Although the Italians were desperately short of goods to sell, their love of color, crowds and occasions still ensured a scene of considerable vitality.

Beccione heard his name called just as he was about to enter the piazza and caught sight of a small boy pushing through a crowd that surrounded a vegetable stall. The boy was half-carrying, half-dragging two large baskets. Relieved that the American had seen him, he let out another shrill cry before taking a fresh grasp of his load. "Hi, Joe. Wait for me!"

Grinning, Beccione called to him in Italian. "Hiya, kid. You buying up the market?"

The boy was panting hard from his exertions. He was nine years old, thinly-built with an attractive face beneath a shock of brown hair. "I'm meeting Maria. She asked me to shop for her so she could get home early." The boy grinned mischievously at the soldier. "I think she wants time to make herself pretty for tonight."

Beccione's expression changed at the reminder. He reached down. "You'd better give me those baskets."

The boy clung to the larger. "I can carry one."

"Sure you can. Only I'm going to look stupid if you carry the bigger one, aren't I? You got to think about things like that, kid."

The boy exchanged baskets reluctantly. His hero-worship for the big American showed in his face as Beccione effortlessly swung the basket to his shoulder. "You're very strong, aren't you, Joe?"

"I get by, kid. Where're you meeting Maria?"

"By the statue." Stephano reached up to glance at Beccione's watch. "She won't be long. The bank closes in five minutes."

The statue, which was of Bacchus, stood on a huge stone plinth in the center of the piazza. Two pigeons, perched on the god's hoary head, watched the tall soldier and the small boy cross the cobblestones and sit on the stone steps that surrounded the plinth. The boy talked heatedly, occasionally gesturing or jumping up in excitement. The soldier nodded and smiled his encouragement. They were both obviously enjoying themselves.

The Town Hall clock began chiming and a minute later a girl emerged from the bank. Before she had time to notice the couple opposite, Stephano put two fingers into his mouth and let out a piercing whistle. As she waved, Beccione grabbed the two baskets and made towards her. "C'mon, kid. I'm short on time."

The boy had to scamper to keep up with his long strides. The girl smiled as they approached. "Hello, Joe. I didn't expect you so early. What's happened?"

"Hiya, kid. I'll tell you later." Beccione made no attempt to kiss her: by this time he had learned the facts of life about Italian country towns.

He had met Maria Marini seven weeks ago when she had been doing voluntary service in a GI canteen. He decided there and then that she was the best looking girl he had ever seen. Taller than most Italians, slim yet shapely, with black hair that fell down to her waist, she had a natural grace that made him feel clumsy beside her. And proud to be seen with her.

With Beccione's entire sexual history one of easy lays and prostitutes, his first approach had naturally been direct and uncomplicated. When she had shown interest in him he had expected sex to follow immediately. When it had not, no one was more surprised than Beccione that he had wanted to continue seeing her.

"I met Joe in the market," Stephano told the girl. "He took one of the baskets. He didn't need to. I could have managed."

"Listen to him," Maria said to the American. "Back home he grumbled I was giving him too much to carry." She turned back to the boy. "What happened to your friend who was going to help you?"

"He went off to play baseball," the boy muttered. "He was given a bat and a ball by some Americans."

"Never mind. You can play with him tomorrow. Did you buy everything on my list?"

"Everything but a cabbage."

Beccione fished into his pocket and pulled out a couple of notes. "Why don't you go and buy it now? And get yourself some candy at the same time."

The boy grinned impishly and pointed at a street that ran parallel to the market. "If you want to give her a kiss, that's the street to take. It's always quiet down there."

"Stephano! Stop talking like that!" Before the girl could say more, Beccione took her arm and steered her away.

"That's some kid brother you've got. Let's take his advice."

She hesitated a moment, then allowed him to lead her down the narrow street. It had no sidewalks and green-shuttered houses rose like walls on either side, keeping out the sunlight and cooling the air. A cat was washing itself on a casement sill but otherwise the street was empty.

They walked for a full fifteen seconds before Maria spoke. "What is happening? Are you coming home with me?"

He lowered the basket and turned to her. "No, I won't have the time. That's what I came to tell you. The dance is off."

She looked disappointed. "Why? Are you on duty?"

"It's that sonofabitch Stanton again." Joe and Maria conversed mostly in Italian, but when he wanted to swear he did it in English—a language she understood imperfectly. "He's fixed me up with escort duty. I might be away three or four days."

"You always seem to be in trouble with Stanton. Are you sure you don't provoke him?"

"Of course I don't provoke him. He just doesn't like me, that's all." His expression softened as his gaze ran down her shapely body.

She glanced nervously down the narrow street. "Not here, Joe. Someone might see us."

"So what?" Lifting her face he kissed her hard on the mouth. Then, pushing her against the nearby wall, he ran his lips down her neck. Her skin felt like velvet and turned his voice hoarse. "It has to be soon, Maria. It has to be."

She tried to push him away but he only moved his lips towards her shoulder. Her voice turned angry. "I said no! Stop it, please."

He drew back. "It's always no, isn't it? What's the matter? Don't you like me enough?"

"It has nothing to do with my liking you. This is provincial Italy, not America. If a girl loses her reputation in a town like this, she is treated as a slut."

"You're using that as an excuse. You act just the same when we're alone." When she did not answer him, his voice rose. "Well! Isn't that true?"

She swung round to face him. "You won't try to understand, will you? I believe it is wrong to make love outside the Church. If I did it, I would feel dirty."

He stiffened. "Loving me would make you feel dirty? Now that's something, baby. Really something."

Before the distressed girl could answer, they were interrupted by the squeal of brakes and the impatient blast of a horn. Turning, Beccione saw a huge automobile standing less than six feet from them. The driver, a middle-aged, balding, expensively-dressed Italian, leaned from his window and shouted at the couple. "You two! Behave yourselves and get out of my way."

To Beccione, in his present mood, no interruption could have been more inflammatory or welcome. He reached the automobile door in two strides. "What was that, you punk?"

Shaken by the GI's reaction, the driver made the mistake of blustering. "You soldiers have been warned about this kind of behavior. If I report you, you'll get into serious trouble. So don't make things worse for yourself."

Beccione had the door open before the man finished his threat. He pulled him up by the shirt collar and savagely slapped his face. To the shocked Maria the blows sounded like pistol shots. Hurling the half-stunned man back into his seat, Beccione slammed the door closed. "Now you get the hell out of here, you sonofabitch. Move it!"

The Italian accelerated away, knocking over the larger of the baskets and scattering vegetables on the cobblestones. Through the heat of his anger Beccione heard Maria's reproach. "Why did you have to strike him like that?"

"Who was the sonofabitch?"

"He is Luigi Zanoni, an important business man in the town. He used to be a Fascist and did business with the Germans. Now he sells to the Americans."

"That fits."

She pulled at his arm. "We must get away. He is sure to tell the Military Police and that could mean trouble for us all."

He picked up the last of the vegetables before allowing her to lead him away. They had barely entered a narrow alley at the far end of the street when they heard the screech of brakes and the shrilling of whistles. The girl led Beccione down two more back alleys. By the time they reached a road intersection the whistles and shouts were faint behind them. Breathless, Maria halted.

"You should be safe now if you go straight to your billet. Don't worry about the baskets. Stephano has to come this way, so I'll just wait for him." When Beccione did not answer, she put a hand on his arm. "I'm sorry, Joe. I know how unhappy I make you."

He shrugged, his eyes withdrawn beneath the scars. "I guess we are what we are."

"You make that sound like an accusation."

He kept his face averted from hers. "What will you do tonight?"

"I won't be going to the dance, if that's what you mean." She tried again to break his mood. "This is so different from America, Joe. Won't you try to understand?"

There was a long silence, then he turned to her. "Shall I come round the house when I get back?"

Relief showed in her voice. "Of course. Nothing has changed." Glancing round, she reached up and kissed him. "Try not to be angry with me. I'll make up for it one day. I promise."

He managed a wry grin. "From the way I'm feeling, baby, you're going to be kept busy."

She laughed. "I won't mind. Not once we're married. Now you'd better go. Take care of yourself and come and see us the moment you get back."

He nodded and moved away down the dusty road that led to his billet. As he passed an alley half a dozen barefoot children ran out. Buzzing like flies, they pestered him for money. He gave them a handful of coins but when they continued to follow him down the road he turned on them abruptly. They scattered when they saw his expression.

A far-off whisper drew his eyes upwards. The contrails of thirty plus B-17s flying at their maximum ceiling were streaming across the evening sky. Squinting, he was just able to make them out, a shoal of minnows in a blue sea.

He reached his billet two minutes later. The sun had dipped behind the western mountains and their shadows lay across the small town. Glancing at his watch, he saw there was barely time to eat before reporting to the transport pool. He paused to take a last look at the contrails above. With no wind to disturb them, they were spread across the sky like the bars of a prison.

4

Beccione watched the tail lights of Stanton's jeep disappear down the mountain road. "I wonder if the sonofabitch will be back tonight."

Rosenberg shook his head. "Not before our convoy arrives. There's trouble in Pinola. A couple of GIs broke into a house, slugged some old guy and took all his savings. The Mayor's playin' hell, so Stanton'll have to stay there awhile." Anticipating Beccione's question, Rosenberg nodded at the MPs' tent near the transport pool entrance. "One of the guys in there told me about it when you were taking a leak. It means Stanton's off our backs awhile." Fumbling in his combat jacket, Rosenberg pulled out a flask and upended it. "Here's to crime."

The two GIs were sitting in a jeep inside the enclosure. Although the night air was chilly, Beccione had insisted on waiting for the convoy in his jeep rather than suffer the company of a bunch of MPs.

Rosenberg, making the best of the situation, was drinking and talking to stay warm. "Ain't this weather something? It frys your ass during the day and hangs icicles on it at night. You think that's because of the mountains?"

Beccione was in no mood to talk about the weather. A shout of raucous laughter had come from the tent. A moment later an MP emerged to relieve himself. Rosenberg grinned at Beccione's disgusted expression. "What is it, kid? They re-

mind you of the cops back home?" When Beccione did not
reply: "I ain't exactly in love with cops myself. Me, a Jew-
boy—they used to shove me around like a beach ball. But
these guys aren't in it for the gravy. They're just here to do a
job, like you and me."

Beccione turned towards him aggressively. "Tell me about
it."

Rosenberg grinned again. "They're here to see we polish
our boots and keep our pants pulled up. That's important,
kid. If your pants fall down when the Krauts are around,
you're in trouble."

Beccione gave him a look and turned away, but Rosenberg
kept at him. "You know your problem—you just don't like
the Army. You think you're alone? There was a day at
Salerno when the shit was flying and I'd just torn open my
shin divin' to escape a mortar when I said to myself: 'Rocky,
why? What the hell are you doin' this for?' "

"You didn't know? You're doing it for Freedom and De-
mocracy, baby. For the rights of the Common Man."

Rosenberg's grin faded. "You sure hate that crap, don't
you?"

"That's right. I hate it."

"Why? Don't you think it's better than the spiel the Krauts
hand out?"

"I don't know what they tell the Krauts. But I know what
we're fighting for. Wall Street, Tammany Hall, and all the
other bastards who've been pushing us around ever since we
were old enough to tell a cockroach from a beetle." Beccione
spat over the side of the jeep. "All the rest's hogwash."

"You're a loner, Joe. Right?"

"Is that bad?"

"It's a hell of a problem. Because as I see it if it ain't one
guy giving you orders, it's another guy. So what's the point
of wearin' out your ass fightin' it?"

"You finished yet, Rosenberg?"

Grinning and shaking his head, Rosenberg handed over the
flask. "I'm just tryin' to figure you out. You hate the Army
but I ain't seen many better soldiers. And wasn't that guy you
saved at Bellazzi a sergeant?" As the flask halted halfway to
Beccione's lips, the Jewish GI made a gesture both wry and
comical. "O.K., O.K. You forgot he was an NCO. Why
didn't I think of that?" He peered down at his watch. "The
convoy's late, ain't it?"

"Only a few minutes."

"You think we'll get a chance to go into Naples? They say the dames there are pretty easy."

"With Stanton fixing the trip? You gotta be kidding."

Rosenberg sighed. "Yeah, you're right. He's probably given orders we're to take Rome before we come back." He took the flask back. "They say it's rough up there. You think we'll break out this year?"

Beccione shrugged. His expression was hard and indifferent. "You think it'll change anything if we do?"

"It could get us out of this goddamned army sooner. Ain't that what you want?"

"No, this is only a sideshow. They'll win the war in France and Germany."

"What makes you so sure?"

"To break the Krauts you have to occupy their factories. With all the mountains between us and Germany, it'd take us ten years to get there. We're just a crowd of suckers they're using to draw off men and munitions."

Rosenberg gave a grin of appreciation. "You're a deep bastard, ain't you? Big words, big talk. I've noticed it before."

The tip of Beccione's cigarette glowed as he inhaled. "What did you use in the Bronx when the other gang started using bricks?"

"That's easy. Bigger bricks."

"That's right. Only the big guys don't use bricks. They use words—the kind you don't understand. So if you're smart you learn those words. Then the bastards can't outflank you."

"You sonofabitch."

There was a shout of triumph from the tent as someone won a jackpot. Over the racket distant music could be heard: the dance in Castelmonte was beginning. Rosenberg jerked his head towards the sound. "Did you see Maria this afternoon?"

"Yeah."

"How did she feel about the dance?"

"O.K."

"How's everything goin'? All right?"

There was a brief silence and then: "You mean have I laid her yet?"

Rosenberg suddenly wished he had never brought the subject up. Although he was the only man in the platoon the big American ever confided in, Beccione would still sometimes turn on him when he was in this kind of mood. To his relief he was saved a reply—Beccione answered his own question.

"Nah. Things are just the same. Hell, you'd think I was asking for the Pope's ring."

"It ain't that surprising in these hick towns, kid. After all, the Church has been threatening 'em with hellfire ever since they were knee high. So how can we expect 'em to change just when we come along?"

There was a brief silence before Beccione shifted restlessly. "Yeah, I guess you're right."

"So just take it easy. Hell, when you feel horny you can always hole up at Carlotta's. As I see it, you're lucky."

"I am?"

"Yeah. Most of the guys stuck with dames back home are always waitin' for Dear John letters. But when we move on—and they gotta move us soon—you'll be laughing. If she says no to you, she's gonna say no to all the other guys who come along, ain't she?"

There was the sound of smoke being exhaled. "Did your momma ever tell you you were a beautiful baby?"

Rosenberg smiled. "All the time."

A sudden ripple of flat reports made both men jerk upright. As they listened the firing came again, single shots and then automatic fire that reverberated through the mountains. Rosenberg turned his startled face to Beccione. "What the hell is that?"

The firing was almost continuous now, distant but clear in the night air. The card players had heard it too and were running from their tent. Beccione shook his head. "That's a real fight. It must be the convoy."

"The convoy? But who would be attacking them? The Krauts are thirty miles away."

Down by the gate a corporal was yelling orders. Two men ran towards a stationary jeep. The corporal and another MP waved towards them. Beccione started the engine, then grinned at Rosenberg. "We don't want company, do we?"

Before Rosenberg could reply, he rammed in the gears and made for the gate, scattering the two cursing MPs. As he swung right and accelerated up the mountain road, Rosenberg stared at him. "What the hell are you doing?"

"We're part of the convoy's escort, aren't we?" Beccione demanded.

"What? Two of us?"

"Two, four, eight. What the hell's the difference?"

The moonlit road unfolded like a ribbon as the jeep built up speed. A jagged cliff of rock reared on its right side, on

the left the mountainside fell away to Castelmonte in silvered
rocks and dark pools of scrub and trees. A bridge leapt
towards them, stripes of jet and silver flashing beneath the
jeep's racing wheels. Then the cliffs closed in, became a tun-
nel whose blackness seemed to defy the headlights.

"How far away do you think that firing is?" Rosenberg
asked when they emerged.

Skidding round a sharp bend, Beccione had to wait a moment to recover control before he answered. "Hard to say.
But it could be another nine or ten miles."

Hanging grimly onto his seat, Rosenberg let out a groan.
"Don't say that. My ring won't stay closed that long."

They were now deep into the mountains. Rounded peaks
soared above them, steep valleys dropped first on one side
and then on the other. They were climbing towards a deep
col in the mountain when Rosenberg nudged Beccione's arm.
Ahead a glow flared against the moonlit sky.

The col led to a pass, then into a narrow valley flanked by
boulder-strewn hillsides. As the jeep came over the crest a
line of stricken transports could be seen stretched out ahead.
Some were overturned and already burned out. Others were
strewn across the road at all angles and still blazing. Rosenberg gave a yell and pointed at the roadside ahead where a
jeep was lying overturned beside a pile of rocks. Two men
were on the ground close by, one motionless, the other waving feebly. Jamming on his brakes, Beccione swung off the
road. He ran towards the wounded man while Rosenberg provided cover from behind the jeep.

The man, an MP, was gasping his life away with three bullet holes in his chest and stomach. Eyeing the blazing
transports ahead, Beccione dropped beside him. "They still
here?" he panted.

The MP, a burly man with heavy eyebrows, shook his head
weakly. "Nah. The bastards took off five minutes ago. Jeez,
am I glad to see you guys. Look at my buddy, will you?"

Beccione rolled the second MP over. One look at his eyes
staring blankly at the moon-washed sky was enough. "Sorry,
soldier, but he's dead."

The man was coughing—Beccione saw a trickle of blood
start from the corner of his mouth. "Oh Jesus! And we were
gonna be relieved at Castelmonte."

"Where's the rest of your escort?"

"Dead, I guess. They caught us in a cross-fire. Then they
set fire to the transports."

By this time Rosenberg was also kneeling alongside the coughing man. "Who were they? Black marketeers?"

The man opened his blood-rimmed eyes. "Hell, no. They were Krauts. . . . At least most of 'em were."

The two soldiers' eyes met. Beccione bent lower. "What do you mean—most of them?"

The MP's breathing was agonized now and his speech difficult to follow. "One was in GI uniform. . . . A guy with a green armband . . ."

"GI uniform?" Beccione said.

"Yeah. At least that's what it looked like. . . . You guys got any morphine . . .? Gotta have something for this pain."

Rosenberg ran back to the jeep. When he returned with a first-aid kit the MP was already unconscious. As Rosenberg slid a needle into the man's arm, Beccione turned towards the jeep. "I'm taking a look at those transports. Wait here until the other guys arrive."

He was back before the MPs' jeeps reached the pass. The light from the burning transports lit up his perplexed face. "They're all dead. Some still inside their transports. Whoever did it didn't aim to take any prisoners."

Rosenberg's voice was hushed. "Who the hell would do a thing like that?"

Beccione shrugged. "A raiding party of Krauts. Who else?"

The Jewish GI nodded down at the unconscious MP. "But this guy says he saw somebody in American uniform."

Headlights could now be seen probing the sky at the far side of the pass. As the sound of engines grew louder, Beccione turned back to Rosenberg. "The guy was delirious. Forget it or they'll say you were drunk on duty. They'll smell that brandy on you."

Rosenberg remained unconvinced. "A party of Krauts wouldn't penetrate our lines all this far back just to ambush a convoy. It don't make sense."

Beccione shrugged as the first jeep came speeding down the pass. "Who cares? Let the 7th Cavalry take care of it." He grimaced at Rosenberg as the two men lifted the MP into the jeep. "As I see it the Krauts have done us a favor. No convoy, no escort duty. You thought of that?"

Rosenberg shook his head as he dropped weakly in the seat alongside the dying man. "Not me. I ain't that hardboiled."

5

The repercussions of the raid were immediate and far-flung. After two months of near idleness in Castelmonte and surrounding villages, Baker Company was put on full alert. Telephones rang and officers in fast cars dashed from headquarters to headquarters. Meanwhile rumors buzzed among both soldiers and civilians. With the worst rumor of all gaining ground—that soon the Germans would be occupying Castelmonte again—candlemakers and churchmen alike profited from the sudden resurgence of prayer.

Among the troops in Castelmonte there was less praying than cursing. By sunrise the following morning every man who could use a rifle was put on search-and-discover duty. Object: to find the mysterious raiders. Every farmhouse within a radius of thirty miles had to be inspected, every copse of trees examined, every cave searched.

Although nothing suspicious was found, the task was not without its dangers. During their briefings men were told it was not unusual for German infiltrators or paratroopers to wear Allied uniforms. They were instructed to shoot on sight if they found any soldier acting oddly. As it was difficult to creep up on farmhouses or caves without acting oddly, search parties exchanged shots on more than one occasion and two soldiers were wounded.

Ten days passed before it was decided the raiders must have left the district and the search was called off. For the townsfolk the news called for a Mass followed by a celebration. For Beccione it meant he would have time to spend with Maria again. It was his last thought before he fell asleep the morning after the search ended. He'd been on an exhausting patrol that night and his body was aching with fatigue.

He awoke late the next afternoon to find Rosenberg shaking him. "What the hell is this?" he demanded irritably. "Can't a guy get any sleep around here?"

"The kid's here, Joe," Rosenberg told him. "Young Stephano. Should I tell him to come back later?"

Beccione sat upright. "No. I'll see him." He reached for a

24

cigarette and was lighting it when the boy appeared. "Hiya, kid. How's tricks?"

The boy looked shy as he entered the billet. "Hi, Joe. Were you asleep?"

"Yeah, I was out on patrol this morning. Musta climbed a dozen mountains."

"Did you find anything?"

"No. Those guys are far away by this time. Probably back in Germany."

"They rang the church bells this morning," Stephano told him.

"They did? What for?"

"Until now they were afraid the *Tedeschi* might come back."

"Nah. That's all over, kid. What can I do for you?"

The boy was looking with some awe at the GI's rifle and combat gear sprawled untidily across the floor. "Momma sent me. She wants to know if you can have dinner with us tonight. She says if you come she'll cook something special for you."

"She will? Tell her I can't wait."

The fact that Beccione liked Agata Marini was, on the surface, surprising. Agata was the archetypal Italian mother, guarding her daughter's virginity with even greater zeal than Maria did herself. In contrast her husband, Pierino, was a gentle, somewhat dispirited man. A metal worker by trade, he had been forced to move south the previous year when the Fascists had taken over the small metal shop where he worked. Offered a job in Castelmonte, although on reduced wages, he had found an empty cottage for his family on the outskirts of town.

None of his family had liked the move. Maria missed the beauty of her birthplace, Stephano missed his friends, and the knowledge they were unhappy in the barren Castelmonte tended only to break Pierino's spirit even further. But the strong and protective hand of Agata had held the family together and guarded its interests. As long as Beccione behaved himself with Maria, he was always made welcome in her cottage.

Beccione noticed Stephano was still gazing down at the floor. "What is it, kid? You want to take a closer look at that rifle?"

The boy started eagerly. "Can I?"

Beccione swung the rifle up and checked the breech. "Sure. Why not?"

To Stephano's delight, the GI showed him how to load and fire the weapon. As the boy was trying to hold the heavy rifle to his shoulder, Rosenberg appeared in the doorway. He smiled at the scene. "What's he doin'? Enlisting?"

Beccione ruffled the boy's hair. "Not if he's smart. You keep out of the Army, kid. It's only for roughnecks like Rocky and me. What time does your Momma want me to come?"

The boy handed back the rifle reluctantly. "She didn't say. Why don't you come back with me now?"

"No. I gotta shave and change first. Tell her I'll be around about six-thirty." As the boy nodded and went to the door, Beccione glanced at Rosenberg. "You still got your can of C-rations?"

"Yeah, I think so. Why?"

"Give it to me, will you? I ain't had a chance to see Koslo recently."

Rosenberg dug into his kitbag. "I've got two cans. You want 'em both?"

"Sure, why not." Catching the cans Rosenberg threw him, Beccione handed them to the boy along with three packs of cigarettes. "Give the cans to your Momma, kid. I know how short food is. The cigarettes are for your Poppa." Searching around him, Beccione threw the boy a towel. "Here, wrap 'em in this or the MPs will skin me alive. I'll pick it up when I come by tonight."

Stephano paused in the doorway. "Will you be able to play baseball with us now that the patrols are over?"

"Sure, kid. Rocky an' me will have a game next week." Beccione rolled his eyes at Rosenberg's expression. "We're both dying for some exercise."

The delighted boy ran out. "You're pretty fond of that kid, aren't you?" Rosenberg asked.

Beccione's face turned expressionless. "He's O.K."

"You notice the way he looks at you? He thinks you're MacArthur, Nelson and Napoleon all rolled into one. You've got something to live up to there, kiddo." Beccione only frowned and Rosenberg went on. "Didn't I once hear you say the family came from someplace called Valderosa?"

"Yeah. Why?"

"I just heard Preti talking about Valderosa—you know, that young Italian in Rice's platoon. He listens a lot to the local radio and says it was mentioned at lunch time today. Ain't there a saint or someone buried there?"

Beccione nodded. "Santa Rosaria. A peasant kid back in the 16th Century who's supposed to have performed miracles of healing. Maria says they parade her embalmed body through the streets on holy days. Folks claim they've been healed just from seeing it, so in peace time the town used to be full of pilgrims."

"Then there must be a parade next week," Rosenberg said. "Because the Church has been asking the Krauts to let pilgrims in again."

"What do the Krauts say?"

Rosenberg grinned. "The Fascist government has said it for 'em. No! You can't blame 'em at that. We might have wheeled in a coupla thousand GIs dressed up as cripples."

Beccione swung his legs to the floor and reached out for Rosenberg's towel. "I'm going for a shave. I'm eating with Momma Marini tonight."

Pulling off his shirt, he walked out into the sunlit yard and made for a tap in the opposite corner. Beneath powerful neck and shoulders, his trim waist was corsetted with slabs of muscle. He had just shaved off a twenty-four hour growth of beard and was drying his face when a jeep drew up. Turning, he saw Stanton, a second MP, and a middle-aged civilian enter the yard. Beccione recognized the civilian almost at once. He continued to dab his face as the trio approached him. Stanton, his belly bulging over his gun belt, halted a few paces away. "You're quite sure this is the soldier, sir?"

Beccione could smell the brilliantine on the Italian's thinning hair. The man nodded. "Quite sure, sergeant. I would know him anywhere. He struck me three times."

Stanton turned to Beccione. Although his fleshy face was expressionless, his small eyes had a prurient gleam. "This gentleman says you struck him without provocation in a street in Castelmonte eleven days ago. You got anything to say?" When Beccione did not answer, he turned to the second MP. "Take him into his billet and stay with him until the Old Man gets the charge sheet."

The MP made the mistake of grabbing Beccione's arm. As the powerful GI swung free, the MP stepped back and dropped a hand to his gun belt. With a last look at Stanton, Beccione started towards his billet.

*　　*　　*

The MP who had been sent to guard Beccione was shortly relieved by a lance corporal, an ugly man who clearly relished whatever authority he could throw around. Rosenberg, who had gone in to try and keep Beccione quiet, had the feeling there was going to be trouble.

The lance corporal sized up the GI from across the room. "You're the guy who knows that Marini girl, ain't you? The one with a kid brother called Stephano."

Beccione's scarred eyes turned on him. "What if I am?"

"The kid's been caught stealin' Army property. Stanton's got him in his tent right now."

Beccione gave a violent start. "What the hell are you talking about?"

"The kid's a thief. Stanton's corporal caught him with two cans of rations and some cigarettes. He brought him in just before Stanton sent me here."

"That's bullshit," Rosenberg protested. "We gave 'em to the kid only half an hour ago."

The MP grinned. "You'd better not tell that to Stanton. Givin' away Army property is a serious offence." Beccione jumped to his feet. "Hey! Where do you think you're goin'?"

Beccione was already in the doorway. "I gave those things to the kid. Stanton has to know that."

The man drew his revolver. "You can tell him that later, buddy boy. Right now you're staying here like Stanton said. So sit down."

Rosenberg was reading Beccione's mind. "Do as he says, Joe. This is a frame-up. Sit down and I'll go find out what's going on."

The MP grinned as Beccione moved slowly back to his bed. "You've got a smart buddy there, buster. I'd have drilled you for sure if you'd stepped through that door."

Reaching his bed, Beccione bent down as if to pick up his cigarettes. Then, seeing that the MP had relaxed his attention, he snatched up Rosenberg's towel and cracked it like a whip into the man's eyes. As the MP screamed and staggered back, Beccione's boot swung up and kicked the revolver to the far side of the billet. Beccione came forward like a leaping cat. A left fist sank deep into the man's stomach, a perfectly-timed uppercut almost lifted him from his feet before he thudded to the ground.

The sheer deadliness of the attack took Rosenberg's breath away. Beccione was halfway across the yard before he could shout his warning. "It's a put-up job, Joe! You're handing it to them! Can't you see that?"

Beccione's retreating footsteps were his only answer. Rosenberg walked back into the billet. Catching sight of the unconscious MP on the floor, he cursed and kicked him in the stomach.

6

Beccione found Stanton sitting behind his desk chatting with his corporal and a third MP. The two cans of rations and the packs of cigarettes were resting on the table in front of him. Stephano, looking pale and scared, was sitting alongside the corporal. He let out a sob of relief when he spotted Beccione, jumped out of his chair and threw his arms around the GI's waist. Beccione gave him a reassuring squeeze. "It's O.K., kid. We'll soon have you out of here."

Stanton was careful to disguise his pleasure at seeing yet another charge racked up against the GI. "I put you under close arrest, Beccione. What are you doing here?"

"You know why I'm here, Stanton. I gave the kid those cans and cigarettes. So let him go home."

"What happened to the man I left guarding you?"

"He fell asleep. Do you hear what I said? The kid's innocent."

The sunlight in the tent entrance dimmed. "The kid's sister wants to see him, sarge. Should I let her in?"

Stanton nodded. "Yeah, that's O.K., Paporelli."

The MP stood aside for Maria to enter. She looked as if she had run most of the way to the pool. As she struggled for breath, Beccione spoke to her in Italian. "Wait outside, Maria. You can't do anything to help him."

"Stephano is my brother," she panted. "I have a right to be here."

Stanton's eyes moved from the girl back to Beccione. "Now she's here, you can tell her something. The Allies are an occupying power, and although her people have signed an armistice with us they're still on trial. So when folks use their kids to steal from us it's a serious offence. It's not just the kid who's in trouble. It's her Momma and Poppa too."

The boy, frightened by so many words he could not understand, ran to Maria and buried his face into her shoulder. Apprehensive now, Beccione turned back to Stanton. "You're talking about two cans of rations and a few cigarettes, Stanton. For Chrissake, these people are short of food—we all help 'em from time to time."

Stanton shook his closely-cropped head. "I ain't talking about two cans, Beccione. My men have been watching this kid for weeks. They say he's sneaked over a dozen food parcels home."

Behind him Beccione heard Maria gasp. "I keep on telling you—I've been giving him the food."

"That ain't what the kid says. He's admitted stealing those cans from your billet."

Beccione swung around. "You told them that? Why?"

Stephano's sobs were muffled by Maria's shoulder. "I did steal them, Joe. You know I did."

Maria shook the boy angrily. "Why do you tell lies like this? Can't you see it is only making things worse for us all?"

Beccione turned back to Stanton. "You know why the kid's saying this. He's scared that I might get into trouble if it comes out I've been giving him food."

"He's dead right, Beccione. Giving away Army rations is a serious offence."

"So it's a serious offence. I gave them. Period."

Stanton grinned at his corporal. "If you want to take the blame it's O.K. with me, but I'll need a written confession." Taking a typewritten sheet from Jackson, he pushed it across the desk. "These are the dates my guys saw the kid carrying food parcels home. Sign in each case you were responsible."

There was a loud sob from Stephano as Beccione scribbled his signature. Stanton carefully blotted the confession and slid it into an envelope. "That about wraps it up, Beccione. Beating up a civilian without provocation, stealing Army rations, breaking out of close arrest—it ain't a bad list. And maybe when we find that lance corporal of mine we might slip in another charge or two." He turned to his grinning corporal. "Put the cuffs on him. We're taking him to the Old Man."

Major Peters glanced down at the charge sheet, gave a grimace of distaste, and walked over to the window. Company Headquarters was on the second floor of the Town Hall and overlooked the piazza, allowing Peters to see one of his transports parked below with a dozen GIs lounging alongside it smoking cigarettes.

It was a sight that wrung a grin from Peters. Carlotta's, the town's main brothel, stood in the Via Reggio just back of the cinema and it had not escaped his GIs that the girls took a stroll around this time before the more serious work of the evening began. During the German occupation Carlotta's prices had been fixed by military statue but now she was taking full advantage of American free enterprise and the GIs were finding it tough to compete with their better-paid NCOs. To counter this they were cutting out the middlemen by making private dates with the girls when they were out of sight of Carlotta or her pimps. While as a good American Peters could not fault their initiative, as an officer he felt his men were making a poor showing before the respectable citizens of Castelmonte. Re-crossing the office, he pressed a bell push on his desk. A sergeant appeared a few seconds later. "Yes, major."

Peters took him to the window. "You know what those men are doing, don't you, Matthews?"

The sergeant hid a grin. "Yes, sir." As he spoke a second transport appeared and parked behind the first. Peters' face darkened. "I'm a tolerant man, Matthews, but those guys are really hanging it out. Get those transports moved. And tell those men to look less conspicuous or I'll put the piazza out of bounds."

"Yes, sir. Right away." As the sergeant passed the desk and his eyes rested meaningfully on the charge sheet, Peters turned irritable.

"Don't worry about that. It won't do Stanton any harm to wait. Get those transports moving before the townsfolk think we're all on the jump tonight."

He moved moodily back to the window as the sergeant hurried out. In his mid-thirties, Peters was a man with the build and face of a New Englander, lean, long-jawed, gaunt cheeks, bony forehead. A lawyer before Pearl Harbour, he had been making good money when his conscience had driven him to enlist. His rapid promotion had been due to his regiment's involvement in the battle for Sicily, followed by Salerno and the northern push towards Rome. He did not consider himself a particularly good soldier or an ambitious one, but he knew he was conscientious and diligent and in

Peters' book as long as a man had those two qualities, bravery was only for the birds.

Yet men often secretly admire the qualities their intellects dismiss and this paradox was at the root of Peters' procrastination now. He had no doubt that Beccione was guilty on some of the charges. Nor did he particularly like the tough GI. With his middle-class background colouring his views, Peters saw him as a bloody-minded sonofabitch who would cause problems in hell if Old Scratchy were fool enough to let him in.

But Beccione had guts. Peters knew it had no bearing whatsoever on the case but the fact still nagged him. Sergeant Suter was an NCO of promise and if Beccione hadn't risked his life to carry him to safety at Bellazzi, all Suter would be today was rotting meat attached to a dog tag. Soldiers like that didn't grow on trees and any field officer worthy of the name fought to keep them out of the hands of MPs like Stanton.

For Stanton represented all the things Peters disliked about the regular army, its petty obsessions, its bigoted and often mindless power structure that lent itself to despotism. While he could not prove it, Peters was convinced that Stanton had laid on an agent provocateur situation to bring about Beccione's downfall.

Then there was the problem of Peters' New England conscience. He himself had a handsome young Italian mistress and he could not count the times he had taken her presents of food, whisky, nylons and cigarettes. Moreover he knew every man in his company had done the same at one time or another. If he had ever bothered to justify the cost to his country, Peters had argued such gestures to needy people could only do good in terms of reconciliation.

Another worrying aspect of the case was its moral side, although Peters knew it was legally irrelevent. It was obvious Beccione was fond of the boy, indeed of the entire Marini family, and there was no doubt his behaviour had improved out of recognition since he had met them. He had probably given the boy food because he believed a growing child needed it. And the reason for his assault on the MP was obvious enough because he had gone straight to the child's defence.

To Peters this brought the case full circle. It had been the act of a man with courage because he must have known he was playing right into Stanton's hands. For a moment the better half of Peters considered calling for an in-depth investigation. Then the lawyer in him killed the impulse. Army law like civilian law was based on what a man did, not why he did it, and no one knew this better than Stanton. All else was speculation and with Beccione's reputation to damn him, the man did not have a chance.

Below the two transports were moving away. The GIs had dispersed but only into hidden alleys and doorways. Walking restlessly back to his desk, Peters gazed down at the charge sheet, gave a grunt of impatience, and rammed his thumb on the bell push again.

"You can send them in now, sergeant."

The NCO's expression was curious. "Might I know what you're thinking of giving him, sir?"

Peters almost told him to go to hell, then changed his mind. "I'm thinking of giving him two weeks detention, sergeant."

The NCO gaped. "Is that all, sir? That's the minimum you can give."

"I know it's the minimum. You questioning my judgment, Matthews?"

"No, sir. Of course not, major."

"Then close it and send them in."

7

To Beccione the MP's face looked like an image in an amusement park mirror. At one moment it was as long and cadaverous as a grinning skull. In the next it was as round as a melon with a stubble of beard, thick lips, and gleaming eyes. The image blurred further as sweat blinded him. He blinked hard, and the MP sneered. "What's the matter, you sonofabitch? Don't you like your own sweat?"

The ground outside the stockade was soft and yielding, pounded into sand by a thousand boots. The overhead sun was pitiless, a demon wielding a white-hot hammer. Dressed in full combat gear, Beccione was standing with his rifle held in both hands above his head. When he squeezed his eyes tightly shut and then opened them again, the parade ground tilted alarmingly. Gritting his teeth, he heard the MP laugh. "What's the matter, Beccione? Aren't you as tough as you thought?"

Beccione tried to bring the MP's face into focus. With the muscles of his shoulders and arms screaming their protest, the rifle already seemed to weigh a hundred pounds.

The mocking voice came again. "You're looking rough, Beccione. You feel like a drink of water?"

Beccione's hoarse reply seemed to come from outside himself. "Get screwed, McCall."

The face distorted grotesquely again, a large ear growing out on one side, the mouth squirting out at the other. "Still sassy, huh? O.K. tough guy. I've broken wilder horses than you. We're going through that dance routine once more. Only this time your knees come right up to your waist. Let's go. One, two! One, two! One, two! I said up to your waist, you lazy sonofabitch. One, two! One, two! One, two . . . !"

Beccione's tortured lungs could not drag enough air through the respirator. He could not see Stanton standing in front of him, the glass of the face mask was opaque from his sweat. As his heart lurched alarmingly from his efforts, he jerked at the rubber straps and tore the mask away.

He had time for no more than two greedy gasps of air before Stanton clubbed his free arm with a rubber truncheon, making it fall nervelessly to his side. At a nod from the sergeant, McCall pulled both of Beccione's arms behind his back and tied his wrists together. Then Stanton seized his head and drew on the respirator again. The man's laugh sounded a thousand miles away as Beccione fought for breath.

"You gotta be fitter than this, Beccione. What if the Krauts use gas and you have to fight with that mask on? Get moving, you sonofabitch. On the double."

His hands tied, Beccione was pushed into the makeshift office by a young MP. Stanton smirked at him from behind a table and then winked at the burly McCall who was standing alongside an empty shell crate.

"We've a new game for you tonight, Beccione. Some simple calisthenics." He nodded at the expectant McCall. "My corporal here uses 'em sometimes. He says if you do 'em properly, you'll go out of here the fittest man in the company."

Another push sent Beccione stumbling forward. McCall led him towards the wooden crate. "You put a foot on it and go up and down on one leg. Our best guy did forty with each leg. We predict a super-tough guy like you ought to do fifty. So fifty's what you're goin' to do. Get moving, soldier."

His face expressionless, Beccione began. The crate was high and with his arms drawn behind his back, he could neither balance himself easily nor breathe with comfort. By the time he had hoisted himself up thirty times he was soaked in sweat. By the time he reached forty his right thigh was burning in protest and he was breathing with difficulty. When, of necessity, he paused to rest, McCall took the rubber truncheon Stanton handed him and swung it behind his right knee. The pain was intense and Beccione swung around on the corporal. His reward was a blow across the stomach that doubled him up. "Ten more, Beccione," Stanton smiled.

Somehow Beccione managed to complete the exercise on both right and left legs although he was retching for breath at the end. When he recovered, his hands were re-tied in front of him and McCall demonstrated the second exercise. "Nothin' to this one, soldier. Just touchin' your toes with your hands. Only you're doin' it a hundred times."

Laughs and prurient remarks came from the three MPs as Beccione commenced the exercise. After he had bent down fifty times his lower back was aching intolerably and he was forced to rest. Immediately McCall swung the truncheon hard across his buttocks. Pain and indignation exploded the restraint Beccione had so far shown. Cursing, he spun around and aimed a boot at the burly MP. Although it missed the man's groin where it was aimed, it caught him on the hip bone and dropped him in a cursing heap on the floor. For a few seconds pain paralyzed him. Then, struggling to his feet, he started towards Beccione in a fury of vengeance. Moving quickly forward, Stanton caught his arm. "Hold it, Mac. It ain't supposed to show."

In spite of Beccione's tied hands and his exhausted condition, it took all three MPs a full minute to wrestle him to the floor. As he was rolled over on his face, Stanton nodded at McCall. "O.K. But remember—I don't want no bruises."

For minutes blows rained down on Beccione's lower back, buttocks and thighs. When the beating was over and not a

sound had broken from him, the younger of the MPs stared
down at him with awe.

They dragged Beccione into his cell and threw him inside.
As he lay retching, the young MP stood for a moment at the
door watching him. "What the hell keeps him going?" he
wondered aloud.

The only man there who knew was Beccione. It had seen
him through his early years with his family, it had seen him
through the children's home. It was hatred.

8

The ache in Beccione's back and ribs was growing and he realized he had been lying in one position for some time. Lifting a leg and turning his body sideways he felt the pain ease.
Across the far side of the field a cow bell tinkled, then went
silent again. The night breeze crept along the hedge he lay
near, rustling leaves and bringing the scent of newly-sprung
furze.

Lying on the poncho beside him, Maria had noticed his
movement. "Are you in pain?"

He shook his head impatiently. "I've already told you. I'm
O.K."

She knew he was lying. Although he had been released
from the stockade five days ago, tonight was the first time he
had visited her. He had given duty as his excuse, but the
painful stiffness of his movements had betrayed him. That
and his mood. Dark and smouldering, it was like a land mine
waiting for one false step to explode it.

"When you didn't come I thought that perhaps you were
blaming us for what had happened," she said. "In a way it
was our fault. We should never have allowed you to give us
food like that."

"For Christ's sake don't start all that again. All the guys do
it. So how could it be your fault?"

"It got you into serious trouble. So naturally we all feel
guilty."

His laugh was harsh. "I was in trouble long before I met

you, honey. Long before I met Stanton if it comes to that. Bolan used to say trouble and me were twins."

"Who was Bolan?" she asked.

He ignored her question and lit a cigarette. In the flare of the match his scarred face looked hard and bitter. He dropped back on his elbows and gazed at her. "You know something, baby? You're a fool."

She pretended not to understand. "Why?"

"Because I'm no good for a girl like you. I'm just a goddamned hooligan."

"So you've said before."

"But it's true, baby. So why don't you get smart and quit?"

"Who was Bolan?" she asked again.

He shrugged impatiently. "An old guy I ran into when I was pushing protection. I was working in another syndicate's part of town and three guys jumped me. As they were roughing me up, old man Bolan drove round the street corner. He had two fighters with him and sent them to help me. Afterwards he took me to his home and patched me up."

"You say he had fighters with him," she interrupted. "What kind of fighters?"

"Prize fighters. Boxers. Bolan ran a stable of them. He said he liked the way I handled myself and offered to manage me. At the time I thought he was crazy—then I thought what the hell and said yes. It was the best move I ever made."

The darkness hid her expression but not her surprise. She reached out and touched his scarred eyebrows. "So that's how you got these injuries. Why have you kept it from me all this time?"

"I don't know, honey. I guess it just never came up."

"Did you box for money?"

"Sure I did. What else?"

"How did you get on?"

With the memory of his best years awakened, he did not notice her subdued voice. "I did all right. It turned out the old man was the best in the business. He got me through to an eliminator for the national title."

"Then you must have been very good. Did you like it?"

"Yeah, I guess I did." His laugh was tainted with irony. "At least it was honest money for a change."

"Did you have the eliminating fight?"

His tone changed. "No. The goddamned Army got me first. I couldn't get in the training, so the old man pulled me out."

"Does that mean you'll go back to it after the war?"

"After the war? I'll be too old, honey. It's over. *Finito*."

She put her head against his shoulder. At first he believed it a gesture of sympathy. She raised her face. "I'm glad, Joe."

"Glad?"

"Yes. I wouldn't like you to be a boxer."

He stared at her, then understood. "I get it. It's too brutal, right?"

She lowered her head. "I'm sorry. But violence has always upset me."

He had a sudden desire to hurt her. "You should tell that to society, honey. And to that Church of yours. It's done its fair share of violence in the past."

Her head jerked up immediately. "Why are you always finding excuses to attack my Church? All I said was that I didn't like boxing. Is that such a crime?"

In the silence that followed there was the cry of a night bird, a harsh and desolate sound. As she shuddered, he turned to her. "Are you cold?"

"No. I was thinking how much I hate this place."

He shrugged. "One place, another place. What's the difference?"

She saw a chance to change his mood and took it. "You wouldn't say that if you saw Valderosa. It's full of trees and flowers . . . it's beautiful. And the people there are so much nicer too." There was a challenge in the look she gave him. "Perhaps that has something to do with Santa Rosaria and the miracles that have happened there."

He opened his mouth to speak, thought better of it and lay back. Opposite them the luminescent light over the mountains was giving way to the rising moon. With spring imminent, new life could be heard scurrying in the hedge behind them. As Beccione shifted his position again their shoulders touched, a contact that seemed to sensitize every nerve in his body. His awareness of life became exquisite, his need for her unbearable. He rolled over and kissed her. For a moment she responded. Then, as he began fumbling with her coat, she stiffened. "No, Joe. You musn't. Please."

"For God's sake, Maria. It hurts! It hurts like hell."

She pushed him away. "That was why you brought me out here tonight, wasn't it? Not just to get away from people."

He wanted to explain his need for a woman's arms after the barbarism of the stockade but pride would not let him. Instead his anger returned. "What are you made of? Stone?"

"I've told you—I can't do it until we're married. I can't break my vows to the Church."

He exploded in frustration. "To hell with the Church. It's those bastards who've screwed you up like this. Can't you see how unnatural it is?"

Her face went pale in the darkness. "You hate the Church because of that home they put you in, don't you? You won't accept they weren't true Christians?"

"True Christians," he spat out. "And where do you find them? Back in the States, if you leave out the blacks, it's mostly the rich who go to Church. And I've figured out why. It's to ask God to protect their loot." Seeing her resentment, his desire to hurt her grew. "Those eunuch priests preach love but what the hell do they know about love? Love's giving, baby, not keeping your ass buttoned up like a miser's purse."

Her eyes flashed. "You talk a lot about giving but what do you give? Understanding? Responsibility?"

He stared at her for a long moment, then dropped back on his elbows. When he spoke again his tone had changed. "It's not that simple, honey. Guys sometimes have to wait months for permission to marry Italian girls. Most likely I'd be posted before mine came through."

"At least you could try," she demanded.

"But, honey, the war isn't over yet. I don't want to leave you a widow saddled with a kid. Not in this country."

"If I let you have your way I could still be saddled with a child. And not even married. Do you stop to think what would happen to me then?"

He gazed at her lovely, accusing face and was lost. "O.K., you've made your point. I'll put in an application."

"When?"

"The first chance I get." He managed a grin. "Then I suppose you'll want to live in Valderosa."

"Of course not. But I'd like you to see it before we go to America." With his promise made, her change of mood was swift, and she leaned forward and hugged him. "Think of it, Joe. All our lives together. In America."

A few feet above them a white owl swept past, silent on its fimbriated wings. His eyes followed it for a moment before he glanced back at her. "You think you'll be able to put up with me, honey? Remember I'm a violent sonofabitch."

She laughed. "I'll put up with your violence. I might even tame you."

Out of the corner of his eye Beccione saw the owl suddenly plunge down into the grass. A second later there was a faint cry of pain. Then the scent of spring drifted back as she reached up and kissed him.

9

Rosenberg weighed the ball in his hand and grimaced ferociously at Stephano on the plate. "Better brace yourself, kid. This is gonna be one of my specials."

From first base Beccione grinned at the boy who was looking both anxious and eager as he lifted his bat. "Don't let him scare you, kid. He's only a powder puff pitcher."

Rosenberg lifted his eyes. "Listen to the guy. One lousy hit and he thinks he's good enough for the Dodgers."

The men's banter brought laughter from watching GIs. The game, long promised by Beccione and Rosenberg, was being played on a piece of waste ground on the outskirts of town. Full of bare patches, with aging goal posts at either end, it was used by the local children for a diversity of games from soccer to cycling. One side was bounded by a wide ditch and stone hedge, the other by a low hill covered in scrub. The road from the south circled round the back of the hill and formed the far boundary behind one of the goal posts.

By popular choice Beccione and Rosenberg were the captains of the two teams. With Stephano and his friends numbering only twelve, the two GIs had enlisted four more soldiers from their platoon, among them Nunez. The game had been in progress for almost half an hour and the delighted shouts of the children had attracted a number of spectators. Maria was among them as were a dozen or so GIs.

Winking at Beccione, Rosenberg swung his arm back and contorted his body as if to hurl a thunderbolt. Instead he lobbed the ball gently towards the plate. Stephano, who was having trouble balancing the fullsize bat, swung with all his strength but missed. Beccione shouted his encouragement. "I told you he was all style and no action; kid. You've still got two more strikes. Watch the ball and you'll be O.K."

The boy swung at the second ball but missed again. This

time there was a murmur of discontent from his team. Scowling at the critics, Beccione turned back to Stephano who was now looking dejected. "It's O.K., kid. I missed too, remember. Just relax and you'll murder him."

He turned his scowl on Rosenberg who grinned ruefully as he caught the ball. The Jewish GI lobbed the third ball squarely over the plate. Gritting his teeth, Stephano swung again and this time connected. The ball sailed over Rosenberg and bounded across towards Nunez who was playing center field. Beccione's whoop sent a couple of chickens running for their lives. "C'mon, kid. Run!"

Astonished at his success Stephano needed a push from the GI catcher to begin running. Beccione was already in full flight, pounding round second base and heading for third. Meanwhile Nunez, keeping an eye on the boy's progress, deliberately fumbled the ball. When Stephano reached second base, Nunez threw it to the boy at first. By the time he had caught it and made his throw, both Beccione and Stephano were safely home. Beccione slapped the boy across the shoulders. "That was a great hit, kid. Two runs! You realize that?"

The panting boy was bright with pride. "Was it really two runs, Joe?"

"Of course it was, kid. The Yankees would have been proud of that one. Now it's our turn in the field." The GIs had agreed beforehand to relax the rules somewhat to keep the game moving fast. "You want to pitch or should I?"

The excited boy gave him the ball. "You pitch, Joe. As fast as you can."

Beccione grinned at Rosenberg who was picking up the bat. "You hear my orders? You're in trouble."

With Rosenberg at bat, Beccione let fly with all his strength and the ball nearly took the Jewish soldier's head off before smacking into the catcher's glove. Rosenberg squawked, "Hey, what was that? Your dipper?"

"Yeah. You can't handle it, can you?"

"Handle it? I can't reach it. Get your sights down, Beccione."

Spitting on his hands, Beccione hefted the ball again. Rosenberg appealed to the amused audience. "Look at the guy. He thinks he's Babe Ruth."

Beccione's second pitch was a better one, homing in three feet above the plate. Rosenberg's huge swing only clipped the ball, but there was still enough power for it to go whistling out of bounds. He grinned at Beccione as he stood at the plate again. "Another one of those, buddy, and you'll need a furlough to get the ball back."

Stephano and two other Italian boys were playing outfield. Seeing the power in Rosenberg's batting, Beccione turned to them. "Better move back a bit, you guys. If he hits one dead center, it's going to travel."

The three boys moved back as far as the goal post, some twenty yards from the road. Satisfied, Beccione turned and threw his third ball. This time it flew over the plate at the height Rosenberg liked. Swinging with all the power in his stocky body, he caught the ball full center and sent it soaring high into the air. As the GI dropped his bat and ran, Beccione turned and yelled encouragement to his fielders. "C'mon, you guys. You can catch that."

Stephano was in line with the hit. Eager to do well with Beccione's eyes on him, he scampered hard after the ball, then turned and tried to gauge its descent. Seeing it would still fall over his head, he ran backwards until he was standing on the road.

The hillside and the shouts of the crowd hid the sound of approaching engines. All eyes were on the eager boy, and when the two vehicles came skidding round the corner it was too late. As the shouts died into a horrified gasp, there was a scream from Maria. "Stephano! Look out!"

The boy turned his head and froze. The first vehicle, an Army transport driven by two drunken GIs missed him by a miracle and sped on down the hill towards Castelmonte. The jeep pursuing it, manned by Stanton and three of his men, was not so fortunate. Following closely behind the transport, the driver didn't even notice the boy until it was too late. He jammed on the brakes and tried to swerve, but his front wheels hit the soft earth at the roadside and he lost control. Screeching hideously, the jeep skidded sideways into Stephano and hurled him a full thirty feet. The jeep ploughed on into the field and righted itself for a moment; then it spun the other way and overturned, spilling its four occupants on the ground.

For a moment both onlookers and players were too horrified to move. Then Beccione began running towards the motionless boy, his arms outstretched as if to will him into movement.

He dropped on his knees beside him. One look was sufficient: the unnatural angle of the boy's head showed that his neck was broken. As men and women, led by Maria and

Rosenberg, began streaming across the field, Beccione's eyes lifted and settled on the half-stunned occupants of the jeep. Giving a cry that made one of the Italian women cross herself, he leapt up and launched himself towards them.

Only Rosenberg guessed his intention. Yelling for help from the other GIs, the Jewish soldier ran frantically after him.

Oil fumes were vaporizing from the jeep and one wheel was still spinning. On its far side Stanton was already on his feet; the other three were sitting up and examining themselves for broken limbs. The driver, McCall, was the nearest MP to Beccione. He had suffered a mild concussion and he peered up blearily at the demented GI. "What happened, soldier? Have the sonsofbitches gotten away?"

A boot smashed into his mouth, hurling him back. Diving on him, Beccione tore the revolver from the man's holster and fired three bullets into his chest. His mouth pouring blood, McCall died with his eyes staring vacantly at the GI.

Rosenberg screamed a warning at the other MPs to take cover as Beccione turned the gun on them. Then in desperation he threw himself at Beccione's knees in a football tackle, but holding him down was like fighting a savage bear. One massive heave sent Rosenberg sprawling at the feet of Stanton who was preparing to fire at Beccione from behind the jeep. Grabbing Stanton's legs in turn, Rosenberg threw the sergeant off balance. Stanton swung the revolver down and put Rosenberg out of commission.

At that moment there was another shot and a second MP screamed and fell. Beccione was turning his revolver on Stanton when Nunez and two other GIs hurled themselves on him. Although they managed to wrestle the revolver from his hand, he flung them off as if they were children. Nunez, seeing that Stanton and the surviving MP were trying to get a shot at the crazed man, snatched up the fallen revolver and brought it down on the back of Beccione's head. To his relief, the GI's legs buckled and he fell face down into the grass.

His fleshy face pale, Stanton pulled out a pair of handcuffs and snapped them on the unconscious Beccione. The surviving MP was stuffing a first aid bandage down the wounded MP's shirt. "How's Stewart?" Stanton demanded.

"He got it in the guts, sergeant. We'll have to get him to the M.O. quick."

Stanton swung around on the group of shocked GIs. "Don't just stand there, you assholes. Nunez, you run over to the transport pool and put out a call for the M.O. The rest of you get this jeep back on its wheels."

As the men obeyed, Rosenberg dragged himself shakily to his feet. "How's Beccione? You ain't shot him, have you?"

Stanton's eyes were feral as he took a second set of handcuffs from the dead McCall and snapped them on Rosenberg. "No. That's a job for the firing squad. I'm taking you in too, Rosenberg. You're an accessory to murder."

No one was listening to them. All eyes were on Maria who had risen from her dead brother at last. Her pale, frozen face told she was in shock. Ten yards away Beccione had recovered consciousness and was struggling to sit up. Her wide eyes were moving from him to the two stricken MPs. When he cried her name, she put a hand to her mouth and backed away.

It was a sight that moved even Stanton to pity. He turned to the nearest GI. "Get that girl away from here," he muttered. "Take her home. We'll see to the kid."

The man nodded and tried to hold Maria's arm. For a moment she fought him. Then, shuddering, she allowed herself to be led away. As the crowd parted to let them pass, the soldier's foot kicked something that until now had lain unseen in the grass. The GI cursed when he saw it was the baseball.

10

Rosenberg peered through the grille set high up on the cell door. Outside a narrow passage ran past the cell. Fly-speckled windows were situated at intervals along it and through one of them Rosenberg could see into the main police office. Its pervasive air of seediness was not offset by the two *carabinieri* present. One, a sergeant with a Zapata-style moustache, was stretched out behind a large desk with a bottle of wine before him. A second policeman, looking shabby and dispirited, was filing correspondence into one of the cabinets. The only smart object in the office was an American MP. He was sitting stiffly in the corner of the office as if afraid of contamination. The muffled music issuing from an old radio only made the scene more depressing.

Rosenberg dropped back on his heels. A small Italian civilian standing at the grilled window on the opposite side of the cell turned towards him. His round face was pitted with small pox scars and he had short blunt fingers with broken nails. His English was good with a light Italian accent. "The American policeman. Is he still there?" Rosenberg nodded. "Before you two came I had two policemen guarding me. Now I have the American Army."

"So what?" Rosenberg asked. "You thinkin' of breakin' out?"

"If I had been, it would not be possible now, would it?"

Rosenberg's eyes moved to Beccione who was slumped down on one of the metal-framed bunks that lined the cell. "You know something, Colenzo? I'm real sorry for you. I truly am." He sat down beside the motionless Beccione. "Kid, you've got to snap out of this. It wasn't your fault; it wasn't anyone's fault. Maria knows that just like the rest of us."

Beccione gave no sign of having heard him and the dusky light hid his expression. Rosenberg shook his head and fell silent. The Italian, intrigued by the silent Beccione, was about to speak when booted footsteps sounded outside and the cell light blazed on. As the door was flung back Rosenberg saw a tall, grim-faced corporal standing inside the cell with a revolver in his hand. The duty MP from the office, also with drawn revolver, stood in the passage behind him.

The corporal's harsh voice gave an indication of the enmity the Military Police felt for the big GI. "Beccione! You're wanted in the cell next door!"

Rosenberg, aware how Stephano's death had massively increased Beccione's hatred of the army, answered for him. "What for?"

The MP's eyes never left Beccione's face. "The boy's mother's in there. Major Peters says she can see him. For five minutes."

Beccione gave a violent start. "Get rid of her. I'm not seeing her."

Disobedience was all the corporal needed. His revolver rose until it was level with Beccione's forehead. "If the Major says you see the woman, you see her, you sonofabitch. Move!"

Beccione hesitated and Rosenberg wondered if he would attempt some further act of self-destruction. Then he cursed and walked out of the cell. When the door clanged shut, the Italian let out his breath. "Santa Maria, who is that man?"

Agata Marini was standing near the far wall of the cell
when Beccione entered. She was a bony, angular woman with
untidy, iron-grey hair. Although her face was drawn and pale
from shock, strength of character enabled her to retain her
customary severe expression and manner. Avoiding her eyes
as she turned towards him, Beccione was the first to speak.
"You shouldn't have come here, Signora Marini. Please go."

She saw a muscle working in his cheek and understood. "I
haven't come to blame you for what happened, Joe. We all
know it was an accident." He tried to reply but could only
manage a gesture. She drew nearer. "Look at me, Joe."

He shook his head. "Go home, Signora Marini. There's
nothing you can do for me."

"There is a great deal we can do. Before this happened you
were victimized and ill-treated. And you loved Stephano so
much the shock turned your mind. If we tell all this, you
must have a good chance. I believe your major is sympathet-
ic."

He wanted to hear only one thing and she was not saying
it. "The major has nothing to do with it. I killed one policeman and shot another. That's all that counts."

Her stern voice turned suddenly fierce. "And do you think
I don't understand why? I, a mother? You were not yourself.
We shall explain that to the court. And we shall get your
friends to speak for you too."

Impatience forced the question from him. "How is Maria
taking it?"

Agata, strong though she was, could not meet his eyes—
and Beccione at once knew the worst. "Violence has always
frightened her, so what you did shocked her very much. But
that is only because she is young. One day she will understand what love can do to a man, as Pierino and I understand." As he turned away, she caught his arm. "I shall talk
to her, Joe. And so will Pierino. But not yet. It is too soon."

"Forget it," he said harshly. "I saw her face after it happened."

In the doorway the corporal was growing impatient.
"You've got two minutes left, Beccione."

Agata pulled at Beccione's arm. "You mustn't give up.
You must fight to save yourself. Will you promise me that?"

Her insistence was puzzling him, as was the way she
turned him until his back was to the doorway. She reached
up to kiss his cheek, he felt her right arm pressing against his
chest and saw a hacksaw blade protruding from her coat

sleeve. With his eyes he tried to signal her to take the blade back, but she shook her head and kissed him again. At the same moment she slipped the blade into his open shirt and pushed it towards his shoulder so that it could drop down his sleeve. Although at that moment he had no thought of escape, the risk she was taking forced him to cooperate. When the blade was safely down his sleeve, Agata drew back. "You still haven't made me that promise."

He wanted her away before the blade was found. "All right. I promise."

Relief lit up her drawn face. "Now I am glad I came. Have you a message for Maria?"

He winced. "Only to say how sorry I am."

There was a thud of boots as the corporal entered the cell. "That's it, Beccione. Time's up."

In the passage Agata turned. "Remember your promise, Joe. *Arrivederci.*"

Guarding him as if he were a savage animal, the two MPs followed Beccione back to his cell. A kick behind the knee sent him sprawling to the floor. Before he could jump to his feet, the door slammed shut and a key rattled in the lock. Still shivering with anger, Beccione went to the grille and peered out. He saw the two MPs enter the office, talk for a couple of minutes, then the corporal left the building. The second MP returned to his chair.

"Don't blame them too much, kid," Rosenberg said, misunderstanding Beccione's interest. "I guess we'd feel the same if someone shot a couple of our buddies."

Beccione stared at him, then pulled the hacksaw blade from his shirt. Rosenberg gazed at it blankly. "What the hell's that?"

Beccione threw it at him. His eyes huge, Rosenberg caught the blade and ran his fingers along its teeth. "I'll be goddamned. It's sharp too." He turned towards Colenzo who had leapt from his bunk in excitement. "What do you think? Will it cut through those window bars?"

The Italian examined the blade, then nodded. "Sure it will. It will take time, but it will cut them."

Rosenberg swung back to Beccione. "Then we're in business again, kid. God bless Mama Marini."

Beccione gave no sign of hearing him. With a warning glance at Colenzo, Rosenberg dropped on the bunk beside him. "You're goin' to help us, aren't you, kid?"

Beccione's eyes lifted. "Where do we escape to? The States?"

Rosenberg's excitement faded. "Yeah, that's a point. If we made it where the hell could we go?" He glanced at Colenzo. "You got any ideas?"

The Italian first went to the door to check they were not overheard. He spoke very softly when he returned. "If we escape from here I can find you both shelter. That I will promise you."

"Where?" Rosenberg asked.

"*Un momento*. First you must both promise that if we fail to escape or are recaptured you will not speak of this to anyone."

Rosenberg glanced at Beccione, who nodded. "O.K. That's a deal."

"You swear it?"

"For cryin' out loud. Yes, we swear it."

"Very well. Now tell me this. Why do you think your company is stationed in this small town?"

"Search me," Rosenberg said. "They say it's to guard our supply convoys."

"But who are you guarding them against? Black marketeers? There are over a hundred of you in the district. The guards on the convoys would be sufficient protection against a few black marketeers."

Rosenberg, who had heard the same question asked a hundred times by the bored GIs, glanced again at Beccione. "O.K., it does seem crazy. But what other reason is there? It can't be the Krauts: their lines are too far away. That raid they carried out just had to be a freak."

Colenzo's voice sank even lower. "You are right. You are not here because of the Germans. Nor was that raid carried out by them. At least not by the German Army."

Both Americans gave a start. "That's crazy," Rosenberg said. "A wounded guy we spoke to said he'd seen Germans taking the supplies away."

"No. He saw German uniforms. A very different thing."

Beccione spoke for the first time. "What the hell are you getting at? Spit it out, for Chrissake."

Colenzo turned to him. "The men who attacked that convoy were a mixture of nationalities. A few might have been Americans."

"Americans?"

"It is possible. Up in the mountains there is a body of soldiers who survive by raiding Army convoys or storehouses. As they are all wanted by their respective armies, they do not mind which side they attack."

Rosenberg was gaping at the Italian. "There's a gang of outlaws out there? Robbing both the Krauts and ourselves? Do the two armies know about them?"

"Their High Commands do. They regularly send out patrols searching for them."

"But how do they get away with it?"

"The mountains are big and empty. And their leader has organized them like a third army. He has spies and collaborators everywhere and he counters every move you or the *Tedeschi* make."

"Who is he?"

"The Padrone? His name is Kessler. Franz Kessler."

"A German?"

"Yes."

"What sort of guy is he?"

The Italian paused, clearly at a loss. "He is a remarkable man. Some say he is *invasato*."

"What's that?" Rosenberg interrupted.

Colenzo hesitated again. "There is no English word for it. I cannot explain . . . he is different from the rest of us. But he is a remarkable leader. Nothing is left to chance."

Beccione's eyes were probing the Italian's face. "You're a member of this gang yourself, aren't you?"

Colenzo smiled apologetically. "I had to let your police think otherwise or they would have stopped at nothing to make me talk."

Rosenberg was still looking astonished at the revelation. "If this gang's the reason we're up in these hills, how come no one's told us about them?"

Colenzo showed his blackened teeth in another smile. "Think, my friend. What does the ordinary soldier in either army get for fighting for his country? The lucky ones get a few lire a week and sometimes a medal. The unlucky ones are wounded or killed. If these men knew that by joining the Padrone they would get the best of food and drink and also have money put aside for them, who knows how many would desert? This is why both High Commands pretend these raids are carried out by the enemy. But you will remember that when you were searching for the 'German raiding party' you were warned that some might be wearing American uniforms. That was the reason."

Rosenberg stared blankly at Beccione. "I'll be damned. It fits. It wasn't the Krauts at all."

Ignoring him Beccione turned to Colenzo. "So you're promising to take us to this outfit if we break out of here?"

"*Si*. Mind you, I cannot promise the Padrone will accept you. That will depend on your convincing him you are prepared to fight against your own soldiers."

Beccione's expression left no doubt of his own willingness. Rosenberg looked more dubious. "I ain't that keen on killing my own guys for loot. But I ain't that keen on being shot by 'em either."

"You must make up your mind before I take you to the Padrone," Colenzo warned. "Because if you changed your mind afterwards it could be very dangerous."

"Why? Would he kill me?"

"His men might. They would think you a spy."

"We'll go," Beccione said curtly. "What time is lights out?"

"It was eleven o'clock last night."

"Then that's when we'll start work."

"Won't they hear us?" Rosenberg asked.

"The corridor should keep the sound from them," Colenzo pointed out. "And their radio stayed on last night until one o'clock."

"So we've got until eleven?" Rosenberg said. "Then I'm getting some shuteye. It could be a long night."

Nodding, the Italian sat on his bunk and lit a cigarette. Opposite him Beccione had lapsed into his private hell again. Watching him for a full minute, Rosenberg could bear it no longer. "Hey, Joe! What about grabbing some sleep?"

The GI gave no sign of hearing him.

11

Beccione dropped the blade. It was time, he decided, to test the bar. Working in ten minute shifts, the three men had been sawing for just over an hour. They had survived three visits by the MP, but Beccione did not want to risk another. Legs braced against the wall, Beccione heaved with all his strength. The bar bent an inch, then held although tiny chips of cement sifted down to the floor. As the big GI paused for breath, Rosenberg took a grip of the bar above Beccione's hands. To obtain purchase, he had suspended himself in midair with his legs braced against the wall. At a word from Beccione both men heaved together.

For long seconds the only sound was their labored breathing and the muffled buzz of the radio. Then, quite suddenly, their handholds gave, hurling both of them painfully to the stone floor. When they climbed to their feet they saw that not only had the bar snapped, but the weakened cement at the base of the frame had broken away as well. Grey dust and pieces of cement littered the floor and a jagged foot-long fissure gaped in the wall.

Rosenberg was eyeing the narrow gap between the bars with some trepidation. "Can you get through?" Beccione demanded.

"I ain't got much choice, have I?" Rosenberg muttered.

"No, you haven't. So get going."

It took the combined efforts of both his companions to push Rosenberg through the gap. The knowledge that the MP's next inspection was imminent added urgency to their efforts, and a minute later the stocky GI dropped with a grunt of pain on the sidewalk. Beccione and Colenzo followed him with less difficulty. Pausing only to make certain the alley was empty, all three men moved cautiously away.

Their objective was company headquarters. Here, Rosenberg knew, were the only vehicles that were left out at night. The local black marketeers, fearful of the harsh measures that Peters' military government would deal out, had unanimously given his jeeps immunity. Rosenberg had learned about this from one of Peters' staff. It was their only chance.

Acutely aware of the passing minutes, the three men crept into the piazza. Although the moon had only just cleared the mountains, there was enough light to frost the statue of Bacchus and the campanile of the Town Hall. Keeping in the shadows whenever possible, they passed a sentry box undetected and crept along the side of the Town Hall until they reached an entrance bay that appeared to be a passageway back inside the building. Here Rosenberg checked them. "I ain't sure whether they post a guard on the jeeps or not. So take it easy."

After the moonlight outside the darkness in the bay seemed almost impenetrable, but twenty yards inside the men reached a small courtyard that opened to the sky. Inside it were standing three shadowy jeeps. Unable to see any sentries, Rosenberg was about to whisper something to Beccione when a distant whistle sounded. As it came again, Beccione pushed Rosenberg forward. "Move it! Once they phone Peters we're dead."

The ignition keys, as they expected, had been removed. With Rosenberg at the wheel, Beccione fumbled inside the engine of the first jeep. The whirring of the starter motor sounded deafening to the three men but the engine would not fire. Hoping the distributor caps had not been removed, Beccione tried again and this time the engine came alive. He quickly ripped out a tire valve from each of the remaining vehicles, then he leapt into the seat behind Rosenberg and thumped his shoulder. "O.K. Let's go."

Shouts could now be heard from inside the Town Hall and a door was flung open. As Rosenberg accelerated along the passageway the stabbing flash of a revolver lit up the darkness. Rosenberg swung the wheel hard over when he reached the street. The jeep lurched drunkenly, then thundered down the street into the piazza. Tyres squealing, it rounded the statue and was heading towards the Via Medici before Rosenberg thought to check the way with Colenzo. To his relief, the Italian nodded and pointed ahead.

The jeep threaded its way through the narrow streets. At every intersection the escapees expected a military vehicle to leap out and intercept them, but it wasn't until they were climbing the mountain road to the north that they saw headlights moving through the town. This brought an alarmed shout from Rosenberg. "They must be sending the whole damn company after us!" He turned to Colenzo alongside him. "How far to Kessler's hideout?"

The Italian's reply made both GIs start. "A long way. Well behind the *Tedeschi* lines."

Rosenberg gaped. "He operates from behind the Kraut lines? Then how the hell do we get there?"

"You will see. It is easy."

"Easy!" Rosenberg peered down at the dashboard. "At least we've got a full tank of gas. Is it going to be enough?"

"I think so if we are careful."

The mountain air, bitterly cold at night, whipped through the thin clothing of the men. Rosenberg and Colenzo gained some protection from the windshield but Beccione was forced to crouch down in the well between the seats to escape the wind.

The road swung into a series of hairpin turns. Rosenberg took them recklessly, relying on the road being empty of traffic at that time of night. Even so, when the road straightened to contour the mountain, the headlights of their leading pursuer had already reached the hairpin turns.

"This as fast as she'll go?" Beccione shouted.

Rosenberg was breathing hard from his exertions. "She don't like these hills. You think that lead car's an automobile?"

"It could be. It's got the legs on us." Beccione turned to Colenzo. "How far before we leave this road?"

"Not far. Eight kilometers. Perhaps less."

Beccione frowned but made no comment. The jeep was now deep into the mountains. Rosenberg floored it on the straightaway. The supports of a bridge zipped past with sharp rushes of sound. The rumble of the tyres turned into a scream as the road surface changed its texture. Just before they reached another bend, Beccione saw headlights sweeping the hill behind him and tapped Colenzo's shoulder. "You'd better find a turn-off soon. That guy's almost got us in his sights."

Aware that if their pursuer closed the gap much more he would be able to see where they turned off the road, Rosenberg took even greater risks. Skidding around a sharp bend, he missed collision with a rock face by inches. A moment later he hit a pothole with such force that Beccione was almost thrown out on the road. Yet each time the tortuous road straightened they saw their pursuer was drawing closer.

Colenzo, who had been paying careful attention to the road for the last couple of minutes, suddenly tapped Rosenberg's shoulder. "Slow down. We turn off in a moment."

A stone hedge was now running alongside the road. Behind it was a steep hillside with bushes and small trees. As headlights began probing the sky behind them, Colenzo uttered an exclamation of relief and pointed ahead. "That gap. Turn through it. *Svelto!*"

Ramming on his brakes, Rosenberg swung through the hedge. Colenzo pointed at a thicket of bushes and trees close to the road. Rosenberg braked behind it and switched off his lights. "What's our move if they see us?" he panted.

Colenzo pointed at the hill behind them. "We go up there."

"In the jeep?"

The Italian gave him an impatient push. "I know what I am doing. Change places with me."

As Rosenberg obeyed, Beccione leapt out and made his

way through the thicket. By this time the pursuing vehicle
had cleared the last bend and its headlights could be seen
bringing out in relief the loose pebbles and uneven surface of
the road. His muscles tensed as it neared the gap. He expected every second that its brakes would slam on. Instead it shot
past, tyres hurling stones into the dry vegetation at the roadside. "Yeah. It was an automobile," he told Rosenberg when
he returned to the jeep.

"You think Stanton's in it?"

"Probably." Beccione turned to Colenzo. "The rest of the
pack can't be far behind. What's our next move?"

The Italian jabbed a finger at the hill. "You mean we still
have to go up there?" Rosenberg asked.

"Yes. On the top there is a trail the shepherds use to take
their flocks to the high pastures. Once we are there neither
the Allies nor the *Tedeschi* will see us."

"And that's the way you're going to Kessler's hideout?"

Colenzo smiled grimly. "That's the way, my friend."

12

Alongside the path trees were threshing like wild horses in
the Apennine wind. As the eastern sky began to lighten, boulders and shrubs on the mountain began to take shape and
substance. Blowing on his hands, Rosenberg glanced down at
the dashboard. "We're gonna be out of gas soon. How much
further?"

"Four kilometers," Colenzo told him. "Perhaps less."

Respect showed in the Jewish GI's glance. Behind him Beccione was also admiring the Italian's navigation and driving
skills. In the hours that had passed since shaking off their
pursuers, Colenzo had kept to the high ground so effectively
that the only German activity the men saw had been distant
searchlights in the direction of Rome.

"You think there's a chance we might see any Krauts now
that daylight's coming?" Rosenberg asked.

"Not unless we are unlucky. The only time they come up
here is when they hear escaped prisoners are around."

Rosenberg nodded at the jeep. "How do they come? In transports?"

Colenzo gave his foxy grin. "Up here? No—they use horses."

Rosenberg blew on his hands again. "Goddamn it's cold."

"That's because we are nearly a thousand meters high. It will become warmer when the sun rises."

The path, little more than two furrows in the turf, led the jeep over a mountain shoulder and into a wide, shadowy valley. As the jeep descended, cultivated fields appeared on bofh sides. The path was wider now and paved with chips of stone. A kilometer ahead, where the ground began rising again, Beccione caught a glimpse of a large, bleak farmhouse.

Colenzo drove as far as a sturdy gate barring the path to the farmhouse. Halting the jeep, he jumped out. "*Un momento*. Stay in the jeep."

As the Italian walked towards the gate, Beccione nudged Rosenberg's arm. In the reflected glow of the headlights the barrel of a machine gun could be seen protruding through a hole in the stone hedge. Beccione noticed a second gun covering them from the opposite hedge. Rosenberg's whisper was apprehensive. "These guys don't take any chances, do they?"

Colenzo was talking to someone at the gate. A moment later it swung back and a soldier wearing a German greatcoat and carrying a machine carbine appeared. He peered at the two Americans and grunted something in German. Rosenberg appealed to Colenzo. "What's he saying?"

Colenzo smiled. "He's telling you he is taking you to the farmhouse. If you try to run away he will shoot you."

"He sounds like a nice friendly feller," Rosenberg snorted. "Are all your Germans like him?"

Colenzo climbed back into the jeep. "He isn't a German. He's a Russian who was conscripted into the German Army. It happened to thousands of them. He deserted soon after they were sent to Italy."

A second sentry challenged Colenzo before the jeep was allowed to enter a large yard flanked by outhouses. The farmhouse itself appeared to be three stories high with a pantiled roof. As Colenzo knocked on a side door, Rosenberg exchanged an uneasy look with Beccione.

Half a minute later the Americans were led into a huge kitchen. A table, running almost from one end to the other, was littered with the remains of a meal: scraps of boiled tongue, hunks of bread, the bones of chickens, and at least two dozen empty bottles of wine. The warmth from a massive oven felt like an embrace to the half-frozen men. At a sink alongside it two women were washing dishes. One was middle-aged and blousy with frizzy, greying hair. The other was a girl in her late teens or early twenties, with a peasant's powerful body and brown hair that fell below her shoulders. The older woman gave the newcomers no more than a cursory glance. The girl eyed them with interest, smiling as her eyes rested on Beccione. It took a sharp word from the other woman to draw her attention back to the sink.

Colenzo had led the Russian guard away and was talking to him in German. His argument seemed to satisfy the man because he nodded and left the kitchen. Returning to the two Americans, Colenzo nodded at the table. "It seems Jean Pierre has been giving a party for his men tonight."

"Who's Jean Pierre?" Rosenberg asked.

"One of the Padrone's commanders. His right-hand man."

"Does that mean Kessler's not here?" Beccione asked.

"No. He is here. But he drinks very little at parties and retired some time ago."

"Has the Russian gone to call him?"

"No. You must first satisfy Jean Pierre."

At the sink the middle-aged woman said something to the girl who dried her arms and started for the door. As she passed the Americans, she smiled at Beccione again. Rosenberg winked at him. "You're in, buddy. She likes you."

The big GI's gaze was roaming around the kitchen. "What the hell is this place? Who owns it?"

Colenzo shrugged. "A landowner who is friendly with the Padrone. They have not all sold out to the Fascists."

Beccione was about to ask another question when a bellow of rage upstairs sent a row of pans rattling. It was followed by a stream of French curses. A few seconds later the kitchen door was flung open. A man raged in and stood straddle-legged at the far side of the table.

An inch or two shorter in height than Beccione, he was a massively built man with a shock of brown hair and a fierce tanned face shadowed by a night's growth of beard. His unlaced boots and shirtless torso showed he had just been awakened. Huge of shoulder, hairy-chested, with enormous arms, he appeared to have the strength of six men. Arms akimbo, eyes bleared with wine, he glared aggressively at the Americans and then at Colenzo. He vented his fury in a colorful mixture of English and American slang.

"Why the hell did you wake me up, you stupid Italian sod? Couldn't you have locked 'em up until the morning?"

Two men appeared in the doorway behind him. One was the Russian, totally unperturbed by the Frenchman's anger, and the other was a young soldier dressed in a khaki shirt and slacks. No more than five feet six, with thin arms and chest, he might have resembled a delicate boy had it not been for his young-old face with its hollow cheeks and sharp features. He had a puckish grin and was clearly enjoying Jean Pierre's anger.

Colenzo, however, was in some awe of the Frenchman. "I thought you would want to see them right away."

Jean Pierre glared at the Americans. "Why? Are they two generals in disguise?"

"No, they are not generals, *luogotenente*. But they are two recruits, I hope."

"You hope? What does that mean? You're not sure?" Striding around the table, the Frenchman walked up to the GIs like a man inspecting cattle. He felt Rosenberg's arms and ran a hand down his ribs. "This one is like all American soldiers. Too fat."

Before the indignant Rosenberg could think of anything to say, Jean Pierre turned to Beccione. His expression changed as he took in the American's rugged body. "What's your name?"

"Beccione."

"I thought you were an American."

"I am an American."

"He is from Italian parents," Colenzo explained.

The Frenchman eyed Beccione with dislike. "Then why didn't he say so?" Walking around the GI, he suddenly smashed a huge fist at his stomach.

It was a blow that would have felled any man but a professional boxer. Reacting entirely on reflexes, Beccione tightened his slab of muscle and half-rode the punch. A split second later he took a step forward and his right hand drove like a piston into the Frenchman's solar plexus. Caught by surprise, the giant staggered back against the table, retching for breath.

Although Beccione's punch would have felled ninety-nine men out of a hundred, the Frenchman took only a few seconds to recover. He snatched up a wine bottle from the table. Beccione grabbed up a chair. In the hush that followed the only sounds were the frightened cries of the woman and the breathing of the two incensed men.

Then the frail, grinning soldier ran forward and tapped the Frenchman's arm. He spoke in French-accented English. "Has the wine taken away your sense of humor? He only did what you would have done in his place. Put the bottle down."

Jean Pierre turned on the man as if about to attack him also. When the soldier only laughed, the giant's expression turned from ferocity to a shamefaced grin. "You are right, Etienne. It seems I have met a man tonight." Returning the bottle to the table he held out his hand to Beccione. "One punch each to the belly. A fair exchange, no?"

Still angry from the attack, Beccione ignored the gesture. As Jean Pierre gave the frail soldier a wry shrug, Beccione heard Rosenberg's hoarse whisper. "What's the hell's wrong with you? This guy matters. Shake his paw, for Chrissake."

Once more the Frenchman held out his hand. This time the scowling Beccione responded but only with the quick touch of a fighter always suspicious of deceit. Jean Pierre lifted a bushy eyebrow. "A man who does not trust others! You could do well with us, American, or you could do badly." He turned to Colenzo. "What is his crime?"

"They say he killed a military policeman, *luogotenente*."

Jean Pierre grinned. "A policeman? He comes with good credentials. What has the other one done?"

"I understand he helped him."

"You understand?"

"I met them both in a prison cell, *luogotenente*. I didn't see it happen."

The Frenchman scrutinized the two GIs a moment more, then turned back to Colenzo. "Take them both upstairs. Nickolai will guard them until we have checked their story."

"How can you check our story?" Rosenberg asked.

He received a fierce grin. "We have our ways, fat one. Now bugger off so I can get some sleep."

Escorted by Colenzo and Nickolai, the Americans were led up a creaking staircase to a bare attic beneath the eaves of the farmhouse. It had no window but a chink of light through the pantiles showed that dawn had turned into day. In the doorway Colenzo looked apologetic. "You should not be here long. Once Jean Pierre has checked you out he will probably allow you to meet the Padrone."

"How the hell can he check us out?" Rosenberg asked again.

"I'm not allowed to tell you that but if you're patient all

will be well. Nickolai will take you down to the latrines. Don't try to go without his permission or he'll shoot you."

With all three men gazing in his direction, Nickolai, who had settled down in one corner of the landing, gave them an amiable grin. When Colenzo closed the door, Rosenberg turned to Beccione with a groan. "Homicidal Frenchmen and po-faced Russians! What the hell have we gotten into?"

Beccione pulled down a pile of flour sacks and spread a couple on the floor. "Maybe this'll teach you not to grab a share of another man's fight!"

Rosenberg knew it was as near as Beccione would ever come to thanking him; but for the Jewish soldier it was enough. "That's for sure. The next time you try to shoot Stanton I'll stand back and cheer."

Outside the dawn wind was tugging and moaning at the eaves. With time to think about Maria and Stephano again, Beccione was beginning to retreat once more into his private hell. He tossed two flour sacks at Rosenberg. "Here, put these down. Then can the noise and get some sleep."

13

Beccione awoke with a start. Thin shafts of sunlight slanting down from the interstices in the tiles dazzled him and it was a moment before he could make out the shadowy figure in the doorway. Then, recognizing the peasant girl of the previous night, he sat upright. Before he could speak she addressed him in carefully rehearsed English. "Good morning, *signore.* Would you like to eat now?"

Beccione glanced at his watch and saw it was almost noon. He answered the girl in Italian. "Hello, *signorina.* Yes, we'd love to eat."

The girl looked surprised. "You speak Italian, *signore?*"

"I ought to. My Momma and Poppa were Italian. They came from Naples. You going to give us lunch?"

"Yes. What would you like?"

"You mean we have a choice? Then what about pasta soup with onion, ham and eggs, and cheese and biscuits. Plus a pot of coffee."

Now that the girl was in contact with him, her previous boldness had gone and she blushed at his grin. "I will do my best, *signore*. Will your friend want the same?"

With a night's sleep to catch up on, Rosenberg needed more than a creaking door and a passing conversation to awaken him. "He eats anything," Beccione said. As the girl nodded and turned to the door, he checked her. "Don't go yet. Tell me what's happening downstairs. It's very quiet."

He noticed her glance back at Nickolai before replying. "Most of the Padrone's men have left, *signore*. And the family and workers are out in the fields."

"Is the Padrone still here?"

"I'm not sure. But I think so."

"Does he come here often?"

"No, not often."

"Then these are not his headquarters."

"Oh, no."

"Do you know where they are?"

The girl hesitated and Beccione could see she had been warned not to answer any questions. "No, *signore*. No one on the farm knows that."

"Then do you know where the big Frenchman has gone?"

"I don't know that either. But I think he wants to make certain you are not spies."

Beccione changed the subject to save her further embarrassment. "What's your name?"

"Elena."

"Elena. That's a pretty name. Is this your parents' house or do you only work here?"

"I only work here, *signore*. With my mother."

There was a grunt of disapproval from the landing. Nickolai was becoming restless at the length of their conversation. The girl backed towards the door. "I had better go and get your meal ready now."

"You'll come up and see us again?" Beccione asked.

Eyes lowered beneath their long black lashes, the girl nodded. "I shall bring your meals up, *signore*. *Arrivederci*."

Rosenberg was awake when Elena returned with a tray twenty minutes later. He brightened considerably when he saw the food. Forestalling another conversation with Beccione, Nickolai took it from the girl and pushed it into the room. "Colenzo wasn't foolin'," Rosenberg whistled. "The chow's really something. Only where's the wine?"

Behind the Russian, Elena had her eyes on Beccione.

When he spoke to her in Italian, she nodded and ran off down the stairs. She returned with a bottle a couple of minutes later and Rosenberg's gratification was complete. "If nobody wants us, this ain't a bad way of showing it."

Beccione grinned. "I guess those rabbis of yours never told you anything about the Last Supper."

Rosenberg glared at him. "You gotta spoil it, don't you?"

It was mid-afternoon the following day when the two Americans heard the sound of approaching engines. Acutely conscious that they were behind enemy lines, they listened with some apprehension. "It couldn't be Krauts, could it?" Rosenberg muttered. "Carryin' out some kind of search?"

The vehicles sounded as if they were entering the farmyard. As their engines died, Beccione shook his head. "They sound like jeeps to me. Two of them."

Heavy footsteps thudded below, then a huge shout boomed up the staircase. Rosenberg showed relief as Nickolai threw open the attic door. "Genghis Khan is back. I suppose we oughta be pleased."

The massive Frenchman met them at the foot of the stairs. Although his expression was as fierce as ever, there was a distinct change in his manner as he greeted them. "*Bonjour*, my two American generals. Have they treated you well in our absence?"

Rosenberg grimaced vindictively at Nickolai. "Just dandy. Thirty-six hours in the sweat box."

The Frenchman slapped him on the back. "What better way of losing your fat? They fed you well, didn't they?"

"Yeah, the chow wasn't bad," Rosenberg conceded. "What happens now? Do we meet the boss man?"

Jean Pierre threw open the kitchen door. "Not yet. I've still got some questions to ask you."

"You mean you still ain't satisfied with our story?"

Jean Pierre pushed the Jewish GI through the door. "Stop talking and sit your asses down."

Three men were already seated at the large table. One was the frail Frenchman, Etienne. The second, wearing civilian clothes, was a thick-set, bespectacled man with a swarthy face and curly dark hair. The third was big and raw-boned with freckled cheeks and a puckered scar at the base of his jaw. Although his hair was receding, what remained was bright red. Like the small Frenchman he was wearing a khaki shirt and slacks with a green band around his left arm. He gave the Americans a nod as they sat opposite him. "Hiya."

His twangy voice drew Rosenberg's attention. "You an Australian?"

The man grinned. "Ain't you been in the war long enough to recognize one, Yank?"

Rosenberg lit up at the chance for some verbal sparring. "You wear those big hats, don't you? Somethin' to do with you not being able to take the sun."

The Australian studied Rosenberg narrowly for a moment. Then his grin came back. "You'll be wearing those hats when you've been in the war as long as we have, cobber. You ain't got your knees brown yet."

"You got a name or a number?" Rosenberg asked.

"My name's Toschack. What d' you mean—number?"

The GI's expression was innocent. "I thought they always gave you convicts a number before they shipped you across there."

The small Frenchman gave a shout of delight and clapped the Australian across the shoulders. At the head of the table Jean Pierre, enjoying the banter as much as anyone, turned to the oven where the middle-aged woman was waiting to serve the men. "We shall eat while we talk," he told her. Jean Pierre took a gulp of grappa and pushed the bottle towards Toschack before turning back to the Americans. "You'll be glad to hear we have now confirmed your story. Berrati here says it checks in every detail."

The swarthy Italian sitting alongside Toschack nodded and smiled, showing a mouthful of gold-capped teeth. Rosenberg looked relieved. "Does that mean you'll take us in now?"

"With reservations, yes."

"What reservations?" Beccione asked.

"That you have certain skills we can use."

"What if we don't have 'em?" Rosenberg asked uneasily.

The frail Frenchman said something to Jean Pierre that brought a huge laugh from him. "Etienne says he thinks you are afraid we will shoot you. We would, of course, if your story was untrue. But from all Berrati has found out, your own Army would shoot you if you went back to them. So why should we waste bullets doing their job for them?"

"So what's the next move?"

The Frenchman's mouth was full of food. "I've just told you—to find out if you're any use to us. If you're not, out you go."

"Where to?" Rosenberg asked in dismay.

Jean Pierre took another draught of grappa before answering. "Hell, as far as I'm concerned." There was a laugh from Etienne. Jean Pierre grinned at Rosenberg's expression. "Well, what do you expect me to say? I can hardly make myself responsible for every Yankee who shoots a policeman, can I?"

"Why don't you cut out this crap and get down to those questions you want to ask?" Beccione barked.

Jean Pierre winked at Etienne. "What's the matter, Yankee? Is the referee keeping you too long in your corner." Seeing Beccione's expression he gave an amused nod. "Oh, yes, you'd be surprised what we've learned about you. I understand you've been trained to handle both machine guns and mortars. So you won't mind answering a few questions on machine guns for us. What types have you handled?"

"Brownings," Beccione told him. ".300 and .500. And Lewises."

Jean Pierre exchanged a glance with Etienne before continuing. "That's good. So let's take the Browning. What faults would cause a first position stoppage?"

The question caught Beccione by surprise and he hesitated before answering. "A broken firing pin would do it. And a broken sear." Then, as memory came back, he continued with more confidence. "A faulty transporter spring and a broken feed pawl. Oh yeah, and chips in the firing pin hole."

The Frenchman pursed his lips in appreciation. "Very good. But what about the transporter claw?"

It was fast becoming apparent to Beccione that there was more to this big Frenchman than a huge body and a fierce sense of humor. "Yeah, a broken claw would cause one too, I guess."

Winking at Etienne, Jean Pierre turned to Rosenberg. "Now you, the fat one. I understand you've been trained as an auxiliary radio operator." When Rosenberg nodded, he went on. "You've also had a course in first aid. Did you volunteer for it?"

Rosenberg looked almost offended by the question. "Me? I ain't volunteered for anything in my life. Nobody does. They picked me outta the hat."

"Can you set broken limbs?"

"Yeah, I think so."

"What do you mean—think? Haven't you had any battle experience?"

"Oh yeah, I had some practice on the guys at Salerno." It was impossible for Rosenberg to be serious for long, even in a situation like this. "I ain't sure how many of 'em died afterwards, though."

Etienne, who had been fighting back laughter for the last couple of minutes, made a choking sound and said something in French to Jean Pierre. The big Frenchman chuckled and glanced back at Rosenberg. "Etienne thinks you're so damn funny that whether you give the guys first aid or not they'll still die—of laughing."

Leaving Rosenberg hanging, Jean Pierre shouted for a bottle of wine. Elena ran towards the Americans with two glasses, brushing her arm against Beccione as she set them on the table. Jean Pierre, whose fierce eyes missed nothing, raised an eyebrow as Beccione turned towards him. "You got any more questions or have you heard enough?"

"I've heard enough," the Frenchman said.

"Then what's your decision? Do we stay?"

Jean Pierre's eyes twinkled. "Let the girl decide. Ask her, Berrati, if we should keep these Americans or throw them out."

The girl blushed deeply as the Italian translated for her. His gold-capped teeth showed in a smile at her shy reply. "She says yes please, *luogotenente*."

"Then there is your answer," Jean Pierre told the Americans. "Providing the Padrone gives his consent, you may stay. But think very carefully before you meet him, because afterwards it will be too late to change your minds."

"Why should we change our minds?" Beccione demanded.

The Frenchman's sudden grimness impressed both men. "Because we are *mauvais sujets*, my friend—enemies of our own people as well as of the *Boche*. That means we must be prepared to kill our own people if called on to do so. If you fail to do this when the moment comes, your comrades will kill you. So think carefully before you accept."

"I've already made my decision," Beccione said curtly. "I've got no love for the American Army. Or any other goddamned army if it comes to that."

Jean Pierre's gaze moved to Rosenberg who was looking pale. The Jewish soldier swallowed before he nodded. "O.K. Count me in too."

Jean Pierre studied him a moment, then rose. "Very well. I will ask the Padrone to see you. Stay here until you are called." He turned to the three men of his party. "You will go now and get the jeeps ready. We shall leave in one hour's time."

14

As the four rebels left the kitchen, Rosenberg turned to Beccione. "What do you make of this set-up, kid?" When Beccione only shrugged, Rosenberg went on. "Even Genghis Khan don't seem so bad today. As for the other guys, I've seen worse-lookin' hoodlums in the Bronx."

Beccione shrugged again. "What do hoodlums look like? I'd say those Frenchmen could slit your throat and use the same knife to finish off their breakfasts."

"Yeah, maybe so," Rosenberg reflected. "I once heard a guy say Stanton looked like his favorite uncle. I wonder what the boss man is like. They sure seem to look up to him. Even Genghis Khan talks as if he were royalty."

Beccione was feeling a certain excitement at meeting a man bold and skilful enough to defy two armies. "Colenzo didn't seem too sure of him. He said he was *invasato*. He didn't think there was a word for it in English but there is. It means possessed."

Rosenberg showed immediate dismay. "Possessed! Jesus Christ. Then maybe that's why the guys treat him the way they do. If he's creepy, maybe they're scared he'll cut their guts out if they step outta line."

There was a growl of anger from the doorway. Turning, both men saw Jean Pierre standing there. From the way his blue eyes were fixed on Rosenberg, it was clear he had heard the GI's last comment. "If you ever speak that way of the Padrone again, fat one, I'll cut *your* guts out. You hear me?"

Rosenberg's Adam's apple bobbed nervously. "Yeah, I hear you."

"The Padrone is a great man, as you will soon find out. So you treat him with respect. Is that clear?"

"You couldn't make it clearer," Rosenberg muttered.

The volatile Frenchman gave him a last glare, then jerked

his head. "He is ready to see you now. So follow me and watch your tongues."

The Frenchman disappeared into the passage outside. As the two GIs moved to follow him, Rosenberg saw Beccione's grin. "What's so funny?" he grunted. "How the hell was I to know the guy was God?"

The door to which Jean Pierre led the Americans was on the first floor of the house. Tapping on it, the Frenchman waited a moment, then peered inside. Although he spoke in French, both Americans recognized the respect in his voice. A moment later he stood aside and motioned the men forward.

The room they entered was large and full of heavy country furniture. A gilded grandfather clock stood in one corner and a huge wood-burning stove in the other. Only the window facing the door was unshuttered. Beneath it a man was sitting behind a large mahogany table. With the rest of the room darkened in the Italian fashion, the sunlight streaming through the single window blinded the Americans. At first they could make out only the man's silhouette. As they both halted he looked up and addressed them.

"Good afternoon, gentlemen. Please come forward."

The words were so precisely enunciated that Beccione believed for a moment the speaker was a well-educated Englishman. When he moved forward, however, he saw the man was wearing standard German battle-dress with a major's epaulets on either shoulder. His rolled-up sleeves revealed lean, tanned arms.

"If you would care to smoke, gentlemen, please do so. You will find cigarettes on the table."

Neither American took up the offer. Beccione moved right up to the table for a closer look at the man and Rosenberg followed a couple of seconds later. He saw now the German was in his middle forties with grey brush strokes in his dark hair. His build was lean and, although he was seated, Beccione could see he was a tall man. His uniform seemed to sit uncomfortably on his slim body, the shirt a poor fit, the epaulets slightly askew.

But it was the German's face that held Beccione's gaze longest. It was a long face with a high forehead, aquiline nose and hollow cheeks. Thin lines ran from the outside of his nostrils to a well-shaped mouth. His eyes, deep-set and

smouldering, had tiny crows' feet in either corner. It was the
kind of face seen in paintings of Quaker settlers, gaunt with
suffering, strong in resolve. In some ways it was a scholarly
face, in harmony with the man's cultured voice.

A sheet of paper rested on the table in front of him. Tapping it with a sinewy hand, he glanced up at the two Americans. "It seems my men have verified your story in every
detail. I am glad because with your qualifications you might
be useful to us. I take it that like most Americans you can
drive?"

Both men nodded.

"Good. And I understand from Captain Moreau that you
have accepted the conditions we impose on anyone who joins
our organization?"

Glancing back at Jean Pierre, Beccione noticed for the first
time that the Frenchman was now wearing captain's epaulets
on his shirt. "Yeah, we know the conditions," he said.

The German's eyes moved to Rosenberg. The Jewish soldier hesitated. "Yeah, that's O.K. But can I ask a question?"

"Of course."

"How does this thing work? I mean, you seem to have
guys from all kinda countries. Do we all fight together against
any target you pick?"

Kessler shook his head and leaned back. "No. I am a realist and know that whatever a man's feelings might be towards
his country, he has tribal loyalties that go deeper than his bitterness. As Americans you will normally be used only against
German or Italian Fascist targets. However, situations will
undoubtedly arise when a special Allied target calls for extra
men or your German comrades need your help. I understand
Captain Moreau has told you the consequences if you were
to refuse that help."

In spite of the warning, Rosenberg was showing considerable relief. "That's O.K. Yeah, that's fine."

The German studied him a moment, then glanced back at
Beccione. "If you are both certain of your allegiances, I will
now explain what will be expected of you during the next
few weeks. Later today we shall take you to my headquarters
in the mountains where you will be given a course of intensive training."

Beccione frowned. "Training?"

"Yes. I know you are both combat infantrymen but that is
not enough for my organization. Remember that every
weapon we use has to be stolen from our enemies and we

cannot always pick and choose what those weapons are. Thus every man must be able to drive tanks and armored cars, to use German and Allied field artillery, and to know all about explosives and methods of sabotage. In other words, we try to produce the complete soldier."

Beccione was fascinated by what he was hearing. "O.K., we're trained. What then? How do you operate? On horseback?"

The German shook his head. "No. We are a fully mechanized company in every sense of the word."

The GI gave a laugh of disbelief. "Mechanized? Up in those mountains?"

"Yes. On foot or on horseback our chances against our enemies would be little more than fifty-fifty. In jeeps we have a mobility they cannot match."

"Jeeps? But you can't use the roads and there can't be that many sheep tracks in the mountains. It's wild country. So how can you be sure you aren't driven off a path and trapped?"

"You don't understand. We use our jeeps as mountain cavalry use their horses. So we are not limited to tracks. We go almost anywhere a horse can go."

"That's impossible," Beccione said bluntly.

There was a growl from Jean Pierre but Kessler silenced him with a gesture. "I assure you it is true. It has always amazed me that you Americans have never realized the true potential of the jeep. Properly driven, it can operate anywhere but in the roughest terrain. By using it as a fighting vehicle we can strike hard and fast and then escape into country where no ordinary mechanized troops can follow. Naturally all my men have to be expert drivers—another skill you will learn during the next few weeks."

The two Americans exchanged glances. Although Colenzo had impressed them with his driving skill, neither man had guessed a reason as dramatic as this. Beccione pursued, determined to know every detail. "You say you use the jeeps as fighting vehicles. What armament do you carry?"

"Two machine guns. A .50 Browning on a swivel mounting at the front and a .30 on a similar mounting at the back. We use Brownings because we have found them efficient and reliable. Also the .50 has the fire power to knock out armored cars and even light tanks. For infantry and for heavier armor we carry light mortars, bazookas or panzerfausts."

"How do you manage for spares?"

"Spares are the least of our problems. All we need do is steal more jeeps which we can use either as substitutes or cannabilise for spares. Breakdowns during patrols present a greater problem but every squadron carries at least one skilled mechanic and sometimes two. For major repairs we have three workshops sited at strategic places within our area of operations."

The size and complexity of the German's organization dumbfounded Rosenberg. "You musta got an army up here."

"On the contrary, a large force would present too many problems. We survive by efficient and detailed planning, not by mere numbers."

"You just said now that we'd be used mainly against the Germans or the Fascists," Beccione said. "Does that mean you operate in two squadrons?"

"In the main, yes. Captain Moreau commands one squadron and Captain Schumann, a German you have not yet met, commands the other. Both squads consist of eight jeeps and two motorcycles for scouting purposes. The complement per jeep varies with the mission but is never fewer than two men, a driver and a gunner. A third squadron provides back-up vehicles such as radio cars and ambulances. It is under the command of Captain Roberts, an Englishman."

"How many men do you have in each squadron?"

"That depends on the operation. But our total strength does give us a reserve over what the jeeps will carry."

Aware that his question had not been fully answered, Beccione was making a quick calculation. Taking a jeep's operational load as four men, and including the motorcyclists, that meant a minimum of thirty-four men per squadron. Allowing an overall reserve of only fifteen men, that still gave Kessler a force of nearly 120 soldiers. And this did not include any technicians, informers, or spies who would be essential to such a clandestine organization.

In spite of the German's tendency to minimize the size of his force, Beccione found the figure impressive. "And you've got all nationalities here?"

"We have a fair number. Apart from deserters from the main armies, we have Yugoslavians, Russians, Poles, Spaniards. . . ." Pausing, Kessler smiled at Jean Pierre. "We even have a few Frenchmen. Ours is a cosmopolitan band, gentlemen."

It was the first time Beccione had seen the German smile and his eyes were held by it. It softened the stern lines of the man's face and yet oddly brought suffering with it. Beccione knew instinctively that at some time this German had been crucified and that the agony remained within him.

"How do you get through to one another?" Rosenberg asked.

"You mean communicate? Wherever possible we use English. It is the most commonly known language and most of the men learn it quickly. For those who do not, we seldom have difficulty in finding an interpreter."

"What kind of guys do you take on?"

Jean Pierre, who was growing more impatient by the minute at the Americans' questions, answered for Kessler. "Hoodlums like you who'd murder their own mothers."

Rosenberg turned and grinned. "Ain't you afraid of trusting guys like that?"

"Why?" the big Frenchman asked. "The bigger their crime, the more they need us."

Kessler's cultured voice recalled the Americans' attention. "This is quite true. We are a small group surrounded by enemies intent on destroying us. Nothing concentrates the mind more or makes men more trustworthy comrades." He paused reflectively. "Sadly, it seems only danger can do this."

"But you do still pick and choose," Beccione said.

"Of course. We must make certain that spies are not planted on us. And men without skills and without courage would be ballast. We have three criteria—that a man has a skill we can use, that he is brave, and that he obeys his orders without question. In a way I suppose we are like the French Foreign Legion. If a man serves us well, his history does not concern us."

"Except you aren't the French Foreign Legion, are you?" Beccione said. "You're a bunch of outlaws who attack and kill the soldiers of both armies."

It was a remark that made Rosenberg stiffen in disbelief. Jean Pierre glared in anger. Only Kessler appeared unmoved. He fixed a long appraising look on the American before answering. "You are quite right. We do attack and we do sometimes kill the men of both armies. But why do you stress it that way?"

"Maybe I like calling a spade a spade. Or maybe because Rosenberg and me were the first guys to find that convoy you attacked near Castelmonte. You sure did a thorough job there, Kessler. We only found one man alive and he died a couple of minutes later."

Kessler glanced sharply up at Jean Pierre and asked him a question in French. The two men exchanged words for a moment, then the German turned back to Beccione. "The raid was carried out by Captain Schumann and his squad. At the moment he is out on another patrol. On his return I shall ask him for more details."

"You do that," Beccione said. "Because it seems to me that robbery is one thing and cold-blooded murder's another."

Kessler seemed to freeze for a moment. Then he leaned forward, his voice low but very clear. "We are at war, Beccione, and every dead soldier is one less to hunt us down. Remember that before you are so critical."

"The Allies and the Krauts are at war too. But they still take prisoners," Beccione said. "As I see it, no one made you fight. You've chosen your own war."

The German's eyes dilated. Behind the Americans Jean Pierre made an exclamation in French that sounded like a warning. Taking a deep breath, Kessler rose and walked to the window. He was obviously struggling to contain some intense emotion. It was a full ten seconds before he turned to face Beccione again. Anticipating his question, Beccione said, "I still want to join. But as I said, I like to know the rules."

Although Kessler's voice was cold, it was clear he had regained his composure. "If you are asking if the rules include massacre, they do not. Without any doubt Captain Schumann must have had a reason for his behavior and I shall learn this reason on his return. But while we are discussing rules, there is one you will both do well to remember. At all times you will show the utmost consideration to the peasants."

Beccione frowned. "Why the peasants?"

Kessler sank back into his chair. "When you get to know them, that question will answer itself. The peasants here are remarkable people. Poor but uncorruptible."

"You believe that?"

"I know it. Perhaps it has something to do with their poverty. They carry it with honor."

"Poor, rich—what's the difference? People are still people. They'll all shake you down if they see profit in it."

Kessler was studying Beccione's hard, sceptical face as he lit a cigarette. On his part the American was thinking how deceptive the German's composure was. Passions boiled as deep within him as molten lava beneath a calm landscape. "You are a city man, are you not, Beccione?"

"Yes. Why?"

"There is a corruption in cities. It runs through rich and poor alike. But those who work on the soil tend not to catch the disease."

"You think so? You think those guys wouldn't sell you out if the Krauts offered enough dough?"

"The Fascists have already done this, Beccione. There is a price on all our heads. Yet, as you see, we are still active."

Beccione shrugged. "O.K., but it still could happen. And it will if you trust those guys too much and the Fascists raise their ante."

"I think you are wrong, but no matter. You will still do as I say. If you need a selfish motive, remember this. Our survival depends on these people. When we need shelter, they give it. When we need information, they provide it. In short we could not exist without them and any man who mistreats them will be summarily shot. I hope I make that very clear."

If he had doubted it for a moment, Beccione knew now that the German had a tempered steel fist inside his velvet glove. "O.K. That's a real reason and it makes sense. But if you're so concerned about the peasants, how do you stop the Krauts from taking reprisals against them? Because after you've carried out a raid, the Germans must think that the local partisans are responsible."

Kessler's expression lost some of its coldness. "We protect the people by leaving behind evidence that we are the guilty party." Jean Pierre murmured something to him and the German reached into a drawer of his desk. "We must leave in fifteen minutes. If you have any more questions they must wait until later." He handed each American a green armband, green epaulets and a green beret. "Take these and wear them on the orders of your squad commander. They will help your comrades and your enemies to identify you."

Beccione noticed that the berets bore a badge depicting a mythological deity wielding a sword. Kessler's voice checked them at the door. "One final thing. You will address me as Padrone, not as Major."

Beccione turned. "Why?"

"Because it is my wish."

"But you've given your squad commanders military titles."

The German smiled wryly. "Regrettably my men are used to them. They can stomach one change but not more."

Before they could ask any more questions, Jean Pierre hustled the Americans outside. He closed the door on them and turned back to Kessler. "I'm sorry, Franz. I thought the big American might be useful to us."

"What makes you think he won't be?" Kessler asked quietly.

The Frenchman looked surprised. "After the questions he asked and the things he said? If he's genuine he could be a firebrand and stir up trouble. But I'm not sure now he is genuine. That fight with those MPs could have been faked."

"No, Jean Pierre. He is too blunt to be a spy."

"Couldn't that be part of his act?"

The German turned to the window and gazed out. "Don't forget intelligent men ask questions as well as spies. It is just possible he is the kind of man we are looking for."

Jean Pierre opened the door to make sure the corridor was empty before he spoke again. "You're not thinking of telling him the truth, are you? If he talked to the others it could be a disaster."

Kessler answered with some irritation. "Of course I shall not tell him. As yet he is far too cynical and would react like the rest. But when he has seen more of what is happening out here, there is the possibility he might change. We shall keep an eye on him to see if that happens."

Out in the farmyard where he could not be overheard, Rosenberg gave vent to his doubts about Kessler and the whole operation. "Kessler ain't a bit like I imagined. But what made him run off the track like that? He talks for fifteen minutes like he was made of ice, then he goes as tight as a mosquito's asshole. Why?"

Beccione had been asking himself the same question. "He sure didn't like it when I said he'd chosen to fight his own war."

"What's so bad about that? It's true, ain't it? He does run this outfit."

"He runs it all right," Beccione said. "From top to bottom and sideways too."

"The guy gave me a weird feeling," Rosenberg muttered. "Like he was wearin' a mask. You notice the way he speaks English? And French? How can an educated guy like that lead a gang of hoods unless he's twisted?"

Beccione shrugged. "One thing stands out a mile. He hates soldiers. All kinds—long, short and tall."

"But why should he hate soldiers? He's got a small army of 'em fighting for him."

Beccione gave the GI a warning look as he spotted Etienne, Toschack and Berrati approach from the rear of an outhouse. The Frenchman climbed into the driving seat of the first vehicle. Toschack and Berrati made for the second, the Australian grinning cheerfully at the Americans. "You got your gear together? We're leaving in a coupla minutes."

"We ain't got no gear," Rosenberg said. "Except these," and he pointed down at the armband and beret he had stuffed into the pocket of his slacks.

Toschack's grin broadened. "So you've been given your membership cards. Welcome to the club."

"You're taking us to your HQ?" Rosenberg asked as the Australian settled behind the wheel.

"That's the ticket, cobber." Toschack gestured to the northeast with a bony, freckled arm. "Right up into those high mountains."

Beccione moved forward. "What's his HQ? Another farmhouse?"

Toschack's loud laugh echoed through the yard. "Farmhouse? It's a bloody town."

Beccione scowled. "Town? Get off it, will you?"

"It's dinkum. We stay in a town."

Rosenberg sounded incredulous. "Behind the Kraut lines and in the middle of a war? C'mon, Toschack. Give us a break."

The Australian grinned. "You gotta understand the politics out here. When the Italian Fascists declared war, they had so many opponents they couldn't build enough concentration camps for 'em all. So they picked the most isolated mountain towns and villages they could find and dumped 'em there. Some of these towns get cut right off in the winter, so they're nearly as good as prisons. You should see the characters we've got. University professors, lawyers, priests, writers, artists—we've even got a coupla opera singers."

Rosenberg whistled under his breath. "A goddamned town! That's just the craziest thing." Then his expression changed. "That means there must be dames there."

"Sure there are dames. But you guys won't be able to enjoy 'em for a few weeks. You'll be too bushed."

"Is the battle course that tough?"

"Tough? We've got a Yugoslav guy who practically tortures recruits." Toschack patted Rosenberg's stomach. "He'll probably take this off with sheep shears."

Before the indignant Rosenberg could respond, Kessler and Jean Pierre emerged from the house and made for the first jeep. Just as Toschack started up his engine, Beccione saw Elena running across the farmyard towards them. She thrust a parcel of food and a bottle of wine at him. And then, impulsively, she kissed his cheek. The next moment she was running back to the house in a confused flurry of skirts. Beccione gazed back as the jeep began climbing into the high mountains. But, within minutes, all he could see was a dwarf house in a spot of green.

Part II

Part II

15

The western sky was aflame when the two jeeps nosed down onto the road. A hawk, patrolling the opposite mountainside, took fright and plummeted down into the shadow of a rock-face. Looming ahead over the twists of the narrow road was a small town perched precariously on a cliff. Its fifteenth century walls and graceful campanile glowed in the last of the sun's rays.

Dust plumed out behind the jeeps as they began their ascent. In the second jeep Beccione and Rosenberg kept catching glimpses of the town as they zigzagged around the hairpin turns. Behind the town the sky burned like an incandescent mantle, then faded to grey. The brief Italian twilight was almost over.

A machiolated tower, half in ruins, stood guard by the roadside. The jeeps crested the hill and entered a maze of narrow streets. Most of the pantiled buildings, with their flaking walls, were shuttered, but here and there lights shone in the dusk. The town appeared almost empty until the jeeps reached an arcaded piazza. Suddenly it seemed to burst into life. Enclosed by the church, a small hotel, a large bar and a dozen or so shops, the piazza swirled with activity. Older men and women were drinking wine at outdoor tables; the young were ogling one another as they paraded around the sidewalks or threaded their way through the rows of naphtha-lit vegeta-

79

ble, fruit and candy stalls. The air was filled with chatter, laughter and music issuing from the shops and bars.

Kessler's driver had to sound the jeep's horn to make its presence known. The effect was dramatic: the sound of gaiety died as if a switch had been thrown. Then the crowd recognized Kessler and relief took the place of anxiety. Men and women crowded round his jeep waving and cheering, and an old man reached up to shake his hand. Rosenberg turned to Beccione. "You see that, kid? They treat the guy like the local hero."

Leaving the piazza behind, the jeeps turned up a cobbled street flanked by old cottages. Here and there black-shawled women and old men sat in rocking chairs outside their doorways. All gave Kessler a nod or a word of greeting as his jeep passed by. As the street grew steeper a large breech appeared in the walls ahead. Passing through it, the jeeps began following a dirt road that led up the mountain. In the dusk larger houses could be seen scattered around the ancient walls.

The jeeps followed the track until they reached a large house standing alone a few hundred meters above the town. With its windows tightly shuttered and emitting no light, it appeared empty. The two jeeps turned down a side path and entered a large yard complete with outhouses and a well.

The others waited as Kessler and Jean Pierre approached a sun-blistered door. The German tugged on an old-fashioned bell and seconds later the door creaked open and an old man in a velveteen jacket appeared. Holding up an oil lamp to Kessler's face, he gave a cry of welcome. The two men exchanged words for a moment, then Kessler turned and signaled for the other men to enter. He and Jean Pierre disappeared at once into the house.

Toschack switched off his engine and turned to the two Americans. "O.K., you guys. End of the line."

"What is this place?" Rosenberg asked as the four men climbed out. "Kessler's headquarters?"

"Naw, that's in town. This is where most of A Squad billet."

"It's quiet, ain't it? You think they've died or something."

The Australian grinned. "Most of 'em will be in town with their girl friends. It livens up when they get back."

Beccione stared around the yard curiously. "Where are your sentries posted?"

Toschack grinned again as he led the Americans and Ber-

rati towards the house. "We've got thousands of 'em, Yank.
A whole townful in fact."

"You mean no one can get here without passing through
the town?"

"That's right. The road we came up is the only way in and
the only way out. But in any case we know in good time if
any suspects are coming. We've sentries down there with radios monitoring the traffic and if they've any doubts they get
in touch with Kessler or Roberts. They've both got guys on a
twenty-four hour radio watch. If they think an orange or red
alert is called for, we slide into the groove. Kessler's got it all
worked out."

He led the two GIs into a long passage with a low ceiling
of untrimmed beams and then up a flight of stairs to a room
off the landing. Entering it somewhat warily, they found
themselves in a bedroom furnished with a huge double bed,
two stiff-backed chairs and a large wardrobe. A wood stove
stood near the door. Setting the oil lamp on it, Toschack
grinned. "It's better than the attic, ain't it? Relax for a while.
I'll call you when dinner's ready."

"I wonder who owns this place," Rosenberg muttered as
the Australian disappeared down the stairs.

Shrugging, Beccione dropped on the bed and stretched out
his legs. "Who cares? When did the army give us a billet like
this?"

Rosenberg rummaged under the bed and pulled out a *vaso
da nòtte*. Setting it on his head like a helmet, he turned to
Beccione. "All the comforts of home. At least we ain't gotta
wander round looking for somewhere to pee." Then, as he
pushed the pot back, his expression changed. "It's still a
queer set-up though, ain't it? We're on the run and yet we
end up like a couple of salesmen in a crummy hotel. Don't it
feel all wrong to you?"

"What did you expect?" Beccione asked. "A cave full of
rattlesnakes?"

Rosenberg looked thoughtful. "Yeah, maybe I did. This
place just ain't in character. And where are the rest of the
gang? We ain't seen any of 'em yet."

Beccione yawned. "Your trouble is you've seen too many
movies."

Booted footsteps on the stairs fifteen minutes later announced the return of Toschack. "O.K., you guys. Chow's
ready."

"Aren't any of the squad here?" Beccione asked as they followed him downstairs.

"Yeah, there's half a dozen playin' cards in the canteen. As I said, the rest of 'em are in town."

"And Schumann's bunch aren't back yet?"

"Naw. Not until tomorrow. Maybe even the day after."

"Do they also billet here?"

"Christ, no. They throw a party here now an' then but they sleep in a house nearer the town."

A moment later the three men entered a large room on the ground floor. With a pool table in one corner and a dartboard on a wall, in some ways it resembled a GIs' recreation room. Light was provided by paraffin pressure lamps. Near the door a table had been set for a meal; at a larger table at the far end of the room six men were playing cards. Etienne was among them. When he caught sight of the Americans, he rose to his feet with mock ceremony. "*Mes amis*, meet our new recruits. The tall one is Beccione. He is clearly insane because he punched our Jean Pierre in the stomach. The fat one calls himself Rosenberg but that is a *nom de guerre*. His real name is Bob Hope." Someone laughed and the Frenchman held up a hand. "It is true I assure you. When he opens his mouth you will see I am right."

While the frail Frenchman was speaking, Beccione was sizing up the card players. The dealer was a fair-headed, square-faced man wearing the shoulder flash of New Zealand on his shirt. He had the appearance of a farmer and his grin was friendly. Next to him, to Beccione's surprise, was a black man in GI uniform. He had good features but his expression was almost hostile as he eyed the two Americans. He was seated alongside a heavily-built man whose head was completely shaven. With slanting eyes, high cheekbones and massive torso, he looked as if he had just stepped out of a Sidney Greenstreet movie. His reaction to the Americans was impossible to determine: his Slavic face was expressionless. Next to him was a soldier from a British infantry regiment. He had the same street-Arab appearance as Etienne with a thin, undernourished face and somewhat shifty eyes. His fingernails were black with dirt. Beccione did not need to take a second look to recognize the type. Products of slums, natural survivors, they made excellent soldiers but only as long as authority was breathing down their necks. The last man in the group was a total contrast to the others. Wearing the uniform of a British armored car regiment, he was a man of medium height with a wiry body and brown hair flecked with grey. His face was lined and a puckered scar running down his right cheek gave him a sardonic appearance. Apart from the bald Slav, he looked at least ten years older than his companions.

Etienne began introducing them. The New Zealander was McAllister, the negro Johnson, the Slav was in fact a Yugoslavian nicknamed Tito, the two Britons were Greyson and Roberts respectively.

The only men to show friendliness by shaking hands were McAllister and Roberts. The other three contented themselves with guarded nods. As Roberts rose to his feet, Beccione noticed for the first time the three stars sewn to his epaulets. "Are you the officer in charge of C Squad?"

The Englishman nodded. "That's right. Have you just arrived?"

"Yeah. Do your guys billet here?"

"No, we have our own house," Roberts nodded at the grinning Etienne. "But I usually come over when Etienne has a poker game going."

Several of the men were scowling impatiently at the disruption of their game, and Roberts returned to his seat. Beccione and Rosenberg, left in the lurch and feeling awkward, were glad when Toschack called them away to dinner.

Rosenberg's mood improved when he discovered a leg of mutton and two bottles of wine standing on the table in front of Toschack. The Australian, who was already eating, smiled as the two men dropped into chairs on either side of him. "What's wrong? Won't they let you play with 'em?"

Rosenberg hacked off two large hunks of meat and dropped one on Beccione's plate. "What's with those guys anyway? You'd think at least that black GI could manage a handshake."

Toschack shrugged as he took a drink of wine. "Why should he? Uniforms don't mean anything here. All he knows about you guys is you've killed somebody, and that ain't exactly a recommendation."

Rosenberg gave a sniff of disgust. "What did that black guy do to get here?"

"Johnson? He didn't like his job in the Army."

"That's all?"

"That's all he's told me."

"That's a hell of a reason. What about the limey, Roberts?"

Across the table Beccione had stopped eating and was listening as Toschack glanced back at the card players. "Some of the guys don't like questions being asked. Hasn't Kessler told you?"

"Yeah, yeah, he told us. What about the Englishman?"

Toschack grinned. "He was in the 12th Lancers—that's a British armored car regiment. From what I gather he hit trouble when he refused to open fire on a peasant's cottage. His officer believed it was a Jerry strongpoint: Roberts believed the Wop family were still inside. It turned out both were right—the Jerries were holding the family as hostages. Roberts never talks about it, but the rumor goes that because a lot of guys were killed taking the cottage, a bunch of his own men jumped him afterwards and did their best to beat him to death. A peasant family found him and, after nursing him back to health, put him in touch with Kessler."

Rosenberg grimaced. "He sure must love the army. What's his job here apart from bossing C Squad?"

"He's one of our explosives experts. He used to be an engineer in a mining company in the north of England. You'll find him a dinkum guy."

"What about the bald-headed character?" Beccione asked.

"Tito? He was a partisan before he was captured and lost his wife and kids in the fighting. They made a slave laborer out of him and he was working on the Gothic Line up north when he escaped. He hates Jerries worse than hell. Watch him when he takes to the bottle. He can go fighting mad in seconds."

"And he's one of our instructors?" Rosenberg said.

"That's right. Physical training. He'll have you running up and down those mountains as if you were goats. At five o'clock in the morning."

Rosenberg looked faint. "Five o'clock?"

"That's the ticket, cobber. So go easy on the vino tonight."

"What about the two little guys?" Beccione asked.

"I don't know what the Frenchman did but don't let his size fool you. He's a hell of a fighting man. Greyson's supposed to have knifed a guy in a card game. I'd watch him. He can be a vicious little bastard."

"And the New Zealander, McAllister?"

"Mac's another one of our mystery men. He's friendly enough but he never talks about himself. They say he got mixed up with an Italian girl down south and had a shoot-out first with her brothers and then with MPs, but no one's sure."

Rosenberg grinned at Beccione. "A guy after your own heart."

Beccione ignored him. "Where's Kessler tonight?"

"He always eats at his place in town."

"Where's that?"

"In a hotel off the piazza. That's his HQ."

"Just like Castelmonte," Rosenberg said. "It gets crazier and crazier."

Beccione pushed the plate of mutton towards him. "Here. Console yourself."

Only too willing to oblige, Rosenberg was lifting another hunk of meat from the plate when Jean Pierre appeared in the doorway behind him. He gave his fierce grin. "So you're feeding your face again, are you, fat one? Make the most of it. Tomorrow the slimming begins."

Rosenberg turned. "You ain't really getting us up at five o'clock, are you?"

"That's why I'm here. To tell you that after your meal you go upstairs. I want you bright-eyed and bushy-tailed tomorrow."

Rosenberg raised a comical eye at Beccione. "He ain't got a bad line in American, has he?"

"I should hope not," the Frenchman grunted. "Seeing as I once worked for a Yankee shipping firm." He glanced at Toschack. "I'm making you responsible for these two. After supper they go straight to bed. O.K.?"

Rosenberg gave a snort of disgust. "You ain't talking to a couple of rookies. We're big boys now."

The Frenchman turned in the doorway. "Wrong. As far as I'm concerned you're rookies until you've finished your training. So it's no leave passes for at least a week. Maybe longer."

"Bromide too?" Rosenberg asked sarcastically.

The Frenchman winked at Toschack. "Four times a day in your coffee, fat one. Mountain air does great things to a man." His tone changed as he addressed the Australian. "I'll be back in half an hour. Make sure they're both tucked up in bed by then."

"Hey, wait a minute," Rosenberg called as Jean Pierre disappeared through the door. "When do we get our gear?"

"You'll get it in the morning," Toschack said when the Frenchman failed to reappear. "The quartermaster issues it before you start training."

Rosenberg blinked. "The quartermaster?"

"Yeah. He's got a store in town, not far from the old man's HQ."

"You sure you ain't got your own Navy and Air Force too?"

Toschack winked. "They tell me Kessler thought about it but decided they might be a flaming nuisance in these mountains."

Fifteen minutes later the Americans were back in their room. Rosenberg couldn't contain his amazement. "A quartermaster, battle training, a gang boss who talks like the King of England. . . . We just gotta be dreaming all this, kid."

Beccione was sitting on the bed unlacing his boots. "Why knock it? It's a great dream."

"But nothing fits. I mean you could slip that guy Kessler into a Congressional Committee and no one would blink."

"Yeah, I wish I could figure out that guy myself." Beccione yawned. "Well, no sense losing sleep over it." He patted the bed. "If they're calling us that early in the morning, we'd better get some shuteye. Which side do you want?"

Rosenberg grinned as he pulled off his shirt. "I'll take the side near the door. Just in case you forget you ain't at Carlotta's."

16

Rosenberg dropped his pack at the foot of the staircase and collapsed with a groan alongside it. "I can't make the room, kid. I'm bushed. Someone oughta shoot that Yugoslav. He's a mankiller."

Beccione smiled down at him. "You ain't even begun yet. Tomorrow we go on right through the day."

Rosenberg, his sweat-soaked shirt clinging to his back, looked up aghast. "Who said that?"

"Jean Pierre, before we drove off. He didn't want to tell you right away in case you had a heart attack."

Rosenberg slumped over his pack. "Let's give ourselves up, kid. What's a firing squad next to this?"

As Jean Pierre had promised, the two men had been awakened that morning just before 05.00 hours. Given half an hour to shave and have breakfast, they had been driven into town to collect their gear. To their surprise it contained two sets of uniforms, German and American, together with all the ancillary apparatus, webbing, packs, and weapons. After helping them take the equipment back to their room, Tito had then driven them northwards towards Kessler's training ground.

As Toschack had told them, it was a good six miles from town, situated at the foot of a particularly barren mountainside. With little grass to sustain sheep or cattle, it was not used by the peasants and as a consequence no paths led towards it. Yet, in a place so difficult of access, the Americans had found facilities and equipment that would have done credit to a first-class regiment. Duly camouflaged from aerial observation were sand butts for small arms' practice and full-size ranges for machine guns and 20mm cannon. In a rebuilt peasant cottage there was a German Panther tank and a British armored car. A small wood gave cover to a German 88 mm artillery gun, a British 17 pounder, small American field pieces and a number of small and large mortars. A few bazookas and a quantity of ammunition for all these weapons were stored in a large cave. In addition to all this weaponry, an obstacle course of exacting design ran up the mountainside. At either end of the training ground guards were on twenty-four hour duty. Considering the location and the circumstances, the facilities were astonishingly comprehensive and clearly designed to produce soldiers of extreme fitness and versatility.

Tito proved to be tough but friendly. In his highly individualistic English he explained that their training schedule was programmed by Kessler, with different instructors stepping in to teach different weapons. As Tito was their physical training instructor, the Americans' entire morning had been spent doing strenuous exercises, long and short runs in full combat gear, and twice surmounting the obstacle course. It was a session that had taxed even Beccione's great strength and he could sympathize with the collapsed Rosenberg. "Never mind, Rocky. Think of the good it's going to do you."

Rosenberg was too tired to raise his head. "Just leave me here, Beccione. Let me die."

"Supposing I get you something to eat?"

Even that made Rosenberg blanch. "Food? You gotta be kidding. I'd bring my ring up."

Grinning, Beccione shouldered the exhausted man's pack.

"C'mon. Just a few more steps and you're in that big feather bed."

Rosenberg tottered to his feet. Beccione pushed him up the stairs and into the room. Sighting the bed, Rosenberg found the strength to stumble forward and throw himself face downwards.

Beccione threw open the shuttered windows and returned to Rosenberg. He pulled off the GI's boots and was about to take off his shirt when he discovered Rosenberg was already asleep. Giving up the attempt, Beccione took off his own shirt and boots and stretched out. He was asleep in seconds.

Beccione awoke just before six o'clock that evening. Still dazed from sleep, he was not certain at first what had disturbed him. Then, as shouts and a huge gale of laughter floated up through the open window, he rose and stared down.

Still bathed in sunlight, the yard was a hodgepodge of color and movement. While he and Rosenberg had been sleeping, two large trestle tables had been set up. These were now surrounded by forty or more uniformed men and almost as many women. The condition of the tables, littered with scraps of food and empty bottles of wine, suggested there had been a banquet earlier in the afternoon. And the feast apparently wasn't over yet: a stream of women moved to and fro, bringing more food from the house and clearing the refuse.

The din that arose was as bewildering as the scene itself. A bearded guitarist, sitting on a log, was surrounded by half a dozen men in German uniform singing bawdy marching songs. Two drunken couples were trying to dance to Neapolitan music that was coming from a radio inside the house. At the tables soldiers and women, pawing one another lasciviously, were laughing and shouting. The entire yard bubbled and seethed; the sounds and smells and excitement rose to the window upstairs like the heat of a fire.

The soldiers present were wearing the uniforms of all the major combatant nations and a few others besides. Some were wearing a mixture of uniforms: an American windbreaker over German field grey, a British combat jacket over Italian slacks. Beccione recognized a few of the flushed faces. Colenzo was there and so were Berrati and Toschack. In another group were Etienne, McAllister, Greyson and Tito. Fa-

natical card players, they were playing poker among the
debris of plates and wine bottles. There was no sign of
Kessler, Jean Pierre, Roberts or Johnson.

With the spring evening exceptionally mild, the women
camp followers, whom Beccione judged to be Italians, were
wearing provocative dresses and many were as drunk as the
men. There was, however, one exception: a strikingly beautiful girl at the head of the nearer trestle table. Although she
was wearing a low-cut, off-the-shoulder, red dress that gave
ample suggestion of a magnificent body beneath, there was
disdain in the glances she leveled at the women around her.
Her long hair was tawny and fell almost to her waist.

She was sharing the head of the table with a man who
wore the uniform of a German Africa Corps officer. Although his dress and manner were casual, he stood out as
distinctly from the soldiers around him as the girl did from
the women. He had a cold, handsome face that was tanned a
deeper hue than his closely-cut flaxen hair. His age appeared
to be around twenty-seven or eight. As he rose to pick up a
bottle of wine from the table, Beccione saw he was tall with a
lean and powerful body. He looked like a controlled, highly-
efficient fighting machine. The American had no doubt that
this was Helmut Schumann.

He glanced back at the girl. The German had apparently
said something to amuse her because she had thrown her
head back and was laughing. Her tawny hair swung silkily
over her tanned shoulders and her teeth shone white in the
sunlight. Without knowing why, Beccione thought of two
sleek animals, beautiful to contemplate and deadly to provoke.

Beccione turned to the bed where Rosenberg was still
asleep and tapped his shoulder. The GI grunted something
but continued snoring. Beccione shook him and this time
Rosenberg stirred and opened one eye. At first it was vacant
with sleep and exhaustion. Then he gave a groan. "It ain't
five o'clock already, is it?"

"No. There's something I want you to see."

By this time Rosenberg had heard the noise outside.
"What's goin' on?"

Beccione moved back to the window. "Come and look."

For a moment it seemed Rosenberg could not find the
strength. Then, moving as if he had arthritis in every joint,
he limped to the window. "What is it, for Chrissake?"

"Schumann's back," Beccione said.

Squinting painfully at the sunlight, Rosenberg peered down. At that moment a soldier further down the table shouted something at the girl. His shout was immediately taken up by other men who began stamping their feet on the flagstones. As the noise grew louder the guitarist walked over to the girl and spoke to her. As if in anticipation, someone inside the house switched off the radio.

By this time every eye in the assembly had fixed on the girl. Twice she shook her head but the clamor grew. Rosenberg, whose eyes had rounded on seeing her, glanced curiously at Beccione. "That dame's really something, ain't she? But what's all the shouting about?"

The guitarist was clearly pleading a case for the entire assembly. Again the girl shook her head but this time the German leaned towards her. His words seemed to annoy her, but after a few seconds she gave a disdainful shrug and rose to her feet. To the sound of resounding cheers she picked up a glass of wine, threw back her head and drained it. Beccione thought he had never seen so much sex in a simple act. Returning the glass to the table, she gave the German a last smouldering glance and walked with the guitarist to a space between the tables. At first she looked imperious and contemptuous, but as the guitarist struck a few dramatic chords and her high heels began to tap the flagstones, her mood changed. Her body swayed and the red dress started to swirl around her long legs. A hush fell and even the card players broke off their game to watch.

The rhythm of the dance quickened and the girl pirouetted, posed and pirouetted again, her arms making arabesques in the evening sunlight. Her voluptuous body and the sexual vibrancy she emanated were holding her audience captive; and every disdainful toss of her head told that she knew it. Rosenberg's voice was hoarse. "I was gonna shoot you for wakin' me up, kid. Now I think I'm gonna give you a medal."

The dance ended in a rapid crescendo of chords. Spinning like a top, the girl suddenly stopped dead, her arms held dramatically above her head. Her red dress, swirling out in a tantalizing glimpse of shapely thighs, rotated a moment longer, then fell back. There was a breathless silence, then a loud roar of applause from the soldiers followed by a stamping of feet for more. The girl, giving no sign that she heard, snapped something at the guitarist and returned to her seat. As men groaned and whistled, other noises gradually began flooding back—the tinny blast of the radio, the clink of plates and glasses.

Letting out his breath, Rosenberg turned. "You seen anything like that before? She could make a million in burlesque. Who's the guy with her? Schumann?"

Beccione grabbed his shirt and began buttoning it up. "He's not Santa Claus, that's for sure. You coming down?"

Rosenberg took another peek out of the window and this time noticed the food. "Why not? I ain't gonna get to sleep again."

In the yard outside the noise was deafening. As the two Americans paused to light cigarettes, they heard a shout from a group of men drinking beer near the water pump. They turned to see the raw-boned figure of Toschack approaching them. "Hiya, you guys. You joining the party?"

Beccione tossed him a cigarette and, ignoring his question, nodded at the blond German at the far end of the table. "Is that Schumann?"

"Yeah, that's him. He's had a big haul. That's why he's celebrating."

"Who's the girl with him?"

Toschack winked. "That's Magda. She's a Yugoslav."

"Since when did Yugoslavs dance the flemenco?"

"That wasn't the flemenco. It's a Yugosalvian folk dance. You ever see anything sexier? She doesn't shed a rag and still she has the boys howling like randy dogs."

"Where did Schumann find her?" Beccione suddenly found himself wanting to know everything about this girl.

"He didn't find her. She found Kessler. She's been working for the gang for nearly a year now."

"Working with them?"

"Yeah. She speaks nearly as many languages as Kessler and is the best actress in the business. He sometimes uses her to get intelligence from Fascist-held towns."

"But what brought her here in the first place?"

The Australian shrugged. "They say she was a partisan once and had to get out of Yugoslavia when things got too hot. I guess it's true, because she handles weapons like a man."

Beccione was watching the girl as she called for another bottle of wine. "But if she was a partisan, how come she's shacked up with Schumann? I always thought those Yugoslavian partisans hated the Krauts worse than hell."

The Australian shrugged again. "She don't talk to guys like

you and me, so how would I know? But if I took a guess I'd say Magda doesn't care whether a guy's a German or an Eskimo, as long as he's got influence and money. Magda's in it strictly for Magda."

There was a chuckle from Rosenberg who had found a large chicken leg on the table. "They're a real Bonnie and Clyde, ain't they?"

"Yeah, but twice as dangerous," Toschack said.

Beccione's eyes were still on the couple. "Does she speak English?"

"Yeah. Very well." Then, seeing Beccione's expression, the Australian gave a start. "You ain't thinking of making a pass at her, are you?"

Beccione grinned. "I like to know I'm understood if I do."

"Keep out of her way," Toschack warned. "Schumann's one hell of a jealous man."

Rosenberg gnawed the chicken leg reflectively. "He's a real clean-cut Aryan, ain't he? Blond and beautiful."

"He's also a killer," Toschack said.

Rosenberg glanced at Beccione. "You hear that, kid. Lay off Magda."

Beccione was no longer listening. His eyes were drawn to a man who had just risen from the far table. Wearing a thick serge shirt, he towered a good twelve inches above the men around him. His features were coarse with thick lips and small malicious eyes. Beccione nudged the Australian's arm.

"Who's the big guy?"

Toschack turned to look. "That's Mogelli. One of Schumann's men."

"Italian?"

"Yeah. A brutal bastard. Schumann uses him to keep discipline in his squad."

The din was growing louder and the litter of wine bottles on the tables mounted. On the bench in front of the huge Italian a soldier had his arm inside a woman's blouse. Grinning at the men around him, the giant suddenly grabbed hold of the couple and toppled them over in a crash of glass. A roar of drunken laughter followed. Beccione glanced back at Toschack. "How long do these parties go on?"

"Sometimes all night if Kessler doesn't stop them."

"Why isn't Kessler here?"

"He's gone out of town with Jean Pierre and a couple of others. Greyson saw 'em leaving two hours ago."

"Do you know where they were going?"

"No. But they often go out. It's probably to meet the black market boys."

"The black market? Kessler?" Rosenberg asked.

"Yeah. How else is he goin' to get rid of the stuff we steal? They pay him for it and he banks the dough for us."

"All of it?"

"Come off it. A third goes to the townsfolk and peasants and a third to running the organization. That way everyone's happy. The old man's got it all worked out, cobber. It's like a flaming business."

Rosenberg nodded at the head of the table where Schumann was whispering something in Magda's ear. "Where's the strength-through-joy boy been? Behind our lines again?"

Toschack nodded. "That's his territory."

"He kinda looks as if he enjoys his work, don't he?"

Before Toschack could reply, Schumann turned his face on the Americans. Magda had noticed their interest for some time and was whispering to him. As the German rose, Rosenberg nudged Beccione's arm. "Get your head down. Here comes *Der Führer*."

Although the German had been drinking heavily, there was no unsteadiness in his step as he rounded the table. He paused two paces away from the men, his eyes moving from Beccione to Rosenberg. Recognizing the latter's Jewish features, he deliberately turned his back on him and addressed himself to Beccione. "What's your name, soldier?"

Beccione understood now why the German's tanned handsome face had such a cold appearance. His eyes were grey with the faintest tinge of ice-blue, the color of gun metal. His English was almost as good as Kessler's, although his s's had a Germanic sibiliance.

"My name's Beccione. What's yours?"

The German ignored the aggressive counter. "Are you one of the Americans who have just joined us?"

"Yeah."

"But Beccione is an Italian name."

Magda, who had followed Schumann across the yard, said something to him in German. Smiling, he turned back to Beccione. "Of course. I am reminded that you Americans are made up of many races."

Meeting the cold eyes behind the smile, Beccione knew that a mongoose and a snake were likely to become better friends than he and the German. "That's right. Italians, Germans, Jews—the whole lot of them. And you know something—it works fine."

Schumann's thinning smile indicated that the point was taken and noted. "I am happy to hear it. I am Helmut Schumann—Captain Schumann. I command our B Squadron here."

Beccione noticed he did not offer his hand. "Yeah, I've heard of you. They say you brought in a good haul today."

"Yes, we raided one of your American base depots. We have brought back many good things. You must join our celebrations."

"Thanks. I might in a moment. Did you lose any men?"

"We had two wounded. But not seriously. The enemy suffered much more."

"Yeah, I'll bet they did." The German lifted a wary eyebrow at this remark. Rosenberg coughed meaningfully. Before any of the men could speak again, Magda moved forward. "Are you the American who used to be a boxer?"

Beccione turned to her. "Yeah, I used to box."

"Were you good?"

Beccione shrugged. "So so."

He noticed that her eyes were green with blue flecks. They were running over his tall, powerful body as if she were valuing a prize bull. "You are being modest. I think you were very good."

He smiled. "You should have been my promoter."

Schumann broke in impatiently. "If you are interested in boxing, we must match you up with one of my men at some time. It would entertain them." He nodded at Beccione and turned away. "Come. Let us get back to the party."

The girl did not follow him. She was taller than Beccione had realized: the top of her head was level with his scarred eyebrows. As she took a step forward, the astonishing aura of sex that surrounded her enveloped him. It was as real as the expensive perfume she was wearing, and made his throat tighten. He knew she could feel his desire—it showed as a mocking light in her green eyes.

"Tell me something I have always wanted to know. Do you have to be brave to be a boxer?"

"No," Beccione said. "Just stupid."

She laughed. "Why do you say that?"

"Because it's true."

"But surely it is dangerous."

"It is. That's why we're stupid."

She laughed again. He knew she was using her sex to bait him and the knowledge both angered and excited him. "Do you make a habit of doing things that are dangerous and stupid?"

"I hadn't thought about it," he said. "But now that you mention it, I've got some stupid thoughts at this moment."

Her expression told him how much she was enjoying the encounter. "What stupid thoughts are those?"

His eyes ran down her body. "Can't you guess?"

Rosenberg gave a cough that had a choking sound. A dozen paces away Schumann had realized the girl was not following him and he turned around. Some of the nearby women were pointing and exchanging giggles and whispers. Schumann's face tightened. *"Magda, was machen Sie? Kommen Sie zurück zum Tisch."*

The girl, aware of the stir she was causing, hesitated for a moment as if pondering whether to exacerbate it by deliberately disobeying the German. Then, as if thinking twice, she acknowledged his shout before turning back to Beccione. "I think we are both right. You are a man who likes taking risks even if they are stupid. Doesn't that sum it up well?"

Beccione grinned. "Not that well. I'd say these risks were worthwhile."

She gave a slight start at his audacity; and then, glancing at Toschack as if warning him to keep silent, she uttered a light laugh. "You are crazy. Go and drink some wine and forget your stupid thoughts. They can only lead you into trouble."

The flash of her eyes as she turned away belied her advice. Rosenberg, looking after her, rolled his eyes in disbelief. "You gone nuts or something? If you start chasin' her, Schumann'll have you gutted for dogmeat."

Beccione was still watching Magda. "She's one hell of a woman."

"Your buddy's right," Toschack said. "She's worse than dynamite. Use your head and leave her alone."

Turning away, Beccione motioned at the nearby table. "How about grabbing some of *Der Führer's* wine?"

Rosenberg cursed, then followed him. "Why should I worry. It's your neck."

17

Beccione sat next to Johnson, the black GI, who was chewing gum rhythmically as he guided the jeep along the bank of a half-dry river. On either side bush-strewn mountains rose into a cloudless sky. The jeep jolted over a network of tree roots, its two machine guns dipping on their mountings.

Six similarly-armed jeeps could be seen ahead. Each one carried a crew of two men, all wearing German uniforms and equipped with automatic carbines and grenades. The spare wheels and jerry cans of fuel and water that hung on racks all around the jeeps made their identification difficult; and to confuse the enemy further, small black crosses were painted here and there on exposed bodywork. Each driver was keeping approximately twenty meters from his neighbor.

Larry Johnson, who came from Chicago, figured he had sized up Beccione's type the night the two GIs arrived. In the half hour of their patrol together, he had seen nothing in Beccione that made him reassess his first impression. Larry Johnson was a man with no occasion to love whites; and as far as he was concerned, this was just another honkie bastard in the long line of bastards he had known. Lost in his own thoughts, he was surprised when Beccione broke the long silence with a question.

"You know what this patrol's for?"

Johnson's jaws ceased chewing. "You don't know?"

"I wouldn't ask if I did, would I?"

Johnson almost told him to go to hell. "We need some more dynamite. So we're raiding a Kraut storehouse."

"Where?"

Johnson jabbed a finger at a range of mountains ahead. "Up in those hills."

"What do we need dynamite for?"

Johnson stared at him. "Dynamite's a way of hitting the sonsofbitches where it hurts."

"You mean sabotage?"

"Sure. What else?"

"But why sabotage? I thought the idea was to grab loot, not destroy it."

Johnson took a closer look at the GI. "You're kinda raw, aren't you? The Krauts and the Allies don't just sit back and take it. There isn't a day when one of 'em hasn't got a patrol out looking for us. So we hit back. If we didn't, they'd be swarming all over us." He showed contempt when he saw Beccione's expression. "What's the matter, buster? Don't you dig fighting when there's no loot in it?"

As was his way, Beccione struck back hard. "You're damned right I don't. That's what I've been doing for the last two years. When I fight now, I want a reason."

"You've got one. Survival. And there ain't a better. Didn't the Frenchman tell you that during your training?"

Beccione and Rosenberg's training had ended two days ago. A week had been spent on navigation and handling the jeeps in mountainous terrain; two weeks learning to operate every weapon on the range. The course had demonstrated the expertise available to Kessler: the Americans had been given a different instructor for every weapon.

Throughout the course Kessler had carefully monitored the Americans' progress and at the end of it, exactly as if they were cadets at a military academy, he had called them to his headquarters and congratulated them on passing its high standards. He had then assigned them to Jean Pierre.

Originally, Beccione was not to be included in the present seven-jeep mission. But after the men had been briefed early that morning, Johnson's gunner had fallen ill with stomach trouble and Kessler, who was leading the mission, had assigned Beccione to take his place. Kessler, conscious of the time already lost, informed the American that he would be briefed when the squad reached its destination. In the meantime, Beccione had been sent to put on his German uniform. Jean Pierre reminded him to take along his green armband and beret.

After months of stress, with its build-up of nervous tension, Beccione was eagerly anticipating the prospect of action. He took a cigarette and shook one out for Johnson. He studied the man's features as he held a match for him.

"You've been to college, haven't you?"

Johnson grimaced at him. "You mean it shows?"

"It shows, even if you talk rough sometimes. How come you got mixed up with this mob?"

"You can't guess?"

Beccione shook his head.

"I'm black, man. Or haven't you noticed?"

"You're saying that's your only reason?"

"*Only* reason? You ought to serve in the black division, buster. We get every dirty job you honkies can find for us. I can't figure out why every guy in the outfit hasn't jumped over the fence by this time."

"You sound like you had it bad. Why aren't you with Schumann?"

"I keep on asking myself the same thing," Johnson said grimly. "Maybe it's because I'm scared I might run into my own guys one day. I wouldn't like killing them."

"You still might have to. Maybe they'll be sent lookin' for us. You say they get all the dirty jobs."

"That'd be different. A guy has the right to defend himself."

Sensing a thaw in the black man's attitude, Beccione decided this might be a good time to satisfy his curiosity about some of Kessler's men.

"Tell me about Schumann," he said. "Is he as mean as they say?"

"Why should he be mean? Because he fights against your buddies?"

"I've got my reasons for thinking he's mean."

"What reasons?"

Beccione told him about the Castelmonte convoy. Johnson nodded when he finished. "That sounds like Schumann. He thinks if a job's worth doing, it's worth doing well."

"Why the hell does Kessler use a guy like that?"

"Why not? Did your company commander get rid of guys who liked killing Krauts? Ours used to recommend 'em for medals. He called 'em good soldiers."

"You know what I mean, for Chrissake."

"O.K. Schumann's a killer. He's also a helluva good soldier and patrol leader. Period."

Beccione thought about that for a minute, trying once more to piece together some explanation for Kessler and his army that made sense. Turning back to Johnson, he asked bluntly, "How about telling me something about Kessler and one or two of the others? Like what they've done and how they got here."

Johnson eyed him warily. Although it had not happened since he joined the group, he knew both the Allies and the Germans had tried to infiltrate spies into it, and this honkie had more questions than a dog had fleas. At the same time Kessler appeared to have accepted his credentials, and the man held the German's judgment in high esteem.

"Most of the guys don't like talking about what they did. I ain't even sure they all use their real names."

Beccione stared at him. "Why's that?"

"Isn't it obvious? When this war's over they want to settle quietly down in some foreign country and spend the dough they've made. If it gets around what they've done it might not be so easy."

Beccione realized this was true. "But Kessler must know their real names."

"Oh yeah. But he'd be the last to talk if a man wanted to hide his identity."

"O.K. What are names anyway? How about Jean Pierre? How did he get into this?"

There was a long pause before Johnson decided to answer him. "He was in Italy on business for the Yanks when Mussolini declared war on France and Britain. They interned him and soon afterwards he got word his wife and daughter had been killed in a British air raid. A few months later he heard the Krauts had shot his younger brother for working in the resistance. Shortly after that he escaped and ran into Kessler. Since then he's been the boss's right-hand man."

Beccione nodded. "What about the Aussie, Toschack?"

Johnson grinned. "He's a crazy man. His platoon commander led them into an ambush and got most of the guys killed, including Toschack's buddy. He was so mad he shot the officer and took off into the hills. He was living with a peasant family when we came across him."

"Who's the guy driving Roberts' jeep?" Beccione gestured ahead to a soldier he hadn't seen before, a big shambling man with a furrowed, worried face. "The one with a face like a spaniel."

"You mean Williams? He's our safebuster."

"Safebuster?"

"Yeah. A London ex-con. He'd just finished five years in the pen when the limeys put him in the army. He reckoned King and Country hadn't done him any favors, but he didn't get a chance to desert until they sent his regiment to Italy."

"What about the South African with McAllister?"

"Russell? He was caught selling ammunition on the black market. There was talk about executing him until he escaped during an air raid."

Beccione grinned. "You've sure got 'em all shapes and sizes. What about the two Italians?"

"Berrati, that's the guy with glasses, got into trouble with the Fascists when they came in power and had to run for it. He hates 'em like hell. Colenzo was a mechanic and small-time con. Kessler uses him to get information from black marketeers. He also knows the district well and scouts for us."

With the river bank becoming fissured and studded with large boulders, the jeeps ahead were forced to take to the riverbed. As their tyres scrabbled over the bleached pebbles, progress slowed down to a walking pace. Once their jeep was back on an even keel, Beccione tried again.

"O.K., let's get back to Kessler. Is it true he was once a professor at Heidelberg University?"

Johnson gave him a quick glance, then his guarded eyes returned to the riverbed. "Who told you that?"

"Toschack. Is it true?"

"It could be."

"Why did he desert from the German Army?"

"Was he in the German Army?"

"C'mon, Johnson. Colenzo thinks he's the greatest leader since Garibaldi. He had to learn it somewhere." As the black shrugged, Beccione turned to him. "Why the cover up?"

Johnson's expression hardened. "You're sure full of questions, aren't you? If you want to know more about Kessler, why don't you ask the guy yourself?"

Beccione thought he understood. "For Chrissake, I'm not a spy. I'm just a guy whose life might depend on Kessler making the right decisions. Do you think he's a commie?"

Johnson appeared to relax slightly. "Why should he be a commie?"

"They say there's plenty of 'em around in Italy these days. And from the way he talks, he seems to think the sun shines out of the peasants' behinds."

Johnson's expression became a mixture of contempt and anger. "And you think that makes him a commie? You met any of these peasants yet? They're decent people trampled into the mud by their own middle class and now by the Fascists. There's another thing—we couldn't operate or even stay alive without their help. So what's wrong with liking them?"

The passion of the man's outburst took Beccione by surprise. "O.K., O.K. I'm just trying to figure out the guy. You and me and the rest are easy: we're either deserters or hoods doing what we've always done. But Kessler seems a different animal. What's his racket? Why does he lead us against his own people? You think it's some kind of revenge?"

"Why should it be revenge? He attacks our guys too."

"But not personally. He uses Schumann for that."

"Not always. If the job's big enough he goes himself."

"You sure of that?"

"Of course I'm sure. I've been along with him."

Beccione frowned. "Then if it's not revenge, what is it?"

Johnson steered the jeep round a large boulder on the riverbed before replying. "You know your trouble? You're one of those people who always sees more in a thing than there is. Kessler and the rest of us are just guys who have run foul of our own kind for one reason or another and jumped the wall. Some of us might have preferred to disappear altogether; some of us maybe like this life—I can't say how many either way. But one thing's for sure—since we can't split, we're making the best of it. And with Kessler leading us, that best ain't bad at all."

Before Beccione could ask another question he noticed that the first jeep had halted beneath a steep fan of shale. His eyes moved up the rugged slope that horses would find difficult to climb. "You ain't driving 'em up there. That I don't believe."

Johnson grinned. "No, we ain't that good. Two of the jeeps are carrying wire ropes, shackles and pulleys. We climb the slope on foot and shackle a pulley to a large rock up there. Then we run a rope through it and down to the first jeep. The other end we fix to two other jeeps and they drive back across the river. By the time they reach the far bank, the first jeep is dragged to the top of the slope. They go on doing the same act until five jeeps are up there. Then we reverse the procedure: the jeeps at the top drag the others after them. We aim to do the job in half an hour."

"You telling me you've done it before?"

Johnson braked the jeep. "Three or four times. The Krauts are active round here—they've got reserves in the area. This way we get right behind 'em without taking any risks. They've never figured out how we do it."

There was an angry roar from the head of the column. Jean Pierre, busy supervising the operation, had caught sight of Johnson and Beccione still chatting in their jeep. The black GI jumped out with a malicious grin. "Here's where you work for your keep, buster. And find out why Kessler keeps us in shape."

18

Nose to tail, the jeeps were descending a grassy hillside. Ahead was a line of trees. One by one the jeeps reached the trees and swung around in readiness for a quick getaway. When the last vehicle was parked, Kessler called all fourteen men to him. His face and cultured voice were disciplined, and yet Beccione sensed that the German was looking forward to the coming engagement.

Kessler pointed at the line of trees. "The stone hedge I spoke about is directly behind there. Keep down and you should not be seen. I shall indicate your objective when you are in position." He turned to Berrati, whom Beccione had learned was trained in first aid. "Berrati, you stay with the jeeps."

During the journey, even during the strenuous hauling of the jeeps over the pass, the men had appeared as relaxed as if on a day's outing. Now, with automatic weapons at the ready, they moved with the caution and speed of highly-trained combat soldiers. Impressed, Beccione stalked with them through the trees until they reached a thirty yard stretch of open country. It terminated in a high stone hedge. Beyond the hedge could be seen glimpses of a road and a few cottages straggling up the opposite hill.

Motioning the men to keep low, Kessler led them out of the trees. When Beccione reached the hedge he peered over it at the mountain village below. A full mile away, it was little more than a few rows of sun-baked cottages radiating from a central piazza. A minor road ran through it from north to south. With the sun still high in the sky, all the inhabitants seemed to be indoors. Even the surrounding fields were deserted. With heat shimmering the outlines, the effect was toylike and unreal.

Then Johnson handed Beccione a pair of binoculars and the scene leapt into life. An old woman, looking like a black crow, shuffled out of a cottage and disappeared down an alley. A dog could be seen in the piazza, sniffing round a bush before settling in the shade of a tree. The piazza, which contained a tiny park of ornamental bushes and dusty gum trees, was surrounded mostly by small shops; but one large stone building caught the American's eye. Its windows had all been removed and replaced by heavy shutters and sandbags. More sandbags stood on the pavement outside and three troop transports were parked before them. A gap between the sandbags suggested a sentry post. In a bay alongside the building were the squat shapes of two armored cars.

Kessler's voice at his elbow made the GI start. "Have you identified our target, Beccione?"

"You're going after explosives, aren't you?" the American said. When Kessler nodded, he went on: "Surely they aren't stored in the village?"

"No. That building in the piazza is where the guards are billetted." The German pointed northwards along the dirt road. "That is the explosive storehouse."

The building he indicated was an old stone barn half a mile from the village. Standing just off the road, it was enclosed by a new chain-mesh fence. A small wooden building, which also looked to be newly built, stood close by. The gate that led into the enclosure was closed and presumably locked.

"What's the smaller building?" Beccione asked.

"It billets the guard of the day, an NCO and three men."

"I can't see them."

"Like the main garrison, they are probably taking a siesta."

"I suppose they are linked by radio or telephone?"

"By radio," Kessler said.

Beccione lowered the binoculars. "What's the point in keeping explosives in a hick joint like this?"

The German pointed north where the road disappeared into the mountains. "A strategic valley runs through there. They are busy fortifying it."

"But why should that concern you?"

The German's glance was both cold and analytical. "No one has said it concerns me. I am here because I need the explosives."

"So what's your plan? To attack both headquarters and storehouse at the same time?"

"No. We shall go straight for the main garrison. Once they are out of the action, the storehouse guards will surrender.

They are not likely to risk a fight when sitting on tons of explosives."

Beccione realized he was right. Down beside the hedge Jean Pierre was talking in low tones to the men and pointing out stragetic objects from a drawing he held. Johnson, who had remained with Beccione, was listening to Kessler's repeat of the briefing he had already given the others.

"Our plan is to wait until midnight when all but the sentries should be asleep. Then one jeep under Captain Roberts and another under McAllister will drive three kilometers north and south of the road and plant mines. As this is a minor road we are not expecting any traffic but we must be prepared. The two crews will then move into prearranged positions outside the mines from which they can see the lights of any approaching vehicles. Both crews are carrying radios and, should any German vehicles pass them, they will report their strength to us. If this should be formidable, the mines will give us time to withdraw. On the other hand, if any civilian vehicles approach they will be sent back."

"What are the rest of us doing during this time?" Beccione asked.

"Berrati will stay behind in the first aid jeep during the action in case anyone is wounded. Later he will bring his jeep down to be loaded up with explosives. The rest of us will move down the hill and attack the garrison. Surprise is essential here because we must try to destroy the armored cars before they can be manned."

"Do you know how many men are in that garrison?"

"Our scouts have counted twenty-four. Excluding the four guarding the storehouse."

"Twenty-eight soldiers and two armored cars," Beccione said. "And you've got fifteen guys and only thin-skinned jeeps. Why didn't you bring more men with you? I wouldn't call those healthy odds."

"We need room in the jeeps to carry the explosives away." Kessler replied, allowing himself a rare smile. "These are still far better odds than we are used to. We are a guerrilla band and can never hope to match our enemies in numbers. Our strength lies in surprise."

Beccione could not resist the question. "Is that how you see yourselves? As guerrillas?"

Kessler smiled again, this time wryly. "I had forgotten. You are the man who likes to call a spade a spade. What word would you prefer? Outlaws? Or criminals?"

"We ain't exactly soldiers fighting for our country, are we?"

"And you think we would be better people if we were? There have been philosophers, Beccione, who have said war is the greatest criminal activity of all. It certainly kills more people than any other."

"That's saying we're better than the guys we kill."

"Not necessarily better. But there are some who would say we are no worse."

Along the hedge Jean Pierre, who had finished talking to the men, moved closer to listen. Beccione grimaced. "I ain't one of 'em. I hate the Army worse'n hell, but I can't pretend a guy who kills for profit is better than a guy who don't. I may be smarter than them but I ain't better."

The German's expression puzzled Beccione as the man turned to Jean Pierre and said something to him in French. Glancing at Beccione, the Frenchman appeared to protest before giving a resigned shrug of his shoulders. Kessler was smiling when he turned back. "Whatever else you may be, Beccione, you are a man who speaks his mind. And they are a rare breed in themselves. You will man the .30 on my jeep tonight. Afterwards you will return with Johnson as arranged."

As Beccione gave a start, the German turned to Johnson. "Colenzo will take his place with you during the action. Tell him when he reports back."

Johnson nodded. With a glance at Jean Pierre, Kessler walked away. The big Frenchman scowled at Beccione before following him. "It's more than you deserve, Yankee. So mind you do a good job. Now get up to those trees and help camouflage the jeeps."

"You know something," Johnson said as the two men walked off, "it must be a hell of a sacrifice for you, fighting for loot instead of principles."

Beccione grinned back. "You can't imagine."

Up the hill men were already backing the jeeps into the trees and covering them with camouflaged nets. When this was done, sentries were posted on the upper and lower fringes of the wood, and the remainder of the squad was allowed to rest. All the men chose to sleep beneath the cool trees. Beccione, lying in the shade of a chestnut, was experiencing the acute awareness of life that the presence of danger brings to some men. Far below, the village shimmered in the sunlight; it was an impossible place to equate with violence

and death. In the chestnut above a wood pigeon's liquid coo-
ing mingled with the rustling of the leaves. They were the last
sounds Beccione heard before he fell asleep.

19

Jean Pierre cut the headlights of his jeep and braked a few
yards from the entrance to the piazza. Like a row of stealthy
Indians, the four jeeps behind him halted one by one. Dark
and shuttered cottages stood on the left side of the road. On
the right side a line of gum trees was threshing in the wind.
The only light came from the bright ceiling of stars.

The wind, cool and easterly, had begun rising just after
sundown and was now blowing a half-gale. It helped to
drown the jeeps' engines but was sweeping clouds of dust
down the road. Sitting behind Jean Pierre and Kessler, Beccione rubbed the grit out of his eyes.

A long minute passed, tightening the mens' nerves. A tin
can, bounding along the road, made drivers and gunners alike
turn sharply. Then a flashlight flickered three times from the
piazza entrance. Nodding at Kessler, Jean Pierre turned to
Beccione. "Etienne says it's O.K. Get ready."

One by one the jeeps crept into the piazza. Circling left,
they kept the tiny park between them and the building that
housed the garrison. The wind sounded louder here, rushing
across the square and shaking the dry leaves of the trees and
bushes. At the far side of the park Beccione saw the first of
the three transports begin to appear. Flicking his tail lights on
and off, a signal for the other jeeps to halt, the Frenchman
crept on while Kessler climbed into the rear seat and uncoupled the heavy .50 Browning. Heaving its mounting over
the driver's head, he nodded at Beccione to be ready.

The three parked transports came level with the jeep. Their
bulk hid the sandbagged entrance of the building, making it
impossible to see whether a sentry was posted there or not.
Beccione felt his nerves tighten a full notch. If they were seen
from the windows of the building or if their engine were
heard through the wind, they would be a sitting target in the
thin-skinned jeep.

Kessler motioned Jean Pierre to continue. As the jeep crept
past the transports, the loading bay with its two shadowy armored cars came slowly into line. Kessler tapped Beccione's
shoulder. "You take the *Kübel*. Are you ready?"

The German gave off an aura of intense excitement, something Beccione had not expected in a man so composed. His
mouth felt dry as he nodded. Settling behind the heavy
Browning, Kessler took aim. Five seconds later its massive
clatter, only three feet from Beccione's ear, shattered the
night like fragile glass.

All hell broke loose as Beccione also commenced firing.
Jean Pierre drove his two gunners slowly past the bay, followed closely by Tito and Etienne who came charging around
the trees to join in the first attack. The machine guns of all
the jeeps had been loaded with incendiary ammunition as
well as tracer and armor-piercing: the effect was dazzling as
glowing bullets ricocheted from the German vehicles' armor
in all directions.

Two jeeps stayed back to concentrate their fire on the three
transports. The rearmost transport burst into flames almost
immediately, lighting up the jeeps and the threshing trees.
The second one lurched sideways as bullets burst its far tyres.
A few seconds later the fuel tank of the foremost vehicle exploded, hurling debris and scraps of burning canvas in all
directions.

Although not thirty seconds had passed since Kessler commenced his attack, there was already frantic activity within
the garrison. Lights kept showing behind shuttered windows,
to be doused immediately as bullets searched them out. From
a side door that led into the loading bay half-clad soldiers
were trying to reach the armored cars. The five yard distance
they had to cover was dense with bullets and man after man
was cut down as he made the attempt.

Although the piazza was a bedlam by this time, there was
little to be seen of civilians apart from a few shuttered windows thrown open and hastily closed again. By this time of
the war, Italians had learned that their wisest course at such
moments was to go to ground and pray to their saints.

Four more Germans died trying to get to the armored cars;
but three others dived for safety into the lee of the larger
one. The dazzling tracer prevented Kessler and Beccione
from seeing them enter it, but Jean Pierre shouted that it was
on the move.

Recognizing the danger, the gunners of all four jeeps gave

it their full attention. Bullets pounded it from turret to skirt, glancing off in a myriad of electric sparks. As Kessler had feared, its tough armored shell turned even the heavy caliber shells. As its 20mm cannon began swinging ominously towards the jeeps, Jean Pierre gave another shout of warning to his gunners and the jeep shot away. The instant response of the other drivers told Beccione the danger had been anticipated and a counter move planned. Tito and Etienne raced around the park after Jean Pierre in a clockwise direction. The two rearmost jeeps, after a final broadside at the shattered windows of the garrison, reversed and joined their comrades at the far side of the park.

In the momentary respite Beccione had time to take stock. All three transports were now burning fiercely. At the far side of the piazza, moving into position to attack the jeeps, the squat black shape of the armored car could be seen appearing and disappearing through the trees. There was no sign of the *Kübel* and Beccione guessed it had been crippled by the heavy .50 Brownings.

The armored car was rolling slowly forward, its crew weighing the situation before they attacked. Kessler signaled the jeeps to retreat and keep the full width of the park between them and the enemy. As the drivers obeyed, the German climbed into the front of the jeep and fumbled down in the well below. Jean Pierre hissed something at him in French and gestured fierce disapproval. Ignoring him, Kessler jumped out of the jeep with a bulky object held in his arms and ran among the trees. Beccione bent forward. "What's he doing?" he shouted.

Jean Pierre was trying to follow the German's movements. "He's going to blow up that armored car."

"What with?"

"A jerry can of petrol with a grenade attached to it. With a seven second fuse."

"Seven seconds? He's crazy," Beccione said.

The big Frenchman turned towards him. "He had no way of knowing those armored cars would be here but he still feels responsible. Go after him and see that he's O.K., will you? He ordered me to stay here with the jeep."

Nodding, Beccione leapt down and ran through the park. Inside there was a patch of baked grass with a couple of benches. Beccione, unable at first to find Kessler, guessed he was keeping to the fringe of the park where there were bushes as well as trees to provide cover.

At the far side of the park the armored car had halted a moment to give both gunners time to test their weapons. The brutal pounding of the 20mm cannon, tearing entire branches from the trees, gave evidence of its fire-power.

When the firing had ended, Beccione ran forward again and caught sight of Kessler behind a bush on the very edge of the road. Before the armored car could begin to move forward, the German darted out and slid the jerry can between its front and rear wheels.

The audacity of the attack caught the gunners by surprise and Kessler was back among the trees before they could react. The driver threw in his gears and tried to pull away, but his wheels had hardly started to roll when the grenade exploded, splashing long tongues of flame out from beneath the chassis. A second duller explosion followed seconds later as the flames reached the ruptured fuel tanks. There was a roar as if a giant blowtorch had been ignited and a sheet of flame leapt up around the vehicle.

Beccione stiffened in surprise at the sight of Kessler. The German had risen from a bush to gain a better view and now, silhouetted against the flames, he appeared to Beccione to be growing taller, as if exulting in his handiwork.

The clang of metal drew Beccione's eyes back to the road. One of the vehicle's crew had managed to push the turret door open. He threw himself out and rolled from the armored skirt to the ground. In an instant his uniform was ablaze and he collapsed among the burning fuel with a thin scream.

The effect on Kessler was as dramatic as his earlier success. He took a step forward as if to try to save the man. Then, realizing such an attempt would be futile, he gave a sharp cry and turned his back on the sight. As he leaned against a tree, the flames showed his face was filled with horror and self-disgust.

Beccione's instinct for survival decided his next move. Drawing back out of sight of the German, he called his name. Fifteen seconds later Kessler appeared, pushing his way through the bushes. His disciplined mask was back in place again—only his pallor and curt voice betrayed him.

"What are you doing here?"

"Jean Pierre sent me."

"Why?"

Beccione shrugged. "In case you needed help, I suppose."

Without another word Kessler pushed past him and made

for his jeep. For the moment the piazza seemed almost quiet, the only sounds an occasional rifle shot, the crackle of fire, shouts and the rushing of the wind. Then muffled explosions began as the intense heat of the fire ate through to ammunition in the stricken armored car.

Jean Pierre's face showed relief when Kessler climbed into the jeep alongside him. "Well done, Franz. With that armored car out of the way, the rest of the garrison can't do us any harm."

"They'll have radioed for help though, won't they?" Beccione asked as he dropped down behind the two men.

The Frenchman shook his head. "Reinforcements can't get here in time, Yankee. And even if they could, those mines will hold 'em long enough for us to get away."

The brusqueness in Kessler's voice told he had not yet forgiven Jean Pierre for sending Beccione after him. "Have you radioed Roberts and McAllister to make for the storehouse?"

Jean Pierre nodded. "Roberts is already there. He says the guards surrendered as soon as they saw the flames in the village. I sent Toschack to help him with the loading."

"And Tito?"

As if in answer there was a sharp burst of firing from the other side of the piazza. "He's in position," the Frenchman said. "He'll keep the rest of the garrison pinned down until we're ready."

Glancing back, Beccione saw there was only one jeep behind them. Jean Pierre flickered his lights in signal and it began to follow them.

To reach the road they had to pass close to the stricken armored car. Red hot by this time, its heat scorched their faces. Beccione saw Kessler shudder as his eyes were drawn to the spot where the soldier had fallen. Then he wrenched his face away as the jeep accelerated towards the storehouse.

They reached it in less than three minutes to find two jeeps already loaded with boxes of explosives. Roberts had wasted no time, even using the German guards as loaders. Two more jeeps, belonging to McAllister and Berrati, arrived shortly afterwards. With four crews to help, the work went quickly. The storehouse contained gelignite, detonators and fuses as well as Panzerfaust and mortar ammunition. Roberts, who was supervising the loading, took large quantities of each. His most difficult task was securing the explosives so that no accident would occur when the jeeps were lowered down the shale slope on the way back. After the last strap had been fastened, Kessler turned to him and motioned at the store-house. "What do you think? Is it safe for the villagers if we blow it up?"

Roberts measured with his eyes the distance to the village. Bursts of machine gun fire could still be heard at irregular intervals. "No. We'd be taking a chance. There's still a lot of explosives in there."

Kessler did not hesitate. "Then we'll leave it."

With Beccione reinstated in Johnson's jeep, the convoy drove back towards the village, leaving the German guards sitting dejectedly at the roadside. Although the red glow over the piazza was beginning to fade, the crews could still see flames licking the hulk of the armored car when they drew near it. There was no firing from the garrison: the survivors, realizing by this time that they were not in danger unless they fought back, were lying low. As the convoy drove past, Tito and Etienne opened fire to give it cover. Then, with the small Frenchman squirting burst after burst at the building, Tito accelerated away and caught up with the other crews half a mile down the road. A minute later all seven vehicles were climbing the hillside. If anything the wind was fiercer up there and Beccione shook his head when Johnson shouted something at him. He waited until the jeep cleared the crest and the wind fell before trying again.

"What do you think of Kessler now? Seven loads of explosives, five Kraut vehicles knocked out, and we ain't got a scratch."

"Not bad," Beccione conceded.

"Not bad? And the guy knocks out an armored car single-handed? You're just naturally tight, man."

Grinning, Beccione was about to tell the black what he had seen in the park but he checked himself and sank back. Whatever the mystery that might surround him, the German was a brave man and his action could well have saved his men's lives. In addition, by accepting Beccione and Rosenberg into his organization, he was giving them protection without which they would be hard pressed to survive. All of this earned Beccione's respect; admiration he would withhold until Kessler's behavior was better understood.

Johnson was tapping the beret he was still wearing. "You can take those things off now. If we see any Krauts on the way back, we want 'em to believe we're just a routine patrol."

Beccione obeyed, then yawned. "You want me to drive?"

Johnson shook his head. "No. You can spell me at the other side of the pass."

Beccione yawned again and tried to make himself comfortable among the boxes of explosives. "Then I'm getting some shut-eye. Call me when you want me."

It was sunrise before the squad reached Kessler's explosive store two miles north of La Capella. As Beccione jumped down from the driver's seat, Kessler approached him and drew him aside. "I want you to know that I am pleased with the way you behaved last night. Captain Moreau feels the same way."

Beccione shrugged. "I'm glad to hear it." He nodded at the cave in the rugged mountainside into which men were already carrying boxes of explosives. "You must have to keep this place well guarded."

"We keep all our installations well guarded, Beccione," the German said dryly. "The men do the duties on a rotating system, although naturally they like to see the new recruits take their turns early on."

Beccione grimaced around at the inhospitable terrain. "Don't tell me. Let me guess."

The hint of a smile twitched Kessler's mouth. "You and Rosenberg will share the duty with two men from C Squad for the next week. You'll report to Captain Roberts at 17.00 hours. He'll issue you with provisions and explain your duties."

"A week," Beccione said. "That's a hell of a spell, isn't it? We ain't seen the town yet."

"You will get your chance for that when the week is over. Your reward will be two days off duty."

"Will you be going out on any more raids while we're here?"

The American's curiosity brought a curtness to the German's voice. "No. I have other work to do."

As he turned away, the beret he was carrying in his hip pocket fell to the ground. Beccione picked it up and was about to hand it back when his eyes fell on the badge with its implacable female effigy.

"I've been meaning to ask you. What does this badge represent?"

Kessler's deep-set eyes turned on him. "You don't know?"

"I wouldn't ask if I did, would I?"

Studying him, the German took the beret. His voice seemed to grind through his teeth. "Nemesis," he said.

20

While Kessler's raids were infuriating local army commanders on both sides of the front, the Allies had decided to take more drastic steps to capture Rome. Held up throughout the winter at Cassino by the immortal German paratroopers of the IV Regiment, the British and Americans had made Operation Strangle their first measure. From March onwards the 1st British and the 12th American Tactical Air Forces had flown daily sorties over central Italy against every conceivable aid to German communications. Goods trains, mechanized columns, road junctions, passes and bridges had all come under an onslaught of bombs and rockets. Similar attacks had been made by heavy bombers against major communication centers like Alpine passes and seaports.

At the same time the Allied 15th Army Group had begun its preparations. The French Expeditionary Force had been shifted to the upper reaches of the Garigliano; the U.S. 2nd Corps to its lower reaches. The Polish 2nd Corps had taken over the hills north of Cassino. The British 10th Corps had been given positions on the upper Rapido. The British 13th Corps and the Canadian 1st Corps had also moved into the battle zone. Thus by May the major part of Montgomery's 8th Army as well as the 5th Army was in the Cassino area, leaving only two divisions and the recently created Royal Italian Army in the Adriatic sector.

Tension was high during the early days of May. Every soldier was waiting for the storm to break. Then, at 23.00 hours on May 11, a radio signal from London opened the floodgates. From the Tyrrhenian sea to Aquafondata, two thousand Allied guns commenced firing. At midnight the dry-throated men of the 5th and 8th Armies climbed out of their foxholes and began their belated attack on Rome.

*　　*　　*

It was an event that did not go unnoticed in La Capella. On the morning of May 12 Jean Pierre entered Kessler's office, an austere room in the hotel. Through an open door that led into an anteroom, a radio transmitter and receiver could be seen.

"You asked to see me, Franz?"

Kessler nodded the Frenchman to a chair. "I assume you have heard the news?"

"Yes. So have Roberts and the others."

"How are they taking it?"

Jean Pierre shrugged. "You can't really tell, and in any case none of the radio bulletins are giving much away. But I think one or two of them are a bit apprehensive."

"That isn't surprising. But they need not be. It means plenty of work for us. I intend taking a scouting party south this afternoon. I'd like you to come with me."

The Frenchman nodded. "Do you think the Gustav Line will crack?"

"Eventually it must. But don't forget there is still the Adolf Hitler Line to break before the Allies reach Rome. It will all take time."

From his expression it was clear Jean Pierre was sharing some of his colleagues' apprehension. "What will happen then, Franz?"

The German shrugged. "If I could read Kesselring's mind, I could tell you. He might stand and fight north of Rome or he might retreat right back to the Gothic Line."

The Frenchman shifted uneasily in his chair. "What happens if he retreats? We won't be able to stay here in La Capella, not once the Allies have occupied the district." When Kessler did not reply, he leaned forward. "How is it all going to end, Franz? Do you ever think about that?"

Kessler gazed at him for a moment, then rose and went to the window. When he spoke, he sounded both grave and amused. "Do I think about it, Jean Pierre? I think about it so much that I keep on having a dream. Do you believe in dreams, Jean Pierre?"

The question caught the big Frenchman by surprise. "What sort of a dream?"

"It is of a small town in the mountains. A rather beautiful town with campaniles and trees and flowers. I do not recognize it and yet when I hear a great bell chiming I know we have reached our destiny." As Kessler turned, Jean Pierre saw he was smiling. "Ridiculous, isn't it? And yet when I have that dream, it is as real to me as this office."

The Frenchman cleared his throat. "What do you think it means?"

"I have told you. It is our destiny." Seeing Jean Pierre's discomfort, Kessler burst out laughing. "Stop looking so serious, Jean Pierre. You and I have far more important things to concern us than a mere dream. Tell Roberts, Johnson and Berrati to be ready to move at 15.00 hours. I expect we shall be away at least a week, so make certain you all have adequate provisions and ammunition."

The Frenchman nodded and rose. At the door he glanced back. Kessler was standing motionless at the window as if staring into another world. With a worried shake of his head, the Frenchman walked quietly out and closed the door.

Beccione nodded at the empty wine bottle on the table. "You getting mean or something? What about another?"

Rosenberg grinned as he motioned to a waiter. "I was thinkin' about your liver. They say too much of this stuff's poison."

"Then with you around I ain't in much danger, am I?"

The two Americans were seated at a table outside the Bar Alberto in the central piazza, the favorite drinking house of the rebels. Having finished their spell of duty in the mountains the previous day, they had spent the morning exploring the small town, an opportunity previously denied them. Both had been agreeably impressed. In spite of La Capella's isolation, there appeared to be plenty of food and wine available and there was a general gaiety that had been absent from Castelmonte.

Without doubt the interned dissidents gave the town much of its vitality, representing as they did a cross-section of Italian society from artisan to artist. That morning they had witnessed an impromptu concert given by the La Scala opera singers in a tiny piazza. Other artists were also in evidence: musicians could be heard practicing in old pantiled cottages, painters lined the cobbled sidewalks with their work. Doctors, lawyers and university lecturers, many of them Jewish, were also well represented. But everyone recognized the real driving force behind the town's self-sufficiency. Without Kessler and his organization, whose raids helped to compensate for what the Fascists had stolen, the situation would have been grim indeed.

Rosenberg was watching an elderly man make his way across the piazza towards the small hotel where Kessler had his headquarters. He nudged Beccione. "You see that guy? He used to lecture at some university out here. You know what Kessler's got him doing now?"

Beccione grinned. "Don't tell me he's in A Squad."

"You're getting warm. Toschack says he gives lectures on modern history to anyone who's interested. Roberts attends them and so does McAllister. There's classes on other subjects too. Art, music, literature, you name it."

Beccione was showing surprise. "And Kessler's organized all this?"

"According to Toschack he has. He's also started classes for the kids again and hopes to stage concerts later in the year." Knowing what a puzzle Kessler and his motives were to Beccione, Rosenberg felt a leg pull and would not come amiss. "Maybe that's it. The Fascists have kicked art and culture in the teeth, so Kessler's fighting back."

"By knocking hell out of the Allies as well," Beccione grinned.

"Why not? We ain't exactly bringing the Met over with us, are we? You heard about Monte Cassino?"

A moment later Rosenberg noticed a girl in an emerald dress crossing the piazza and nudged Beccione. "Watch it, kid. There's Schumann's girl coming over."

Beccione looked round and saw the girl, who was carrying a raffia bag, make straight for their table. Men were turning to watch her as she passed by. She was bare-headed and her long hair, glinting amber in the sunlight, rose and fell to her springy walk. Beccione thought again of a beautiful untamed animal. A warning whisper from Rosenberg snapped his trance. "Keep it cool, kid. You don't want trouble with Schumann."

The two men rose as the girl reached their table. She gave both of them a smile, then spoke to Beccione. "May I join you?"

A hovering waiter, recognizing the girl, hurried to fetch her a chair and a glass. Beccione poured wine and offered her a cigarette. Magda's green eyes acknowledged him. "*Salute.*"

"*Salute.* What are you doing in town today?"

She motioned at the raffia bag standing beside her chair. "A little shopping."

"Did you get any bargains?"

She laughed. "In war-time Italy? Hardly. But I have got what I wanted."

Two middle-aged men passing the table were staring at her. "Do you always go shopping on your own?" Beccione asked.

"Yes. Why?"

"Don't you have trouble fending off the wolves?"

She looked amused. "It's most unlikely anyone would dare to molest me. They know who I am."

He nodded at the raffia bag. "Is that where you keep your gun?"

She laughed again. "Where else?"

His eyes wandered over the tight-fitting bodice of her dress. "There sure ain't room anywhere else, is there?"

Rosenberg gave a warning cough at the direction the conversation was taking. Magda glanced at him. "Your friend is very quiet. Doesn't he approve of me?"

"As a matter of fact, I don't think he does." Grinning at the kick Rosenberg gave him under the table, Beccione went on, "He thinks you're bad medicine for GIs like us."

"Why is that?"

"You're Schumann's girl. And he has a lot of muscle in this town. They also say he's a jealous man."

Her mood changed in a second. "Why are you Americans all alike? Why do you see women as possessions instead of people? I belong to no one but myself. Which means I do as I please."

"So I've noticed. But that doesn't mean Schumann goes along with it."

"Why do you talk about Schumann? Are you afraid of him?"

Beccione turned and waved at the surrounding mountains. "That's what I'm afraid of, baby. Getting thrown out there to the wolves. It's a hungry world when you've got no friends."

"Helmut couldn't do that. Only Kessler can get rid of men once they've been accepted."

Beccione smiled at her. "I feel better already."

"What do you know—there's Schumann now," Rosenberg muttered.

A jeep had entered the piazza and halted outside the hotel. Three men jumped out, Schumann and two members of his squad. One was the massive Italian Mogelli whom Beccione had noticed at the party.

As yet Schumann had not noticed the trio at the table and was busy giving his men orders. As they saluted and turned away he caught sight of Magda. He looked startled and immediately called Mogelli back.

Magda, who had shown no surprise at seeing the German, turned back to Beccione. "Helmut arranged to pick me up here after I'd finished my shopping."

Schumann and Mogelli were in close conversation. Twice Beccione saw the huge Italian glance across at him. When the German finally turned and started across the piazza, Mogelli followed him.

Halting at the table, Schumann ignored the two Americans. *"Wie lange sind Sie schon hier?"*

Magda answered him in English. "I've been here about ten minutes."

"You told me 12.15."

"I know that. But I finished my shopping early. Does it matter?"

Giving her a stare, Schumann turned his cold eyes on the Americans. "What are you two doing here at this time of the day?"

"We're off duty," Beccione told him.

"Off duty. What does that mean?"

Schumann was frowning heavily as Beccione explained. "New recruits do not get days off. They have too much to learn. You should be up in the battle training ground, not sitting here drinking wine."

"What for? We've finished our training."

"No one here ever finishes his training. That is why we are such an efficient force. Your training taught you to handle new weapons, but proficiency requires constant practice. That is why you should be on the range today."

"O.K.," Beccione said. "Only you explain that to Kessler. Because he told us to take the two days off."

The German's face tightened. "I shall speak to him. We are a fighting force, not a wine-swilling rabble. Is that understood?"

Beccione reached for the bottle of wine and filled his glass. "Yeah, it's understood. Is that all?"

Aghast at Beccione's insolence, Rosenberg was afraid Magda was going to break into laughter. Instead she hid her amusement by reaching down for her shopping bag. "Helmut, are you ready to go?" she asked innocently.

Fighting for control, the handsome German did not at first

answer her. For a prolonged moment the only sound was the laughter and chatter of voices inside the bar. Then Schumann took a deep breath and motioned Mogelli to his side. "I want you to do something for me, Beccione."

"You do? What's that?"

"My men have heard that you were a professional boxer and have asked me if I will match you against Mogelli here. With all our squads in town at the moment it would be a good time for the contest."

Beccione's heavy-lidded eyes moved over him. "This is your idea, isn't it?"

"Originally, yes. You will remember at our first meeting I said a fight would provide good entertainment for the men."

"That's right, you did. Only you forgot to ask how I felt about it. I'm not fighting to entertain your men, Schumann. Not now or any other time."

Magda, who had released her hold on the shopping basket, was showing excitement as she glanced rapidly from face to face.

"Perhaps you are afraid Mogelli will be helpless against a professional boxer," Schumann said. "If you are, let me reassure you. He used to be an all-in wrestler, so is quite able to take care of himself."

"I don't care if he used to be a Samurai swordsman," Beccione said.

"You will be well paid. I will personally guarantee your purse."

"I said no."

"But don't professional puglists fight for money?"

"Not your money, Schumann. So forget it."

The German said something to the huge Italian whose brutal features broke into a grin. Turning, he spat on the cobblestones alongside Beccione's chair. Without glancing at him, Beccione said in Italian, "You spit at me again, you slob, and I'll rub your ugly nose in it."

Mogelli took an eager step forward. "Then you'll fight me?"

"No, you sonofabitch. I'll put a bullet in your belly. Now get your fat ass out of here."

Schumann, who knew enough Italian to grasp the gist of the exchange, said something to Mogelli that instantly restored the stupid grin to his face. The German then turned back to the table. "You disappoint me, Beccione. I took you as a man of spirit who would enjoy a good contest."

"We all make mistakes, don't we?" Beccione said.

There was both mockery and triumph in the glance Schumann gave Magda. "Yes. Everyone of us. However, as you are a new recruit, I think we shall have to make certain your reluctance to fight doesn't go beyond a contest with Mogelli."

"Why not try pistols at dawn?" the American asked savagely.

The German smiled. "I don't think that will be necessary. We have better ways of finding out than that." He turned to Magda. "We must go. I am late already."

The girl rose and, with an enigmatic glance at Beccione, allowed Schumann to lead her across the piazza to the jeep. Mogelli followed them for a few feet, then turned and gestured obscenely at Beccione. Rosenberg released his breath. "You goddamn fool. Why'd you have to goad him like that?"

Beccione did not hear him. He was staring fixedly after Schumann as if he and the German were the only two men in town.

21

Beccione found the garage in a street that ran near the central piazza. Four men were standing in a service pit examining a dusty jeep. Ducking his head, he saw they were Kessler, Jean Pierre, Berrati, and a man in mechanic's overalls he did not recognize. He spoke to Kessler.

"Toschack says you want to see me."

From the stiff way Kessler climbed out of the pit, Beccione judged his recent journey had been a long one. "What's wrong with the jeep?" he asked as the German led him away.

"We cracked the sump on our way back. We're seeing if it can be repaired." Kessler took Beccione into a tiny office full of oil-smeared books and closed the door. "I asked to see you because of a request Captain Schumann has made. He appears to think the matter is urgent."

Beccione gave a laugh of contempt. "He doesn't waste much time, does he? Don't tell me you also want me to fight the guy."

Kessler frowned. "Fight whom?"

Realizing he had made a mistake, Beccione had no choice but to explain the events of the previous morning. Kessler shook his head when Beccione finished. "No, I knew nothing about this proposed fight between you and Mogelli. But it might go some way towards explaining this demand Schumann has made."

"What demand?"

Weariness made Kessler look his age as he sank down on a stool. "He is asking for proof you are not a spy planted on us by the Allies. It is relatively easy for them to do this: that is why we spend so much time checking on a man's background before we accept him. Even then we are aware that that background might have been artificially created. The only way we can be tolerably certain a man is genuine is to see him in action against his own countrymen. I believe Jean Pierre told you this before you joined us."

Beccione nodded. "So?"

"Normally I make my own judgments. And in your case I have found no reason to doubt them. But we have an unwritten law that if one man suspects another, he can demand that the suspect be put to the test. This makes the men feel secure. And it is the demand Schumann is now making."

Beccione wondered if Kessler knew of Magda's part in Schumann's hostility. "What excuse does he give for suspecting me?"

"He was under no obligation to give a reason. However, I think he feels you dislike Germans too much to be genuine."

"Dislike Germans? You're the first Germans I've met. The guy's twisting his reasons around. He's the one who dislikes Americans."

Kessler made no attempt to deny the allegation. "Who dislikes whom is not the issue. I made the rule, so I must abide by it. Moreover, three of Schumann's squad have added their names to his request."

"So what happens now? Do I have to go with his squad on an operation?"

"Yes, but not alone. I shall be coming along and so will others from my squad."

"That's a relief. I guess you could kiss me goodbye if you weren't." Ignoring Kessler's frown, Beccione went on, "What's the job going to be?"

"Schumann has information that a large shipment of drugs is to be taken from Bari to the Allied forward field hospitals.

As drugs fetch a high price on the black market, the Americans are certain to put on a heavy guard. Probably there will be armor as well as soldiers. So we shall need a large force to attack it."

Beccione relaxed. "That doesn't sound too bad. What about Rosenberg? Schumann's got no quarrel with him."

"He asked for you both. As you are friends and arrived together, it seems reasonable enough."

"He's a real reasonable man," Beccione said. "What will our jobs be? Or hasn't Schumann worked that out yet?"

Kessler rose from the stool and reached for the door. "It will have to be something that demonstrates very clearly that you are at war with your countrymen. But we will decide your role later when our battle plans are drawn up."

Jean Pierre gave a growl of discontent. "Schumann admits himself the convoy will be well guarded. Take the full squad with you, Franz. C Squad can take care of things here while you're away.

Kessler shook his head impatiently. "We're not attacking a battalion, Jean Pierre. At the most the Americans will only be sending an armoured car and a couple of dozen soldiers."

"You can't be sure of that. You've said yourself what a prize all that sulphanilamide would be on the Black Market. After Schumann's raid at Castelmonte and then on the base depot, the Yanks might decide to play safe and pack the convoy with troops."

"Even if they did, they wouldn't be able to engage us with their full strength."

"What if they put all their troops in the front of the convoy? Your plan wouldn't be much use then."

Kessler smiled. "It's hardly likely. But if they did we should simply withdraw."

The Frenchman, who was facing Kessler across the desk in the German's office, gave a laugh of derision. "With all that sulphanilamide about? That could save dozens of sick kids' lives. You'd attack an army for that. Take the full squad, Franz. Another twelve men could make all the difference."

Kessler rose from his desk in a gesture of finality. "No. We may be away a week, even longer, and I need you here. Your job is to find out if there is any foundation to these rumours we keep hearing. If the Germans intend carrying out reprisal raids against farms and villages suspected of harbouring partisans, we need to know in good time."

"Nothing's going to happen until Rome falls," the Frenchman grunted. "The Germans need every man for its defence."

"Perhaps they do. But Rome could fall very soon and we must know the Germans' intentions when it does."

"None of this is going to happen in the next week or two," Jean Pierre grumbled. "You're being over-protective towards these people."

At any other time Kessler would have punished the remark, particularly as it concerned his well-beloved peasants. In this instance, however, he knew the cause of Jean Pierre's discontent. His driver and comrade in dozens of skirmishes, the Frenchman was now imagining he, Kessler, might be at risk without his presence.

"I don't intend arguing any longer, Jean Pierre. I must have you, Roberts, and my other lieutenants here to organize help if the worst happens. Send Colenzo and Berrati into Florence to see what they can find out. Threats to anyone giving shelter to enemies of the Reich are being broadcast every day, so it's not a subject that should be dangerous to discuss provided they act like Fascists themselves. If they're careful, they'll probably learn something from these New Republican SS and police. They'll be the ones who'll accompany the Germans if they carry out reprisal raids."

Jean Pierre gave a gloomy nod. "They say they're everywhere in the cities these days. Berrati heard the other day that a young boy was kicked to death because he was carrying an Allied leaflet in his pocket. Apparently the bastards were all carrying whips."

Kessler's dislike of all things Fascist showed in his expression. "Oh, yes, they are aping their SS masters very well." Then, noticing Jean Pierre was still looking worried, his voice softened. "Try to understand, Jean Pierre. I can't take you on this raid because I need you here. Haven't you realised yet that you are my right-hand man?"

No words of Kessler could have moved the big Frenchman more and for a moment he was defenceless with pleasure. Then, aware he was betraying himself, he gave a fierce scowl. "I can't see why you have to go on this raid in the first place. Any one of us could have gone and made sure Schumann didn't throw Beccione to the wolves."

"Never mind why I'm going, Jean Pierre. Just do as I ask and take care of things here."

"Who's going to drive for you?" the Frenchman muttered.

Kessler's eyes twinkled. "Toschack. And I shall take Beccione as my second gunner."

Jean Pierre gave a non-commital grunt. "And you think you'll be gone a full week?"

"That depends on the amount of activity at the front. We'd better keep radio silence now we know the search patrols are carrying D/F equipment. Of course if an emergency should crop up here let me know at once. But keep your transmission as short as possible."

At the door the Frenchman turned. "Will you be in charge or are you leaving it to Schumann?"

"That's something I shall decide later. If his plan looks like it's working out I shall let him handle it. If it doesn't, I shall take over."

The Frenchman could not resist a last warning. "He's a bloodthirsty bastard and likely to show off if you're around. So keep an eye on him."

Kessler lifted an arm and the jeeps halted behind him. It was near sunset and blood-red light was drenching the mountainside. The convoy was following a mule track that ran north and south, to the west was a panoramic view of mountains and narrow valleys falling through thousands of feet to long ridges of beech and chestnut. Apart from the deeper hollows where twilight was already established, the entire landscape was aglow in the ghostly light.

But it was not the view that was drawing Kessler's attention. Turning to Beccione, who was seated behind him, Kessler handed him a pair of binoculars and pointed at a path contouring the mountainside opposite. "Do you know the artist Goya, Beccione?"

"No," Beccione said.

"He is a man who has painted the suffering of the innocents in wartime. He would make a masterpiece of this."

Focusing the binoculars, Beccione saw that a seemingly endless procession of peasants was shuffling along the path. All were carrying heavy loads, some of these loads looking almost as large as those borne by the donkeys that occasionally punctuated their column. With their backs bowed and their tattered clothing blowing out in the wind, they all appeared unbelievably weary.

"What are they doing?" Beccione asked.

"They are carrying locally-made merchandise in exchange for food. With all their vehicles requisitioned by the armies, it is the only way they can survive. They return by another path at the far side of the mountain. Take another look at them."

Beccione obeyed. He saw now there were women and even children in the procession. Some had fallen by the wayside and were leaning against their loads in postures of extreme fatigue. As he lowered the binoculars again, Beccione saw Kessler's eyes were scanning his face.

"This is what war does to the peasants, Beccione. It rapes them, it robs them, it starves them, and as a final mockery it forces them to give their sons to its noble cause."

"You really hate war, don't you?" Beccione said, handing back the binoculars. "That's why I can't understand what you're doing with your own army."

The German's eyes glowed with a sudden and unexpected passion, arousing Beccione's hopes that he might at last hear something that would help explain this strange and complex man. Instead, after giving him another look, Kessler turned and waved his arm forward. As the jeeps began moving again, Beccione found his gaze drawn back to the pitiful column. Too weary even to lift their heads to watch the jeeps, the tiny figures were stumbling onwards like the actors in a Greek tragedy. As the wind wailed mournfully through the rocks, a shudder ran through the American.

22

The silence had the calm of a sleeping woman. The effect of the sun was balmlike; the scent of wild mint and thyme as soothing as incense. To Beccione, stretched out with closed eyes, his purpose there seemed like the projection of a fevered mind. Death would not visit so tranquil a valley.

His illusion vanished the moment he raised his head. The bridge lay to his left, a two-hundred foot span that straddled a steep dried-up watercourse. The road it supported came looping around the mountain opposite, crossed the bridge, passed below along the foot of a rock-strewn hillside and disappeared. At the moment it was free of traffic and the entire

landscape was motionless in the sunlight. Even the hawk that
hung over the bridge, watching for the lizards that darted
over its baked surface, seemed hardly to move its wings in
the warm lifting air.

Three men and a girl shared the nest of rocks where Beccione was hiding: Kessler, Schumann, a young Italian called
Rossi and Magda. The main force, comprised of Schumann's
entire squad and ten men from A squad, was hidden in ambush in the valley beyond. Toschack, McAllister and Rosenberg were among them. Two medical orderlies and a radio
operator completed the raiding party. They were guarding the
thirteen jeeps that were hidden in a beech wood at the back
of the valley.

Beccione wondered how Rosenberg was doing. To make
sure the Jewish soldier played his full part in the ambush,
Schumann had put him under the surveillance of one of his
lieutenants, a slim sardonic German named Weiss. Not trusting Schumann or his lieutenant, Beccione had asked Toschack and McAllister to keep an eye on the GI.

The raiding party had left La Capella nearly three days
ago. Their progress over the mountains had been slower than
expected because of the heavy Allied air activity that they encountered as they neared the front. A second factor had been
a German patrol their scouts had reported. Its presence in the
mountains behind the German lines almost certainly meant it
was searching for Kessler. The rebels' greater mobility and
skill had easily enabled them to evade it, but still more time
had been lost.

Lying watching the road Beccione could feel the sun soak
through his shirt. Kessler, Schumann and Rossi occupied the
nest of rocks on his left side. Magda, dressed in American
combat dress like the rest of the raiding party, lay smoking a
cigarette on his right. Throughout the journey her attitude
towards Beccione had been ambiguous: friendly one moment,
offhanded the next. How much of this was due to the tight
surveillance Schumann kept on her, Beccione had been unable to guess. Now, however, with her green eyes assessing
him closely and then moving away, he knew that he was on
trial. After his refusal to fight Mogelli she had decided to
keep her options open. This raid was his chance to redeem
himself.

Rossi, the nearest man to Beccione, was asleep. A slim
youth no older than nineteen or twenty, good-looking in a
boyish way, he had the most calculating eyes Beccione had

ever seen. When they were closed in sleep, he might have been a girl with his smooth cheeks and long dark eyelashes. When they opened, he looked like a baby-faced killer. According to Johnson he had been a tout in Naples before the war. Now he was Schumann's explosives expert.

The second man from Beccione was Kessler. With his gaunt body turned away, Beccione could not decide whether he was asleep until a fly settled on his neck. The sinewy hand that rose to slap it away gave him his answer. At the start of the raid there had been some speculation as to why Kessler had left behind Jean Pierre, his customary driver. According to rumor, the Frenchman was initiating a special operation to check on reprisal raids carried out by the Germans against peasant villages suspected of harboring partisans. It was the kind of scheme that, more and more, Beccione was learning to expect from Kessler.

The third man, laying at the very edge of the hideout where the hillside fell fifty feet to the road, was Schumann. With the prospect of action near, there was no possibility of Schumann falling asleep. Fighting and killing were as compulsive acts to the handsome German as sex; and today the prospects of combat were excellent. With the wonder drug, sulphanilamide, still in limited production and therefore more valuable than gold, there was every chance the Americans would have laid on a substantial escort.

Feeling his stomach tighten in anticipation, Schumann glanced at his watch. It was 14.20. The convoy was not due at the bridge until 16.30 at the earliest but the rebels' preparations necessitated an early arrival. These would begin as soon as the men had rested.

The glint of sunlight on glass made Schumann duck his head. An open-topped automobile had appeared at the far end of the looping road and was making for the bridge, dragging a trail of dust behind it. Kessler, who had also spotted the vehicle, glanced warningly back at Beccione and Magda.

Edging forward, Schumann watched the automobile as it crossed the bridge and passed directly below. It was chauffeur-driven with two American Army officers occupying the rear seats. In his mind's eye Schumann picked off the three men with his machine carbine. In another time and place he would not have hesitated: single vehicles offered good practice and usually provided weapons and ammunition. Today, however, there was bigger game afoot and he watched the automobile disappear behind the slash in the hillside. He had no fear of its occupants sighting his main force further down the valley. Discipline among A and B squads was that of an élite force and all men had been ordered to keep out of sight until the ambush was sprung.

Once again the long loop of road beyond the bridge became empty of traffic. Schumann, whom Kessler had allowed to retain command of the raid, decided he would wait five more minutes before beginning his preparations. His pale eyes, keen with anticipation, stared back at Beccione. The American had popped a stick of gum into his mouth and was chewing rhythmically, an act that could be interpreted as nervous or relaxed according to the bias of the witness. Watching him, Schumann found it difficult not to smile. The ambush alone was a thing to relish: the test he was setting the American added to it a new dimension of pleasure. If Beccione was a genuine deserter he was soon going to pay his proper dues for full membership in the organization. If he was a spy, he was about to discover the price of treachery.

Schumann's dislike for Beccione was not, as it appeared, a wholly personal matter. The situation with Magda had in fact hit a particularly sensitive nerve. Years ago, when Schumann was just beginning his career as a group leader in the Nazi Youth Movement, his first love had left him for an American—the son of a diplomat living in Munich. Losing the girl was bad enough; but facing the jeers and taunts of his Nazi friends—who whispered that Schumann had been humiliated by a member of an inferior race—had scorched the young man's pride. He secretly vowed that he would avenge himself on both women and Americans.

Women became available to him first. Schumann made the wives of other men his special quarry. It was adultery that led to his final disgrace in the German Army. The woman involved was the wife of an elderly Italian brigadier, a man who had the misfortune to return home too early one night Finding his wife and Schumann in the thick of things, he had drawn his revolver and taken aim. Schumann, ever cautious, kept a gun of his own handy for just this eventuality; he put a bullet neatly and quickly between the Italian's eyes. Rumor insisted that Schumann had then rolled over and completed intercourse with the shocked woman. Whatever the truth of it, the Italian authorities, furious that one of their senior officers had been disgraced and then killed by a German NCO, demanded the full penalty for the crime.

With Axis relations already under heavy strain, Schumann

had known that this time not even his war record would save him. Accordingly he killed his two guards and deserted into the mountains where he ran into Kessler. A pragmatist when it suited him, Schumann realized that membership in the organization would not only provide his best chance of survival but ensure him personal profit as well.

He was fortunate to have met Kessler just when he did. Kessler's problem, unlike orthodox military leaders, was primarily one of communication. Operating as he did behind enemy lines, he needed section leaders who, while obeying the wider concepts of a mission, could use their own initiative to achieve success. In addition Kessler had just created B Squad and was looking for a man to lead it.

As an ex-paratrooper Schumann had been ideally suited for the role. And since Kessler was a German himself, Schumann had not found it difficult to take his orders. Indeed his first impressions of Kessler had been wholly favorable. He could think of no other man who could have built up such a network of collaborators, informers and fences in so short a time. He admired Kessler's command of strategy and tactics that made every raid a small masterpiece of planning and execution. He also admired Kessler's courage, although the recklessness the German often displayed when leading his men into battle sometimes made Schumann wonder if the man had a death wish.

His first serious doubts about Kessler were aroused by his attitude towards the peasants. Why, he wondered, would an obviously educated and refined leader bother with this class of scum. Indeed Kessler often treated them with a far greater consideration than he showed for his own men.

Then, two months after his inauguration, Schumann had received the shock of his life. Realizing the younger German's role as a section leader had left him no choice, Kessler had drawn him aside and explained to him the real reason for his, Kessler's, presence in the mountains. He had also warned him he was to keep this reason a secret from his rank and file followers under pain of death.

It was an astonishing revelation that had burst on Schumann like a bombshell: its entire import was in direct conflict with everything he had been taught to believe in. His judgment had been immediate, although he was careful to keep it to himself. The entire concept was insane, the product of a brilliant but sick intellect.

At the same time the sheer audacity and magnitude of it

could not fail to excite a man as power-hungry as Schumann, just as the rancor in him found satisfaction in some of Kessler's acts. Moreover his sharp self-centered intelligence quickly realized that Kessler's mad ideas would not necessarily interfere with the profits to be made through the organization. Accordingly, Schumann decided to keep his peace and play his part as before. There would be time enough to bail out if the need arose.

Schumann shook off his reverie and returned his attention to Beccione. Magda, he knew, found something attractive in the American, although he also knew that she was the kind of woman who enjoyed playing off one man against another. Both thoughts made Schumann's handsome face tighten with resolve.

The dull rumble of engines drew Schumann's gaze back to the road. Two Allied transports emerged from the slash in the hillside ten seconds later. They were filled with soldiers, many of them stripped to the waist. From their carefree appearance and their singing, Schumann guessed they were a platoon moving south on rest. As the transports crossed the bridge he saw Kessler glance at his watch. In order to prevent Kessler from interfering in the operation, he turned to him. *"Ich denke, es ist Zeit zu beginnen."*

Guessing the meaning of Schumann's words, Beccione felt his muscles tighten. Alongside him Rossi, who appeared to sleep as lightly as a cat, opened one eye, then sat upright. "Is it time?"

"In a moment," Schumann told him. "When those two transports have gone."

The young Italian watched the second transport disappear around the far corner, dragging its trail of dust behind it. Then he picked up a haversack and dropped one alongside Beccione. "One for you and one for me," he smiled.

Beccione, who would rather have shared the job with a scorpion, gave him an expressionless stare as he shrugged on the pack. He turned to find Schumann smiling triumphantly at him. "Very well," said the German with a nod at Rossi. "You can go now."

Kessler, who had noticed the look that Schumann had given Beccione, caught Rossi's arm as the youth was about to jump out of the nest of rocks. "One thing before you go. You have plenty of time. So I don't want either of you taking any risks. Is that understood?"

"*Si*, Padrone."

"I also know you have an odd sense of humor. As the American is new to this kind of work, you will not play any tricks on him. Is that also understood?"

From the way Rossi's eyes fell, Beccione knew he was afraid of the German. *"Si, padrone. Ho capito."*

"Make certain you do," Kessler said dryly. "Very well; you can go now."

The youth, who like Beccione was wearing rubber-soled shoes, began running down the rock-strewn hillside. As Beccione moved to follow him Magda, now sitting upright, gave him a bright excited smile. "Good luck."

He ignored her. Acutely conscious what his pack contained, he began moving carefully down the slope. Ten seconds later, soaked in sweat, he was crouched with Rossi alongside one of the main pillars of the bridge.

Glancing up, he saw that the spider's web of trusses was badly rusted. Pointing to the tiny flakes of rust floating down in the sunlight, he said to the Italian, "This goddamn thing looks like it might fall down on its own!"

Rossi flashed his bright, deadly smile. "No, it needs our help. Are you ready?"

"When you are," Beccione said.

Heaving his haversack higher, Rossi leapt up on one of the metal stays and began climbing.

Beccione followed more slowly. Rust flaked away under his hands and the pack impeded his movements. Already fifteen feet above him, Rossi, whose agility suggested he might once have been a cat burglar as well as a tout, grinned down. "Do you need help?"

Beccione heaved himself bodily onto a cross-member. "Get your ass moving and don't worry about me."

The web of the arch bracing began to thin out towards the center of the bridge. Soon there was little left but the main metal beams and a kind of catwalk that supported the concrete span. To move along it the two men had to shuffle with bent knees, grabbing for handholds on the vertical members. To Beccione's disbelief, Rossi was humming a popular song. As the American reached for a stanchion, his fingers sank into something soft and a second later a huge spider scurried down his bare arm and leapt for the girder below. Releasing his grip instinctively, Beccione felt himself swaying and he grabbed for the stanchion again. His fingers closed around it just in time: the haversack was unbalancing him and half a second later would have dragged him to his death.

Fighting vertigo, he clung on hard. A hundred feet below the bleached rocks of the watercourse were throwing up dazzling waves of light. Through his nausea he heard Rossi's taunting voice. "You're not going to fall, are you?"

Beccione could only croak his reply: "Get on with it."

When his eyes cleared he saw the youth was already at work, binding a bundle of brown sticks to a girder above him. Aware what would be wanted next, the American clung to the stanchion with one hand and maneuvered his haversack around with the other. To his dismay he discovered he needed both hands to unfasten the buckle. Taking a deep breath he let go and made a quick grab at the buckle in the hope the strap would jerk free. Instead, he found himself swaying and had to grasp for a handhold again. Heart hammering, he considered trying to free the strap with his teeth when the grinning Rossi noticed his antics. "You would not make a good circus act, would you, Americano? Hand the pack to me."

With no choice but to obey, Beccione wriggled out of the pack and held it out with one hand. Replacing his own haversack on his shoulder, the youth reached out for it and crouched without a handhold on the girder while he unfastened the strap. He then handed the pack back to the American. "Do you think you can manage now?"

You gutsy sonofabitch, Beccione thought. "What do you want?" he asked aloud.

"First a detonator. Then pass me the cable."

Gingerly Beccione obeyed. Fixing the detonator into the bundle of gelignite, Rossi attached the end of the electric cable and then waved the American back. Unable to turn on the narrow girder, Beccione retreated backwards paying out the cable from his haversack as he went. Following him, Rossi tied the cable to a couple of trusses to prevent it from swinging out, then paused and drew a second bundle of gelignite sticks from his haversack.

"Another?" Beccione asked hoarsely.

Rossi nodded. "Some of the blast will go downwards. Pass me your pack again. I shall need more gelignite than this."

The process was repeated with the Italian splicing the cable to accommodate the second charge. By this time Beccione's bent back and legs were aching intolerably. Yet he still had the long shuffle back as he carefully unrolled the cable. When they reached the network of trusses, Rossi swung past him, grinning as he went. By the time Beccione reached the foot of the main pillar the sweat was running in rivulets down his face.

He found Schumann waiting there. The German had run a second cable down from the nest of rocks and as soon as Beccione dropped alongside him he snatched the spool from the American's haversack and tossed it to Rossi. The Italian deftly clipped the cable and grafted it to the second one; then he gave the German a nod. Checking to see that the road was clear, Schumann led the men back to the hideout.

23

Kessler was waiting for them in the hideout and spoke first to Rossi. *"Gli esplosivi sono in posizione?"*

Rossi nodded. *"Si, padrone.* Everything is ready." Moving to the rear of the hideout, he drew an electric generator from the third haversack and began attaching the cable to it.

Kessler turned to Beccione who had flung himself full length to the ground. "How are you feeling?"

The American lifted his sweating face. "I feel great. I always get a kick out of high wire acts."

The German smiled. "You did well. It was a difficult climb."

Beccione nodded at Rossi who looked as if he had just been on a gentle stroll. "You should get yourself another monkey for these jobs. One ain't enough."

The young Italian scowled at him as he sank back to the ground again. A moment later he felt a hand on his shoulder and saw Magda leaning over him. She was holding a lighted cigarette which she put to his lips. "Thanks," he said.

Schumann was watching them from across the hideout. "I think that was very clever of you," she said. "And very brave too."

Aching from head to foot, Beccione was in no mood to bandy compliments. "The hell it was. I'm on trial, remember? If I'd refused to go your boy friend would have had me shot."

Seeing Kessler turn, he expected a curt reprimand. Instead

the German picked up a pair of binoculars and began scanning the road.

Schumann moved within earshot as Magda reached for a water bottle and offered it to Beccione. "You must be thirsty."

Beccione believed her real purpose was to tease Schumann and he decided to play along. "You remind me of my mother."

She glanced down at the curves of her body that even her battle-dress could not hide. "I hope you have poor eyesight."

With a sharp exclamation, Schumann said something in German to her. Without turning her head, she answered him as sharply. "What's the matter?" Beccione said maliciously. "Is lover boy getting angry?"

Face thin with anger, Schumann was about to move towards them when Kessler spun around. His measured voice was icy with anger. "That is enough! All of you. Do I need to remind you this is a military exercise?" His gaze moved on to the girl. "You are allowed to come on these patrols because until now you have behaved like a soldier. If you behave like a whore, you will stay behind in La Capella. Is that understood?"

"I was only giving the American a drink, Padrone."

"Don't argue with me. Do as I say and behave yourself."

Nothing could have illustrated more clearly Kessler's extraordinary power to dominate men than the reaction of the trio. High-spirited although she was, Magda looked subdued as she sank down on the ground alongside Beccione. Schumann, still pale with anger, met the German's gaze for a moment, then cursed and turned back to the road. Beccione hid his own reaction behind a yawn. "I'm getting some shuteye. Someone wake me when the convoy comes."

He closed his eyes and lay back. A minute passed and then he felt something brush his ankle. Without looking he knew it was Magda's foot. As the pressure came again he opened his eyes and saw she was lying on her side facing him. Her green eyes, flickering towards Kessler, warned him to be careful and at the same time challenged him.

Unable to hide a grin, he shook his head and lay back again. Once more her foot touched his leg and this time ran along it for a few inches. His skin seemed to burn at the point of contact and an ache came into his groin. Pushing her foot away impatiently, he turned on his side away from her.

The first breeze of the evening wafted down and brought

with it the smell of wild lavender. The shadows of the mountains, reaching across the valley, touched the hideout and changed the color and texture of its rocks. A goldfinch rose from a bush and flew off to find the sunlight. The breeze came again, rustling the dry vegetation. The melancholy sound changed Beccione's mood and he saw again the endless chains of peasants struggling through the mountains. Kessler was right. As a soldier you never gave them a thought. It was you and the enemy and if the poor sonsofbitches got in the way it was their tough luck.

The breeze subsided and Beccione heard the distant sound of engines. A few seconds later a word from Kessler made him sit upright. A jeep had appeared on the far side of the gorge. It was followed by an armored car, then by a large troop carrier. After a short interval, three canvas-covered transports appeared, lumbering around the bend in a cloud of dust. Two armored jeeps followed, each carrying four soldiers. In turn they were followed by three open-topped transports with a final jeep bringing up the rear.

Both Kessler and Schumann were examining the vehicles through field glasses. Behind them Rossi was pulling up the plunger of the electric generator. Once again Beccione sensed that Kessler was unnaturally excited as he turned towards Schumann. "My guess is the drugs are in the first three transports. That is why the escort is positioned that way."

Schumann nodded. "I think the same."

"Then what do you want to do? Blow up the bridge after they have crossed it? Or not take the chance and let them all through?"

Although the men were speaking in German, Beccione could understand their problem. If the entire convoy was allowed to cross the bridge before the road was sealed, the size of its escort might possibly outnumber the raiding party. On the other hand, if the drugs were carried in the rearmost transports and the bridge was blown before they crossed it, the ambush would be an expensive and dangerous waste of time.

With the leading jeep no more than three hundred yards from the bridge, Schumann had to make up his mind quickly. "We'll blow it after the first transports are across." Kessler nodded and Schumann turned to Rossi who was crouched over the generator with a grin of anticipation on his face. "What are you doing?" the German barked. "You heard my orders!"

Looking crestfallen, the young Italian drew back. Schumann's gaze settled on Beccione. "Have you forgotten why you are here? Or are you unable to kill your friends?"

Taking a deep breath, Beccione moved forward and kneeled over the generator. In case the American's nerve cracked at the last moment, Rossi stood beside him, intent on the task at hand. Schumann glanced back. "Remember! You explode the charge when I drop my arm."

Beccione fixed his eyes on the road. The first jeep, well ahead of the armored car, was across the bridge before the heavier vehicle reached it. A hollow rumble sounded as it slowed and began making its way across. Kessler and Schumann meticulously assessed its fighting strength as it passed below them. Kessler said something to the younger German who nodded his head.

Laughter and men's voices resounded as the large troop carrier followed the armored car towards the slash in the hillside. From his position Beccione could not count the number of soldiers but guessed there were nearly twenty. At the far side of the bridge the first transport had slowed down as it approached its narrow span, causing the others to close up behind it.

Everyone's attention was now on the three transports that were just beginning to cross the bridge. Beccione, concentrating deeply, heard a low voice in his ear. "Think of that young boy they killed in Castelmonte, Beccione. And of those peasants you saw struggling to survive. It will make it easier for you."

Turning, Beccione saw Kessler's face only inches from his own. He was about to speak but the German shook his head and turned away. At the edge of the hideout, Schumann had raised his right arm.

The first transport was already rumbling below. It was followed five seconds later by the second. The dust from their heavy wheels billowed up to the hideout. The third transport, with an armored jeep fifteen yards behind it, had slowed down slightly and was just clearing the bridge.

Beccione was sweating freely. Kessler's words had brought back memories he had tried to suppress. Schumann glanced back over his shoulder and dropped his arm. The American threw his weight on the plunger.

The two bright explosions split the bridge in two. One half reared up, hung a moment, then toppled into the gorge. The other half sagged down, was held a few seconds by its arch bracing, then with a weird screeching and rending of metal, broke away and fell. A great cloud of dust rose from the riverbed and joined the black smoke of the explosions.

The first armored jeep was lucky: its momentum carrying it to safety before the bridge collapsed. Its companion and the first of the open-topped transports were less fortunate. Like a toy tossed away by a petulant child, the jeep plunged down, spilling men out in all directions. The transport, catching the full force of one explosion, almost disintegrated. Wooden boxes and scraps of metal were flung high into the air, the mangled bodies of two men fell from the shattered cab, and the remainder of the chassis exploded in a ball of flame on the riverbed below.

Reverberations from the surrounding mountains drowned for several seconds the shouts of the soldiers across the gorge. When the dust and smoke began to disperse, the men could be seen again; some were running towards the collapsed bridge, others taking cover behind their vehicles that were strung out in an exposed line. A heavy explosion to the north ripped through the brief calm. The rebels turned to look and Schumann's laugh broke out triumphantly. "That's Krankl sealing off the northern road into the valley. Now we have them in a trap. Let's go and finish the job."

Soldiers were shouting and pointing towards the rocks and there was the rattle of automatic fire. The rebels had been spotted; there was no time to lose. Exchanging his green beret for his American cap, as did the other rebels, Schumann pushed Magda from the hideout and motioned Rossi and Beccione to follow her. As he came abreast with the German, Beccione, who had felt numb since destroying the bridge, saw that his eyes were glittering with excitement.

24

The valley at the far side of the slash in the hillside was in evening shadow by this time and the flashes of gunfire could be seen clearly. The battle seemed to radiate from a huge, overhanging bluff that stood half a mile away where the road rounded another bend. Between the slash and the bluff, the

road was littered with crippled vehicles. A jeep, with two
dead men alongside it, was ablaze. The troop carrier, riddled
with bullets, was buried to its engine in a clump of bushes.
One transport was overturned; the other two were askew and
abandoned. Soldiers lay like dropped sacks among the vehicles. Most of them appeared to be dead although Beccione
could hear one man screaming.

Yet the resistance of the convoy was by no means over. In
order to protect the vehicles from the scorching fire being
poured down at them, the armored car had driven beneath
the overhanging bluff. It was soon joined by the armored jeep
whose fire power had given its occupants some protection.
From that position the two vehicles were able to cover the
entire stretch of road and the hillside opposite, effectively
protecting the survivors of the convoy from front and rear as
well as above. The ambushers, under fire now from the soldiers' carbines as well as the 37mm gun of the armored car
and the jeep's two heavy machine guns, were pinned down on
the opposite side of the valley and unable to maneuver their
bazookas and panzerfausts within range. In addition, the
overhanging bluff precluded the use of mortars.

From Schumann's point of view it was a stalemate that had
to be broken quickly. The armored car almost certainly carried a radio and it was likely that Allied fighter bombers had
already been alerted. Moreover, the rubble that an explosive
charge had brought down on the road a mile to the north
would not hold up ground reinforcements indefinitely. Had
the gunfire that was sweeping the road not prevented the un-
loading of the transports, it was likely even Schumann would
have broken off the engagement and been content with the
spoils. As things were, it had to be all or nothing and the
German was the last man to admit failure.

Beccione watched the two Germans consulting up ahead.
Kessler frowning heavily, appeared to be censuring the
younger man. Magda, pausing alongside the American, spoke
in an excited and apprehensive whisper. "We must hurry or
the Jaboes will be here."

Beccione watched a 37mm shell burst on the hillside. "You
know something? I think this time your boy friend's bitten off
more than he can chew."

She was quick to defend Schumann. "If it were not for
that bluff, the fight would have been over by now."

Beccione grinned and nodded at Kessler. "Maybe so, but

he should have taken it into account, shouldn't he? That's
what Kessler's telling him."

The brief conference between the two Germans ended.
Waving the others to follow him, Schumann began running
along the hillside towards his pinned-down men. Rossi and
Magda moved after him along an animal trail that contoured
the hillside. Beccione was about to follow when Kessler
checked him. "Come with me and take a closer look at those
transports. We must get the drugs out of them before the
fighter-bombers arrive."

Whatever the differences between the two Germans, it was
clear that Kessler had confidence the action would quickly
end once Shumann took direct charge of his men. Beccione,
glad to avoid joining in the fight, was content to follow
Kessler down the hillside. They reached a clump of bushes
above the first of the stricken transports just as a shell
screamed towards them. Beccione at once dived for cover;
the shell exploded thirty yards away, uprooting bushes and
throwing up a fountain of earth. Kessler did not move a
muscle but as the American picked himself up and started
forward again, the German caught his arm. "They've sighted
us. Wait until Schumann engages them."

Relieved, Beccione peered through the foliage. "You're
never going to get that stuff away. They'll be strafing you in
ten minutes. Maybe less."

"We have to get it away, Beccione. There is sulphanilamide
in those transports."

"Maybe. But how are you going to get it up to the jeeps in
time?"

A heavy burst of automatic fire from the armored car
seemed to ask the same question. Less than fifty yards from
his men's position, Schumann had been spotted by the Americans and his progress could be traced by the spurts of dust
that bullets were kicking up around him. To cover him, his
own men opened fire with every automatic weapon they had,
and a few seconds later the German dived for shelter among
them. With a nod of appreciation, Kessler turned back to
Beccione.

"It will soon be over now. Then we can get to work."
Kessler pointed at the dense trees opposite. "We'll hide the
boxes over there until the aircraft have gone and then take
them up to the jeeps. It will be dark in half an hour."

Down the valley Schumann was already in action. Under a
shield of covering fire, half of his men were running forward

into new positions. No sooner had they dropped behind trees or boulders than they opened fire and the second line came leap-frogging forward. Beccione saw one rebel drop and roll down the hillside in the loose-limbed way of men who have been instantly killed. The tactic, however, was working: one more rush and Schumann would be within rocket range of the armored car. Conscious of their danger, the Allied crew was loading and firing like man possessed and the valley filled with the explosions of shells and the rattle of automatic fire.

Kessler moved to the fringe of the bush to gain a better view of the fight. One of Schumann's men must have crawled ahead of the others because there was a sudden streak of flame and a dull explosion—a bazooka rocket had struck the jeep and exploded its fuel tank. Burning fuel drenched the armored car and Beccione knew that in another minute, perhaps less, its crew and the soldiers behind it would be forced out into the open.

The gunfire from the bluff was already faltering as smoke blinded the American soldiers. Realizing what had happened, the rebels left their cover on the hillside and, urged on by Schumann, ran forward, pouring volley after volley into the smoke. When Kessler made no move to check them, Beccione caught his arm. "Kessler, those guys have had enough! Call Schumann off." The German neither moved nor spoke. "You hear me? Schumann's *murdering* those men."

Kessler, as if in a trance, turned a pale, implacable face on the American. His eyes seemed to burn in the dusk, his voice was harsh and toneless. "Tell me, Beccione, why should I stop it?"

"Because it's over, goddamn it! Those guys are helpless."

"Those men are soldiers. Men dedicated to violence. Isn't it just that those who live by the sword should die by the sword?"

Beccione shouted at him over the roar of the battle. "You're crazy, Kessler. Most of those guys are just drafted kids. In a minute they'll be walking out of that smoke blinded. And Schumann's going to mow them down. For God's sake, you're not a butcher like him, are you?"

His protest seemed to reach the German at last. With an exclamation Kessler swung away, pulled the Very pistol from his belt, and fired a red flare in the direction of the bluff. As it soared upwards the firing of the rebels ceased. A few seconds later Beccione saw the first of the American soldiers run out coughing from the smoke, their hands in the air.

Before Beccione could speak, Kessler slipped another cartridge into the Very pistol and fired again. As a green flare rose over the valley Schumann could be heard shouting orders. Four of his men ran forward and disarmed the Americans. The rest began running down the road towards the transports. Without glancing at Beccione, Kessler returned the pistol to his belt and started down the hillside.

There was already activity below. Those of the raiding party who had lain in ambush on the opposite side of the valley had reached the transports by now and were feverishly dragging out wooden crates. Watching them for a few seconds, Beccione started after Kessler. He pushed through a large clump of bushes where he'd seen Kessler disappear. He stopped dead when he reached the center. A young American soldier, his shirt stained with blood, was lying on a patch of bare ground with a huge top sergeant crouched protectively over him. They were men from the troop carrier who had been cut off from their comrades by the ambush. The young soldier had been hit badly in the stomach. The sergeant, a man of massive strength, had dragged the youth minutes before up the hillside into cover.

Time stood still for Beccione as he took in every detail of the scene. The youth looked no more than nineteen, a slim boy pouring his blood out into the dry ground. His blood-drenched shirt was torn open and a field dressing was strapped to his stomach. The sergeant was bull-necked with spiky brown hair and hairy arms. Beccione had seen dozens of his type before: NCOs who bawled out their men like felons on the parade ground and nursed them like children in combat.

The man was armed with an M3 carbine and it was pointed straight at Beccione's belly. Had Beccione been a German, he would have been dead as soon as he emerged on the pair. As it was, the sight of his uniform confused the NCO: for a moment his sweating face showed relief. Then he caught sight of Beccione's green beret and his bloodshot eyes blazed with fury. "You're one of them? You fuckin' treacherous sonofabitch. Ah'm gonna blow your guts out."

The man's hesitation had given Beccione time to swing up his own carbine. There was no time to protest. In a second, perhaps later, he would be cut in half unless he fired. Yet, to his horror, his finger froze on the trigger.

Time halted again. He saw the NCO's face contort and knew what it signaled. Closing his eyes tightly, he heard the deafening hammer of automatic fire. He felt no pain, but he knew when the injury was mortal a man did not. He opened his eyes and glanced at his belly, expecting to see a bloody pulp. Instead, he heard the sergeant make a choking sound and topple over the ashen youth.

Spinning around, Beccione saw Kessler standing three yards away, a Sten gun in his hand. At first the American did not notice the German's expression—finding himself still alive was surprise enough. A rattling sound from the sergeant drew his attention away from Kessler. The NCO's bloodshot eyes rolled up in their sockets. Then his legs kicked and he was dead.

A half-muffled exclamation made Beccione turn. Kessler had swung away and was supporting himself against a tree. Thinking he must have hurt himself in some way, the American moved towards him. Then, as the German motioned him away, Beccione saw his tortured expression.

Beccione returned to the two American soldiers. It was a full thirty seconds before Kessler recovered. He spoke without turning. "I want you to say nothing of this, Beccione. Do I have your word?"

"You've got it," Beccione said.

"Is the sergeant dead?"

"Yes."

The German was fumbling with a cigarette. Seeing how his hands trembled, Beccione struck a match for him. The German still appeared unable to turn and face the man he had killed. "What about the young soldier?"

"He's in a bad way. He looks as if he's got half a dozen slugs in him."

"Then we must get him down to the road as quickly as we can. Stay here and I'll send someone up to help you."

Beccione checked him before he could move away. He searched the German's face for a long time before he spoke. "I don't get you, Kessler. I don't get you one bit. You nearly let Schumann butcher a bunch of kids ten minutes ago, and now when you kill one man to save my life, you look as if you're about to puke. What's your problem? Don't you like doing the killing yourself?"

"That man I killed was not taking life. He was trying to save it." Kessler avoided Beccione's eyes.

"He was going to take mine," Beccione persisted. "And he was a soldier like the rest."

Kessler shrugged him off and started forward again. "If we don't get help for that young man he is going to die."

Before Beccione could reply, the bushes closed behind the German, hiding his tormented face. Beccione shook his head in bewilderment and returned to the two stricken Americans. The dead sergeant had fallen with one arm sprawled over the youth. Fearful that its weight might be too much for the wounded soldier, Beccione was about to move it when he noticed that the boy's eyes were gazing up at him with neither recognition nor enmity. Leaving the sergeant's arm where it rested, Beccione closed both men's eyelids and followed Kessler down to the road.

25

The fighter-bombers came six minutes later, snarling into the valley and rocketing out across the evening sky. There were six of them, sleek shapes with clutches of rockets and bombs beneath their tapered wings. Sighting the wrecked bridge, the flight commander led the line of aircraft in a tight, determined circle.

Dusk had now overtaken the valley and the shadows were dense beneath the trees on the western hillside. Beccione could see the aircraft clearly, gleaming like beautiful but deadly insects through the black filigree of the treetops.

Rosenberg, having rejoined the main rebel force, was crouched alongside Beccione. The Jewish soldier's part in the operation had been less exacting than he had feared. Luck had been with Rosenberg. Weiss, the man assigned to watch him, had been called away to repair a jammed machine gun. And so, by the time the convoy had entered the valley, no one had noticed that the American's enthusiastic fire was striking nothing but bushes and rocks. Then, before Weiss could find a way under the bluff that sheltered the Allied crews, Schumann had won the battle.

Consequently Rosenberg survived the ambush with hardly a shot fired in his direction. But, glancing at the aircraft that now circled above, he was apprehensive that his luck might have run out.

"You don't think they're gonna waste their bombs on this timber, do you, kid?"

"I wouldn't bank on it," Beccione said. "They must be fed right up to here with us by this time. And they know we haven't left."

In the few minutes remaining before the fighter-bombers' arrival, the patrol had worked like galley slaves. Identifying the crates of sulphanilamide first, they had torn them out of the transports and tossed them from man to man until they were hidden among the trees. When no more could be found, they had then turned their attention to the other drugs. In all, about half the contents of the transports had been dragged away before the fighter-bombers appeared. Now the panting, sweating men were dispersed in the woods, waiting to see if the attack came or whether the Jaboes would give up and return home. Kessler, examining the aircraft with field glasses, had little doubt about the flight commander's orders.

He knew he was right a few seconds later when a parachute flare was released, illuminating the half-unloaded transports and the dead soldiers sprawled on the road. As if frenzied by the sight, the first fighter-bomber launched itself down like a wild cat. Schumann was shouting over the scream of its engine and airfoils. "*Achtung*! Take cover."

Men flattened themselves and cushioned foreheads on arms against concussion. Teeth bit into lips and drew blood as the scream grew louder. No man, however battle-seasoned, could escape fear during a strafing attack. The noise was too terrifying for human nerves to bear, the sense of helplessness too great.

The first aircraft released two rockets at the trees, then opened fire with its 20mm cannons. The ground kicked twice, then a swath of boiling destruction swept along the hillside. The second Jabo dropped two 250 pound bombs. Massive boulders were uprooted and sent crashing down to the road. Trees sailed into the air and rained down like matches from an open box. The third aircraft released phosphorus bombs. Their weird white quills (with the capacity to cling to a man's flesh until it was devoured) radiated out and created more fires where they landed.

The fighter-bombers came again and again, blanketing the entire length of the hillside with their bombs and rockets. Branches were sliced off trees, spurts of fire ran along the undergrowth, dust rose in clouds and choked the prostrate men. Someone screamed but no man dared to raise his head.

The last attack was the worst as the aircraft released all their remaining stores. The hillside became alive, heaving with the agony of the assault. A path of bursting shells came boiling towards the prostrate bodies of Beccione and Rosenberg. The shells missed both men by a few feet but struck a nearby tree, hurling fragments of wood and steel in all directions. As the murderous sound died away, Beccione heard a groan and saw Rosenberg curl up in pain. He leaned over him in alarm. "Where're you hit?"

Rosenberg indicated his right thigh. Pulling out a knife, Beccione ripped open his slacks and saw that a large splinter of wood was buried deep in the flesh.

As he ran up the hillside for help, he heard a whistle shrilling as the sound of engines and airfoils died away. After the hideous din, the shouts of men answering Schumann's roll call sounded thin and distant. With the raiding party dispersed widely among the burning vegetation, it took the German some minutes to find out his losses. Grimed with dust and smoke like his men, he returned to Kessler. "We've lost two more men: Scheinder and Klein. Both of them dead."

Beccione found the two Germans and reported Rosenberg's wound.

"How badly hurt is your friend?" asked Kessler.

"He's going to need attention," Beccione said. "He's bleeding freely."

Kessler turned back to Schumann. "Send Schiller back with Beccione. He can give first aid until we can attend to him properly. We'll take the bodies of the dead back with us."

Schumann met his eyes meaningfully. "I wouldn't try to do that, Padrone."

Like most of the men present, Beccione knew what the German meant. The bodies were too mutilated for removal. Kessler frowned, then nodded. "Very well. Bury them here." He glanced around at the circle of silent men. "I want the rest of you to get the crates up to the jeeps as quickly as possible. Although it will soon be dark, there is still the possibility more aircraft might be sent."

With the men still reacting to the intense strain of the attack, it was a necessary warning. While Beccione and Schiller hurried down to Rosenberg, men pulled themselves together and began carrying the crates up the smoking hillside and into the wood that lay beyond.

* * *

The first shells fell just after 20.30 when there was little more than an afterglow in the western sky. Beccione heard a whispering sound first, like a tree being gently shaken in a breeze. The next moment there was a bright flash and an explosion on the hill crest. Rosenberg lifted his head from the rear seat of a jeep. "What the hell's that?"

Beccione heaved another crate into the passenger seat. "They must have gotten heavy mortars up."

Rosenberg stared up at him in shock. "You think they're broken through the road block?"

"Maybe. We'll know in a minute."

Shouts sounded down the line of jeeps as a second explosion came. Schumann, who like Kessler was working as hard as his men, dropped a crate and ran through the trees towards the hill crest. As he disappeared, a cluster of rockets came sweeping across the darkening sky, dragging fiery tails behind them. The rushing sound they made caused every man to stiffen with terror. They screamed over the wood and burst in a series of bright flashes and heavy explosions on its far side. "Rocket projectors," Rosenberg muttered. "Christ, they must want us bad."

The direction of the rockets' trajectory made the warning clear. Heavily-armed troops had broken into the valley and would soon be swarming up the hillside.

Kessler's authoritative presence helped restore order, and men began frantically heaving aboard the last of the crates. Another salvo of rockets arced up and overshot just as Schumann returned and confirmed the threat. The jeeps must leave at once or they would be annihilated.

Kessler brought Schiller over to Beccione's jeep as the American was starting up the engine. The medical orderly was a plump German with a round, good-natured face. "I shall travel back in Captain Schumann's jeep. Schiller will ride with you. You'll follow us until we reach a peasant cottage where we have friends. You'll stay there overnight while Schiller attends to Rosenberg's wound. If he is fit to travel tomorrow, make your way back to our base. If you are unsure of your way, Schiller will help you. You may stay a second night if you must; but return as soon as you can."

Half a minute later the jeep containing Kessler and Schumann moved out of the wood and up towards the barren slopes that lay ahead. Nose to tail, the others followed. They

were only just in time. Mortar shells and rockets were now
falling freely among the trees. But, seconds before the jeeps
crested a stony ridge a quarter of a mile to the north, the
barrage ceased. All the men knew what it signified. Allied infantrymen had cleared the hill crest and were about to swarm
into the wood.

26

The attic smelled of wheat and antiseptics. Sacks of grain
were heaped in one corner and flitches of bacon and strings
of onions dangled from the rafters. A small table supported
the paraffin lamp that was casting shadows on the white-
washed walls. Schiller was curled up asleep on a couple of
empty sacks. Beccione sprawled in an old chair alongside the
pallet on which Rosenberg was breathing stentoriously. Outside a wind had been rising steadily since nightfall; occasionally Beccione felt it buffet the pantiled roof as if trying to
gain ingress.

A sound on the staircase made him turn. The door creaked
open and an old woman appeared, her wrinkled face and
iron-gray hair illuminated by the oil lamp she held up. Seeing
Schiller was asleep she tiptoed towards the bed. *"Come sta il
giovane Americano? Sta ancora dormendo?"*

"*Si.* He's still asleep. But he's doing fine," Beccione said.

"Good. As soon as he wakes up, I will give him food."

"You should be in bed," Beccione told her. "It must be
past three o'clock."

The woman shrugged. "What does sleep matter when one
of Signore Kessler's men is wounded? We can sleep when you
have gone."

Over the last three hours Beccione had grown accustomed
to this sort of selfless attention. The raiding party had arrived
at the farmhouse just after midnight. It had taken Kessler
some time to rouse the elderly couple from their bed; but
once they understood the situation they had been kindness itself—solicitous and efficient in tending to Rosenberg's wound.

The operation proved messy but not dangerous. Schiller
anesthetized Rosenberg with morphine and eased the splinter

out with a pair of tweezers. It was four inches long and at least half an inch thick at its widest section, and it left a considerable hole on extraction. Nevertheless it was virgin wood, so infection was unlikely, and no artery had been pierced. After dusting the wound with sulpha powder—the first benefit of the raid—Schiller had bandaged the leg with a strip of sheeting.

The woman had been in constant attendance, fetching more hot water when required and showing great anxiety for the unconscious Rosenberg. When the bandages were finally in place, she had gone downstairs to prepare a meal. Now she had returned, to find Schiller sleeping and Beccione sitting up in the only chair in the attic.

The woman crept nearer the bed. "He is very pale. Did he lose much blood?"

Beccione nodded. "It took us two hours to get here."

Her frail, wrinkled hand stroked Rosenberg's forehead. "I could see Signore Kessler was worried about him. Poor boy. You must not move him until his fever is down."

Beccione shook off his drowsiness and studied the woman, really seeing her for the first time. Her body was gaunt and shapeless beneath a faded blouse and patched skirt: a lifetime of labor had worn away the curves of her womanhood as the sun and rain erode the soil. The same harsh elements had hollowed and wrinkled her face, and yet had done nothing to dim a smile of extraordinary gentleness. Beccione glanced across the room. Schiller, still asleep, could speak neither English nor Italian. He turned back to the woman. It was safe to speak openly.

"You seem to know Signore Kessler very well, *signora*."

She clearly took the remark as a compliment but shook her head. "No better than many others, *signore*."

"Yet I saw you kiss his cheek."

"I kissed him because the Padrone is a good man. Sometimes it seems there are not many left in this world."

"Why is he a good man, *signora*?"

She showed surprise at the question. "You do not know? I thought you were one of his followers."

"I am. But my friend and I have only recently joined him. So we have much to learn."

Her puzzled face cleared. "He is the benefactor of the poor, *signore*. These are very hard times for us. Everyone steals our food, the *Tedeschi*, the *Fascista*, even our own *giovanotto*. Our children and grandchildren grow sick because they are hungry and then we cannot afford medicine to cure them. But the Padrone understands and helps us. Many people light candles for him and pray for his safety. Many, many people."

"Yet are we not thieves ourselves?" Beccione asked, watching her face.

"That is what the soldiers and the *Fascista* say. That is because the Padrone only steals from them. He takes back what they have taken away. Is that stealing, *signore*? I do not think so."

Here was one indomitable old peasant who would never betray Kessler, Beccione thought. Over on the bed Rosenberg gave a groan and stirred restlessly. The woman bent over him and stroked his forehead again. "*Povero ragazzo*," she whispered. "*Sei al sicuro qui.*"

Although clearly in pain, Rosenberg was still asleep. The woman gazed down at him. "We have relatives in America, *signore*. My sister and her husband went there after the first war. But we do not hear from them any more. We think the Germans must be sinking the ships that carry the mail. Do you think that is likely?"

"Perhaps," Beccione said.

She sighed. "War is madness, *signore*. Life is hard enough without it."

Gazing into her wrinkled eyes, Beccione saw the long and stony road she had traveled. "Do you have any children, *signora*?"

"We had a son. But he died eight years ago."

"Did he have any children?"

Seeing her eyes suddenly fill with tears, he understood and turned away. Then, as he fumbled for a cigarette, he heard her give a tut of impatience. "Here I am chattering away and you have not eaten yet. Will you come downstairs or would you rather stay here with your friend?" Beccione's glance at the bed decided her. "You would rather stay here. What about your other friend? Should I wake him?"

Beccione leaned over Schiller and shook his arm. As the weary German's eyes opened, Beccione made a feeding gesture with his hand. His face brightening, Schiller rose to his feet. Beccione turned to the old woman. "If he returns downstairs with you, he can bring my food back with him."

She would have none of it. "No, poor boy, he is tired like you are. He will eat downstairs with us and Antonio will bring up your food."

Unsure of what was happening, Schiller followed her to the door. She turned as he held it open. "Your American friend must stay with us until he is better. We insist on it. And if he should want anything during the night you must call us. We will not be asleep."

The old man came upstairs a couple of minutes later with a tray. His leathery face was as wrinkled as his wife's. A night's growth of beard shone silver in the lamplight. Somewhat unsteadily he set the tray on the table, then turned to the bed. "How is he, *signore*?"

"He seems all right," Beccione said. "I guess it'll be safe to drive on with him in the morning."

The peasant looked surprised. "You are leaving tomorrow, *signore*?"

"We must. There might be a search for us and you could be in serious trouble if we are found here. Don't tell your wife. It might worry her. But there'll be no danger if we leave early."

"My wife already knows, *signore*."

"You mean she knows what we did?"

"Of course. The Padrone would not put us in danger without telling us everything first."

"Doesn't it worry you?"

The old man replied with great dignity. "We are not fools, *signore*. Nor are we brave. But there are worse things, are there not? Surely the man who turns his back on those who have been good to him is in the greatest danger of all."

Beccione took a deep breath. "We'll leave at first light. Make sure you wake us in case we oversleep."

"We will see, *signore*. Now have your meal before it grows cold."

He shuffled from the attic and closed the door. Beccione crossed to the table. The tray contained a bowl of hot bean soup, a large plate of polenta, and a bottle of wine. He drew the chair up to the table. Although hungry, he ate mechanically, his thoughts elsewhere.

He did not open the wine until he had finished the food. Outside the wind seemed to be speaking to him in a language he could not understand. He poured himself a glass of wine and settled back in the chair, watching the oil lamp flicker in a draught and Rosenberg stir restlessly in his sleep. The bottle was empty on his lap by the time Schiller returned, but he did not answer when the German spoke to him. Eyes withdrawn beneath their scarred lids, he was staring into his mind as he listened to the wind.

They left the following morning just as the sky was turning red over the eastern peaks. They were late. The old couple had not awakened them and they had overslept. Fearing for their safety, Beccione refused the breakfast the old woman had prepared.

They carried Rosenberg down to the foot of the stairs, then Beccione crossed the yard to the barn where the jeep was hidden. It had rained during the night: there were pools standing among the cobblestones. The last gray clouds were clearing from the sky, and the odor of straw and manure permeated the damp air. As Beccione jumped into the jeep and began arranging blankets in the back for Rosenberg, he found the old woman standing next to him, a parcel of food in one hand and a bottle in the other. "You will be hungry later," she told him. "And the spirits will keep you all warm."

The bottle contained home-made brandy. Beccione felt his throat tighten. "You have been good to us, mother. I shall not forget you."

His words of affection delighted her. Reaching up, she kissed his cheek. "I shall not forget you either, *ragazzo mio*. Take care of yourself."

The old man shook hands formally with all three men and helped lift Rosenberg into the back of the jeep and cover him with blankets. The woman slipped one of her pillows beneath his head. Although still under sedation, Rosenberg managed a smile. "You're a real momma, lady, you really are."

She did not understand him but gave him a kiss just the same. Then it was Schiller's turn and finally she turned to Beccione once more. This time she gripped his hand and whispered, *"Vai con Dio"* as she kissed him again. The two old figures stood in their yard and waved until the jeep vanished over the mountainside.

The wind was still blowing and the morning air was chilly. Below the jeep the farmhouse was shrinking into the vast perspective, a tiny quadrangle in the desolate mountains.

It happened quite suddenly as Schiller was offering Beccione a cigarette. There was a cry from Rosenberg followed by the paralyzing snarl of an engine. Glancing back, Beccione saw a blurred silhouette diving at incredible speed straight at them.

His reaction was entirely automatic. He spun the wheel, straightened it and shifted gears. The jeep skidded ninety degrees, found traction on the wet ground, and shot off towards the wood below. At the same moment a blast of cannon fire raked and pulverized the mountainside where the jeep had been seconds before.

The Mustang went into a steep climbing turn. Rosenberg pushed himself up and leaned over the front seats. "How does he know who we are?"

Cursing, Beccione tore the green beret off Schiller and hurled it away. "Who else would have a jeep this high in the mountains? They must have put up a patrol at first light."

The morning sunlight caught the Mustang at the apex of its climb. Dropping a wing with breathtaking grace, it came plunging down again. Beccione was controlling the jeep with difficulty. The mountainside at this point was too steep for a direct descent: moreover the rocks and thin soil were slippery from the night rain. Yet his only chance was to reach the flat plateau and the wood at its far end. As the scream of airfoils and engine came again, he ran parallel to the declivity and at the last moment swung the jeep downhill.

The desperate maneuver caught the Mustang pilot by surprise. The rocket he released snaked past and exploded against an outcrop of rock; the raging trail of cannon fire leapt out in the same direction. In the jeep Beccione was fighting desperately. The vehicle skidded downwards with all four wheels locked; not responding at all to Beccione's frantic pumping at the brake. Slamming over rocks, the vehicle careened on two wheels, perilously close to overturning—and certain death for the passengers. Then, as the ground leveled a few degrees, its wheels gained traction again and Beccione was back in control. Shouting encouragement to his ashen-faced comrades, he made for the trees ahead.

The Mustang came down furiously for a final try. But the jeep had made it to the trees now and the canopies of leaves and branches were providing cover. A rocket struck a beech and the entire upper trunk toppled down as if felled by an axe. The jeep escaped unhurt, and by the time the frustrated pilot was climbing over the mountains again it was safely hidden under a huge chestnut.

Suffering reaction, all three men could do nothing for a moment but fight for breath and self-control. They could hear the Mustang circling above as its pilot searched for them. When at last it began moving back to the south, they all relaxed, believing the danger was over.

It wasn't. Instants later they heard the scream of diving airfoils. Beccione's exclamation was hoarse and shocked. "Oh, my God." As he spun the jeep around there was a heavy thud in the distance.

They reached the edge of the wood just as the Mustang was banking back to begin its second attack. Below them on the plateau a thick column of smoke was shredding in the morning wind. The Mustang dived again and released three more rockets. Bright flashes followed, tossing bricks and tiles high into the air as if scattered by some giant's hand. The ground kicked violently, rocking the jeep from side to side.

Beccione reached for the gears. Seeing his intention, Schiller caught his arm, only to be thrown savagely against the door. Behind Beccione, the white-faced Rosenberg added his own plea. "It'd be suicide, kid. No one's alive in there. Look at it."

Fire was now visible through the dust and smoke, consuming fire that was licking up into the morning air. Above it the Mustang was circling, checking to see if a further attack was necessary. "He must've seen us drive out," Rosenberg muttered. "He probably thinks it's one of our bases."

Beccione ignored him, gazing down at the scene with helpless rage. There was no way the American could express his hatred. It went beyond the droning aircraft to hammer on the doors of heaven and hell. A dense pall of smoke was now hanging over the blazing ruins. Deciding his work was done, the pilot of the Mustang turned for home.

27

Jean Pierre tapped gently on the bedroom door. "Franz!" When there was no reply he opened the door and peered inside. "Franz," he whispered again. "Are you all right?"

This time he heard a muffled exclamation and the creak of bedsprings. Glancing down the empty corridor, the Frenchman stepped into the room and closed the door behind him.

The room was dark save for a moonbeam slanting through

an open window and falling across a bed on which a man was lying. The acid smell of whiskey filled the air. Hesitating a moment, Jean Pierre approached the bed.

"Franz, you have not eaten a thing since yesterday. Let me get you a meal."

Kessler cursed thickly in German. "Leave me alone."

The Frenchman's deep voice had the gentleness of a woman as he moved up next to the bedside. "Franz, you did it to save a man's life. One of your own men." Seeing the German wince, he went on. "I'm sorry, Franz. But I know this is what has upset you."

There was silence for a moment. Then Kessler's voice lashed out like a whip. "Upset me? Stop talking like a fool. Go away and leave me alone."

"It was not your fault," the Frenchman insisted. "Any one of us would have done the same thing."

Kessler swung his feet down to the carpet, an act that brought his face into the moonlight. It was sweat-stained and tortured, the face of a man on the rack. He reached for his glass and drained it before glancing back at Jean Pierre. "Do you know what that American sergeant was doing? He was trying to save a young boy's life."

"I know that, Franz. But what happened was not your fault."

"Not my fault? If I had not allowed Schumann to attack that convoy, the man would still be alive. And so would the boy."

"But you had no way of knowing that. And without those drugs many children would die. If you must have regret, keep it where it belongs."

The Frenchman's admonition drew Kessler's stare. Then he laughed, a sound so full of self-loathing it made Jean Pierre wince. "You are a fool, Jean Pierre. You believe I hate killing. You are wrong. Sometimes I want to kill the world. If I had the power, I would kill it."

"You forget I know why, Franz. But it is you who are wrong. Men like Roberts and Nickolai would not follow you if you were a killer. They know you save far more lives than you take."

The German's hostility suddenly fell away. With a sigh he dropped back on his elbows. "Why is the world like this, Jean Pierre? Why does it destroy all that is pure in us and then turn us against the ruins of that purity?"

"Perhaps only God can answer that, Franz."

It was a mistake. Kessler's voice again lashed out like a whip, taunting and scourging. "God? The fount of love and mercy? The great pacifist? Tell me something, Jean Pierre. Did God make this world?"

"I believe he did, Franz."

Kessler leaned forward. "Then explain something to me. Why is the design based on killing? The chameleon kills the fly. The bird kills the chameleon. The cat kills the bird. And man—he kills the cat. Man kills everything, including his own kind. Isn't that true?"

"Yes, Franz. But . . ."

"But what, Jean Pierre? Do you think I am saying man is the greatest killer of all? If so, you are wrong. The greatest killer must be the one who made us all what we are. Your God, Jean Pierre."

The Frenchman crossed himself. "No, Franz. God gave us free will. We are what we choose to be."

The tremor of hatred in Kessler's reply opened to Jean Pierre a sudden vision of the deep black waters into which he was treading. "Are we, Jean Pierre? Are you sure of that?"

The night was not warm but the big Frenchman was sweating. "Life can make a mockery of our ideals, I know that. But man is aware of his loss. Isn't that a gift in itself?"

In the moonlight Kessler's eyes looked like burning coals, the eyes of a man who believed himself irretrievably and eternally damned. "The man who knows his sins and still commits them is the greatest sinner of all. Isn't he like the fallen angel? Doesn't your holy book tell you God sees him as a mortal enemy?"

"No, Franz. If he turned against the things he believed in because he was wronged, God would know and forgive him."

Kessler's laugh made the Frenchman wince again. "Let us hope you are right, Jean Pierre. Because he has still to forgive the fallen angel, hasn't he?" When Jean Pierre failed to answer, the German laughed and reached for the bottle alongside him. "I love your simple soul, Jean Pierre. But you are wasting your time. Go back to the others and forget about me."

"At least let me get you something to eat," the Frenchman begged again.

Kessler cursed and his voice rose into a shout. *"Verdammt, ich sagte: Gehen sie weg!"*

Kessler flung himself back on the bed. Jean Pierre, hesitating at the door, heard a sob of agony break from the shadows. Blindly, he hurried down the corridor.

From his seat outside the Bar Alberto Beccione could hear the Litany being chanted. The heavy studded doors of the church opposite were wide open in an attempt to combat the early summer heat. In the cantina behind him the scene was somewhat less pious: men and women crowded around a radio, intent on a tinny voice half-drowned by static. Clandestine BBC and Allied broadcasts were always eagerly awaited by the inhabitants of La Capella even though reception was poor in the high mountains.

At least half of those present were Kessler's men. Their various attitudes towards the progress of the war betrayed differences between them that their collective activities tended to hide. Some listened to the bulletins because they knew that once the war ended their wild and irresponsible lives would end with it. Others listened because, although they would sooner die than admit it, deep-seated tribal loyalties still made them hope for the success of their own kind. Yet another group took a purely academic interest in the news. Beccione was one of these. His recent experiences had consolidated his belief that the world had no time or mercy for the defenseless. Whoever won the war, the old predators and the old injustices would still be there—even if they took on a different name. Now an established member of the gang, Beccione was living from day to day and letting the future take care of itself. His one and only departure from this philosophy was the hope that sometime somewhere he would see Maria again.

A loud and excited cheer from the bar drew his glance. Men and women were embracing and kissing one another. Rosenberg, grinning broadly, pushed through them and limped toward Beccione. He plonked a bottle of wine on the table. "It's all happening. Monte Cassino's fallen."

Beccione reached for the bottle and filled his glass. "Bully for Monte Cassino."

"Ain't you glad?"

"Why should I be glad? I like it here."

Rosenberg's face fell. "You think we might have to move out?"

"As I see it, it depends on whether the Krauts defend Rome or declare it an open city. If they don't defend it and they can't hold us north of Rome, they might decide to fall right back to the Gothic line. And that would put *us* behind the Allied lines."

"Would it matter that much? We're high up here and most of the fighting's on the west coast. Why should the Allies bother us more than the Krauts? At least they'd leave the Jews and the anti-Fascists alone."

Beccione gave him a pitying look. "You must be kidding. Wherever they go they slap in their Control Commissions. You think Kessler could go on operating here if the place was full of Whitecaps?"

Alongside the bar two pretty giggling girls were struggling to put up a poster. Rosenberg glanced at them and sighed, "Why did I move over here? I was happy until you cheered me up."

Beccione followed his eyes. "What's the poster for? Another concert?"

"Yeah. This one's in the bar next weekend. They say Magda's agreed to dance." When Beccione made no comment, Rosenberg went on: "I guess that means we'll be going, uh?"

Beccione shrugged and toyed with his glass. "Maybe."

Rosenberg eyed him with some concern. Since the killing of the two old peasants, there had been a subtle change in Beccione. He was quieter, more reflective—his flame seemed to burn deeper inside him and more intensely. Rosenberg was about to speak when a jeep halted at the curb and Jean Pierre jumped out. "*Bonjour, mes amis.* I thought I would find you here."

"It is Sunday morning," Rosenberg pointed out.

The Frenchman's eyes twinkled. "So it is. And I see the two of you are sitting very sensibly on the fence."

Rosenberg glanced around. "What fence?"

Jean Pierre's eyes moved from the bar to the church opposite where the congregation was now singing heartily. "The fence between heaven and hell. What else?"

Rosenberg grinned. "That one? Oh yeah. We always like to hedge our bets."

Jean Pierre snapped his fingers for a waiter to bring another glass, then addressed Rosenberg again as he dropped into a chair. "So they've let you out of the hospital. Does that mean I can put you back on duty?"

Rosenberg looked shocked. "Me? I'm still on the danger list."

"The only danger you're in is from that red-headed nurse. Is she still taking care of you?"

Rosenberg grinned. "All the way."

"You got wounded in the right place," the Frenchman grunted. He filled his glass and turned to Beccione. "I've got a job for you, *mon ami*."

"I thought you might," Beccione said.

"Relax. You're going to enjoy this one."

"I can't wait. What is it?"

The Frenchman took a sip of wine before answering. "Do you remember that place where I first interrogated you?" Beccione nodded. "Schultz, one of our German boys, has found three potential recruits and taken them there. One's a German, the other two are Yugoslavs. Schultz has sent word he believes they're O.K. but the Yugoslavs can't speak any English or German, so he wants Magda to go and interrogate them. She'll take two jeeps from my squad, one as a backup in case of trouble."

"Why doesn't she use Schumann's jeeps?" Beccione interrupted.

Jean Pierre nodded at the southern mountains that overlooked the small town. "He and the Padrone are out on a job and they've called for Schumann's squad to back them up. This rumor about the Boche and the Fascists carrying out a purge on the peasants is growing stronger by the day. Colenzo and Berrati tried to find something out last week but security's as tight as hell." A momentary frown betrayed the Frenchman's concern for Kessler. "So the Padrone and Schumann are going into Ancona disguised as S.S. officers. They figure a couple of our captured *Kübels* manned by Schumann's Germans should fool the garrison there without any trouble."

Kessler's readiness to take extreme risks for the peasants impressed Beccione more than ever. "So what's my job?" he asked.

Jean Pierre's grin returned. "Magda feels she needs someone who speaks unaccented Italian for a trip like this. I said she could take her pick and she chose you."

Beccione shook his head. "I'm not interested. Tell her to find somebody else."

"It's not that simple, *mon ami*. Roberts is going along as a back-up: he wants to check on the Boche activity down there. As he hardly speaks any Italian, he'd also like you to go along."

Beccione, who liked Roberts, hesitated before shaking his head again. "You've got plenty of Italians, for Chrissake. What about Colenzo or Berrati?"

"They've both gone with the Padrone." Uncharacteristically patient so far, the Frenchman now made it clear the argument was over. "You'll leave in the morning at first light. Roberts and Toschack will lead in the first jeep, you and the girl will follow in the second. You'll have to keep to the high ground until you get near the house. It never was that far from the front and now that Nonce Cassino's fallen the Boche could be active around there. You should reach it tomorrow but you'll probably have to spend the night there."

"What if Magda's not satisfied with the Kraut or the Yugoslavs?" Beccione asked.

"If she's not, you'll leave them there with Schultz. He'll lock them up again. We'll decide what to do with them once we've got Magda's report."

Quiet so far, Rosenberg could hold back his protest no longer. "Schumann ain't going to like this. You thought about that?"

Beccione wondered how much of the Frenchman's tongue was in his cheek as he glanced at the Jewish soldier. "It is a military exercise. So why should Captain Schumann mind?"

"Ah, come on," Rosenberg grunted. "It ain't no secret the guy don't like Joe. And he ain't gonna like him any more when he finds out they've all spent the night together."

"But there will be two other men present to vouch that Joe has been a good boy." Draining his glass, the Frenchman rose and winked down at the frowning Beccione. "Just the same, never let it be said your commander does you no favors. I am told even a ride with Magda can be a delightful experience."

Beccione's scarred eyebrows rose. "I'll let you know later on just how much of a favor you've done me."

Jean Pierre laughed and climbed into his jeep. His reply was drowned out by the engine as the jeep accelerated away.

28

Beccione could see the flight of Allied bombers clearly through his binoculars. They were peeling off one by one and diving out of sight behind the ridge of mountains to the west. The thump-thump of bombs came pulsing through the hot still air and made his eardrums contract. He passed the binoculars to Magda. "Isn't there a main road beyond those mountains?" he asked.

She brushed a fly from her cheek. "Yes, but it won't be the road they are bombing. They'll need it for their advance. The Boche must have dug into a strongpoint. Or perhaps they have a gun battery covering the road."

It was 14:30 the afternoon following Beccione's talk with Jean Pierre. The three men and the girl had left La Capella just after dawn and, apart from a short stop at 10:00, they had driven all morning. There had been only one incident: Roberts' jeep had stalled in an irrigation ditch and had been dragged out only with great difficulty. They had spotted Allied aircraft at irregular intervals, mostly heavy bombers pounding German reserves deep behind their front line. Since no notice so far had been taken of the two camouflaged jeeps treading their way through the mountains, the crews had decided it was safe to stop for rest and food.

They were parked inside an old castle, a place of crumbled stone walls and great clumps of furze and bramble. Roberts and Toschack, both excellent cooks, had volunteered to stay with the jeeps and cook the meal. Beccione had been posted on the outer walls as a sentry. After a few minutes Magda had joined him.

Taking the binoculars back, Beccione lifted a mocking eyebrow at her last comment. "Boche! I hope you don't use words like that in front of Schumann."

She gave him a steady look. "I say what I like to Schumann. He is not my master."

"He's your lover," Beccione said.

"What if he is? I still say what I please."

Like him, she was wearing a khaki shirt and slacks—a uniform that should have hidden her femininity, but instead seemed to accentuate it. The top two buttons of her shirt were open, making it obvious that she wore no brassiere. It was impossible to guess whether she had unfastened the buttons as a sexual provocation or whether, indifferent to its effect on the men around her, as a simple response to the heat: she was capable of either type of behavior. In the sunlight Beccione could see the golden down on the nape of her neck; he felt again his desire for her.

"I get the feeling sometimes you don't like Germans," he said.

She was gazing straight in front of her. "Germans are just men like any other."

He cared nothing about her feelings towards Germans: his aim was to learn more about her. "Yet if it wasn't for Germans you wouldn't be a refugee up in these mountains, would you?" he said.

She gave him a cold, hard stare. "No, I would not. I would be a provincial lawyer's daughter living in a provincial town. You see how I must hate the Germans."

He laughed in disbelief. "You're a lawyer's daughter?"

"Yes. Is it so hard to believe?"

He smiled at her. "I guess not when you stop and think about it. A guy I used to know always said the professional classes make the best gangsters because of the practice they get."

In spite of her haughtiness, she did have a sense of humor. "Thank you for the compliment."

"Is that how you come to speak English so well?" he asked. "Special school and the rest of it?"

"Yes, I had a good education."

"And yet now you're up in the Italian mountains with a crowd of deserters, hoodlums and murderers. How come?"

"How come?" she repeated.

"Yes. Tell me what happened."

"Why?"

"I'm curious, that's why."

She took a cigarette, then offered him one. A frown marred her perfect features as she inhaled. For a moment it seemed she would refuse him. Then she shrugged. "Have you heard of Mikhailovitch?"

"Yeah, I think so. Wasn't he the first guy to organize partisan resistance in Yugoslavia?"

"Yes. One hears nothing about him now: the Communists have destroyed him and taken over his leadership. But to people of our class he was our one hope of survival."

"Was it his partisans you joined?"

"Yes, when the Germans reached our town. Many of the young people took to the mountains and I went with them. With Mikhailovitch leading us we fought as well as we could, but we were always short of food and arms and the Germans never stopped hunting us."

Beccione was aware that of all the partisans fighting against the Germans, none fought harder or suffered more than the Yugoslavs in the bare Balkan mountains. "Did many girls become partisans?"

"Many. They fought just like the men. Do you know what happened to us after nearly a year of those conditions?" When he shook his head. "We stopped having our periods. At the time we thought we were pregnant but it wasn't that. We were living like wild animals and so nature adapted us to survive like animals. Had we become pregnant we would have been helpless."

"How are you now?"

"I am normal again. This life is nothing like as severe as the life over there. The winters were the worst and when the Communists took over it became impossible. They commandeered the food and got whatever arms and ammunition the Allies sent over."

"You didn't consider joining them?"

Her green eyes flashed at him. "The Communists! Never! A dozen men and myself managed to reach the coast where the captain of a Turkish ship offered to take us to Egypt. Two days after sailing one of our men who could understand Turkish heard two of the crew discussing what share of the money they would receive when the captain delivered us to the Italian Fascists. I knew the captain desired me and that night I agreed to go to his cabin. When he fell asleep, I looked for the key to his arms cupboard. A few minutes later all our men were armed and we forced the crew to take us to Alexandria."

Beccione had been watching her closely. "What happened to the captain?"

She stared straight at him. "We killed him. He was a filthy treacherous pig and a knife in his heart was too quick a death."

"Go on," Beccione said.

"We arrived at Alexandria safely, only for the British to intern us. Tito was in favor by this time and the British wired his forces to ask what should be done with us. The Communists said we were traitors and demanded our extradition. Fearing the British might appease them, we managed to break out one night. We stole some money and bribed an Egyptian fisherman to take us to Albania. On the way an Italian naval ship intercepted us. When they tried to board us we put up a fight. All our men were killed or wounded but one of the Italian officers protected me and put me in his cabin. When we docked in Ancona he wanted to get an apartment for me but I ran away. Shortly afterwards I met Helmut and then Kessler."

With her beautiful face gone hard from the memories she recalled, Beccione had no doubt that everything she had told him was true—if anything greatly understated.

"I'd say you were a survivor," he said.

She shrugged. "Aren't we all?"

"How do you feel about Yugoslavia now?"

"How do I feel about any country now? Aren't they all the same? Don't they all use people like pawns and then throw them away when their use has gone?"

"I'm not quarreling with that. Tell me something. Why didn't you become Kessler's girl?"

She turned and frowned at him. "Why should I have become his girl?"

"Because he's the boss man and you're a survivor."

She stiffened. "You do realize you are being rude?"

"C'mon, baby. You've always gone to the top, like all smart people do. So why not with Kessler?"

She stared at him for a moment, then her anger receded. "Kessler never wanted me. Does that satisfy you?"

"Yeah, that's better—though I can't think why. Do you know?"

"How could I know a thing like that?"

"Doesn't he like women?"

"I can't say. But I've never seen him with one."

"Is that why you're scared of him?"

The unexpected question made her eyes flare again. "What do you mean—scared of him? I'm scared of no man."

"Yes, you are. You're scared of Kessler. I saw it at the bridge. Is it because you've got no power over him? Or is it something else?"

She sat upright with a jerk. "That is the stupidest thing I've ever heard."

"It is? Then why are you getting so upset about it?"

Her beautiful face was sharp with disdain. "I thought you were intelligent. Instead you talk like a fool." Beccione was finding something aphrodisiacal in her anger. As he grinned at her, her mood changed to sullenness. "It is true he is different. I could tell it from the beginning. He is not one of us."

His tone also changed. "What does that mean?"

"I don't know. It is something one feels."

He knew it was true. "Do you know anything about his background?"

"Nothing the others do not know. Only that he was once a university professor."

"You don't know what he did to become a deserter?"

"No. But if he is in fact a deserter, he cannot have come from the Italian front. The German Army only entered Italy after Badaglio signed the Armistice in February, and I know he was in these mountains last year."

"Then where the hell *did* he come from?" Beccione muttered.

She had been watching his expression. "He fascinates you, doesn't he?"

He was saved from making his reply by a shout from the ruins behind them. As they rose, he nodded at the western mountains. "How much further do you figure we have to go?"

"Not far. Perhaps twenty kilometers."

"How long's your interrogation going to take?"

"It's difficult to say. If you are wondering if we shall have to stay the night, I would say yes." He nodded and she pursued: "Does that worry you?"

He frowned. "Why should it worry me?"

Her smile taunted him. "You might be thinking of Helmut."

"Helmut? Why should I think about him?"

"Some men would. Some men would be afraid of him."

"Some men might have cause. But I've done nothing to annoy Helmut, have I?"

She laughed and tossed her silky bronze hair over her shoulder, a characteristic gesture. "Not yet. But I have a feeling you might."

"Have you now? What will I do?"

Her green eyes challenged him for a moment, then she laughed again and moved away. "Perhaps I am wrong. We shall see. Let us go now and eat."

His desire for her came alive again as he followed her. Behind the ridge of mountains the bombers had finished their work and disappeared. They left behind a pall of black smoke that floated like an omen in the bright, blue sky.

29

Roberts's jeep reached the hill crest that overlooked the valley, halted abruptly, then backed away to avoid making a skyline silhouette. Beccione halted alongside the Englishman. "What's wrong?"

Roberts leapt out. "I don't know yet. Let's take a look."

Followed by the rest of the party, the two men ran back to the hill crest. Beccione recognized the view of square fields and stone hedges. But he stiffened with shock when his eyes turned on the large farmhouse. "What's happened, for Chrissake? It wasn't those bombers, was it?"

Gazing down through his binoculars, Roberts shook his head. "No, they were bombing something along the highway. Fifteen miles or more from here."

Beccione saw that although the outhouses that enclosed the farmyard appeared to be intact, the main building itself had been gutted by fire. Its stone walls were still standing but most of the roof had collapsed, exposing its charred interior. In the late afternoon sunlight a faint blue haze hung over the valley.

Beccione shifted his binoculars to the farmyard where a number of men and women were congregated. The horses and carts standing along the cobbled roadway indicated that they were local tenants visiting the stricken house. Black-shawled women were gathered in small groups while cloth-capped men probed gingerly among the smoking ruins.

Roberts's lined, thoughtful face was showing distress. "It's been a raid. And it hasn't happened that long ago."

"You mean by the Germans?" Magda asked.

"The Germans or the Italians. They probably found out we've been using the house. If they have, God help the family."

Like the others, Roberts was searching the valley and the surrounding hillsides for any trace of soldiers. A couple of carts could be seen passing one another on the lane that ran through the fields but they were being drawn by civilians.

Roberts lowered his binoculars. "If the Jerries did it, they appear to have gone. Let's go down and find out."

The two jeeps descended the hillside cautiously. Toschack and Beccione drove, Roberts and Magda manned the machine guns. Tiny figures could be seen below pointing excitedly upwards. Men were running across the farmyard, herding their women folk towards the waiting horses and carts. Toschack glanced back at Roberts. "The poor sods think the Jerries are coming back!"

The Englishman took off his beret and waved it above his head. The others did the same and gradually the commotion died down and peasants began drifting back into the farmyard.

The two jeeps circled the house cautiously before approaching the main gate. There they halted, their machine guns trained on the outhouses. A balding man in peasant dress emerged from one of them, his arms above his head. He joined the rest of the peasants who, made nervous again by the militant posture of the jeeps, were huddled together in the center of the farmyard. Beccione glanced across at Roberts. "What do you think?"

"I think we're all right. But let's hear what happened first."

Beccione gave a shout. *"Chi ti manda?"*

There was a moment of hesitation, then the thick-set balding man detached himself from the group and made for the jeeps. His distress and his thick local accent made it difficult for Beccione to understand him, and it was several minutes before the American turned back to the others.

"It was a raid but it's O.K. now. They left some hours ago."

Roberts relaxed. "Who were they? Germans or Italians?"

"This guy says there were both."

"Both? Then it must have been a tip-off. Do they know what happened?"

"Yeah. They released an old woman before they left the valley. She says the German deserter who Schultz found with the Yugoslavs must have been a plant. He escaped from the house during the night and just after dawn brought the raiding party back with him. They took away both Schultz and the Yugoslavs."

"What about the owner and his family?"

Beccione lit a cigarette. "They were taken away too. Everybody was taken away except this old woman and the three others who were killed."

Roberts gave a start. "Killed? Who were they?"

"It seems two of the men tried to escape and were shot." Beccione inhaled smoke, his eyes bleak. "The girl, Elena, killed herself."

"Elena? Why, for God's sake?"

"Two of the Fascists raped her. When they'd finished she cut her wrists. There was no one to attend to her and she bled to death."

Toschack cursed. "Elena wasn't involved. The poor kid only worked here."

The balding peasant was talking to Beccione again and pointing at the outhouse from which he had emerged. "He says they left the bodies in there for the peasants to bury," Beccione said.

Toschack glanced at Roberts. "What do we do now? Go back?"

Roberts checked the Australian as the peasant said something else to Beccione. The American pointed up at the hillside. "He says the Krauts are checking all the farmhouses in the district. A party of them went up there before noon and haven't returned yet. It's a wonder we never ran into them."

"Ask him if he knows how big the party was," Roberts said.

The peasant spread out his arms. "Someone told him it was a big one," Beccione said. "They had horses carrying machine guns and mortars."

Roberts grimaced. "If it's that big we'd better lie doggo for a while. Let's hide the jeeps and play it from there."

The peasants clustered around them as they drove into the farmyard. Many of the women were still crying bitterly. The smell of smoke was strong in the late afternoon air. The cow shed and the pigsty were empty of animals: the raiding party had taken all the cattle with them. A large cart had also been stolen. While Toschack backed his jeep into the stable, an old woman led Beccione into a barn full of fodder and straw. Crossing herself, the woman pointed at three bodies covered by tarpaulins at the far end. Beccione, followed by Magda, approached them and drew back the coverings. The first body he did not recognize. The second belonged to a burly young man who had acted as relief guard when he and Rosenberg had been kept in the house. Beccione found himself hesitating before drawing back the third tarpaulin. The girl's clothing had been decently rearranged and her face had the tranquillity of death. Its bloodless appearance startled him, however:

in his mind's eye he had been seeing the healthy smiling face of the living girl. Moreover she looked much younger than he remembered her: her face had the innocence of a sleeping child. His breath caught in his throat when he realized Magda was at his elbow.

Without a word to her he replaced the tarpaulin and walked out into the sunlight. Roberts was standing in the yard, trying to make sense of something the balding peasant was telling him. Beccione stepped forward to help. "He says they're all worried that we might run into the Germans. They want to hide us in their homes until they've gone."

Roberts showed no surprise. "That's typical. They're scared to death but they won't leave us in the lurch."

There was a frown on Beccione's scarred face. "You're not going to accept? Not after what's happened."

"Of course I'm not," the Englishman said curtly. "Thank them but tell them we shall stay here tonight. But ask them if they'll bury the dead for us."

The balding man nodded when Beccione made the request. "They are our people, *signore*, and we will take care of them. But may we leave them until the morning? It is getting late and the men must get back to their cattle."

Before the peasants left, everything they had found in the gutted house was placed reverently in the outhouses. A middle-aged woman ran to her cart and handed Roberts a quarter of cheese. Another woman gave Magda two bottles of wine. Their spokesman, the last man to leave, told Beccione more food would be sent to them later in the evening. He also asked that their Padrone, Kessler, should be told of their sorrow at the loss of his Italian friends and that the villagers' blessing be conveyed to him and his men.

The carts began to creak away down the cobbled lane; one by one they disappeared into a magenta mist that was filling the valley. The three men and the girl stood at the gate watching them go. Beccione's harsh laugh made all of them glance at him. "They give us their blessing. Now that's really something."

Roberts, busy packing his pipe, gave a shrug. "Did it surprise you?"

"Surprise me? For Christ's sake, those three people in that barn would be alive tonight if it wasn't for us. If I were those peasants I'd hate our guts. And Kessler's most of all."

The Englishman struck a match and applied it to his pipe. He pressed down a rising flake of tobacco before answering.

"As you see, they've a different view of Kessler. They consider themselves in his debt."

"Some debt," Beccione said. "As I see it, all he does is compensate them for the risks they take in helping him. And how do you compensate for the dead?"

Roberts's eyes rose from his pipe. Without knowing why, Beccione had the feeling the Englishman's answer was only a substitute for the one he wanted to make. "If you prefer it, forget all about debts. When a man's in need, these people help him, friend or stranger. I know. A family once gave me food and shelter when their own kids were half-starving. They don't care about race either. They'll help a hungry German just as readily as any of us."

Magda nodded. "It's true that many of them don't seem to know what the war's about."

The girl's words were offered in sincerity, but they brought out all Toschack's dislike of her. "Don't know what the war's about? With their friends shot and their kids starving? Don't talk like a fool."

Roberts's quiet glance made the Australian turn away. "You're right they've no strong feelings towards their country, Magda. You'd hardly expect it when for centuries they've been ground into dust by landowners, priests, and the Italian upper classes. What I find amazing is they're not embittered. Nothing seems to deter their generosity: it is as simple as that. I've always felt it a privilege to meet such people."

It was praise made the more impressive by the Englishman's quiet way of speaking. Beccione, watching the last cart disappear into the mist, turned from the gate. "I'll get my jeep out of sight."

"Then we are definitely staying?" Magda asked.

Roberts nodded. "Yes. With any luck the Jerries will be out of the mountains by the morning."

"Then if you like I'll cook supper."

Roberts's eye crinkled at her. "It'll taste nicer if you do. But wait first to see what the peasants send us."

With room for only one jeep in the stable, Beccione was forced to back his vehicle into the outhouse that contained the three bodies. Toschack walked after him. He bent down and picked up a handful of straw. "It starts getting dark around eight and light about four. So if we do a two hour shift apiece, that should see us through."

"You think the girl should do one?"

The Australian's expression was hard. "Why not? She's always bragging she's as good as a man." His eyes challenged Beccione. "And it'll help to keep her out of mischief."

The group gathered to draw straws five minutes later. Picking the shortest, Beccione gained the first watch. Toschack got the second, followed by Roberts and Magda. Beccione offered to change watches with the girl and smiled at her sharp refusal.

They decided the small cemetery a quarter of a mile up the hillside made a good sentry post. It gave cover and if the night were still and starlit, as it promised to be, it would be possible both to hear and see horses long before they reached the house.

Beccione made his way up to it a few minutes before eight. Settling behind its low stone wall, he watched the Italian night close around him. The purple sky darkened and stars appeared one by one. As the afterglow faded over the western mountains, phosphorescent flashes could be seen running over them like summer lightning. Beccione thought he heard the far-off rumble of gunfire.

It was a night that brought back memories, both bitter and sweet. Beccione wondered how old man Bolan was getting on, whether he had any new fighters bidding for ring honors. The last letter he'd received from the old man had said he was thinking of retiring, but Beccione knew he never would. The ring was in his blood and he'd probably die of a heart attack one day while yelling for some kid to get back on his feet and fight.

He wondered what Baker Company was doing and whether they were back in action yet. He was aware that his nostalgic mood was leading him down the road to Maria but tonight he seemed to have no defenses. Now and then, in moments of optimism, he had drawn hope from Agata Marini's parting words—but tonight he knew that optimism had come from the heart and not the mind. Maria had known nothing of McCall's behavior in the stockade. To a girl of her temperament and upbringing, his act must have seemed inexcusably brutal.

Nor was she wrong, Beccione thought. His ordeal in prison had not justified murder, and yet he had not only killed McCall but would have also killed the other MPs had not Nunez and Rosenberg stopped him. Violence was as much a part of him as the blood in his veins. Even if he and Maria could have married, it would have inevitably come between them.

He dropped back on his elbows and gazed up at the brilliant stars—wondering at their icy indifference to the suffering they witnessed below. Up until now, indifference had been in accord with all his experience of the world: it was something he had borne without complaint. Tonight, however, he felt rebellion. He and his kind might deserve no mercy, but a world outrageous enough to destroy people like the two old peasants and Elena was foul beyond toleration.

Although quick to ridicule his thoughts, he also knew they alarmed him. In Beccione's world the man who began to feel compassion was like the wolf who began to bleed. The rest of the pack would soon smell his weakness and turn on him with fang and claw. Searching for help, his mind turned towards Magda. Surely the man who took her in his arms would never be unmanned by sentimentality.

Earlier on he had half-expected the girl to join him during his watch. Now he realized he had underestimated her. However else she might use her sexuality, she was far too good a soldier to endanger her unit.

The clink of a pebble made him grab for his machine carbine and peer over the wall. He could see no silhouettes on the hillside above but he clearly heard footsteps. He relaxed when he realized they were coming up behind the cemetery. A few seconds later he heard a low, twangy voice. "Where are ya, cobber? It's me, Toschack."

The American was surprised to find two hours had passed. "I'm over here."

Toschack swung his raw-boned body over the wall. "How's it gone? You heard anything?"

Beccione nodded at the shimmering flashes on the horizon. "Nothing but those guns."

The Australian followed his gaze. "Looks like all hell's busted loose. I wonder if the bastards will crack?"

"We'll know soon enough. Is the chow ready?"

"Yeah. A kid brought some meat and vegetables. We've had ours. The girl's kept a bottle of wine for you."

As Beccione turned to climb the wall, the Australian caught his arm. "You know what my advice is, don't you, cobber?"

"I ought to. You've dished it out to me often enough."

Toschack's voice turned hard. "O.K., Yank, it's your head. Just don't come running to us for help if Schumann wants it for a football."

Beccione broke away and walked slowly back to the farm.

He found Magda waiting in the deep shadow of an outhouse. "Joe! I'm over here."

He followed her into the barn where his jeep was parked. At first the only light came from a spirit stove on which a pan was simmering. Swinging the heavy door closed, she lit a paraffin lamp she had found in the barn. Its yellow light spread outwards, touching the three tarpaulin-covered bodies lined against the far wall.

"Where's Roberts?" Beccione asked.

"He's sleeping in the stable. We've all eaten." She led him around the far side of the jeep where the pan was hissing and poured its contents on a tin plate. "You must be hungry."

He found the goulash she had made with the meat and vegetables delicious. Without speaking or looking at her, he finished the meal and accepted a glass of wine. He drained it and set the glass on the ground. Only then did he allow his eyes to be drawn to her.

The paraffin lamp rested on the cobbled floor between them. At some time during the evening she had released her long bronze hair and the lambent light burnished it. The same light was adding a bloom to her tanned cheeks and shapely mouth. As she leaned forward to pour him more wine, her hair brushed his bare arm and an electric shock seemed to pass through him. "Did you enjoy the meal," she asked as he pushed away his plate.

"Yes, it was great. Thanks."

There was tension between them. He finished the second glass of wine without another word. By this time he could feel the alcohol in his bloodstream. He noticed that her shirt was unbuttoned again and the deep curves of her cleavage were accentuated by the light and shade. His desire for her grew painful and her eyes told him she was aware of it. Then he remembered the dead at the far end of the outhouse and something rebelled inside him. Magda looked startled as he jumped to his feet. "What is it?"

Without answering her he walked around the jeep. Kneeling down, he drew the tarpaulin back from Elena's face. In the soft light she looked less bloodless: she might almost have been sleeping. He was startled to hear Magda's voice at his elbow. "Did you make love to her."

He took a deep breath, replaced the tarpaulin and straightened. "No."

"Then why do you keep on looking at her?"

He turned away. "She was just a kid. They shouldn't have done that to her."

"She wasn't a member of the household, you know. She lived on a peasant farm with her father and two brothers."

"What's that got to do with it?" Some kind of rage, raw and uncontrollable, was rising up in Beccione.

"It makes you wonder if there wasn't another reason why she killed herself. If the stories you hear are true, not many of these peasant girls get the chance to stay virgins, in spite of the Church. Not on lonely farms with fathers and brothers about."

At another time or place he might have realized she was only speculating or even trying to ease his feelings. But now, something in her words and manner enraged him. He cursed and struck her hard across the face. She lifted a hand in surprise. "What was that for?"

He struck her again. This time she staggered back and fell on a pile of straw. He saw he had hurt her and his anger died at once. "I'm sorry," he muttered. "I don't know why I did that."

She lay watching him, a trickle of blood showing at the side of her mouth. Her voice checked him as he turned away. "Come here, Joe."

He hesitated, then obeyed. "I'm sorry," he said again.

To his surprise her arms reached up, clasping around his neck, pulling him down. He tried to draw back, feeling the act profane in the surroundings. But he discovered his desire seemed inflamed by the presence of the dead.

Magda deftly removed her clothing and in seconds was naked beneath him. Her probing fingers ran down his sweating back, then slid beneath his belly and freed him. As her body arched, he gave a cry and drove into her. It was not an act of love: he was punishing her for his shame and it brought a gasp of pain from her. Yet her bruised lips lifted and crushed against his own. Her tongue circulated within his mouth and he tasted the salt of her blood. "Everything, *cara*," she breathed. "Give me everything."

Driven on by the madness that possessed him, Beccione thrust and thrust again. In turn, crying with desire, she urged her body towards him. Accompanied by the distant ominous orchestra of guns, their shadows danced on the cobwebbed walls. To Beccione, with guilt fueling his desire, they seemed to be writhing and straining like creatures in purgatory.

30

The recreation room was packed with men from all three squads. Although it was only 08.30, it was already stiflingly hot. The increasing humidity of mid-summer was one factor: another was tension. Rumors had been circulating among the outlaws for weeks that something big was afoot and the size of the briefing suggested this could now be it. Although every window was open, there was no movement of air to lift the dense pall of cigarette smoke that hung over the assemblage.

With Rosenberg behind him, Beccione was standing near the front beside an open window. Never having seen the entire company together before, he was fascinated both by its size and the variety of nationalities present. With most of the men wearing the customary uniforms of their native armies, the effect was both colorful and bizarre, a tiny rebellious League of Nations army.

One thing was common to every man present, however: they were all freshly shaven. No tidy military figure himself, Kessler cared little about uniform unless it served his ends. But he was fastidious about personal cleanliness and men were punished by heavy fines if they appeared before him unwashed and unkempt.

Magda was present. Wearing German battle dress, she was standing among a group of Schumann's men. As she exchanged glances with Beccione, Rosenberg nudged the GI in the back. "Watch it, pal. Schumann's got his eye on you both."

The German was seated with Kessler's other lieutenants near the end of a row of chairs at the far side of the room. Kessler, standing with his back to the wall, faced the main assembly with Jean Pierre in attendance beside him. A large map of Italy was pinned to the wall behind the two men.

Kessler had a pointer in his hand. Tall, lean, academic in appearance, he might have been a professor lecturing a class of students had it not been for his uniform.

"I have called you in here this morning, gentlemen, because we have now confirmed the rumors that have been

174

spreading in the towns for some time. The Germans and the
Fascists are about to launch a large punitive operation
against isolated villages and farmhouses behind their front
line. Indeed, as some of you might have heard, some raids
have already taken place. Because the area in question depends to some extent on where the Germans stabilize their
new line, we cannot say for certain how far north they will
strike. Some believe they might reach back as far as Cantone."

A loud murmur broke out. Cantone was not that far south
of La Capella. Kessler allowed the murmur to continue for a
few seconds before holding up his hand. "For those of you
who do not know the background to this decision, I will
quickly explain. When, on September 8 of last year, Badoglio
asked the Allies for an armistice, thousands of Allied prisoners of war either escaped or were released by their Italian
guards who believed the War was over. The Germans, however, who had been expecting such a move, immediately
poured their armies down into Italy, took over the Italian
front line positions, and then began rounding up the escapees
again. Many were recaptured, but others were given food and
shelter in mountain villages and farms. The Germans made
this a capital offense but the peasants have continued to ignore their threats—even though many of them have been ex-
ecuted as a consequence. The peasants have also helped many
young Italians who have taken to the mountains to avoid reporting for military duty. In some cases they and the escapees
have joined together to form local resistance groups."

Kessler's deep-set eyes moved from face to curious face.
"Now it seems Kesselring is taking his revenge. No doubt the
need to make his rear positions secure now that his front line
is crumbling has also influenced his decision. The areas
shaded on this map show where we are expecting the raiding parties. As you can see, they are primarily remote farms
and villages. If the inhabitants don't betray the escapees, they
will be punished at the discretion of the German commanding officer. As the S.S. have been put in overall charge of the
operation, it should not be difficult to guess what that punishment will be."

A more insistent murmur broke out among the men. If
Kessler noticed it, he made no comment. "Which brings me
to the reason for this briefing. By this time there cannot be a
man among you who is unaware of the debt we owe the
peasants. They have always helped us in time of trouble—it

is no exaggeration to say we could not have survived without them—and now it is our turn to help them. This is not going to be an easy task. We are few in numbers and the area involved is huge. But on the other hand, we are skilled in traveling over the mountains and can cover ground far more quickly than the Germans. Our help, therefore, will not be as ineffective as it might first appear."

Beccione was watching the faces of the men as Kessler translated first into German and then Italian. Some were clearly in agreement with Kessler's decision; others looked like soldiers anywhere, indifferent to the issues involved. Some, however, were becoming restive as Kessler completed his translations and returned to English again.

"You are all aware that the Germans have firm control of all means of communication, telephone, postal services and the radio. Consequently, in spite of their highly developed grapevine, many of the peasants and the villagers in isolated areas will have no idea of their danger until raiding parties descend on them. Our job, then, is to give them advanced warning so they can hide any escapees who might be living with them. This will probably mean the escapees having to take shelter in woods or caves until the Germans have gone. Unfortunately, if informers have been at work, it will not always save the peasants themselves. But in many cases a timely warning might mean the difference between life and death."

As whispering men translated his words to one another, the restive murmuring grew louder. Watching the German, Beccione sensed that he had expected trouble, although his disciplined face gave nothing away.

"This is how we shall give them that warning. I have already spoken to your squad and sectional commanders and they will split you up into units of two jeeps each with a specific area to cover. Wherever possible, each unit will carry at least one Italian speaking crewman. As for the areas, we have worked out routes which will enable you to get from farm to farm in the quickest time possible. One jeep will pass on the warning while the other one provides cover outside. Both vehicles will be stocked with food and protective clothing that escapees can take with them if the peasants have no provisions to spare.

"The procedure in the villages will be slightly different because there is always the possibility of a Fascist informer being present. Wherever possible, you will be given the names of people you can trust before you leave here and will pass your warning to them only. They will then take the appropriate action and also let you know if any extra food or clothing is required. Where we don't have such information, you will make discreet enquiries first. If you run out of provisions, finish your rounds nonetheless: your most important task is to spread the alarm. If you make a list of what is required, you can always return with the provisions at a later date."

Grumbles prevented Kessler from beginning his translations. A hand rose. "Can I ask a question, Padrone?"

The speaker was an Italian named Razzoni who had relatives in La Capella. Kessler gave a terse nod. "Yes, Razzoni."

"If the Fascists are starting this operation soon, is it safe for us all to leave La Capella? Shouldn't we stay here in case we are needed?"

There were shouts of assent. Checking them with a heavy frown, Kessler glanced back at the man. "I am hardly likely to abandon La Capella, Razzoni. During the time we shall be away, our emergency plan will be in operation under the command of Captain Roberts. The sentries at every access point will be on orange alert and in some cases doubled. These men will be drawn from the townsfolk and a few from C Squad. If the need should arise, Captain Roberts will put into motion our withdrawal plans. However, we have no reason to fear the Germans will be coming here yet. We are still well north of their front line and their first raids will be concentrated in the areas shown on the map."

Another hand rose. "How can you be sure of this, Padrone?"

Kessler glanced at the silent Schumann. "Captain Schumann and I have spent a few days around the German area headquarters in Ancona. We cross-checked the information we picked up very carefully before coming away."

"But the risk is still there, Padrone." The protestor this time was Weiss, Schumann's right-hand man. "Are we justified in taking it just to warn the peasants? Why not let them do the job themselves?"

Shouts of agreement ensued. Prominent among the dissenters was Mogelli. Although his complaint was not meant to reach Kessler, the giant's rumbling voice carried further than he intended. "Why the hell should we help the damned peasants? What's in it for us?"

Jean Pierre, moving towards Beccione for a translation of the complaint, let out a growl of rage and started at the Italian. Seeing his intention, Kessler rapped out something in French that halted him. The admonition brought silence to the room.

"I find your question contemptible, Weiss. These people give charity for no other reason that it is needed. Since we have the means, the least we can do is warn them when their lives are at risk because of that charity."

Through force of personality Kessler managed to subdue his audience, although here and there men could still be seen whispering.

"That is all I have to say to you now. Your squad and section commanders will brief you on the details of your patrols. Afterwards you will take your jeeps to the storehouse where they will be loaded with food and clothing. I want every man and vehicle ready to move away by 11.00 hours. Off you go."

Although there was a general movement towards the doors, an angry mutter of complaint could be heard again. With an exclamation Kessler spun around.

"If any man among you still questions my orders, let him stay behind now and voice them personally. If he does not and he leaves with the others, I shall expect him to carry out my orders to the letter or his punishment will be severe."

Tall, gaunt, the German stared at the dissenters with a gaze so icy that even Beccione could feel its chill. Glancing nervously at one another, the dissenters went silent and followed the others outside. As Beccione was about to follow them, Jean Pierre called him back. "You are going with the Padrone and me. Come over here and I'll show you our sector."

"Just the three of us?" Beccione asked as he moved to the map.

"No. We're taking Toschack, Johnson and Etienne. I've sent them to load up the jeeps."

31

The atmosphere was sucking up humidity the way blotting paper sucks up water. It showed in the copper tint of the sky and the burning glare of the sun. Beccione was lying behind

a clump of bushes on a shallow hillcrest. Kessler and Jean
Pierre were on his left, Toschack, Johnson and Etienne on his
right. All six of them were wearing German SS uniforms. Below, a dirt road wound through the foot of the hill. A small
village—a cluster of pantiled hovels, farmhouses and stone
barns—lay sprawled across it. A row of gum trees looking
like old and tired sentinels lined the road at its eastern end,
and there were a few splashes of color from flower pots and
tiny gardens. Otherwise the village looked as arid as the sun-
baked fields that surrounded it.

Ordinarily the village would have surrendered to the heat
of the mid-afternoon sun. Instead it was a scene of violent
activity: uniformed men were running from cottage to cottage, hammering on doors with rifle butts, dragging peasants
out to the street. The heavy silence was jarred by harsh
shouts and the thin screams of women. The transports that
had brought the soldiers were parked in the center of the village: two large troop carriers and a scout car.

Kessler, who was wearing the cap and uniform of an SS
major, turned to the men on Beccione's right side. His expression was as grim as Beccione had ever seen it. "You three
will drive round to the far side of the village and hide there
until you hear our firing. Then you'll go in fast and destroy
their transports. Ignore everything else until they are on fire
because they will contain machine guns and mortars. Then
you can join us if we are still engaged."

Beccione turned his binoculars back on the village. By this
time all the cottages appeared to have been emptied and the
Germans were herding the peasants towards the road flanked
by gum trees. Two thirds of them were women, some with
babies in their arms. The rest were middle-aged and old men.

Beccione was trying to count the grey-clad figures that
were following the column of peasants. Lowering the glasses,
he turned to Kessler who was already rising to his feet. "How
are we going in? Straight down that road?"

"Yes. Why?"

"There must be thirty Krauts down there. You think we
can take 'em all that way?"

"With the advantage of surprise, yes."

"I hope you're right."

The iciness of the German's voice betrayed his pent-up
emotions. "Are you afraid?"

"You're so right. I'm terrified."

"Then perhaps you would like to be relieved of your duty. Make up your mind quickly."

Beccione took a deep breath. "No, I'll go along for the ride. But I hope you're a good actor."

Without another word, Kessler motioned the men to follow him and began running towards the two jeeps that were parked below the crest of the hill. The two jeeps, festooned with fuel cans, had black crosses conspicuously displayed at both front and rear. Toschack took his jeep along the hill range towards the western end of the village. Jean Pierre, disguised as a massive German corporal, drove down to the dirt road that skirted the eastern hillside. With Kessler urging him to make all speed possible, the jeep bucked and rolled like a wild horse, forcing Beccione to cling hard to the rear gun mounting.

Once down the road, Jean Pierre reduced speed in an effort to keep their approach as silent as possible. As the jeep reached the last bend before the avenue of trees, Kessler, who was now standing behind the heavy machine gun, leaned forward and ordered Jean Pierre to halt. The act reassured Beccione. The German, though in the grip of some fierce emotion, was still exercising the restraint of a leader.

The three men got out of the jeep and peered round the bend through a clump of brambles. The sight that greeted them was harrowing. The peasants were now lined up with their backs to the trees and facing a row of soldiers. At the far end of the line, an old man was being interrogated by an SS officer. It was clear he gave nothing away because the officer suddenly raised his cane and struck him across the face. When the old man still shook his head, the officer shouted an order and two soldiers stepped alongside him and raised their carbines. A second later there was a burst of firing and the old man slumped down to the road. As women screamed, the soldiers dragged two more men from the line, kicking and pushing them towards the officer. Beside him Beccione heard a voice he barely recognized.

"Routine SS methods against suspects, Beccione. They will shoot the men in pairs now until someone talks or until there are no men left. Then they will start on the women. Are you still worried about the odds?"

Beccione would not have believed a man's voice could contain such emotion. Before the American could answer, Jean Pierre gripped his arm tightly and shook his head.

The two men climbed into the jeep after Kessler. Before

Jean Pierre started up the engine, Kessler glanced back at the American. Everything gentle and humane in his face had disappeared. The muscles were bunched into hard, tight slabs from which his eyes burned with an old and uncontrolled hatred.

"Keep out of sight until I give the word. Then aim at this end of the line and swing your fire towards me. You're to show no mercy. Remember these are the killers of women and children."

Mouth dry, Beccione cocked the .30 Browning and sank down in his seat. A moment later the jeep rounded the corner and the twin lines of peasants and soldiers stretched out ahead.

For Beccione it was a frozen moment of time. Every head down the road appeared to have turned to stare at them, the terrified peasants, the soldiers, the SS officer, even the two hostages and their bullying escort. Crouched in his seat Beccione had stopped breathing. For all its iron crosses, the jeep was still a jeep and at any second he felt the spell must break and thirty soldiers would pour fire at them.

But Kessler was playing his part to perfection. Immaculate for once in his SS cap and uniform, erect and motionless behind the heavy machine gun, he radiated a disdain and arrogance that was quickly turning bewilderment into respect. As the jeep reached the first of the soldiers, the man hesitated, then sprang to attention. In a chain reaction the rest followed suit. In that moment Beccione realized the vulnerability of disciplined men to boldness and enterprise.

Yet he was close enough to Kessler to see things the soldiers could not. The German's left hand was gripping the gun breech so hard the knuckles showed white against the tanned skin. Beccione felt he was sitting behind a time bomb. Packed with murderous explosives, it was waiting only for the right moment to explode and kill.

The SS officer at the far end of the line was as deceived as his men, but the anomaly of the situation aroused his curiosity. Motioning two soldiers to his side, he started towards the approaching jeep. His shout broke the silence. *"Welches ist Ihre Einheit, Major? Warum fahren Sie in einem amerikanischen Jeep?"*

The jeep was almost halfway down the line of soldiers by this time. Beccione could feel the sweat trickling down his face as the staring eyes moved past. Up ahead, the SS officer had decided enough was enough and shouted an order to the entire platoon. The men stared at one another in bewilderment and began swinging up their rifles and carbines. It was then that the time bomb that was Kessler exploded. Shouting at his two crewmen, he tilted the heavy machine gun down and fired a burst straight at the SS officer.

Once again time became a slow-motion film for Beccione. The officer's expression turned from suspicion to horror and then to blankness as the heavy bullets smashed the life from him. Hurled to the road like a broken doll, he was followed a second later by the two soldiers next to him. Without taking his finger off the trigger, Kessler swung the Browning down the line of men.

Beccione had also opened fire on the rear end of the line. In his trance-like state the murderous machine guns sounded like jackhammers. As he pivoted the Browning, images came and vanished as if in a giant kaleidoscope: a soldier doubling forward, a carbine being ripped away by the impact of a bullet, a man turning to run and being driven broken-backed against a tree. To Beccione the slaughter seemed to go on for minutes while screams as thin as needles pierced the pounding of the guns.

In reality it was only a few seconds before the two lines of fire converged and the last remaining soldier fell. Yet it took a shout from Jean Pierre, who had augumented the fire of the Brownings with a Sten gun, to make Kessler release his trigger.

Beccione had already ceased firing and for a moment the silence was deafening. Down the road a black cloud of smoke rising from the center of the village told that Toschack and his men were successfully destroying the enemy transports.

The action had been so sudden and unexpected that many of the peasants had not left their assigned places at the roadside. Totally bewildered by the turn of events, unable to believe the threat was over, they were staring with ashen faces at the jeep as if expecting their turn would come next.

The sharp crack of a rifle and the scream of a ricochet from the tailboard of the jeep suggested their fear might have some foundation. The shot came from the stone hedge that ran behind the opposite row of trees. Somehow three soldiers had managed to avoid the hose of fire long enough to leap over the hedge into the field behind. Two had wanted to do no more than hide until the jeep had gone, but the third, an arrogant and ambitious young Nazi, had derided their cowardice and opened fire with his rifle. With their hiding place exposed, the other two men had no option but to follow suit. One soldier, a corporal, was armed with a machine carbine and he was edging it through a chink in the stones.

He was given only seconds to fire it. Spotting a gap in the hedge thirty yards down the road, Jean Pierre sent the jeep accelerating towards it while Kessler fired a long burst to give cover. As the jeep's left wheels struck the dead SS officer, Beccione was almost flung over the tailboard.

The jolt probably saved his life because the German soldier fired at the same moment. Grabbing onto the tailboard, Beccione heard a low gasp from Kessler and saw the man's right arm had been flung away from his machine gun. A moment later the jeep swung to the right and skidded through the gap into the field.

Seeing resistance was futile with two machine guns covering them, the three soldiers raised their hands. Beccione, relaxing, turned his attention back to Kessler. The German, his right sleeve soaked in blood, was leaning on his Browning with his back to the American. Beccione bent forward. "Are you all right, Kessler?"

There was no reply. The jeep bumped forward across the field. "Kessler! How bad is it?"

By this time the SS soldiers were no more than twenty paces away, walking towards the jeep with arms raised. Swinging the Browning forward, Kessler had raised his head and was staring at them. He was shivering now as if with acute fever. Suddenly uttering a hoarse cry, he lowered the machine gun and opened fire. Stunned, Beccione grabbed at him but the man's left arm flung him back with unnatural strength. When the American regained his balance, the three soldiers were lying on the dry ground like butchered cattle. "Oh, my God," Beccione said.

Jean Pierre had jammed on his brakes. The glance he threw back at Kessler was a mixture of shock, reproach and compassion. The German had dropped his head on the gun breech, his breathing painful and labored. Outrage brought a shout from Beccione. "O.K. So they were SS murderers! They kill old men and women and children. But where does this put us, Kessler? Tell me!"

A deep shudder ran through Kessler as he turned to face the American. Beccione stared him down and watched his aggression dissolve into horror and finally despair. Crying something in German, he jumped down from the jeep and began stumbling towards the hedge.

"He's crazy," Beccione said. "You know that, don't you?"

Jean Pierre flinched. "No, *mon ami*. In torment, yes, but not crazy."

"Crazy," Beccione said again. "He kills these Nazis as if they were animals and then pukes in remorse. In my book that's crazy."

The sound of firing in the village had ceased. Smoke was still billowing up into the humid sky. Jean Pierre jerked a thumb. "Go and tell the peasants they must hide all traces of what's happened today. Everything—the bodies, the vehicles, every sign the Boche were here. And then those who can get shelter from friends or relatives should go at once. The Boche will be back and we can't defend every village."

Beccione's eyes were fixed on the tall figure of Kessler supporting himself against the hedge. "I want to know everything about Kessler. You hear me? I've a goddamn right to know."

There was understanding in the Frenchman's sigh. "Yes. After this you have. But not until tonight. Do as I ask first."

When Beccione reached the gap in the hedge he glanced back. Jean Pierre had gone over to the German and was standing protectively alongside him. Shaking his head, Beccione joined the peasants who were making their way back to their homes.

32

In the darkness the broken pillars of the old pagan temple looked like admonishing fingers. Here and there they appeared to be supporting the heavy clouds. The steady build-up of humidity had lowered the sky down to the mountain tops and it draped itself there like the pelt of a black animal. Beneath it the heat was stifling, an unusual occurence in the mountains. Twice in the last ten minutes the grumble of thunder had been heard.

Seated amid the temple ruins, four men were sipping wine. One of them—Beccione—abruptly stood. Toschack gazed up at him. "You going anywhere near Kessler?"

"Maybe."

"Ask him if he'd like some coffee, will ya?"

"I'm not doing Kessler any favors. Ask him yourself."

The other two men, Johnson and Etienne, were staring at Beccione now. Toschack swore. "So he gunned down a pack of Hitler's killers. He saved those poor bastards in the village, didn't he? Which was more important?"

Turning his back on the Australian, Beccione walked out onto the temple terrace. The mountainside was precipitous here, dropping down to a huge plain backed by mountains. As smooth as black velvet, with only two tiny lights moving across it, it looked like an enormous mountain lake. The only sounds were the faint soughing of the wind and the distant murmur of the crews' voices. It had taken the rebels most of that afternoon to cross the plain and well into evening to reach this mountain hideout. Peasants had led Kessler here months before after a narrow escape.

The terrace was littered with fractured slabs of marble and broken pillars. At some period in the Christian era a monk's cell had been built almost at the edge of the cliff and Beccione picked his way towards it. As the murmur of the voices died away, another rumble of thunder sounded in the distance. Although miles away, a storm was approaching.

As he neared the cell Beccione heard men talking. He could not make out the words, but their inflections—one voice slurred and full of despair, the other hushed but compassionate—told him all he needed to know. Sitting on a broken plinth of marble, he began to throw stones over the cliff edge. The first made no sound but the second caused a tiny avalanche of pebbles. The voices ceased instantly and he waited. He heard nothing move but ten seconds later there was a fierce growl behind him. "What are you doing here?"

He spoke without turning. "We made a deal earlier today. Remember?"

The big Frenchman had clearly had second thoughts. "Why don't you get back to the others? They've got plenty of wine, haven't they?"

Beccione turned. "The others weren't with him this afternoon. I was. You forgotten that?"

There was a silence, tense with disdain and indecision. Then: "If you say a word about this to your buddy or anyone else, I'll kill you. Understand that?"

"I guess that's fair enough."

"Then wait here."

The Frenchman's shadowy figure disappeared. Beccione heard the murmur of voices again. Then Jean Pierre came out of the cell and jerked a thumb at the broken terrace that lay beyond it. When they were out of earshot, he turned on Beccione with hostility. "I've only got a few minutes. It's time his wound was dressed again."

"I thought you said it was only a flesh wound."

The Frenchman scowled. "You've always got an answer, don't you?"

"Not this time. Until I met this guy I thought I'd met them all, the big ones, the bad ones, the ugly ones. But this guy's out on his own. How can a man care about the peasants the way he does and then turn into the killer he became this afternoon? How can he lead hoods like Schumann and retain the loyalty of men like you and Roberts? I'm not saying those Nazis didn't deserve what they got—there was a time this afternoon when I hated them more than he did. But in his case it goes beyond that. Maybe he's got a good reason. I hope so, because at times I actually like the guy. But right now I feel dirty and I need some clean water to wash myself in."

Jean Pierre stared at him, then sank down on a slab of rock. He sat brooding at the blackness below, muttered something, then lit a cigarette. "I'm not sure I know everything."

"You know enough," Beccione said with conviction. "Or you wouldn't hold the guy's hand when he's on the rack, like he is tonight."

The Frenchman's cigarette glowed in the still air. "Kessler's saved my life twice, Beccione. The first time in a way you wouldn't understand."

"I believe you and I think I do understand. I bet he's saved plenty of other guys too. We're in his debt ourselves. Maybe that's the reason I need to understand him."

Appeased, the Frenchman's mood changed. "He was in a bad way when he talked to me. We'd been forced to kill a lot of men, like today, and he'd hit the bottle. That's the only reason it came out. So there'd be plenty I didn't hear."

Beccione squatted down on a rock in front of the Frenchman. "O.K. Give me what you did hear. It seems to have convinced you."

Jean Pierre knit his brows. "Where the hell do you begin a story like his?"

"Why not try the beginning?"

"Where is the beginning? A million influences make up a man and as I see it he's only responsible for a few of them. The rest come from his parents or from what life does to

him. So do you start with his parents, his birth, or the time
when life begins to rough him up?"

"Let's start with his parents. What do you know about
them?"

"Not much except they were both German and middle
class. I'm not sure what his father did—I think he was a
businessman. I got the impression his mother was religious.
Like most of their generation, they must have been patriots
because when the First War started Franz said they were
proud that their two sons volunteered to fight. The elder son,
Wilhelm, was in at the beginning and was killed at Verdun in
1916. Franz couldn't get in because of his age until late
1916, but he fought against the British at Passchendaele and
our Army on the Aisne. When things got bad in 1917 the old
man joined up as well and was killed in the big push of 1918.
Franz was wounded twice and was in the hospital when the
Armistice was signed."

"Father and brother killed—he had a rough war," Beccione said.

Jean Pierre's cigarette glowed again. "He must have had
more than a rough war. Because when it was over he had become a dedicated pacifist."

Beccione wondered why his surprise was not greater. "A
pacifist? Kessler?"

"Yes. He'd grown to hate war and everything connected
with it. In 1921 or thereabouts he married a girl who was
also a pacifist, a girl called Eva. She was Jewish and, from
the photograph Franz showed me, a beautiful woman."

"Jewish?" Beccione said hoarsely.

A flash of lightning lit up Jean Pierre's grim face. "Yes.
They had two children. The first was a boy they called
Johann. The second was a girl, Astrid. This was during the
time Germany was starving. I don't know what Franz did
during those years—he has never talked about it—but his father must have left something in trust because when things
picked up Franz was able to go to university. He got a degree
in archaeology and later a seat at Heidelberg where he lec-
tured until this second war began."

"What about Eva? Did the Nazis find out she was Jewish?"

"Of course they found out. They did a census not long after they got in power. At first she was shielded to some extent
by his standing at the university but that didn't stop the whispers and innuendoes. Her name began to be left off invita-
tions and some of the wives snubbed her in the streets. But

according to Franz she had all the courage in the world and her only concern was for Johann. He'd joined the *Jugend*—that's the Nazi youth movement—and the bastards were doing a first-class job with him. Franz and Eva had tried to bring him up a pacifist like themselves, but the Nazi creed says a man can find no greater glory than dying for his Fatherland and the boy was already contemptuous of his parents. Now he was taking in the poison about the Jews as well."

"What about the girl?"

"From what I gather she was the only comfort they had. She was three years younger than Johann and so far the Nazis hadn't got through to her. But it doesn't take much imagination to guess the misery they must have gone through waiting for her to go the same way."

The storm was drawing nearer, showing its white teeth in the sky and snarling in the valleys as the Frenchman continued. "They knew they'd lost Johann when he came home from one of the *Jugend*'s weekend camps and started spewing the Nazi line about the Jews and their grip on the German economy. He said they had to be driven out of their rat holes and kicked out of the country. When Franz demanded that he apologize to his mother, the boy shouted he was ashamed of his family. His mother was a Jewess and both of them were pacifists, enemies of the Fatherland. He told them he'd already lost promotion in the *Jugend* because of them: if he stayed home any longer he'd come under suspicion."

"How old was he?" Beccione interrupted.

"As near as I can make out, around sixteen. Anyway, he left that same night and went to live with a senior Nazi who ran his section. Neither Franz nor Eva saw him again, nor did he have any further contact with them."

A spot of rain fell on Beccione's face but he was too engrossed in the Frenchman's words to notice it. "What about Astrid?"

"The bastards didn't fare so well with her. She was still attached to her parents, although Franz said they had enough arguments with her to make them fear for the future. With Hitler grabbing chunks of Europe and yelling threats, the persecution of the Jews was in full swing now and Franz was in daily terror that Eva would be arrested, particularly because of her beliefs which she'd never tried to hide."

"Had Kessler let it be known that he was also a pacifist?"

Jean Pierre uttered a snort of contempt. "If you knew the

man at all, you wouldn't need to ask a question like that. The Nazis knew all right and soon after the war started they asked him to volunteer. He was over enlistment age at that time but they used the excuse that they needed men with combat experience. When he refused they asked him to sign a statement of his reasons. He knew they'd use it against him later but he still signed it."

"What happened to Johann?"

"He was one of Hitler's storm troopers when the war broke out. Just eighteen and dying to fight for the Fatherland. He died all right. In Russia in 1941. But not before he had won a row of medals in Poland and France. They sent the medals along with his ashes back to Franz and Eva."

"And you say they hadn't seen him again?"

"No. There'd been no chance of a reconciliation. And what pride could they feel in his death? He had wasted himself for a tyranny that was persecuting Eva's people. I'll never forget how Franz put it. He said a light went out inside Eva that day and in the time left to her she lived in darkness."

Sitting motionless, Beccione was listening intently to the Frenchman's bitter voice.

"There was an air raid the night they heard of Johann's death. Until then most of the raids had been hit-and-miss affairs, but this was the first of the big ones. As Franz was an air-raid warden, he was called out to help.

"He said there were dead everywhere: children, women and old men. After Johann's death it put a final seal on his pacifism. The Germans had crushed Europe into the mud and were savaging Russia. Now the Allies were retaliating and killing the innocents also. War was an obscenity and he made a vow that night that no power on earth would make him kill again."

"He's religious, isn't he?" Beccione broke in. "He must be."

"Not now. But he was then. I'm sure of it although he has never said."

"Go on."

"He hadn't, however, taken the Nazis into full account. With their losses growing in Russia, they were calling up older men and they came back to him. Most of his colleagues were either exempt or drafted into industry, but they told him they had no place for an archaeologist and with his combat experience he would have to serve in the Army. When he refused they warned that not only would he be punished, but his Jewess of a wife would be treated like the rest of her kind and sent to a concentration camp."

A wind was rising as the storm drew nearer. Distant at first, it sounded now like a tormented soul as it wailed through hollows and valleys. The Frenchman lit another cigarette.

"It must have been the hardest decision of his life. He said war had become anathema to him. He knew that if he were to kill again it would destroy him."

"You say he was drunk when he told you all this?" Beccione interrupted.

"Oh, Christ, yes. You don't think a man like that would bare his soul if he was sober, do you?"

"Go on," Beccione urged again.

"Eva wouldn't hear of his giving in but how could he let her suffer for his principles? She begged and prayed for him to hold fast but in the end he made a deal with the bastards. He said he would enlist if they would drop their persecution of Eva and give him a medical, non-combatant role.

"He'd have done better from a deal with the devil. He'd hardly got his uniform on before he was sent off for intensive military training. Then he was sent to a special combat unit in the Balkans that was used to hunt down partisans. The Nazis would not recognize partisans as soldiers and the fighting was bloody with no quarter given on either side.

"Aware that the Nazis were taking their revenge on him, Franz refused to fight when he reached the unit. They'd been expecting it and they knocked hell out of him before slapping him in the can. A few days later he was told that Eva had been arrested and sent to Auschwitz. He knew it was a death sentence for her but he said in some ways it was a relief. Now that she was no longer a hostage, he could spit in the faces of the bastards."

The storm was upon them now, an awesome cannonade of lightning bolts and ear-splitting thunder. Large drops of rain were splattering down, disturbing the dust and wetting the shirts of both men, but neither one noticed. Beccione leaned nearer his companion. "What about Astrid?"

"By this time she was nursing in a military hospital. With casualties pouring in from Russia, nurses were in short supply. He felt certain if they intended to act against her they would have told him already."

Beccione nodded. "So he was free to make his big gesture. What happened?"

The big Frenchman stared at him, then lifted his cigarette to his mouth. Finding it was soaked, he cursed and hurled it away. "There was one thing he hadn't taken into account. How could he—he hadn't fought since the last war? After Eva was arrested they let him out of the can and sent him with a small force to an area where the partisans were particularly active. One morning at dawn the Yugoslavs launched a surprise attack and for a while it looked as if the Boche unit would be overrun. When Franz still refused to fight, an officer rammed a revolver into his back and drove him to the front of the action. He was still refusing when the officer fell dead alongside him. At the same moment three partisans came at him from a cluster of rocks. It was the situation he had been dreading ever since the Nazis forced him to enlist. He had gone through it a hundred times in his mind: rather than kill, which he knew would torture him for the rest of his life, he would offer no resistance. If he were killed, he would at least die with a clear conscience."

A bolt of lightning lit up the scene, the ruins of the temple, the two seated men, the sweating face of Jean Pierre. As blackness flooded back, the Frenchman sounded as if he too was enduring Kessler's moment of crucifixion. "It happened and was over in seconds. As the partisans ran towards him he tried to drop his M.40. Instead, when the leading man took aim at him, he opened fire and cut all three of them down. He said he even went on firing after they were dead."

A crack of thunder sounded, a wild voice echoing away through the hills. Frozen for a moment, Beccione stirred. "Yeah, that fits."

Jean Pierre nodded bitterly. "That's the purpose of training. To give a man a gut reaction. And don't forget Franz had had a double dose."

"What happened then?"

"That's the part he wouldn't talk about. But from what I gathered he didn't disobey orders any longer. I believe he killed along with the others but only until the Nazis decided he was beaten and lifted their surveillance on him. Then he escaped and made his way to Italy where at that time there was no real German presence. That was where I met him." Lost in memory, Jean Pierre's voice was grim. "He had only one thought in his mind and, Christ, it was an obsession. The war lords and their kind had put the curse of Cain on him as they had to millions of others. Now he intended to harass them with every means in his power."

Beccione frowned. "What does all that mean?"

The Frenchman's prevarication escaped the GI. "Those are his words, not mine. You see, one last thing happened to him not long after he shot the partisans. His daughter was killed."

"Oh Christ, no," Beccione muttered.

"Yes, but not by the Nazis this time. She was killed by American bombers when they were raiding Stuttgart." The Frenchman leaned forward. "So is it surprising he hates war and all those who make war?"

Beccione's laugh of disbelief sounded through the drenching rain. "But he's the guy who's got himself a small army together! Goddamn it, he's making war all the time!" Then the American went suddenly quiet. He believed he finally understood. "You're really saying what I said this afternoon, aren't you? That all this has turned his mind."

Jean Pierre's reply was fierce and full of contempt. "You think war's sane, Beccione? When men put on uniforms to hide that they're human beings and burn one another alive with flame throwers? Or drop bombs on women and kids? You call that sanity?"

"You know what I mean," Beccione protested.

"Like hell I do. Sometimes, like tonight, Franz is tormented to the point of suicide, as any sensitive man would be in this filthy world. But I'll tell you this, Beccione." The sudden simplicity of the Frenchman was moving. "I love that man, both for his guts and his ideals. He's the sanest man I know."

"Like in that village today?"

The Frenchman spat a curse. "Who have you lost in this war that you care for?"

"Nobody," Beccione confessed.

"Then stop acting like Christ almighty and throwing stones at a man who's lost everything."

The rain was torrential now, plastering the men's hair down on their foreheads and turning their clothes sodden. Beccione made a gesture of defeat. "O.K. He's got his reasons. But how did you come to help him?"

"Maybe I had my reasons too."

"Yeah, I'd forgotten. They say you also had a bad war. Was that why?"

"Not altogether. It just made sense to me. Bright, terrible sense. And it still does."

"You can't mean that. Even if the man's sane, it's still a crazy gesture."

"Don't all gestures of this kind seem crazy? Until the world catches up and realizes how sane they are?"

Beccione was struggling to understand. "How could the world think this gesture's sane? Unless there is something else." As lightning betrayed the Frenchman's expression, he gave a start. "That's the answer, isn't it? There *is* something else."

There was grim amusement in Jean Pierre's laugh. "There's something else all right, Beccione. More than you could ever imagine."

The American leaned eagerly forward. "What else?"

Jean Pierre gazed openly at him for a moment, then took control of himself. "No. First I'd need Franz's permission and he won't be sober until the morning. Then we'd need to talk to the others and we can't do that until this patrol's over."

"Others? Are you saying all the guys know?"

"Of course they don't. How could they? But a few know and they've a right to be consulted." Jean Pierre rose to his feet. "You'll have to wait until we get back."

By this time Beccione's curiosity was intense. "What the hell's going on? What else do you do?"

Ignoring him, the Frenchman turned and made for the cell. Beccione went after him and caught his arm. "What else do you do? I've got to know!"

Cursing, Jean Pierre flung off his hand. "You'll wait until I get Kessler's permission. Now get the hell out of here. I don't want to see you again tonight."

Before the American could argue further, he ducked into the cell. Listening outside, Beccione thought he heard a groan, then the Frenchman's comforting voice. For a moment his burning curiosity tempted him to enter. Then a bolt of lightning and a simultaneous peal of thunder seemed to crack the sky apart. Beccione stood transfixed until the immense reverberations echoed away, leaving only the hiss of rain, the sobbing of the wind, and a low despairing voice. That faint sound changed the American's mind. Turning, he began picking his way back over the broken stones of the terrace.

33

After the fall of Rome on June 5, 1944, the German XIV Army was in disarray. Three of its divisions were almost destroyed and the rest were of little more than battalion strength. Worse, their X Army, which had at last been forced to abandon the Cassino front, was still out of contact. Had the Allied 5th Army driven straight out of Rome in pursuit, they could well have overrun the XIV Army west of the Tiber and then been able to turn northeast to cut off the X Army. They could have achieved the same ends had they driven northeast through Terni. Instead the 5th Army chose first to build up protective positions immediately north and northwest of Rome.

This delay was a godsend to the Germans. Although it had always been Field Marshall Kesselring's intention to retreat to the Gothic line after the fall of Rome, its fortifications were not expected to be completed until the autumn of that year. Consequently, a slow and orderly retreat was essential if the line was to serve as the barrier the Germans hoped for.

The 5th Army's pause at Rome played right into the Germans' hands. Panzer and panzer grenadier divisions were rushed up to occupy Tiber crossings between Rome and Orviesto and the X Army was able to make its escape. Although a general retreat was still the order of the day, it could now proceed in a planned and disciplined manner.

Yet one thing obsessed Kesselring: the existence behind his armies of groups of partisans and escaped prisoners of war. In order to extirpate this threat most effectively, he ordered his raiding parties to use the harshest measures against any Italian found harboring them. As his troops retreated doggedly northwards, the area of his raiding parties moved north with them.

Kessler was watching the situation with his customery vigilance. He heard from one of his informers that Livello was to be raided next. Acting quickly as always, he made plans for the town's protection and then told Jean Pierre and Beccione he wanted them to accompany him on a mission the following day.

The sleeping girl's hair lay like a bronze pool on the pillow. Early morning sunshine was slanting through the window and splashing on the far wall. Beccione glanced at his watch and lit a cigarette. His movement awakened Magda. Her voice was drowsy as she stirred. "What time is it?"

"6.15. I'll have to leave in a few minutes. Kessler wants me at his headquarters at 7.00."

"What for?"

He felt a throb of excitement at her question. The previous day Jean Pierre had drawn him aside and told him Kessler had agreed to his request. He was to be taken on a special mission, after which Kessler's true purpose in the mountains would be explained to him. "I don't know. Jean Pierre didn't say."

"How many of you are going?"

"Just the three of us. Kessler, Jean Pierre and myself."

Her green eyes turned on him mockingly. "You're becoming one of Kessler's favorites, aren't you?"

"Am I?"

"He's probably going to see one of his black market contacts. Do you know how long you'll be away?"

"No."

"Then you might not be back tonight?"

"Possibly not."

She sat up. The single sheet covering them fell away, exposing her perfectly-formed breasts. "Can't you find out?"

"Yeah, I suppose so."

"Don't sound so enthusiastic," she said.

He grinned. "O.K. I'll ask them and get a message to you." As he turned to jump out of bed, she pressed against him. "You can be there in fifteen minutes. So what's the hurry?"

He glanced down. One of her breasts was pressing against his arm. He felt his groin harden, but he shook his head impatiently and swung his legs to the floor. "I can't risk being late. Jean Pierre said it was important we got an early start."

Her eyes followed his powerful, naked body to the window. "Why did they have to take you today?" she asked resentfully.

He was gazing down into a small garden that contained a well and two gnarled old olive trees. Small pantiled cottages were pressed around it. "What's so special about today?" He heard her light a cigarette and inhale smoke impatiently, and he turned towards her. "It's because Schumann's away, isn't it?"

She met his gaze defiantly. "What if it is?"

He walked towards the chair over which his uniform was draped, pulled on his slacks, then turned towards the bed again. "Schumann's someone you and I have to sort out. I'm not happy sneaking in here like a thief when he's away. When are you going to tell him about us?"

She drew in smoke. "I'll tell him when I'm ready."

"And when's that going to be?"

"I don't know."

"What is it? Are you scared of him?"

Her slender body stiffened. "I'm scared of no man."

"They why don't you tell him and get it over?"

She turned away to hide her expression. "Because I like going on patrols with him. If I tell him he'll stop taking me."

Sitting on the bed, he began pulling on his boots. "Do you expect me to believe that?"

"I don't give a damn what you believe. It's true."

"All right, then come with us instead. What's the difference?"

"Jean Pierre wouldn't take a woman. Particularly when Kessler goes with him."

"Then you'll just have to turn into a good girl and stay at home with the others, won't you?"

"Go to hell," she said.

He grinned, tugged on his other boot, and tucked in his shirt. At the door he turned back. "I'll tell you something, baby. You're the first girl I've shared with another guy and I don't like the feeling. Particularly with a sonofabitch like Schumann. You tell him or I will."

She stared at him narrowly. "You know what'll happen to you, don't you? His pride won't let you get away with it."

Beccione opened the door. "Tell him. I've had a bellyful of feeling I'm short-changing the bastard. Tell him as soon as he gets back."

Her voice rose. "All right, get yourself killed. Do you think I care?"

Her hostility subsided the moment he closed the door. A deep furrow of anxiety appeared between her eyes and she dragged fretfully on her cigarette.

*   *   *

Jean Pierre cursed and brought a huge hand down with a slap. As he lifted it the remnants of a horsefly could be seen crushed among the glistening hairs of his forearm. "*Mon Dieu*, the bastards have sharp teeth today."

Kessler smiled at him. "It's the rain, Jean Pierre. It has given them all new life. And there's more to come yet."

Beccione glanced up at the sky and saw the German was right. There was still humidity up there: the afternoon sun was a copper coin floating in an alloy sky. The three men were lying behind a clump of rocks high above a wide valley. With Jean Pierre at the wheel they had driven out of La Capella just after 08.00 hours and kept on the narrow mountain road for the first twenty minutes, during which time they had encountered nothing more threatening than peasants' carts bringing supplies up to the small town. Ignoring the occasional side roads that led into the maze of mountains, they had continued south until they had joined the major road linking Rosaro with Aspiro. From this point Jean Pierre had taken to the hillsides, driving with great skill along cow paths that laced their lower slopes. Judging from the occasional glimpses of mechanized traffic moving along the major road below, it had been a move both timely and necessary.

At the same time, because the tracks had been made slippery by the heavy rain of the last few days, their progress had been slowed down almost to a snail's pace. Every few minutes Jean Pierre had been forced to use the telescopic runners he carried, and his two passengers were kept busy helping haul the jeep on to firmer ground. As the morning wore on, a certain urgency had crept into the behavior of Kessler and Jean Pierre; but once the sun rose higher the mud began to dry out and the jeep made better time. Now the men were in a position that gave them a panoramic view down the entire length of the valley. Beccione could only guess its length—the road seemed to wind for at least eight kilometers before disappearing around a large mountain spur.

Kessler and Jean Pierre had their binoculars trained on the far end of the valley. With no idea what they were waiting for, Beccione glanced back at the jeep that was covered by a camouflage net behind the boulders. It was a vehicle he had not seen before: a jeep equipped with a large radio transmitter and receiver that took up the place of one rear seat. As

yet neither Kessler or Jean Pierre had used the radio and its purpose was intriguing the American.

Noon came and went. A blue-crested bird landed on a nearby rock, cocked a bright eye at the three men, then darted away. Occasional vehicles looking as small as toys appeared on the road below: peasants' carts, civilian trucks and military transports. Kessler and Jean Pierre took no notice of them. No one was talking now: the heat made the act too much of an effort. Only the insects seemed to draw energy from the oven-like atmosphere, and with no role to play in the long watch, Beccione finally succumbed to their shrilling and fell asleep.

A sudden grunt of satisfaction from Jean Pierre awoke him. "I think they're coming now, Franz." Lifting his own binoculars, Beccione tried to see what had caught the Frenchman's attention. At first only a faint dust cloud was apparent at the foot of the mountain spur, but a few seconds later he could just make out four tiny shapes entering the valley.

Kessler, apparently satisfied that the vehicles were the objects of the long wait, was now scanning the mountain peaks opposite. With a word to Jean Pierre, he moved back to the jeep and ducked beneath the camouflage net. A few seconds later Beccione heard the tapping of a transmitter key. Puzzled, he glanced at Jean Pierre. "What's going on?"

The Frenchman flashed his fierce grin. "Patience, Yankee, and all will be revealed to you."

Beccione lifted his binoculars again. The impression that the trucks were moving slowly proved deceptive: swift dust clouds billowed behind them. Already they were far enough into the valley for him to recognize the shapes of open-topped troop carriers. Alongside him, Jean Pierre shifted his binoculars to the mountain peaks opposite just as Kessler had done. Muttering something in French, he rose and walked back to the jeep. Beccione followed him and saw through the net that Kessler had a map of coordinates spread out on the seat beside him. He had stopped transmitting and, with his hands pressed against the earphones, was taking a reply. As the sound of morse ended, Jean Pierre lifted the camouflage net. "Are they coming?"

Removing the earphones, Kessler nodded. More mystified than ever, Beccione followed the two men back to their vantage point. By this time the four troop carriers were visible to the naked eye, and as Beccione focused his binoculars he saw they were packed with uniformed men. The soldiers in the first three vehicles wore black uniforms, those in the last one wore grey. A small scout car was leading them. "Three loads of Italian Fascists and one load of SS," Jean Pierre told him. "All heading straight for Livello."

"What's Livello?"

Kessler answered for the Frenchman. "Like La Capella, it is a small mountain town where dissidents and Jews have been banished. Now that the Germans are retreating, they intend taking all important anti-Fascists to concentration camps further north or to Germany."

"Is this something you found out when you went into Ancona?"

"It is a consequence of it. We made contacts there and had a tip-off."

Beccione was struggling to understand. "But how are you going to stop them? None of our squads have gone out, have they?" Then he remembered. "Or is that the job Schumann is doing?"

To his surprise Kessler shook his head. "No. This time we are calling on other help."

"What other help? Partisans?"

The German shook his head again. "I understand from Jean Pierre that you have expressed a wish to know more about my organization. That is why we have brought you today. But you must be patient a little longer."

Unable to read the German's expression, Beccione turned back to the road. The transports were barely two kilometers away now and the soldiers packed inside them could be seen clearly. In the hot still air Beccione heard a siren demanding right of way for the convoy. He could feel the tension mount in Kessler and Jean Pierre as they searched the mountain peaks again. "What's holding them up?" the Frenchman growled.

Kessler did not answer. Fifteen seconds passed, then Jean Pierre made an exclamation and pointed. Following his outstretched hand, Beccione saw three black shapes flash like arrows over the mountain range. They dived into the valley for a quick scan of the road and then made a steep climbing turn. The American's voice was hoarse with astonishment. "Those are Allied fighter-bombers. What the hell's going on?"

Kessler and Jean Pierre were too busy following the flight path of the aircraft to reply. Reaching the zenith of its climb, the leading Mustang came plunging down and flattened above the road. A thousand yards from the convoy it released two rockets. Both missed, but a long burst of cannon fire ripped open the macadamized road. Shells mowed through the packed men in the rear troop carrier, hurling them aside like broken dolls. The shells missed the second and third vehicles, which had pulled sharply off the road, but struck the leading transport. Seconds later its fuel tank exploded in a ball of fire and smoke.

The valley was alive with the massive reverberations of aircraft engines. Men were leaping out of the transports in an effort to find cover. But the second Mustang was already skimming along the road. A rocket struck one abandoned vehicle, hurling fragments in all directions. Automatic fire followed, hosing from side to side among the fleeing men.

Although by the time the third aircraft had completed its strafing run all four transports were ablaze, the Mustangs had not finished yet. Like wolves who had tasted blood, they came plunging down again, this time going after the men who were trying to find cover on the roadsides. When they were finally satiated and nosed back in deadly formation over the mountains, only a few soldiers could be seen stumbling through the smoke.

Beccione let out his breath. "That was some clobbering." Then he turned on the two men alongside him. "What the hell does it mean? You were waiting for those aircraft, weren't you?"

Neither man answered him and Beccione's voice rose accusingly.

"You brought those Mustangs here, didn't you? You led them into this valley. For Christ's sake, what's going on? Don't tell me that you're a plant and you work for the Allies."

At that Kessler turned towards him. "I know how puzzling this must be for you, Beccione. But be patient a little longer. It is going to rain again soon and before it does we must reach firmer ground. Also there is the possibility the Allies might send aircraft looking for us now the convoy is destroyed. They might have located our position from the messages we transmitted."

"Looking for you? After you've helped them?" Frustration was making a vein swell on Beccione's forehead. "What are you trying to do, Kessler? Drive me crazy?"

Ignoring him, the German nodded at Jean Pierre and the two men moved away. Beccione paused a moment to watch the smoke from the burning transports drift up the hillsides. Then, with a gesture of defeat, he followed the men to the jeep.

34

Outside the cave the tap-tap of a morse key could be heard through the dripping of the rain. Beccione's glance at Jean Pierre was heavily sarcastic. "Who's he signaling to now? Eisenhower? Or the British Navy?"

The Frenchman grinned. "Neither. He is making sure that all is well in Livello. If it is, he will tell Roberts to go home."

"What's Roberts doing in Livello?"

"The Padrone sent him there on the chance that the fighter-bombers missed their target. In that case Roberts would have led the dissidents to a shelter in the mountains where we could help them with supplies."

With the short Italian twilight almost over, the inside of the cave was dark with shadows. As Jean Pierre shoved a supply pack towards Beccione, Kessler ducked through the entrance. "How many blankets do we have?"

"Three," the Frenchman told him.

Kessler shrugged. "They'll have to suffice. We'll get no further tonight. Shall we have coffee?"

Nodding, Jean Pierre pulled a paraffin stove from a second pack and pumped it vigorously. As he struck a match there was a high-pitched squealing from bats hidden in the deeper recesses of the cave. The Frenchman then laid a pan of water on the stove, flattening its flame so that it barely illuminated the faces of the three men. Beccione's patience finally ran out. "When I joined you I understood you led a gang that raided Allied and German storehouses and convoys. Yet today you guided three Allied aircraft down on a raiding party of Fascists and wiped them out. That had to be arranged beforehand with the Allies. So just what are you? Is your organization a cover-up for some cockamamie the Allies are pulling?"

Kessler showed no surprise at the American's aggression. "Not in any way."

"Are you saying you didn't signal those aircraft to attack?"

"Oh, no. I made contact with them. And I planned the raid

with the Allies beforehand. But I am not working for them. At least not in the way you are thinking."

"You're in touch with the Allies to the point where you can tell them to lay on an air strike but you're not working for them! At least be straight with me, Kessler."

"I am being straight with you. What would you say if I told you that a month ago I informed the Germans of a major attack the Allies were preparing to make. And on the strength of that information the Germans brought up reinforcements that prevented the attack being made."

The sheer audacity of the German's claim took Beccione's breath away. Then he gave a laugh of derision. "I'd say you were a liar. Or crazy."

Jean Pierre growled in warning and half-rose, but Kessler waved him back. "I know how bizarre it must sound to you. But nevertheless it is true."

There was a hush in the cave as Beccione realized the German meant what he said. "You're telling me you have enough influence with both armies to make them do as you say? For God's sake, Kessler."

The German shrugged. "You saw those fighter-bombers today. If you do not believe me, ask Jean Pierre or my other close associates."

Beccione did not even glance at the smouldering Frenchman. "Jean Pierre would say anything for you. But I don't believe you're God. I don't even believe you're Napoleon. And even if you were, what would be the point of it all?"

Kessler lit a cigarette. The flare of the match betrayed the emotions the conversation was arousing within him. "Did not the killing of those two peasants have any effect on you, Beccione?"

The American's scarred face tightened resentfully. "What's that got to do with it?"

"Everything. I am told you fought in North Africa before you came to Italy. Try to remember something. Did your Army show any consideration for the Arabs in whose land they were fighting? Were they even mentioned when you were briefed for combat?"

Beccione frowned. "No; I don't think they were. But what's the connection?"

The German leaned forward. "The connection is this. Throughout history, whenever armies have fought on foreign soil, they have robbed and abused its people. It happened in Roman times. It happened in the Middle Ages. It happened when your Union army marched from Atlanta to the sea. And it is happening today. First it was my race that ravaged the whole of Europe and much of Russia. Now it is the Allies' turn. It was not a German aircraft that killed those two old people but an American one. While my countrymen strip the peasants of their cattle and shoot those who do not cooperate with them, yours destroy a treasure house like Monte Cassino and rape the Italian women they have liberated. When armies march, destruction and rapine become causes in themselves. War gives man a license for violence and with that license every dark aspect of his nature comes to the fore. Be like me, Beccione, and hate war that tells man only brute force deserves respect and the meek shall never inherit the earth."

Beccione took a deep breath. "I'm lost, Kessler. I'm as lost as hell. You're sitting here talking like the greatest pacifist of all time and yet you run an outfit that does nothing else but plunder and kill."

In the dim light Kessler's eyes shone with a black piercing bitterness. "Perhaps I was a pacifist once, Beccione. But always remember no sword is bloodier than the sword of the idealist whose faith has been betrayed. Only the strongest can withstand that pain. The weak ones like myself take their revenge."

"Revenge? But that's crazy. It's also pathetic. You couldn't kill as many soldiers or steal as much equipment in a year as the armies lose in five minutes."

Jean Pierre could contain himself no longer. His anger was directed at Kessler. "Why do you always paint the blackest picture of yourself? You are not doing this for revenge. So why tell him differently?"

Kessler turned slowly to face him. The self-hatred in his voice chilled the night air. "Am I not? Are you so sure of that, Jean Pierre?"

"Of course I'm sure. Haven't I worked with you all this time and seen everything you have done?"

"If only a man's motives were as black-and-white as you paint them, Jean Pierre."

Ignoring Kessler's comment, Jean Pierre swung back to Beccione. "He saw terrible things in Yugoslavia. Whole villages wiped out, with children blinded or wandering about in the ruins with their minds destroyed by the horror. He also witnessed the massacre of San Pietro when the Germans and the Americans fought over the town like dogs over a bone. It all made him swear that whenever possible he would try to prevent such atrocities."

"But how, for God's sake? By raiding a few convoys with a handful of men? I tell you it's *pathetic*."

The Frenchman gave a grim smile. "Is being a puppet-master pathetic, Yankee?"

"What do you mean—a puppetmaster?"

Jean Pierre made expressive gestures with his fingers. "He pulls the strings and the armies jump one way or the other."

About to curse the Frenchman for mocking him, Beccione remembered the fighter-bombers and his tone changed. "You're serious, aren't you?"

"We're serious all right. If you don't believe us, ask those Fascists we clobbered this afternoon."

Head reeling, Beccione turned back to Kessler. "Those armies out there are enormous! How the hell can a few men manipulate them?"

With great effort Kessler pulled himself out of the mood he had plunged into. "We use their strengths against one another. Otherwise, as you rightly say, we could not have an appreciable influence on their conduct."

Beccione's voice was hoarse with insistence. "But how, Kessler? How?"

"To understand you must first remember our advantages. Even before the Allies landed in Italy I had nearly a dozen nationalities in my command, men who could mix freely in either army or be at home with civilians. We had also perfected our method of moving with speed among the mountains. As the Apennines run from north to south, that is from army to army, it was and is relatively easy for us to ferret out information from one side and pass it to the other."

"Easy? How does anyone pass information on to Kesselring or Alexander?"

Kessler permitted himself a rare smile. "We are not that ambitious. A staff officer on either side serves our purposes adequately."

"O.K., a staff officer. You're still only the leader of a gang of outlaws. So how do you get in touch with staff officers?"

The German nodded. "It proved quite simple. Our first task was to establish credibility. Therefore every time we carried out a raid, we left behind detailed information about the enemy unit we had destroyed and its objectives. We knew that army intelligence on both sides would check our information and find it accurate. Our next step was to reap the benefits. As you probably know, the communications in Italy were in chaos after the Allied landings. By offering an official in the telephone company a large bribe, I persuaded him to link me up with both Allied and German field headquarters. It took patience but eventually I contacted an officer on either side and told him that from time to time I would supply him with information that would prove highly advantageous to him and the units he commanded. Naturally they were sceptical at first, but after I gave them information that proved correct they began putting out cautious feelers. My next move was to ask for a code and special wavelength from both sides."

"You're telling me you've got your own codes and wavelengths?" Beccione interrupted.

"Of course. I had to be certain the other side could not overhear. Naturally I didn't forget to point out to each officer that if he granted me these facilities, any advantage he gained from the arrangement would be his and his alone. In other words, he would be able to take the full credit if my information gained him any military success. I think we can safely claim responsibility for a number of illustrious promotions in both the German and Allied armies."

The magnitude and yet simple brilliance of the scheme had again taken Beccione's breath away. "Are you saying these officers have your wavelengths monitored day and night?"

"Yes. Twenty-four hours a day. I have only to pass on information and invariably they respond."

"But you're giving information to both sides. So how can they do business with you?"

"Governments often employ spies who are double agents. What is the difference?"

"There's a hell of a difference. You're not just playing one off against the other: you're also attacking and killing their men. How the hell can they play ball with you?"

"How can they afford not to? They would immediately put their army at a disadvantage against the other. This is one of the weaknesses of the war lords. Beccione. They must always be as dirty as the enemy they face. We use that weakness against them."

Beccione was still floundering. "But I've heard you say yourself that both sides send out patrols searching for you."

"Of course they do. If they could destroy us; the disadvantages would cancel out. Also, they have a deeper reason for fearing us. As we are the only combatant, anti-war faction in Italy, if not in Europe, men of conscience from either army could join us and fight with clean hands."

The American's expression changed. "Clean hands? Come on, Kessler. You might be helping the peasants but aren't you pushing the conscience bit? You still enjoy your revenge. Don't forget I've seen you in action. Anyway, if guys came jumping over the fence to join you, they wouldn't be coming because of their consciences. They'd come like I did, either to escape punishment or because they prefer to fight for loot instead of medals."

The accusation abruptly halted Kessler's flow of rhetoric. He shrugged in resignation. "You are probably right. This might well be the way I appease my conscience. But doesn't every man hide his mark of Cain one way or the other?"

Beccione ignored Jean Pierre's growl of protest. "There's something else too. And if you weren't so crazy for revenge, you'd see it. As far as the ordinary people of this country are concerned, the quicker the Allies win the war the better. I'm not denying some might get killed in places like San Pietro, but who started the war? In the long run they'll only get a square deal from an Allied victory and they know it. So how are you helping them by playing off one army against the other?"

Jean Pierre leapt to his feet. "Why don't you keep your mouth shut until you know everything, Yankee? Do you think Franz is such a fool he doesn't know it's essential the Allies win? It's *how* they win that concerns him. The only time he gives the Germans information is when he feels the Allies haven't taken civilian losses into account. He acts as their conscience and don't you think they need one?"

"He didn't tell me that," Beccione stammered.

"You never gave him the chance, did you?" the Frenchman snarled.

In the silence that followed the hissing of the water in the pan could be heard. Beccione frowned and gave a nod of acknowledgement. "Yeah, that's true. That's the difference that makes all the difference. Yeah, I see that now." When he glanced back at Kessler his tone had changed. "How many of your men know what's going on?"

"Eight. Roberts, Johnson, Berrati, Etienne, Nickolai, Williams, Tito and Schumann."

Beccione gave a start. "Schumann?"

"Yes. As a squad leader, he had to know. And he is useful to us."

"Can you trust him?"

"Providing he does not lose by aiding us, yes. And so far he has not."

"What about Williams? He's an ex-con, isn't he?"

"Yes, but quite trustworthy. His argument goes that he stole because the system kept his family poor. As he sees the peasants here being treated the same way, he relates to them. Johnson, while more intelligent, has similar views. He sees the peasants living under the same injustices as the blacks in America. As for Etienne, who is a product of the slums of Marseilles, his reasons hardly need emphasizing."

"What about Nickolai and Tito?"

"Both are from peasant stock, so their affiliation is basic. Nickolai's earliest memories are of Cossacks riding through his village, looting and raping in the name of the Czar. It is hardly surprising he sees the peasants here as his brothers."

"Is he a Communist?"

The German gave a shrug of indifference. "I have never asked him but I suppose he is. After all, it was the Communists who freed his people from the tyranny of the Cossacks. But Nickolai is above all a simple soul: he does not view people as causes but as human beings. The world would be a better place with more men like Nickolai."

"And Roberts and Berrati?"

"Roberts witnessed the crushing effect of poverty in the north of England, but his main motivation is a sense of fair play and gratitude to the peasants. Berrati is the easiest of all to understand. He is an intelligent peasant who suffered exploitation from the Italian upper classes until the war came. Since then he has lost everything: his home and his family. To him the ruling classes and the armies are all part of the same disease and he fights them both with equal vigor although by nature he is not a soldier."

Beccione pondered a moment. "So, including yourself and Jean Pierre, you are only ten men. You're light on the ground, aren't you? Why haven't you brought in guys like McAllister and Toschack? For that matter, why haven't you brought all the men in?"

"McAllister is a comparative newcomer but we have him ear-marked as a possible recruit. Toschack we feel is too great a risk. Although he is a fine soldier, he talks too much when drunk."

"But why does it matter if the other guys find out?" Beccione asked again. "What could they lose? They'd still get all the loot they get now."

"You answered that question yourself a moment ago. My present company did not join me because of their consciences. They joined first to ensure their survival, then they looked for gain which, to achieve my purpose, I have to give them. If they knew my real reason here they would feel unsafe."

Beccione knew the German was right. "So in effect you're using them?"

Kessler's deep-set eyes lifted. "Yes. But I feel justified. I am giving them the things they want."

Beccione eyed him a moment, then rose and walked out of the cave. Although water was still running down the hillside, the sky had cleared and far across the wilderness of mountains and hollows, flashes like summer lightning were illuminating the sky. Kessler's voice sounded at his elbow.

"They are retreating along their entire front, and as the Allies pursue them they will use every village and town as strongpoints. If we are to save lives in the time left us, we shall be stretched to the limit."

"In the time left us," Beccione repeated curiously. "What does that mean?"

The German shrugged. "Like all things we shall come to our destiny, Beccione. My hope is that it will be a worthy one."

The American inhaled, then let his cigarette drop and hiss out on the wet rocks at his feet. He turned towards Kessler. "O.K., I'm convinced. If you can use me, count me in." Giving the German no time to reply, he went on. "How many men do you have altogether."

"One hundred and twenty-four."

"A hundred and twenty-four," Beccione repeated. "And yet you're doing things Hitler, Churchill and Roosevelt can't do. Even they can't manipulate the enemy's armies."

Kessler smiled. "Perhaps they have not analyzed the weaknesses of the mailed fist. Perhaps they are too much a part of it."

A short silence followed before Beccione gave a laugh of disbelief. "You're really playing God, Kessler. Have you ever thought that?"

Although his face was in darkness, the German's somber change of mood could be felt. "Often. And I know what the penalty can be. But after sights like San Pietro, it will be a small price to pay."

Behind them Jean Pierre had overheard the American's remark. "*Mais oui*, Yankee. I like that. *Un Dieu de Guerre!*"

Kessler swung around on him. "Stop talking like a fool, Jean Pierre."

For once the Frenchman took no notice of the German's anger. As a vivid flash and then a red glow lit up the horizon, he gave a deep chuckle of delight. "Yes, I like that, Yankee. A God of War. I like that very much."

Part III

Part III

35

The road from the pass bent sharply to the right, ran beneath a massive dam wall, then wound down a long narrow valley in a series of hairpin turns. Half a mile down, it passed through a small village that was still in shadow. It was early morning.

From the pass above, the reservoir looked like a blue mirror in its frame of mountains. A secondary road ran along its near shore, linking with the main road beyond the barrage. Eastwards it contoured the lake until it disappeared around a hill shoulder.

Both roads were empty of traffic. The previous day a formidable rearguard of German troops had dug in at the head of the valley, their task to check the advance of an Allied regiment known to be approaching the pass. But late that evening they had begun withdrawing, moving their heavy artillery out under cover of darkness. Now there was no sign of them. Nor, more surprisingly, was there any sign of the Allied column, although the previous evening it had been reported only eight miles from the pass.

An early morning breeze moved across the water, ruffling its surface. A few seconds later it reached the hillside below the pass and rustled the dry bushes where two men were hiding. Alongside them were a couple of jeeps, one empty, the other containing radio equipment.

The men were Kessler and Beccione, disheveled and weary from two sleepless nights. Along with the rest of their small party, they had reached the dam two days ago and since then had been keeping a close watch on the German activities. Their attention now was focused on the eastern approaches of the lakeside road. The sudden buzz of a radio telephone made both men turn. Kessler answered the call, then turned to Beccione. "It was Roberts. He believes all the cables are cut."

Beccione showed relief. "What's taken him so long?"

"He's been trying to make sure the two outposts we've located haven't laid on any hidden cables to the charges. If they had, they might still be able to blow up the dam."

"He said *believes*. Isn't he sure?"

"Not entirely." Kessler nodded at the eastern approaches of the lake. "But if we wait any longer the main force might wonder what's happening and send back a reconnaissance party."

"What happens now?"

"Roberts is joining us here. In the meantime Nickolai is taking the R/T set to Jean Pierre who'll then make for the outpost on the opposite side of the barrage. As soon as they're in a position to attack, they'll contact us. That'll be our signal to go down and attack the outpost on this side. When Jean Pierre hears firing, he'll move in himself. In this way both positions should be taken by surprise."

The radio telephone buzzed again ten minutes later. As Kessler was answering the call, Roberts came pushing up through the bushes, his wiry body drenched in sweat. Breathing hard, he grimaced at Beccione and threw a small haversack of tools into the empty jeep. He waited until Kessler took off the earphones before addressing him. "Was that Jean Pierre?"

"Yes. He says they have their position surrounded."

The Englishman glanced again at Beccione. "He's too damned keen. I could have used a rest. All right. Let's go."

Slinging machine carbines over their shoulders, Kessler and Beccione followed him down the hill. As they neared the barrage they began moving with great care to avoid the dry twigs that littered the ground. Pausing two hundred feet above the great wall, Roberts cautiously parted the bushes and motioned his two colleagues forward. The men peered down on half a dozen German soldiers seated in a clearing below them. The clearing had been the site of heavy artillery: the marks of tyres and trunnions were still visible.

The soldiers had not long finished breakfast, mugs and eating utensils were scattered around them. At the far side of the clearing a middle-aged sergeant and a corporal were speaking animatedly beside an electric exploder that was braced on a makeshift stand. With surrounding bushes cleared by the artillerymen, the post commanded an uninterrupted view of the road that zig-zagged up to the pass.

A quick glance was all Kessler needed. Obeying his signals, Beccione and Roberts skirted the post until they had it covered on three sides. When they were in position Kessler cocked his machine carbine and leapt to his feet. "Don't move, any of you! Put up your hands!"

Seeing Beccione and Roberts, who had also jumped to their feet, five of the Germans obeyed. The sixth man, the grizzled sergeant, pretended to obey, then at the last moment spun around towards the exploder and dragged up its plunger. All three men fired at the same moment, but the weight of the German's body drove the plunger down.

Expecting a massive explosion, the German engineers dived for cover. Kessler glanced anxiously at the dam wall. When no explosion came, his lean body relaxed and he ordered the German captives up the hill.

Across the dam a green Very light announced that Jean Pierre's party had been equally successful. Five minutes later the Frenchman, accompanied by Johnson, Nickolai, and four more German captives, returned to the jeeps. His laugh echoed across the deserted hills. "That was like taking candy from a baby, Franz. Have you given the Allies the go-ahead yet?"

Kessler nodded and pointed down the valley. Following his finger, Beccione saw distant clouds that marked the ascent of the Allied transports up the pass. The glance he gave Kessler was full of disbelief. "The damnedest thing is they trust you!"

The German shrugged. "If we did not keep our word to both sides, our work would become impossible."

Jean Pierre grinned at Beccione. "Well, Yankee, do you still think we're only capable of pin-pricking? We've just opened an important pass for the Allies and maybe saved half an infantry regiment at the same time. Not bad for six men and two days work, is it?"

Beccione grinned back. "Not bad at all."

The sudden anger in Kessler's voice made the Frenchman

turn in dismay. "You talk like a fool, Jean Pierre. We didn't come here to save half a regiment of soldiers. We came so that a village should live and the thousands of peasants in the district can continue to water their crops and feed their children. We exist not to help armies but to protect the populace from them. Keep that in mind in the future, all of you."

The Bar Alberto was as packed as Beccione had ever seen it. Every table was occupied and men were lined four deep along the bar. The congestion was made even worse by the roped-off area provided for the entertainers. On one side of it Beccione shared a table with Rosenberg and Toschack. On the opposite side was Schumann, cutting an elegant figure in bush jacket, silk scarf and polished boots. He was sitting at a table with Weiss and two other members of his squad. The empty bottles on the table suggested all four men had been drinking heavily, but Schumann gave little indication of it. Only a close observer would have noticed the suffusion of his cold eyes.

The occasion was the feast of San Gennaro, the patron saint of La Capella. All day townsfolk had been trooping to church and, with the coming of darkness, a candlelight procession headed by an effigy of the saint had threaded its way through the narrow streets to a special mass that had overflowed into the piazza. Afterwards, in the Italian way, the evening had been given over to festivities; as usual the Bar Alberto had acquired most of the available talent. With an excellent piano and guitar accompaniment, the opera singers had sung two arias to an audience of rapturous Italians. A Jewish psychiatrist who had once practiced in one of Rome's leading hospitals had given a demonstration of the art of hypnosis; a violinist had given a virtuoso rendering of the *Valse Paganini*. In between these acts, to placate the soldiers who thronged the bar, half a dozen girls in scanty costumes had danced and sung popular hits of the day.

The most recent performance, Beethoven's *Moonlight Sonata* played by a Jewish ex-member of the Italian Academy, had brought some restless shuffling among the soldiers, but their mood changed the moment the bearded guitarist walked out on the floor. As the guitarist released a crescendo of chords, they gave a cheer. The cheer became deafening when Magda appeared. She was wearing a dress with a tight-fitting bodice and flared skirt. Emerald green, it set off her bronze hair to perfection. Her shoes were the same color with high, slender heels. The guitar throbbed again, she stamped her feet imperiously, poised like some volatile statue, then began to pirouette in a style that was all her own. The sex and artistry of her movements claimed the attention of even the women spectators, although some showed jealousy and dislike.

"Where the hell did she learn to dance like that?" Rosenberg muttered.

Toschack's reply was aimed at Beccione. "I guess she's had plenty of practice entertaining the troops."

Beccione gave no sign of hearing the Australian. Across the floor Schumann was angrily admonishing one of his men for talking. Each time the girl's dance took her near his table, the German tried to catch her eye but she pretended not to notice him. Toschack leaned towards Beccione. "First she chooses you as her driver and now she insults Schumann in front of his men. I'm warning you, buddy boy. She's setting you up."

Beccione shrugged and lit a cigarette. "There's worse ways of dying."

The girl's dance was reaching its climax. Stamping her feet to the music, she began revolving on her high heels, slender arms held high. As she spun faster and faster her skirt swung out, revealing her long tanned legs. Sex was spraying from her like sparks off a catherine wheel, exciting and inflaming her audience. When the last chords died away and she posed motionless, there was a great roar of applause.

Across the floor Schumann had risen to his feet and was clapping. Meeting Magda's eye, he waved her to his table. As the girl took a step forward, the German turned to his men and said something that made them laugh. Magda abruptly checked her stride, and Schumann frowned and shouted at her in German. Stiffening, the girl deliberately turned her back on him and crossed the floor to Beccione's table. A hush fell in the bar—the significance of her act was apparent to everyone.

Beccione, who had risen to his feet, grinned as he offered her a chair. "That's as good a way as any, baby."

Both Rosenberg and Toschack were looking shocked. Toschack, whose eyes were on Schumann, cursed under his breath. "Have you two gone insane? Look at the guy!"

His face pale, Schumann had taken a few steps after the girl before Weiss caught his arm. For a moment it seemed as if Schumann would tear himself away. Then, as Weiss whispered urgently in his ear, the tall German turned back to his table. He dropped into his chair and a loud hum of vicarious excitement filled the bar.

Only Toschack seemed to realize how dangerous Schumann's self-control really was. "You're crazy," he told Beccionne. "He'll have you killed as sure as Christ."

Magda, already regretting her act, took a sip of grappa from Beccione's glass. "He's right. Only he was so arrogant I acted without thinking."

Beccione shrugged. "Stop worrying. I asked you to tell him."

Toschack made an exclamation. "In front of all his men? You've humiliated him."

Beccione turned on him fiercely. "If that's all you have to say, why don't you get your ass out of here?"

The Australian jumped to his feet. "That's O.K. with me, cobber. I'd be as crazy as you if I got myself killed over a two-timing dame who enjoys setting her boy friends up."

As Beccione slammed back his chair, Magda caught his arm. "No, please. He's right. I shouldn't have done it. Only he made me so angry." She appealed to Rosenberg who was looking dismayed. "You think I was wrong too, don't you?"

Beccione swung towards the Jewish soldier. "You want to leave too? If you do, nobody's stopping you."

Rosenberg managed a weak smile. "I ain't said a word, remember. And I ain't got the guts to leave. I'm paralyzed."

Across the floor Weiss had risen and gone to the bar. A moment later the giant figure of Mogelli detached himself from a group of soldiers and returned to the table with the German. Rosenberg saw Schumann whisper something to the giant, who turned to stare at Beccione. When a few seconds later all the men rose together, the GI turned uneasily to Beccione. "Watch it, kid. They're headed this way."

Beccione shook his head and nodded at a table by the wall where Jean Pierre, Roberts and Johnson were seated. "They won't start any trouble with those guys here."

Unconvinced, Rosenberg watched Schumann lead his four men across the roped-off section of the floor. "Let's hope you're right, kid. Because they're makin' straight for us."

Beccione's legs braced beneath his chair as Schumann paused beside the table. The German's eyes, lit by cold flames, moved from Magda to Beccione and then to Rosenberg. When they paused on the Jewish soldier, Beccione felt a sudden chill of apprehension. Before he could speak, however, Schumann turned and made for the door. The others followed him but Mogelli, passing the table last, appeared to stumble. In regaining his balance he knocked over Rosenberg's glass. As wine spilled over the Italian's slacks, he let out a bellow of fury—shouting Italian at the uncomprehending Rosenberg. He grabbed the GI by his shirt and heaved him to his feet.

Everything was suddenly crystal clear to Beccione. Jumping up, he grabbed the Italian's massive arm. "All right, you sonofabitch. I got the message. Let go of him while I talk to Schumann."

Grinning brutally, the giant flung Rosenberg back in his chair. Beccione motioned Magda to stay with the GI, then went to the door where Schumann had paused. Silence had again fallen over the bar.

"Call that hatchet man of yours off Rosenberg," he said. "Otherwise I'll shoot the bastard."

Triumph glowed in the man's icy eyes. "It isn't my quarrel, Beccione. He says Rosenberg insulted him two nights ago."

"That's a lie. He's picking a fight. Call him off."

"I can't do that, Beccione. We are a fighting unit, not a pack of women. If your friend cannot take care of himself, he shouldn't be here."

"Supposing I say I'll fight the sonofabitch instead. He'll change his mind fast enough then, won't he?"

Schumann smiled. "Yes, I think he might. Is that the arrangement you would like me to make with him?"

"Make it," Beccione said tightly.

"When? Tomorrow night?"

"Tomorrow night, any night."

"Very well." Turning, Schumann gave a signal that brought a savage grin to Mogelli's face. Weiss opened the door and Schumann turned back. "As you are the challenger, I take it you will accept the rules we draw up. We shall make sure they give your skills their full expression."

"I'll accept them," Beccione said. As Schumann nodded and disappeared through the door, a blow on the shoulder sent Beccione staggering and he saw Mogelli push past him.

About to pursue, Beccione felt a restraining hand on his arm. It was Magda. She studied his face and in seconds read there what had happened. "You're fighting Mogelli, aren't you Joe?" Beccione tried to shrug her off, but she gripped

him tighter. "You fool. That's just what Helmut wants. He'll
tell Mogelli to kill you."

He felt the need to punish her. "What's wrong? Would you
prefer Schumann did it himself?"

She flinched at his tone. "When will it be?"

"Soon. Probably tomorrow night."

She gasped in dismay. "But Kessler isn't in town. You
must wait until he gets back."

"It's too late. I've already agreed." With that Beccione
shook himself free and strode back to the bar.

36

The inside of the warehouse was a scene straight from
Gustave Moreau. Packed with men wearing uniforms of a
dozen nationalities, it seethed and bubbled like a cauldron as
the figures frantically exchanged bets and fought for better
vantage points. Pressure lamps, dangling on ropes from the
timbered roof, swayed somewhat perilously in heat intensified
by the excitement. Cigarette smoke, drifting around them,
added to the surrealism of the scene.

A large ring had been roped off in the center of the floor.
Two ranks of chairs surrounded it. Behind them men sat or
stood on ammunition boxes, packing cases, benches or any
other kind of support they could find.

The two contestants were already in the ring. Stripped to
the waist they were a striking contrast in appearance. Tall
though he was, Beccione was dwarfed by the giant Italian.
Moreover he appeared at least a hundred pounds lighter. But
every slab of muscle on the American's body was as clearly
defined as if cut by a chisel, while rolls of fat wreathed the
arms and stomach of Mogelli. Some men, who had not
witnessed the giant's strength, laid their bets against him on
this score. Others, aware that bulk and weight were advantages for an all-in wrestler, made him their favorite. A
few used other criteria, such as the belief that a wrestler
would always beat a boxer. Adding the intrigue aroused by
the difference between the fighting styles to the rivalry be-

tween the squads and the hatred known to exist between the
two contestants, it was hardly surprising that almost the entire contingent of rebels was present. Among them were a
few friends and favored townsfolk—most of them relegated
to inferior seats.

Although the partition was not absolute, most of the members of A squad were packed at one side of the ring with B
squad on the other. C squad members were mixed among
them. The two tiers of chairs were filled by officers and their
NCOs. Jean Pierre was among them, with Etienne, grinning
impishly at the prospect of violence, on his one side and
Magda on the other. Inconspicuously dressed in a khaki shirt
and slacks, she was hiding her apprehension well. The one
notable absence was Kessler, who had driven out of La
Capella two days earlier and informed his lieutenants he
would not be back before the weekend.

Schumann was sitting almost directly opposite Magda. On
her arrival five minutes ago he had changed seats with one of
his men to gain this position. Every now and then his eyes
would settle on her, their triumphant threat more expressive
than words. In the main she avoided him, but when their
glances did meet, she gazed back with cold defiance.

The preliminaries were almost over. Two stools were set in
opposite corners and buckets of cold water placed outside the
ropes. Three men were acting as seconds in Beccione's corner, Rosenberg and Johnson had been automatic choices;
Williams had also volunteered. Mogelli was being served by
Rossi and Weiss. A thick-set German from C Squad called
Rubermann was acting as timekeeper, his bell having been
provided by a local blacksmith. To preserve his stance of
neutrality, Schumann's only official part in the proceedings
was that of presenter. Bassa, the referee, was a Spaniard with
cauliflower ears who claimed knowledge of both boxing and
wrestling codes. As an ex-member of Hitler's Spanish contingent, it was felt by many that his prejudices would lean
towards Mogelli. However, since no one else had wanted or
felt qualified to take on the task, the Spaniard's claim had
gone unopposed.

The buzz of excitement died as Bassa leaned over the ropes
to address Schumann and the German climbed into the ring.
Casually but elegantly dressed, speaking first in his excellent
if sibilant English, he was playing his part of the sporting
presenter to perfection.

"Good evening, gentlemen. It is my pleasure to introduce

the contest you have all been waiting for." The German's cold smiling face turned to Beccione. "As you all know, we have in our midst one of America's leading heavyweights. After considerable persuasion he has agreed to give us a demonstration of his skill. Obviously we have no boxer among us who can match him, but we do have in Mogelli a man who until the war was one of Italy's leading all-in wrestlers. Sportingly, the two men have agreed to fight for your entertainment."

There was an outcry of cheers, counter-cheers and cat-calls when the German paused. His smile did not falter as he held up a hand for silence.

"The rules of the contest, which both men have accepted, are simple. The rounds will be four minutes long, a compromise between the wrestler's five minute rounds and the boxer's three. Although both men will endeavor to fight under his own code whenever possible, each may change his style if the situation demands it. In fairness to the boxer there will be no shoulder falls. The fight will be decided when one or the other is counted out. As in these circumstances gloves would be a handicap to both men, they will not be used. That is all. I hope you enjoy the contest."

Although most of the men had heard the rules before entering the warehouse, fierce arguments broke out as Schumann repeated his announcement in German. Magda, looking puzzled, turned to Jean Pierre. "I don't understand. No gloves and no shoulder falls—doesn't that favor Joe?"

The Frenchman scowled. "No. Schumann's just made it sound that way. If Joe puts the Italian down for a count of ten, it's not going to do the slob much damage. But to stop Joe his way, the Italian will have to cripple him."

In Beccione's corner, Williams was giving the boxer advice in his sing-song Welsh voice. "Remember what to do if he gets a bear hug on you, boyo. Get your knuckles under his nose and push like hell. He's got nerve points there and he'll have to back off. Do the same if he gets a strangle hold on you. If he goes for your neck, lock your hands like this and twist, see? And don't let the bastard get a Boston crab on you. With that weight he could break your back."

Rosenberg, who was looking as scared as if he were fighting the giant himself, gazed at the Welshman's portly figure and lugubrious face in surprise. "I thought you were an ex-con. You never told us you'd fought Norman the Butcher."

The Welshman grinned. "Some people keep their eyes and ears open, boyo. You ought to try it sometime."

Beccione, whose heart was beating as hard as he could remember, tapped his stool. "You wouldn't like first crack at him, would you?"

Williams patted him paternally on the back. "Not right now, son. Maybe when you've softened him up."

Rosenberg was staring across the ring at the massive figure on the stool opposite. "Why did you fall for this, kid? Look at the sonofabitch. He's bigger than Carnera."

Johnson was quick to counter the GI's pessimism. "Yeah, and look what happened to him."

Rosenberg brightened. "Yeah, that's right. Maxie Baer half-killed him." Leaning forward, he dug Beccione in the ribs. "You remember that, kid, and what Maxie said. 'The last man up's a sissy.' "

Beccione gave him a look but before he could answer the referee called both men into the center of the ring. Mogelli grinned at Beccione over the stocky Spaniard's head. Seeing his height and bulk alongside the American and the malice in his small eyes, men murmured to their neighbors while others hastily changed their bets. Magda looked frozen as she waited for the fight to begin.

The bell rang fifteen seconds later. Winking at Schumann, Mogelli rose from his stool, hitched at his belt, and began advancing across the ring. With his massive arms outstretched he was a figure of such menace that a hush fell over the audience.

Keeping well on his toes, Beccione circled him warily. Mogelli, his thick lips parted in a sneer, revolved with him. For a full fifteen seconds neither man made an aggressive move. Then, as quick as a cat, the giant feinted at Beccione's head, and tried to grab his right leg. Taken by surprise, the American escaped only by leaping backwards. In doing so he collided with the ropes which flung him forward a couple of feet.

The Italian was swift to take advantage. He grabbed Beccione, swung him around and a second later wrapped a meaty arm around the American's throat, cutting off his breath.

The grip was so powerful that Beccione feared his neck would break. Knowing it was an illegal hold, he tried to catch the eye of the Spaniard but the man gave no sign of interfering. His eyes bulging with the pressure, Beccione realized he had only seconds to act. He tried to reach Mogelli's face with his free hand but the man kept his head well away. Desperate, the American drove an elbow back with all his strength. The choking grip slackened only momentarily, but it was long enough for him to twist sideways and break free. Choking and coughing, he retreated around the ring to the shouts and jeers of the Italian's supporters.

Flushed with the success of his first attack, Mogelli tried to pin him in a corner. As he dived for his legs, Beccione side-stepped and smashed a fist to the side of his head. The blow jarred his arm but brought only a grunt of pain from the Italian. Next Beccione drove two solid punches into his stomach and a roar broke out from the American's supporters, but he was still too winded to sustain the attack. Seeing he was in no immediate danger, Mogelli paused against the ropes to recover.

A few seconds later the men were circling one another again. Beccione saw that Mogelli's left ear was beginning to swell and blood was trickling down his cheek. Sweat poured off both men. Twice Mogelli tried to grab Beccione's legs but each time the American evaded him. Knowing he must keep away from the Italian until his strength returned, he ignored the jeers from the giant's supporters and kept on backing away. The round, which seemed endless to him, ended with Mogelli attempting to catch him in another headlock.

A quiet voice sounded behind him as he dropped on to his stool. "Honors even, I'd say."

Beccione saw Roberts had joined his seconds. "Honors even like hell! He nearly broke my neck. All I gave him was a bloody ear."

Rosenberg was running a cold sponge over his face and shoulders as gently as a mother washing her first born. As Bassa paused nearby, the Jewish GI glared at him. "What's wrong with you, you fink? Couldn't you see that sonofabitch was trying to choke him?"

Pretending he did not hear, the Spaniard walked away. Across the ring Mogelli was exchanging a joke with Weiss. Ten seconds later the bell sounded.

As if under instructions, Mogelli came out of his corner fast, but Beccione had now recovered his breath and was able to side-step and slip away along the ropes. With arms weaving like an octopus, the giant went after him. Beccione ig-nored the loud booing from the Italian's supporters and continued retreating. Realizing he was in danger every time

he extended an arm, he had decided his only chance was to
tire the heavier man before making his own attack.

He evaded contact for over a minute before he was
trapped in a corner and forced to fight. He landed three
heavy body blows before Mogelli managed to grab him and
jerk him forward. A split-second later the giant's arms closed
tightly around him, his huge biceps swelled, and Beccione
was caught in a bear hug.

The Italian's strength was frightening: the American felt as
though his ribs were snapping and the intestines bursting
from his body. For a moment he was paralyzed by pain and
panic. Then he remembered Roberts's advice. Realizing his
arms were free, he fumbled up for the giant's face.

The grip around his waist slackened for a moment but only
to give Mogelli more purchase. An instant later it tightened
again like a crushing noose. Although the crowd was shouting
and yelling, Beccione could hear nothing but the leaden
pounding of his heart. As the bear hug tightened, lifting him
from the ground, his hands found their target. Clenching his
right hand into a fist, he drove his knuckles hard beneath the
wrestler's nose.

The effect was immediate, although Mogelli's arms
tightened again almost at once. Heartened, Beccione dug his
knuckles in once more and ground them with all his strength.
He heard a grunt of pain and felt the Italian's head draw
back. At the same time the interlocking hands slipped apart
and Beccione was able to break free.

The respite was short-lived however. Before the American
could recover, Mogelli leapt forward, caught him in a crutch
hold and lifted him bodily above his head. Helpless, Beccione
had a lurching glimpse of the hysterical audience and the
smoke-wreathed lamps. Then he was slammed to the floor
with an impact that made Magda grip Jean Pierre's arm and
close her eyes. In almost the same movement the wrestler
flung his full three hundred pounds on the supine man.

Only one thing saved Beccione. His feet had struck the
ground first, partly breaking his fall. As a result, although
half-stunned, he still had the reflex to draw up his knees.
With Mogelli fully committed and with his great weight com-
pounding the effect, they drove into the Italian's stomach and
landed him alongside Beccione with a force that made the
nearby seats dance.

Winded, both men stayed down a few seconds to recover.
The warehouse was a bedlam of noise as the crowd waited.

Mogelli's behavior, displaying openly his intention to maim or kill Beccione, had ended all pretense that the fight was a sporting contest. Some men—and there were Germans of Schumann's squad among them—were showing concern and even protest. The majority, oblivious to the pain of the contestants, were merely aroused by the increasing violence of the match. Many, among them Greyson, were on their feet and screaming with excitement.

The bell sounded as both men were climbing to their feet. Beccione dropped thankfully on his stool and motioned Rosenberg to massage his back. Roberts bent over him. "I'm going to talk to Schumann. If this goes on, one of you will be killed."

Beccione caught his arm as the Englishman was about to duck through the ropes. "No, leave it." When Roberts pulled impatiently away, the American's voice rose. "I said leave it! I'm O.K."

Roberts studied him, then nodded at Rosenberg. "We'll give it one more round."

Rosenberg groaned in disappointment. "What's wrong with you, kid? You tired of life or something?"

The bell rang for the third time. Beccione was caught only a few seconds after leaving his corner. Ducking beneath his left jab, Mogelli grabbed a leg and twisted his full weight over it until Beccione was sure the knee joint had gone. It hadn't, yet, and Beccione pushed himself up and struck with all his strength at the man's grinning face. Riding the blow, Mogelli shifted his weight and half-turned the American on his face. As the wrestler tried to straddle him, Beccione knew the man had spotted his back injury and was going for the dreaded Boston crab.

Conscious that if three hundred pounds were dropped on his spine it might snap, Beccione fought desperately to avoid being turned over. The audience knew what was happening and the tension grew unbearable. When the wrestler failed to reach the American's free leg, he tried to swing him over by drawing back on the leg he held.

It was a trial of pure strength with Mogelli's skill and posture giving him all the advantages. As Mogelli heaved again and Beccione countered by dragging himself painfully forward, the GI caught sight of the blurred faces that lined the ringside. One came into focus through the sweat that burned his eyes, a handsome face glowing with triumph.

The sight revived the American. Gaining a few inches of

purchase, he twisted his head and saw that Mogelli's lower back was within his reach. Taking a deep breath to anchor his body, he struck full at the man's kidneys and felt the agonizing drag on his left leg momentarily weaken. Muscles cracking with the strain, he raised his shoulders a couple of inches higher and struck again. This time the giant grunted and reached back to slam him down. Knowing it was his last chance, Beccione heaved with all his remaining strength and, as Mogelli lost his balance, drove another blow into his back and broke free.

He discovered he could barely stand for the pain in his leg—knowledge that added to his desperation. Mogelli, his small eyes feral, was still sitting on the ground rubbing his back. When he caught sight of Beccione limping towards him, he rose quickly—but not before the American had ripped two blows into his stomach. The man dropped his guard and Beccione unleashed a right-hand punch to the jaw. It was a blow that would have felled ninety-nine men out of a hundred, but to Beccione's dismay the Italian appeared only to wince.

Yet the effect was deceptive: the punch had stunned the nerve centers that carry messages to the body. With the giant's arms now pawing the air helplessly, Beccione was able to hit where he pleased.

He finished him off like a woodsman chopping down an oak tree. As three consecutive punches smashed into Mogelli's jaw, he quivered, swayed, then his massive legs buckled and he went down.

In the awed hush that had filled the warehouse, the thud resounded like a poleaxed steer hitting the floor of an abattoir. The giant lay motionless and a roar broke out that made the pressure lamps swing crazily. Jean Pierre bellowed delightedly. Magda was looking stunned with relief and joy. Rosenberg, yelling like a madman, was thumping Johnson on the back. "He's done it! You see that! He licked the sonofabitch!"

There was no exultation in Beccione. Nauseated, unable to believe the fight was over, he had dropped on his knees beside the stricken giant. When at last he realized the man was unconscious, he glanced up at Schumann. With a dozen things to say, he opened his swollen mouth to speak but the only sound he could make was like the croak of a raven. Rising painfully, he limped back to his corner.

37

On Kessler's return to La Capella three days later, Beccione was called to his office. Still achingly stiff from his fight, the American believed he was summoned for a reprimand. The German's heavy frown reinforced his belief as he limped into the office. "When you first mentioned this contest to me I believed it was a sporting one. Had I known it stemmed from rivalry between you and Schumann, I would have forbidden it."

Beccione sank into a chair next to the German's desk. "That's the reason I couldn't tell you. Schumann would have claimed I was afraid of the sonofabitch."

Kessler controlled his anger only with difficulty. "This organization doesn't exist for men to prove their manhood, Beccione. Nor will I tolerate two of my men fighting like dogs over a bitch. I have told Schumann that if there is any more trouble between you, you will both regret it. You'll be wise to keep that in mind."

About to reply, Beccione shrugged instead. The angry German eyed him for a moment, then walked behind his desk where an open map was resting. "However, that is only one reason I've called you in this morning. The other concerns news Colenzo has just brought me." Kessler glanced sarcastically at Beccione's outstretched legs. "If you are able to stand, perhaps you will glance at this map."

Rising with an effort, Beccione moved next to him. The German's forefinger drew a circle around a maze of mountains north of La Capella. "This is where Colenzo has been, in the northern Marche. It is very wild country and what roads there are run through narrow valleys that are easily defensible. That is why the Allies have ignored this area. At the same time, fearing the Allies might try a seaborne landing to outflank them, as at Anzio, the Germans have been forced to keep a mobile reserve there." Kessler's forefinger stopped at a point near the Umbrian border. "This has been its center. As you see, there is a road running north and south and another running east and west, which means the reserve could easily be rushed to whichever coast the landing is made from. There is also a small town at the road junction where the troops have been billeted. However, ten days ago almost the entire reserve was withdrawn, presumably to man the Gothic Line further north. All they left behind was a large battery of mobile artillery sited on a hill that overlooks the town. At first I believed it was left only to provide rearguard cover and would be withdrawn a day or two later. Yet Colenzo has just brought back the report the battery is still in position."

Beccione studied a photograph of the hill that Colenzo had taken. Perhaps eight hundred feet high, it was steep-sided and heavily wooded. Small buildings were dotted among the trees. Only one of the four valleys that intersected there was visible—it looked no more than half a mile wide. Beccione shrugged as he handed the photograph back. "Perhaps they think the Allies might still send a large force up through the Apennines."

"In that case why have they withdrawn their main reserve?"

"Search me. It makes no sense."

Kessler's intellectual background was evident in the pleasure he took in solving the mystery. "To attempt an answer one must examine Kesselring's problems. Although he is working his slave laborers to death, they still have not completed his Gothic Line. So somehow he has to slow down the Allied advance. If he can do that and the Line can be completed, he has every chance of holding the Allies until the winter. After that he is safe until the spring. Four, even five months of stalemate could make a massive difference to Germany's fortunes. So isn't it likely he will take almost any risk to gain that time?"

"Yeah, that sounds reasonable. But where does a gun battery in the heart of the Apennines fit in? It's a hundred miles from the real battle."

"It makes sense only if Kesselring has changed his mind," Kessler said dryly.

Beccione stared at him. "You mean reoccupy the town?"

"Yes. But for an entirely different purpose than before."

"You're going to have to explain," the American said.

Kessler laid his finger on the map again. "Supposing Kesselring could take Siena from the French. Or even have a division in that area. Wouldn't that check the Allied advance on the west."

"Sure. They'd have to stop and secure their flank. But how

does Kesselring get a division there? It's behind the Allied front line."

Kessler motioned him to be patient. His finger moved eastwards. "Now take the situation here. General Leese of the British 8th Army has been secretly moving a massive number of troops across Italy to the Adriatic coast. The plan is obviously to attack the Gothic Line on two fronts: the Americans on the west and the British on the right. As my informers have brought this move to my attention, it is reasonable to suppose the Germans have heard about it too. The date of Leese's offensive is still a secret, but would not that offensive be thrown into complete confusion if a German division suddenly appeared or was even reported on his left flank?"

"But how would that division get there?"

Kessler traced his finger along the northern road that led down to the fortified hill and town. "They travel along here at night and stay under camouflage by day. To secure their rear they reoccupy the town and then, with the battery sealing off the Allies' only approach from the south, they are free to strike east or west as the situation demands."

Beccione took a deep breath. "You've worked all this out just from one gun battery left on a hill?"

The German looked surprised. "What other explanation could there be?"

"Christ, there could be a hundred. They could be short on fuel and be waiting for supplies. Their commanding officer could have a girl friend in town he just hates leaving. You want me to go on?"

Kessler smiled. "Of course it could be a hundred things. But not strategically."

"Always assuming Kesselring's as smart as you are."

The German's voice turned dry again. "In war it is always wise to assume one's enemy is smarter. But I accept there could be a simpler explanation. That is why I want you to go there and find out all you can. Since at the moment Italian Black Shirts are providing the infantry shield for the battery, you'll take Colenzo, Berrati and Alfredi with you. As I shall want immediate news of your findings, Rosenberg will take one of the radio jeeps. You'll also need Magda."

Beccione frowned. "Why Magda?"

"Because she is the only one of us with a chance of infiltrating the battery."

Beccione gave a start. "You want her to get inside the battery? That's too dangerous a job for a woman."

Kessler nodded coldly. "This is precisely why I am against personal relationships within my organization. Why do you think I allow Magda to be a member? Certainly not for the jealousies she causes. I keep Magda because she is a born actress and with her good looks has little difficulty in making men talk." Seeing Beccione's expression, the German's tone changed. "If it is any comfort to you, she will be taking risks in an excellent cause, although she must not be told this. If the Germans are allowed to reoccupy this town, it could become a second San Pietro."

"Why is that?"

"Because if Kesselring's plan succeeds and his division breaks out east or west, the only sensible Allied response would be to chop off the threat at its source. They would drive up the center of the Apennines and try to take the town. As the German's main force would be trapped if they lost the base, both sides would fight to the death and the town would be obliterated."

Beccione realized he was right. "Assuming you've guessed correctly, what's your solution?"

"I shall warn the Allies of their danger and tell them they must at all costs occupy the town first. And with a force large enough to make the Germans abandon their plans and withdraw. But first I must be certain I am right. As there is no time to waste, I want you to leave today."

Beccione gazed at the map with its maze of mountains. "If the Germans have retreated, won't it be safe to use the main road? We'd make better time."

"No. They are certain to have mined it. In a moment I'll call Weiss in. After his desertion he spent some months hiding in the northern Marche and he knows the district well."

"How are you going to explain all this to Magda?" Beccione asked. "You're giving her a hell of a job. She's sure to be curious."

Kessler gave an impatient shrug. "I realize she will be curious but she knows better than to ask questions. In any case she enjoys this kind of assignment. The danger is a challenge to her."

Beccione nodded and turned back to the map. Its scale was small and no name showed on the intersection of the roads. "What sort of a town is it? Did Colenzo say?"

Kessler, who was reaching for his telephone, paused. The slow musing smile he gave puzzled the American. "He says it is very beautiful. A mountain town with tall campaniles, trees and flowers."

"What's its name?"

Kessler turned away. "Valderosa," he said.

38

Across the cobbled market place the tradespeople had loaded their bread and provisions into one horse-drawn cart and were preparing to climb into a second. The stocky Italian Black Shirt in charge of the ration party, bad-tempered because of the earliness of the hour, shouted at them to hurry.

Beccione turned to Magda. "Are you ready?" When she nodded, he hesitated, then gripped her arm. "Be careful."

The gesture appeared to please her. Smiling, she held his eyes for the briefest moment. Then, as coolly as if she were going shopping, she stepped out into the open and began crossing the piazza.

Alongside Beccione were Colenzo, Berrati and Alfredi. All four watched Magda breathlessly. Her appearance was a work of art. Subtle touches of make-up added hardness to her expression without marring her good looks. A tight sweater outlined her superb breasts. A beret sat cheerfully on her long amber hair. Her affected walk made her tight skirt twitch provocatively.

The reconnaissance party had arrived within sight of Valderosa the previous evening. Hiding their jeeps in the woods and leaving Rosenberg to guard them, they had made for the town on foot along paths Colenzo had already mapped out for them. All were wearing civilian clothes and carrying forged papers and travel documents.

Avoiding Black Shirt sentry posts and patrols, they had reached the town in darkness and gone through its deserted alleys to the market place. Colenzo had discovered that a ration party left there for the German battery at sunrise every morning. Magda, in the role of a foreign prostitute, was to attempt to gain entry to the battery by begging a lift in the ration convoy. Beccione and the three Italians had a simpler task. To bring their provisions to the market place, the trades-

people used young assistants who returned to their places of
employment when the ration party moved away. Each rebel
was to tail one of these assistants back to his shop or store
and there try to ferret out from the staff information about
the length of the battery's stay. Beccione was also to take detailed photographs of the hill and the terrain around it.

Busy bullying the tradespeople, the Black Shirt in charge
did not notice Magda until she was only a dozen paces away.
Instead of pausing at his challenge, she smiled and swung
towards him, every movement of her body a sexual promise.
As the Italian scowled and shouted at her, she leaned against
him and murmured something in his ear.

Her murmur proved a trump card. Flashing a sudden grin,
the man led her towards the second cart. Two blowsy women
sat among the six tradesmen in the cart and their protests were
loud and shrill as the man helped the girl aboard. There, to
the delight of the six men, she thumbed her nose at the
women, pulled up her skirt, and sat with her shapely legs
dangling over the side of the cart as it rolled away. Colenzo
showed his blackened teeth in a smile as he turned to Beccione. "That's one hell of a woman, Joe."

His eyes following the cart, Beccione did not hear him.
Across the piazza the young assistants were beginning to disperse. Beccione pulled himself together and turned to the
three Italians. "O.K., so far so good. Pick yourself a guy
apiece, follow him and see what you can find out. If you
have no luck, try other tradespeople but watch your questions. Remember I want you all back at the jeeps by dusk.
Let's go."

Beccione felt like a man in a dream as he climbed the
worn cobbled steps of the alley. Alongside him a patch of
bougainvillaea ran up a wall like a cool crimson fire. An old
man, enjoying a pipe in a shaded doorway, gave him a nod
as he passed by. A linnet was chirruping in a cage above one
of the shuttered windows. As he climbed higher a donkey
carrying a large pannier came around a bend above him.
Leading the animal was a young boy, as brown as an Arab,
who showed his white teeth in a smile as he passed by.

The alley led into a tiny piazza. Small cottages rose on
three sides. Pots of flowers stood before them, their blooms
great splashes of color. A campanile stood on the fourth side.

Beccione walked across to it, drawn by the incense of heliotrope.

The ground beyond the clock tower fell away, giving glimpses of further campaniles, pantiled roofs, and the old walls of the town. Beyond them neat villas clung to the shallow hillside. On the floor of the valley vineyards slept in the midday heat. In the sunlight the air shimmered with a million specks of gold. The silence was like crushed velvet, broken only by the crying of a child and the clip-clop of a horse on a distant road. Beccione listened, feeling an odd excitement and an eagerness he did not understand.

A whirring of wheels and cogs made him start and turn. A few seconds later the clamor of the clock tower bell sent a flock of pigeons scattering high into the air. Deeper, more sonorous chimes followed almost immediately and his eyes lifted. High above the cobbled roads and piazzas, the great campanile of the cathedral of Santa Rosaria rose into the azure sky. Each of the twelve chimes that struck seemed to echo down the hushed corridors of the American's mind.

He glanced back at the valley. The hill he had first seen on the photograph stood about two miles from the town. In shape it resembled a minor mountain peak, its summit being steep on both north and south sides. Its eastern side, which faced the town, was less severe and a road could be seen winding upwards through the trees. Beccione had already learned that the tiny buildings dotting its summit were ancient monks' cells. He could see no sign of the German battery.

His gaze moved to the mountains that hugged the east-west valley. All were heavily wooded. The entrances to both the northern and southern valleys looked to him like deep folds in crumpled lengths of cloth. Roads emerged from them and came winding through the fields and vineyards towards the town. The one from the south crossed a dried-up river that ran from east to west.

A miaow made him turn: a white cat was eyeing him from a low wall that stood in front of one of the cottages. It made no attempt to run away as he approached, but nuzzled its head into his hand. In the sunlight a nearby pot of geraniums appeared luminescent. The ornamental facing of the clock tower shone like burnished gold. Maria had not exaggerated, he thought. This town was a jewel. Walking back to the tower he gazed again at the vineyards and the valleys that ran to the four points of the compass. A jewel set in an emerald cross, he thought, smiling at his rare whimsicality.

The sound of an engine changed his mood. Below, an open-topped truck was moving along one of the narrow streets that led towards the town center. Half a dozen black-shirted militia were lounging in the back. Although the Germans might have left the town, it was still in the hands of the hated Italian Fascists, which meant it was wide open for re-occupation should that be Kesselring's intention.

Beccione waited until the truck disappeared. Then, hoping no one was watching him from the cottages, he pulled out a small camera from his jacket pocket and began taking detailed photographs of the hill and the terrain around it. When he finished he saw he had only twenty minutes left before he was due to meet Magda. Pocketing the camera, he began walking up the cobbled alleys towards the cathedral that dominated the town.

It took him less than ten minutes to reach the cathedral. It stood on one side of a large piazza lined with small cafes. Its facade was faced with white marble and above its portals was a magnificent color mosiac of the Apostles. Higher still was a mosiac of the Ascension. A long portico flanked the piazza. The great bell tower, crowned by merlons, rose from a cloistered garden full of ornamental bushes, oleanders and benches.

The activity in the piazza surprised the American. Eating lunch-time sandwiches, men and women filled the benches that ran in front of the portico and were also seated on the steps of the cathedral. The cafe tables were occupied as well. Yet although the scene looked peaceful at a distance, it was deceptive. As Beccione moved into the piazza he saw men talking agitatedly and here and there women dabbing their eyes. A couple of discreet questions confirmed his suspicions: rumors had been circulating in the town for days that the *Tedeschi* were returning.

He could see no sign of Magda and since he was still a few minutes early, he decided to take a look inside the cathedral. Its portals of richly carved wood had a frame of blue stone adorned with cherubs. As he passed through them the shade inside was like a cool hand on his forehead.

He paused a few seconds for his eyes to adjust. Ahead the central nave was supported by a double series of ornamental pillars. His footsteps sounded loud and hollow as he turned down one of the aisles that skirted the chapels.

Expecting to see treasures everywhere, he gazed around him in surprise. Both the aisle and the chapels looked as if they had been pillaged. Stains on the walls betrayed the one-time presence of works of art. Empty plinths proclaimed the removal of statues and priceless ornaments. For a moment he wondered if the German Army was responsible. Then he understood. Fearing the worst, the clergy themselves had removed the treasures and hidden them.

Some hint of the wealth of the cathedral was given by the objects that had defied removal. One chapel had an exquisite altar-frontal of carved marble depicting the Madonna and Child. Close by was a baptismal font adorned with the figures of the Apostles. A second chapel had a magnificent lunette of blue glazed earthenware celebrating the Annunciation. Within was a marble bier surrounded by dozens of flickering candles. The discoloration of its flat top suggested it had recently supported a casket, and Beccione had little doubt what its precious burden had been.

Beccione found the calm of the cathedral disturbing, and it was a relief to emerge into the sunlight and bustle of the piazza. Still seeing nothing of Magda, he found room on a bench in front of the portico, hid his face behind a newspaper and waited.

As the lunch period ended and the benches began to empty, he began to feel conspicuous. Moving to one of the cafe tables, he ordered a bottle of wine. The clock above chimed the quarter hours, his anxiety grew. He emptied the first bottle of wine and ordered another.

It was 4:30 before she appeared, walking down the line of tables with quick graceful strides. Men turned to watch her pass. Showing relief at the sight of Beccione, she dropped into the seat opposite him.

"How did it go?" he muttered.

She recovered quickly. "Very well." She leaned forward to examine his face. "You've had a lot to drink, haven't you?"

"So what? Why are you so late?"

She laughed. "Have you been worried?" When he did not answer she said, "The work was difficult. It could not be hurried."

"Did you get all we wanted?"

"Yes, I think so. But before I tell you more, please give me a drink."

He ordered another bottle and a glass. She took the drink he gave her and sat back. "I am certain a main force will occupy the town in four days."

He started. "Four days. How can you be so sure?"

She gave an amused laugh. "I slept with the commanding officer, his adjutant and half a dozen gunners. How else could I find out?"

He answered without meeting her eyes. "I figured you'd have to sleep with somebody. Who was it?"

She sat looking at him for a moment. Then she lit a cigarette and inhaled deeply. Her tone was harder when she spoke again. "As it happens, it was not necessary. I simply made a date with the commanding officer."

"What does that prove?"

"A great deal. Our date isn't for four days. So we know right away the battery is not withdrawing during that time."

"How did you get him to wait that long?"

"I said I was unwell. And that I slept with the mayor every weekend."

"The mayor? And he believed you?"

She smiled. "He could hardly phone the mayor to ask him, could he?"

Beccione was frowning. "But this doesn't prove a main force is coming."

"Let me finish. When the commanding officer was called out from his office, I offered his adjutant a date."

Beccione was beginning to understand. "After the date with the C.O.?"

"Exactly. Instead he tried to sleep with me first. When I asked why, he said soon there would be so many Waffen SS and high-ranking officers about that there would be no opportunity for us to meet."

"Waffen SS," Beccione muttered. "They must mean business."

"That's what I thought. And it can only mean the main force is due in four days time. Not earlier or the C.O. would have quibbled about waiting so long."

"Not necessarily. Maybe he doesn't give a damn about Waffen SS officers."

"No. This man is the sort who likes to keep a pure Aryan image. I am certain the arrival date is four days."

Although Beccione was impressed by the girl's handling of the task, his moody face gave no sign of it. "None of this explains why you've been away so long."

"It took a good deal of argument and persuasion before I was allowed to meet the C.O."

"A whole day of persuasion?"

She began to show anger. "If you must know everything, the C.O. is a gentleman. He invited me to lunch."

"To lunch? A German officer? Where did you have your lunch? In his office or his bedroom?"

She was on the verge of losing her temper. "What is the matter with you? Are you jealous? Or are you drunk? The lunch was in the mess with four of his officers. We talked until 3.30. Then I was driven back to town in the C.O.'s car. That is all that happened."

Beccione muttered something and drained his glass. Across the piazza the last rays of the sun, which was dipping behind the mountains, had caught the tall campanile and set it aflame. The girl's explanation appeared to have changed the American's mood—he motioned at the shadowy church garden with its oleanders and quiet cloisters. "What do you think of this town? Isn't it beautiful?"

She was more interested in his change of mood than his words. "Yes. It's very attractive."

He became immediately aggressive again. "Attractive? It's beautiful. The most beautiful town I've ever seen."

"Very well, it's beautiful. But why are you so hostile tonight?"

She saw he was not listening to her. A tall, dark-haired girl with a young boy at her side had emerged from behind one of the cafes and was crossing the shadowy piazza. Giving a violent start, Beccione jumped to his feet. Magda rose with him and caught his arm. "What is it, Joe?"

Pushing her away, he began running towards the couple. When he was a few yards from them Magda heard him call out and saw the girl turn. Beccione stared at her, then muttered something and swung away. He pushed his way back to the table, his face dark with disappointment.

"What was all that about?" she asked as he dropped heavily into his chair. "Did you think you knew her?"

Ignoring her, he reached for the wine bottle. She snatched it away. "No. You've had too much already. We must get back to Rosenberg."

He moved to take the bottle from her, then cursed and turned away. Holding his arm tightly, she led him down the quietest alleys she could find. To her dismay the last one brought her out opposite the *palazzo communale*. A dozen Italian Black Shirts were talking and laughing before its main entrance, all heavily armed and one man carrying a whip. About to draw back, the girl saw they had been noticed. She

clenched her teeth and led Beccione past them. As the man
with the whip nudged a comrade and started after her, she
put her arms around Beccione and kissed him firmly on the
lips. The Black Shirt took a few more steps towards them
then, taking the advice of his companions, leered and drew
back.

Five minutes later the couple were out of town and heading through the vineyards for their rendezvous. Peasants
trudged past them, weary after a long day in the fields. All
gave them courteous greetings, but their eyes moved with
curiosity from the beautiful girl to the moody silent man at
her side.

39

Although the western sky was still aflame, the wood of the
southern valley was in deep shadow when the couple
reached it. They stopped abruptly when, a few minutes later,
a flashlight beam blinded them. Rosenberg's relief was heart-
felt. "Where the hell have you been? Colenzo and the others
have been back over an hour."

"Never mind that," Beccione said. "Have you been in
touch with Kessler yet?" He was considerably sobered by the
long walk.

"No, I've been waiting for you. Did you find anything
out?"

"Magda did. She's certain a main force will be here in four
days time."

"That's what Berrati heard. A storekeeper's been told to
buy up all the flour he can for Tuesday."

"O.K. that settles it. Get your code book out and get the
word to Kessler."

The rest of the party gathered around the jeep to await
Kessler's reply. Beccione held a flashlight while Rosenberg
decoded it. Peering over the stocky GI's shoulder, Beccione
got the gist of the message and turned to Berrati. "He wants
you and Alfredi to take the radio jeep down the northern valley and to watch out for the Kraut main force. As soon as
you sight it you're to let him know."

"How far down does he want us to go?" Berrati asked.

Rosenberg, who had finished the decoding, turned to him. "As far as you safely can. He wants an assessment of their strength and if possible he wants you to trail 'em so he'll know when they reach the town."

Standing beside Beccione, Magda was looking puzzled. The big American drew Berrati aside. "In case he didn't tell you, Kessler's going to try to get the Allies here first. So he's going to need all the information possible about the Krauts. Otherwise the Allies might not take the threat seriously."

The Italian nodded. "He did explain to me. Tell him not to worry. I will do my best."

"You'd better take all the food and provisions we've got. Just leave us enough for a cup of coffee later on." Beccione glanced at the crimson sky over the mountains. "You'd better get started. You'll have to drive pretty far east before you cross the valley. Those Black Shirts have every approach road to the town covered."

With Berrati driving, the radio jeep moved off six minutes later. Beccione stood listening to its fading engine and Magda, her curiosity growing, came up to him. "Kessler is taking a great interest in this town, Joe. Do you know why?"

He was only surprised that she had not asked him the question before. "No," he lied.

"I don't believe you. Kessler trusts you these days. He would not have put you in charge of this mission without giving you a reason." When he did not answer she went on. "Have you ever visited the town before?"

Beccione, wanting to avoid what he knew was coming next, moved towards Colenzo and Rosenberg. "We'd better get moving. You two ready?"

"How're we riding?" Rosenberg asked.

"The same as we came. I'll ride ahead with Colenzo, Magda can drive the middle jeep, and you can act as rearguard."

Magda, who had followed him, touched his arm. Her tone was exactly the right blend of apology and weariness. "I know it's stupid but I think I'm feeling some reaction. Won't you drive for me?"

It was an admission of fraility so unlike her that he was suspicious. But he acknowledged that the risks she had taken would have exhausted most men. Beccione jerked his head in assent. "O..K, if that's what you want. In that case we'll act as rearguard."

The route they took back led them along foresters' tracks through the dense woods. The night air was cold in the open-topped vehicles and Magda huddled against Beccione to keep warm. Her sudden question, after fifteen minutes of silence, startled him. "You never told me if you had visited that town before. Have you?"

"No I haven't," he said.

She shifted her head to see his face. "That wasn't how it sounded. You talked as if you had known it all your life."

His laugh was dry. "Hardly."

"And you thought you recognized that girl. Why was that?"

"I was drunk. You said so yourself."

"Not that drunk. Just drunk enough to give away your feelings."

"What's that supposed to mean?"

She shrugged. "I wish I knew."

The track, muddy from heavy rain, ran in a series of undulations parallel to the road below. The trees and bushes on the rising ground caught the last of the crimson light; the depressions were full of shadow. Ahead of Beccione, the headlights of the other jeeps were slicing paths through the night and leaving a wake of darkness behind them.

A steeper rise made Beccione drop down a gear. As he crested it, his headlights shone down into a steep-sided clearing. Stumps of trees lined its sides and piles of logs awaited removal. A hundred yards ahead Colenzo was beginning to ascend the opposite rise. He was a third of the way to the crest when there was the sudden hammering of automatic fire. With its headlights and windshield shattered, the jeep slued violently and halted. A few seconds later its fuel tank exploded.

Beccione, who had braked immediately on hearing the firing, saw stabs of flame coming from a pile of logs high up on the right-hand bank. Lines of tracer revealed why Colenzo's jeep had burned so readily. Ahead, Rosenberg had also braked and was trying to bring his .50 Browning into operation. Before he could uncouple the heavy gun, a burst of bullets hurled him away. He fell in a heap on the muddy track below.

Beccione saw the Jewish GI hit as he was frantically backing the jeep in reverse up the rise. It skidded down the far side, momentarily out of sight of the gunmen. He jammed on the brakes, seized his Sten gun, and leapt out. "Keep going," he yelled.

The suddenness of the attack was too much even for Magda's nerves: she was staring at him with a dazed face. Cursing, he ran around the jeep and pushed her roughly into the driver's seat. "Get the goddamned thing away!" he shouted. "Drive back a mile and then wait for us."

Without glancing back, he ran up the rise. For the moment the firing had ceased. In the light from the burning jeep the motionless figure of Rosenberg could be seen on the road. Beccione took a deep breath and began running.

For the first thirty yards he was able to keep in the shadow of the trees. Then, as he began sliding down the muddy bank, he entered the revealing pool of light. As two guns began hammering immediately, he dived for cover behind a pile of logs.

Bullets drilled into the soft wood, others ricocheted away in shrill screams. Panting for breath, he tried to gauge the distance to Rosenberg. Twenty yards, maybe a few more. Damning the flickering light, he launched himself forward.

Bullets splattered him with mud, then screamed off the reinforced sides of the jeep as he flung himself down behind it. He crawled towards Rosenberg. "How bad is it, Rocky?"

Although the GI appeared too shocked to speak, his eyes showed he was alive. But his body was unnaturally twisted and his shirt soaked in blood. Beccione cautiously tried to assess the damage to the jeep. One look at the shattered dashboard was sufficient. As a means of escape it was useless.

He tried to guess how long it would take the gunmen to work their way around the clearing. Probably three to four minutes if they wanted to keep out of range. Only one man would stay behind to keep him pinned down. To test his theory he cocked his Sten, jumped up and fired a quick burst at the pile of logs. As he ducked back, bullets hammered on the jeep again. He knew the gunmen were searching for the fuel tank, but the jeep's angle to the line of fire was keeping it protected.

There was no point, then, in dragging Rosenberg towards one of the piles of logs. If they were not mown down on the way, they would be just as exposed when men moved in behind them. Their only hope lay in the fire dying down and that was raging more fiercely than ever.

The sudden crack of bursting shells made him stiffen until he realized it was the ammunition in Colenzo's jeep explod-

ing. The noise hid from him the sound of the jeep that came
backing down the rise at breakneck speed. As it halted with a
scream of brakes, Magda leapt out and dived alongside him.
"Get in! Quickly!"

"For God's sake," he hissed. "You gone crazy?"

Face pale but determined, she tugged at Rosenberg's legs.
"Stop talking and get him into the jeep!"

With desperation adding to his strength, Beccione picked
up the GI and toppled him over the armored side of the vehicle. The crack of the exploding shells hid from him the fact
the gunmen had ceased firing. Seeing Magda turning towards
the driver's seat, he grabbed her and swung her up after
Rosenberg. "Keep down and you've a chance," he shouted.

Certain that the real test would come when he dropped behind the wheel, he turned and fired a long burst to give himself a few seconds protection. Then he leapt into the jeep and
slammed in the gears. As its spinning wheels hurled back
mud and gravel, he heard the hammering of the .50 Browning
behind him. Magda had risen to her feet and was raking the
bank above.

The few seconds it took the jeep to reach the crest of the
rise and to skid down to safety seemed like minutes to the
American. He could not understand why they were still alive.
Behind him Magda had ceased firing and was trying to lift
Rosenberg onto the seat. Conscious there might be other gun-
men around, Beccione dared not stop to help her.

A track turning to the right and climbing the hillside appeared in his headlights. On an impulse he swung into it, his
wheels skidding in the mud until they found traction. He
climbed for a couple of minutes, then turned right at another
intersection. Twisting his head, he gave a shout, "How's
Rocky?"

The girl had to lean forward to be heard. "He's badly hurt.
You must stop as soon as you can."

He drove on for another minute, saw a gap in the trees,
and backed into it. As he switched off the lights and engine,
the silence seemed as dense as the shadows around them.
They spread a blanket on the ground and lowered Rosenberg
onto it. He was a dead weight—his arms and legs as limp as
a doll's. Magda shone a flashlight on his face; its pallor made
Beccione wince. He began gingerly lifting the GI's bloody
shirt, but she pushed him away. "I will attend to him. You
go and make sure we're not being followed."

Remembering she had nursing experience, he took his Sten

from the jeep and walked fifty yards along the track. He could see and hear nothing: the woods seemed empty of life again. Fear of what might await him burdened his steps as he walked back.

With the flashlight nuzzled into her shoulder, Magda was plugging Rosenberg's stomach wounds with bandages. Finishing the task and laying a blanket over the GI, she drew Beccione aside. "I think he is recovering consciousness. So keep your voice down."

"What are his chances?" he muttered.

She turned and faced him. "He has no chance. He is bleeding internally and I believe a bullet has broken his back. That is why he is in no pain."

He gave a grunt of shock. "Are you sure?"

"Take a look for yourself."

"Supposing we get him back to La Capella?"

"He wouldn't last ten minutes in the jeep."

"Then you go. That's it." His voice was eager; his grip on her arm painful. "You drive there and bring back a doctor while I stay with him."

Weariness and distress turned her impatient. "Can't you understand? He is dying. I don't think he will live half an hour."

A low moan took them back to the stricken GI. The girl set the flashlight so that it illuminated his face without blinding him. Seeing his eyes were open, Beccione leaned over him. "How're you feeling, Rocky?"

Rosenberg's voice was little more than a croak. "What happened, kid?"

"You fell outta the jeep and bruised yourself. Don't you remember?"

The cords of the GI's neck stood out as he tried to lift his head and failed. "It musta been a hell of a bruise. I can't move anything."

"It was a hell of a fall. But you'll soon be O.K."

"Aw, quit kiddin' me, Joe. I know what my chances are." Although clearly afraid, the GI attempted a grin. "You know how I'm feelin', kid? I'm scared to death."

Magda saw Beccione swallow. For a moment his face lifted to her as if he were asking for help. Then he leaned over the dying man again. "That's a hell of a bad joke, Rocky."

"Yeah, I know. Like all my jokes." Rosenberg paused for

breath. "How did you get me outta there? Those guys were zeroed in on us."

"Magda brought the jeep back."

"Magda? On her own?"

"That's right. She saved both our skins."

Rosenberg tried to focus on the girl. "You gotta be kidding. I thought she had no time for ordinary GIs like me."

The girl moved forward and wiped his forehead with a damp cloth. "You're no ordinary GI, Rocky. You're something special."

Rosenberg's blood-rimmed eyes moved back to Beccione. "You hear that, kid? Ain't it my luck? Just as she falls for me, I can't move a whisker."

Magda, stained with blood and dirt, looked close to tears. "Don't let that worry you, Rocky. I'll be waiting for you when you're well."

The banter had drained the GI's remaining strength. Magda had to bend lower to catch his whisper. "You know something, kid? You've got what it takes. You're O.K."

She kissed him full on the lips. Then she swung sharply away. Astonished at what he had seen, Beccione took her place. Rosenberg was breathing with difficulty now and his face was the color of marble. When he spoke again he was half-delirious. "That you, kid?"

"Yeah, it's me, Rocky."

"Kid, I've just seen Maria. She was bendin' over me. I said she'd forgive you, didn't I?"

It was Magda's turn now to watch Beccione. He took one of Rosenberg's limp hands and gripped it tightly. "You did, Rocky. How're you feeling now?"

"It don't hurt." Without the restraint of his will, the GI's fear of death was naked now. "Except it's cold. And it's gettin' dark. I'm scared, kid. I ain't never been so scared before."

The girl saw Beccione swallow again. She had not believed a man's voice could be so gentle. "You've got nothing to be scared about, Rocky. Not a guy like you. Just take it easy, buddy. Just take it easy."

Rosenberg died two minutes later with Beccione still gripping his hand. Magda stood a distance away, listening to the faint soughing of the wind and the rustle of leaves. When she returned Beccione was still bending over the dead GI. Then he heard her, took a deep breath and straightened. She reached out and touched his arm. "I'm sorry, Joe. So very sorry."

He did not pull away as she had half-expected. Instead he reached back and gripped her hand. "You did all you could, kid. And more. I'm grateful."

They barely spoke another word as they lifted Rosenberg back into the jeep and drove away. There was a shyness between them now as if, in spite of their love making, they had discovered they were strangers and, when their sorrow had eased, they would need to make new assessments of one another.

40

Kessler rose to his feet as Magda moved away towards his office door. It was not his act of courtesy that was significant: the German was always courteous to the girl unless inflicting a reprimand. His change of heart towards her showed in his words and tone of voice. "You've done well, Magda. The information you've gathered will be more than useful to me. It also seems Beccione owes you his life." When the weary girl did not answer, Kessler nodded at her blood-stained clothes. "I'm sorry I gave you no time to wash and change on your return but the matter was urgent. I won't need you again until 11.00 hours when I shall be briefing the entire company."

Magda indicated she understood, went out and closed the door. Sinking back into his chair, Kessler glanced at Beccione who was seated before his desk. "It took great courage to enter that camp. And brains too."

Beccione, dull with fatigue and grief, nodded but did not answer. About to discuss Rosenberg's death, Kessler took another look at the American and decided against it. "I could not tell you while Magda was here but I have already been in touch with the Allies."

Beccione stirred himself. "What did they say?"

"They sounded disturbed. They believed the Germans were in full retreat and never dreamed Kesselring would take a gamble like this. They were sceptical enough to say they would send a reconnaissance aircraft over the hill at first light."

Beccione took a sip of the cognac the German had given him. "You could hardly expect them to divert an entire combat division without verification."

Kessler drummed his fingers on the desk. "Perhaps not. But they are going to have enough trouble reducing that battery when they arrive without wasting time like this. Remember, they cannot enter Valderosa until they occupy that hill."

Beccione shrugged. "They'll clobber it with aircraft. They've got total air supremacy now."

"Air power did not succeed at Monte Cassino. And these guns have equally good protection from the caves that honeycomb the hill. I believe that battery can be reduced only by infantrymen. Moreover the minefields the Germans must have laid along the approach road could be extensive. I take it you did not see any of them?"

"No. We did as Weiss said and kept on the forest tracks all the way."

"And now the Allies will have engineers examining that road," Kessler mused. "It is a pity: those minefields could be the key to the entire operation."

Beccione was trying to understand. "One way or the other, you're making it sound as if the Germans are still going to be first in Valderosa."

"It takes time to assemble and move the equipment the Allies will need to hold the town. Their earliest ETA is daybreak on Tuesday."

"Tuesday? But that's when the Germans are due."

"Precisely. That is why I have decided to take the battery myself. With luck its loss will discourage the Germans and could turn them back."

Kessler's statement, delivered in a matter-of-fact way, took a moment to register on the weary American. "Do you know what you're saying? That battery's sited to hold up an army."

"I know that. But I have had this in mind for some time and now, thanks to Magda, I believe we can pull it off."

"How, for Chrissake?"

"By using the Trojan horse technique." Seeing Beccione's expression, Kessler smiled. "Let me explain. My men dress up as German soldiers and we drive quite openly to the gates of the battery. There I tell them we are a mixed unit of engineers and signalers whose task is to reinforce the gun emplacements and to check that communications are adequate before the main force arrives. Once we are inside the rest should be easy."

The boldness of the plan roused Beccione from his grief. "Easy? What if the battery phones or radio checks on you?"

"We must hope our acting ensures they do not."

"What time of day is this?"

"Midday."

"Midday? Then they'll see you approaching from the wrong side of the valley. You'll never get past the Fascist outposts. And when they discover who you are, the battery will slaughter you before you can turn your transports around."

Kessler gave a wry smile as he pulled a map out of his desk. "I had hoped by this time you would trust me to take care of such elementary points. We shall not come out of the southern valley. We shall use minor roads and tracks to work ourselves around Valderosa until we can emerge from the same valley the German main force will eventually use. This way our only obstacle will be the Fascist outpost on the hill itself and this I want you to take care of. Only, to be successful, you will need to hire a horse-and-cart in Valderosa."

"A horse-and-cart?"

"Yes. This is what you will do." When the German had finished outlining his plan, Beccione was looking more impressed.

"Yeah, that might work. But won't we be seen by the battery above?"

Kessler reached into a tray on his desk where a pile of newly-developed photographs were lying. He selected one and handed it to the American. "We believe the trees between the curves in the road will give you cover. If they don't, you will have to do the job without arousing suspicion. It should not be too difficult. No one is likely to be paying attention to an old peasant cart."

"Let's hope not. Because if they can see us, they can also shoot us."

Kessler raised an eyebrow. "If you don't want the assignment, say so now."

"No, I'll go. But why take Magda?"

"Because the presence of a woman always allays suspicion. Moreover the sentries will probably remember her and think she is going up to the battery for her date with the commanding officer."

"You don't miss a trick, do you?" Beccione said. "What

about the infantry shield of Black Shirts? If we take the battery, isn't there a danger of them using the townsfolk as hostages?"

His concern for the civilians clearly pleased the German. "You are quite right. If that were allowed to happen, the mission would lose its purpose. As I shall need all my men with me, I intend using a detachment of Italian partisans who have been thirsting for a major action for some months now. Under the overall command of Jean Pierre, they will attack the outposts and the Black Shirt garrison in Valderosa the moment they hear firing on the hilltop. They must not attack before or they will alert the battery. For the same reason you must take great care that no shots are fired when you overcome the outpost."

"But what if things go wrong—if you fail to take the battery? Or if they catch on to your scheme before you reach it? They'll have you, the partisans and the rest of us at their mercy."

The German shrugged. "The partisans know the risks. And we shall have our jeeps hidden nearby in the hope we can reach them. But I am not contemplating failure, Beccione. It must not happen."

In Beccione's earlier state of grief he had failed to notice the excitement behind the German's disciplined exterior. Now it seemed suddenly to crackle in the air like a static charge. "This is the big one for you, isn't it? The perfect set-up."

A shield appeared to fall over Kessler's eyes. "What does that mean?"

"This town is another San Pietro. Only this time you've got a chance to save it. Isn't that right?"

The German rose and went to the window before answering him. "Yes, I suppose it is. But is that a bad thing?"

"As far as you're concerned it's great. It's your reason for being out in these mountains. But what about your men? You make it sound simple but in fact it's as dangerous as hell. That battery could slaughter every man jack of you if they get suspicious. Your men aren't fools—they'll figure it out."

Kessler turned. "What is your point?"

"My point is that this is by far the most dangerous job you've ever given them. It could be their last. And yet there's nothing in it for them. So why should they go?"

The German appeared to relax. "Isn't there? Are you sure of that?"

Beccione believed he understood. "Unless you're thinking

about the treasure in the cathedral. If that's your bait, forget it. It's all been hidden away for the duration."

"But hidden where, Beccione?"

The American gave a start. "Not up the hill?"

"Where else? The caves provide excellent hiding places. My men will have the time of their lives searching them."

Beccione eyed the German suspiciously. "How did you find this out?"

Kessler's sudden curtness dampened his curiosity. "I have my informants, as you well know. Now you had better go and change. As I told Magda, I am holding a briefing at 11.00 hours."

"You're not thinking of leaving then, are you?"

The German frowned. "I wish we could. Every minute might be important. But we must hide all signs of our presence here before we leave. That will take time."

"You sound as if we're not coming back."

"The German front line is crumbling fast and I shall need all my men with me. If the Allies should occupy La Capella during our absence we must be sure the people here do not suffer for giving us hospitality."

"So when do you hope to get away?"

"My target is tomorrow night."

Beccione gave a start. "That means we'll only get there a day before the armies are due."

"Yes. But it should be enough." Kessler walked forward and picked up his telephone. "You must excuse me now. Thank you again for all you have done."

Beccione shrugged and made for the door. As he reached it, Kessler put his hand over the mouthpiece and glanced up. "I am sorry about your friend. He was a good man."

Nodding, Beccione walked out into the corridor where Magda was waiting. "What's happening?" she asked as he led her away. "Why did he want all that information about the battery?"

With the entire contingent to be briefed on the mission shortly, he could see no point in not telling her. When he finished she looked puzzled. "But why is he so interested in that town?"

For an instant all his old distrust of her was back. "Don't people and kids mean anything to you?" Then, as he remembered her conduct the previous night, his tone softened. "You saw the town. Isn't it worth saving?"

"Of course it is. But you say he's committing his entire

company. If the Germans or the Allies arrive before we evacuate, we could all be captured."

Beccione shook his head. "No. He'll get us out long before that." He was paying only partial attention to her questions; with the rest of his mind he was gazing through a door he had been hammering on since Rosenberg's death and which had just suddenly swung open. As they came out on the piazza, he turned to her. "There's something I have to know. How did you and I get out of that ambush alive? They had automatic guns zeroed in on us and they got Colenzo and Rocky before they could spit. Yet you and I got out without a scratch."

She stared at him. "Are you saying they weren't firing at us? That's ridiculous. They had you pinned down. That was why I came back for you."

"I'm not saying they weren't firing at me, baby. Only that they took it easy when you were around."

She halted, her mud-stained face showing disbelief. "That's absurd. Why would Germans want to spare me? They wouldn't even know I was a woman."

"Always assuming it was a German or Italian outpost."

She gave a violent start. "You don't think it was? But that's not possible."

He walked on a few paces before he turned to her again. "Isn't it, baby? You think about it again because it's the only thing that makes any sense."

41

The horse pulled the cart up the narrow road that climbed the shallow side of the hill. It had five occupants, four men and a girl. The sun was overhead and the horse's plodding feet were stirring up tiny clouds of dust.

A hundred yards ahead two structures of barbed wire blocked the way. Beyond it the road could be seen for another fifty yards, then trees closed around it. The lower slopes of the hill had been cleared for vineyards, but the less negotiable upper reaches had been left with their natural covering of spruce, birch and pine.

Beccione, the driver of the cart, was taking in the details of the road block. On one side a machine gun covered the road beneath a makeshift sun awning. On the opposite side was an open-sided command post that the American knew would be linked by telephone to the battery above. Behind the barbed wire three men wearing the black uniforms of the Fascist militia were chatting to one another as they watched the slow progress of the cart. Nudging Magda who was sitting beside him, Beccione addressed the men in the rear without turning his head. "Those trees must hide 'em from the battery. I think we're going to be O.K."

The men were Etienne, Razzoni and another Italian called Luigi. The Frenchman gave his street-Arab grin. "What if the Boche have thought of that and put a sentry lower down the hill?"

Beccione scowled. "Then in a minute or two you could be moving your ass down this hill with twenty plus 88s trying to blow it off you. I hope you can run fast."

Etienne chuckled. "I used to outrun police cars, *mon ami.* So what are Boche 88s to me?"

Expecting a laugh from the other two men, Beccione turned his head when it did not come. "You're supposed to be half-drunk, you bastards. So relax and show it."

The cart was now four hundred feet above the valley. Valderosa below was a conical cluster of pantiled roofs, trees and campaniles; the fields and vineyards that sustained the town reached out on either side to the flanking mountains. A line of stunted trees followed the dry course of the river to the south. The entrances to both the north and south valleys were clearly visible. Beccione, his eye fixed on the northern entrance, could see no sign of Kessler's column. He glanced at his watch and then at Magda. "I hope to Christ he hasn't been held up."

Ahead, one of the Black Shirts had hoisted his rifle to his shoulder and was walking around the road block. A second man, cigarette dangling from his mouth, moved leisurely to the machine gun and sat beside it. The third man, a corporal, yawned and supported himself against the command post.

Alongside Beccione, Magda began humming a popular song. The foremost Black Shirt turned and said something to the corporal, who laughed. All three Italians were eyeing the girl. As the cart came within fifteen yards of the road block, the first sentry held up his hand. "*Ferma!*"

Beccione reined back the horse. The Black Shirt, a big sallow man whose breath smelled of garlic, drew near him. His accent was of the Marche. "What are you doing here?"

Beccione jerked a thumb over his shoulder. "The commandant asked for wine this morning. We're bringing it up to him."

The man's eyes moved from him to the three outlaws in the back who were grinning and passing a bottle of wine. "I haven't seen any of you before."

"We're from Magliano," Beccione explained. "We brought a consignment of wine in this morning and when we heard the commandant wanted some, we thought we'd deliver it ourselves.'" He winked at the sentry. "Why give middle men the profit?"

The Italian peered over the side of the cart at the crates of bottles stacked inside. "What's wrong with the local wine?"

"Ours has more body. You want to buy a few bottles?"

Ignoring Beccione, the Black Shirt walked to the other side of the cart and stared up at Magda. "You're the girl who came up here a couple of days ago, aren't you?"

Magda, who had lit a cigarette, blew smoke down at him. "That's right. You asked me for a date."

The man grinned. "Have you changed your mind?"

"Not yet. Ask me when you're an officer."

There was a loud guffaw from behind the road block. The sentry scowled. "You're one of those, are you? Officers' pets."

The girl blew smoke down at him again. "No, I'm the commandant's pet. Do you want me to tell him you've been rude to me?"

The sentry's face darkened and the girl carefully changed her tone. With a laugh and a flash of tanned legs, she reached out to the man. "Help me down, soldier."

The Italian sullenly obeyed, but his expression brightened when Magda pressed against him a moment. As she was taking two bottles of wine from the cart, two distant but heavy explosions rumbled from the southern side of the valley. Magda and Beccione exchanged a glance, and the sentry swung around to his two colleagues. "What the hell was that?"

The corporal ran into his command post and grabbed the field telephone. Cursing inwardly, Beccione signaled Magda with his eye. Still carrying the two bottles of wine, the girl began edging towards him. If the partisans had been careless and given the game away, their only hope was to shoot the sentries and then try to find cover among the trees.

With Etienne and his comrades crouched tensely in the back of the cart and everyone else gazing at the corporal, the scene froze into a tableau. The corporal waited for a reply from the battery. An endless minute passed before it came. Relaxing, the corporal replaced the receiver and rejoined his machine gunner behind the barbed wire. "It's nothing. Our outpost over there's been in touch with the battery. It was only a couple of mines exploding down the road. They think goats or deer must have set them off."

As cool as if nothing had happened, Magda turned towards the first sentry and offered him a bottle of wine. "A consolation prize, soldier. Until you are an officer."

Laughter came again from the road block. Forced to grin, the sentry took the bottle from her. The girl then walked towards the other two men, her hips swaying provocatively. Pausing opposite them she glanced at the single bottle in her hand. "Bring me another one, Mario," she called back to Beccione.

Beccione jumped down with a third bottle, winked at Etienne and approached the girl. With a laugh she threw the first bottle over the barbed wire to the corporal. As the man caught it, she tossed the second bottle at the machine gunner. It was a high throw that forced the man to step backwards to catch it. When he recovered his balance he was staring down the barrel of an automatic pistol that Beccione pointed at him.

At the same moment the outlaws had snatched Sten guns from beneath the crates of bottles and were covering the other two startled Italians. Etienne leapt to the road and pushed the first sentry towards his colleagues. "There's only one problem now, Joe. Whose uniform do I wear?"

Relieved that the incident had passed off without a shot being fired, Beccione grinned back at him. "That's the price you pay for being a short ass, Frenchy."

The rebels drove the Italians into the trees, stripped, bound and gagged them. Then, dressed in the Fascist uniforms, they returned to the road block where Beccione and Magda were waiting for them. Beccione pointed to a heavy dust cloud rising from the northern valley entrance. "Kessler and company. Right on time. Don't waste a second once you get his all-clear. You might get other Fascists using this road before Jean Pierre's had time to round them all up. So go straight up and join Kessler."

Turning the cart, he and Magda started back towards the

town. Both were conscious of the one flaw in the operation: that German observers above might question where the other three civilians had gone. An earlier suggestion that the three sentries be forced into their clothes and made to ride back to town had been discarded: it was felt that under binocular surveillance the chance of the switch being noticed was too great. Instead it was hoped that if the Germans missed the civilians at all, they would assume they were being interrogated by the sentries.

By this time Kessler's convoy could be clearly seen streaming across the floor of the valley. Knowing it would shortly leave the main road and branch off towards the hill, Beccione drove the cart off to the side and halted. He was now in full view of the German battery, so he jumped down and pretended to be giving a wheel hub his attention.

The leading vehicle, Kessler's automobile, reached the cart two minutes later. Nickolai was driving; Roberts sat next to him. Kessler, as befitted the commanding officer of the unit, was sharing the rear seat with Schumann. Every inch a Wehrmacht officer, Kessler did not even glance at the cart as he passed by. Magda, however, turned and blew the officers a kiss, a signal the outpost had been taken.

Six large transports rumbled past after the automobile. Kessler was using almost every man in his organization. Crouched beside the cart wheel, Beccione was half-blinded by dust but here and there he caught sight of the men's faces. All shared one common element: tension. There was not a man among them who was unaware that if the Germans on the hill top turned suspicious, their guns could blow them and their transports to fragments. Their tension showed in the cheers they gave Magda as she turned and blew her kisses at them. The sound did not alarm Beccione: he felt certain the Germans would accept it as an entirely natural reaction.

When the last transport had passed he climbed back into the cart. "So far so good. Keep your head down and let's go and see what Jean Pierre is doing."

With her back to him, Magda was watching the convoy climbing the hill. Her voice expressed her change of mood. "I've never known Kessler to use all his men like this. He's taking a terrible risk."

Beccione shook the reins and the cart eased back on to the road. "You heard him at the briefing. This is the big one. Those cathedral treasures must be worth millions."

There was scorn in her voice. "Do you think I'm that stu-

pid? Kessler would never risk his entire organization just for
money. That is his secondary reason. He is really here to save
the town."

He glanced at her. "So what? Is that so bad?"

"I didn't say it was. But it seems to matter as much to you
as to him. Is that girl involved in some way?"

He was listening for telltale sounds from the hill top that
could bring a rain of shells down on them. A spasm of anger
made him turn towards her. "You pick one hell of a time to
ask about her, don't you? If you must know, I was drunk and
that girl and kid reminded me of people I knew in Castelmonte. That's it. Period."

"A girl you were in love with," she insisted. "Why don't
you admit it."

He cursed. "O.K., a girl I was in love with. So what? It's
over. I blew it."

"What happened?"

He glanced back at the hill. The convoy had disappeared
among the trees, making it impossible to know whether it was
still climbing the hill or had reached the German sentries.
With tension sharpening every nerve end, he discovered it
was a relief to be absorbed in talk. When he finished his story
a minute later she raised her eyebrows in disbelief. "She left
you because of that?"

"That? I'd murdered McCall, an innocent man."

"Innocent? After what he'd done to you in the stockade?
He was a sadist."

"That was something else. It wasn't his fault he killed Stephano."

"What had blame or right or wrong to do with it? You
loved the boy? That was your reason."

"The reason to shoot a defenseless man?"

Her voice turned suddenly fierce. "Yes. Because love leaves
hate when love is destroyed." An unexpected image of
Kessler flashed into Beccione's mind as the girl continued.
"The girl's mother understood this. But the girl herself—
she was nothing but a shallow fool. She didn't love you. She
loved the thought of marriage and a life in America. When
both these chances were lost, she deserted you."

He cursed. "What the hell do you know about her?"

"You have just told me everything there is to know. Now
I will tell you something. It wasn't the girl you loved. It was
the boy."

He gave a violent start, then recovered himself. "How do you work that out?"

"Because if you had loved her you would have moved heaven and earth to see her again."

His frown deepened. "How could I have done that?"

"You would have found a way. You are that kind of a man."

"You think you know me pretty well, don't you?" he sneered.

"Until two days ago I didn't know you at all. I thought you were callous and incapable of love. Now I know differently."

He stared at her, swore again, then flicked the reins aggressively. The cart was passing through a cluster of attractive cottages. Ahead was a small park and beyond it the old walls of the town. As the horse sensed home and began quickening its stride, the sudden rattle of automatic fire from the hill made Beccione haul back on the reins. "It's started," he muttered. "Now keep your fingers crossed."

Like myriad echoes, automatic fire started up from a dozen different points as the couple listened. With the Black Shirts hearing the firing as well, Jean Pierre and his partisans were being compelled to launch their attack regardless of the outcome of the hilltop battle. As mortar shells began exploding in the fields, dogs barked and startled women ran out of their cottages. An old woman screamed *"Tedeschi!"* and crossed herself. Magda was gripping Beccione's arm so tightly that her hand appeared bloodless.

Within minutes the firing had closed around the town, suggesting that the Black Shirts had already broken under the surprise attack. Yet both Beccione and Magda knew that unless Kessler captured the battery the partisans' success would be short-lived.

The rifle and automatic fire from the hilltop had almost ceased by this time, but there was no way of knowing its significance. Then a green Very light soared into the bright sky. As a second one followed it, Beccione's arm tightened around the girl. "He's done it," he said hoarsely. "My God, he's done it."

Seeing the Very lights, the exultant partisans renewed their efforts. Burst after burst of firing came from the southern boundary of the town; mixed with the din were the sounds of racing engines and bloodthirsty shouts and cheers. Beccione turned to Magda. "The Black Shirts must have gotten word that the battery's fallen and collapsed. By the sound of it the partisans are already in the town."

"Shouldn't we go and help them?" she asked as he reached into his shirt pocket.

He lit a cigarette for her. "Kessler said the partisans were thirsting for action. Let them have their fun and take the *palazzo comunale* first."

The firing began to die down. It ceased altogether a minute later, but the shouting continued unabated. It was reinforced by cheering that grew louder and louder as if the entire town were going wild with joy. As the couple listened, there was the snarl of engines overhead: four RAF fighter-bombers were crossing the valley. As aggressive as hunting hounds, they leapt over the northern mountains and disappeared. Beccione shrugged at Magda's questioning glance. "Search me. It's all happening. Let's go and see what gives in town."

They entered the central piazza on foot. It was a great tossing sea of color and excitement. Men and women were cheering, crying and kissing their neighbors in hysterical abandon. The heroes were the partisans, picturesque figures wearing the red scarves of the Garabaldi Brigade and heavily armed with captured German weapons. They were intermingling with the crowd and unashamedly enjoying the adulation the townsfolk were pouring on them. Magda showed her contempt as she and Beccione pushed their way to the *palazzo comunale*. "They defeat a couple of hundred Black Shirts and swagger about as if they have won the War."

Beccione grinned as a plump girl hurled herself at a tiny partisan and buried him in mounds of palpitating flesh. "Don't be like that. They've done a good job. According to Kessler, this outfit hasn't been formed that long."

They found Jean Pierre on the steps of the *palazzo comunale* alongside a tubby, red-scarved Italian with a florid complexion and a fierce moustache. The Frenchman introduced him as *Comandante* Brosio, the leader of the partisans. Gallantly kissing Magda's hand, the Italian proceeded to plant kisses on Beccione's cheeks before addressing the two in English. "This is a great day for us, my friends. Valderosa belongs to her people again. And the enemy's day of defeat grows near."

At the far side of the piazza the crowd was swaying like a field of corn as a truck pushed its way through. It was manned by two partisans who gestured excitedly at Brosio. The Italian excused himself and ran down the steps towards

them. Seeing his expression as the partisans addressed him
and the way the crowd around the truck had gone quiet, Jean
Pierre turned to Beccione. "See what the trouble is, will
you?"

Beccione returned a minute later. Jean Pierre cursed and
Magda showed distress at the news he brought them. "Are
they sure?" the Frenchman muttered.

"They seem to be. They've sent some guys to get them and
there's a truck standing by. It might take some time because
of the minefields."

Jean Pierre nodded. "It's a hell of a thing but I suppose
there's nothing we can do."

"What's the situation with the Black Shirts?" Beccione
asked.

The Frenchman grinned. "What's left of 'em are in the
cells. Brosio's bloodthirsty bastards wanted to lynch 'em but I
said Kessler wouldn't like that."

"What makes you so sure? Since when has Kessler been
gentle with Fascists?"

Jean Pierre gave the American a scowl, then changed the
subject. "Brosio can take care of things down here now. Let's
get up to the battery and see how things are shaping up."

42

The large hut stood in a clearing on the eastern sector of the
hilltop. From the widely-scattered monks cells, tracks ran
through the woods towards it as if it were the center of a spider's web. At sunset Kessler's men began converging along
these tracks. Still wearing their German uniforms, sweat-
stained, dirty and tired, some were looking puzzled and others disgruntled.

The hut, built of rough unsized stone with moss and lichen
filling every crevice, looked strong enough to stand a siege.
Centuries ago, to insulate it against extremes of temperature,
its roof had been piled with earth. Now this earthen covering
had become a solid thatch of vegetation. Small apertures in
each wall served as windows. It had a single doorway with a
lintel so low a man had to duck his head to enter.

Until that afternoon it had been used as the command post for the German battery. Now the Germans, with one exception, were imprisoned in one of the many caves that honeycombed the hill. Three tables stood on the bare flagstones. A large German radio stood on one. A second was littered with field telephones. A pressure lamp was on the third, its bright light pushing back the evening shadows. Empty ammunition boxes served as chairs. Nickolai, with a Sten gun lying across his knees, was seated on one; a sullen-looking young German officer was seated on a second close by him. Usually the most amiable of men, the Russian's expression boded ill for the German if he moved as much as an eyelid without permission.

Five other men, all Kessler's lieutenants, shared the hut: Roberts, Johnson, Etienne, Williams and Beccione. Except for Beccione, all were still wearing their German uniforms. Johnson and Beccione were smoking cigarettes, Roberts was puffing thoughtfully on his pipe.

The sound of a jeep made them glance at the entrance. Half a minute later Schumann ducked inside. "Where's Franz?"

Roberts removed his pipe from his mouth. "He's gone off with Jean Pierre and Tito to check on the sentry posts. What's your problem?"

The German dropped on one of the ammunition boxes. "I suppose he has notified Brigadier Hutchinson that we have taken the hill?"

The Englishman's voice was dry. "It was the first thing we did. If you hadn't been so busy looking for that cathedral gold you'd have heard him."

He received a sharp look from the German. "What did Hutchinson say?"

"It looks as if the Allies have got their finger out since their recce planes confirmed our reports. They've rushed up troops and armor and their fighter-bombers are harassing the Jerry main force. As that kind of a clobbering must slow them down, it now seems certain the Allies will get here first."

Schumann opened his mouth as if to speak, then turned instead and motioned towards the young German officer. Beccione wondered what he was keeping back. "Why is he here?"

Roberts nodded at the array of telephone equipment. "He's

their signals officer and as we haven't been able to sort out how this lot works, we're making him earn his keep."

Voices could be heard outside as men began congregating in the clearing. Schumann glanced at one of the open windows. "Why has Kessler told everyone to assemble here?"

Roberts shrugged. "My guess is he's going to organize them into search parties."

"He hasn't told you his reason?" When Roberts shook his head, the German leaned forward. "Don't you think he is acting very strangely? He asks us to carry out the largest and most dangerous operation in our history and yet he appears to have no precise knowledge where the treasure is hidden. Don't you find it out of character?"

"Perhaps he couldn't find out," Williams said.

"Perhaps not, but then why did he not tell us so at the briefing? And why did he not organize search parties the moment we occupied the hilltop? Why has he wasted over three precious hours. Why hasn't he been trying to find the treasure himself?"

Seeing the glances men gave one another, Beccione knew others had shared the same thoughts. He broke in abruptly. "What are you getting at, Schumann? That he lied to us and the treasure isn't on the hill?"

"No, the treasure might well be here. But because Kessler does not appear to have found out its exact location, one wonders if for once he has allowed his heart to rule his head."

All eyes were now on the German. "What does that mean?" Beccione asked.

Schumann shrugged. "As he is wasting so much time, which is not his way, could he be intending to stay on the hill as long as possible to make certain the Allies occupy it?"

There was a loud murmur. Johnson looked puzzled. "Why would he need to do that? With the Black Shirts taken care of, it's here for the Allies anyway."

"Unless the German main force wins the race," Schumann reminded him.

"How can they do that? You've just heard Roberts say the Air Force is pounding hell out of them. All the Allies have to do is move their butts and they're here."

Once again Beccione imagined he saw something move behind the German's eyes. "Odd things can happen in war, Johnson. And remember Kessler is a German. He knows full well it is not the habit of German soldiers to give up easily once they've been given an objective."

"O.K. supposing that happened. What would be the point of Kessler keeping us here? All we'd do is end up in a Kraut bag instead of an Allied one."

Schumann shrugged again. "When anyone is as fanatical about the welfare of civilians as Kessler, one has to look at all possibilities. Particularly when he is acting as much out of character as he is today."

"You're talking bullshit, Schumann. For all you know he might have been making enquiries about the treasure while we've been up here. And now he's called the guys together to give them the score."

The black American's contempt brought a coldness to Schumann's eyes that betrayed the racist in him. "Let's hope you are right. Because my men are growing more restive by the moment."

Kessler arrived when the sun was almost down on the rim of the distant mountains. Shining red through the trees, it fringed with fire the black silhouette of Kessler's figure as he pulled up his jeep before the curious assembly. The German had a few words with Toschack, who nodded emphatically and then pushed his way through the murmuring men. He disappeared inside the command post. "Kessler's here, you guys. He wants you to join him outside. Nickolai has to stay here and look after the German."

Schumann passed the order on to Nickolai in German and the Russian sank back on his seat. The others followed Toschack outside. Magda, waiting impatiently near the entrance, caught Beccione's arm. "Kessler looks very serious. What is happening?"

Beccione shook his head. "I can't even guess."

He could see no sign of Jean Pierre as Kessler motioned his lieutenants into a line before his jeep. When Magda followed Beccione, the German offered no objection. Standing on the driver's seat, Kessler faced the sea of curious and excited faces.

"Good evening, gentlemen. You will be wondering why I have ordered you to break off your search and join me here. The answer is I have received news of the utmost importance that concerns you all."

There was a murmur of expectation through the packed

crowd. "Some of the things you are going to hear will puzzle you. However I am going to ask that you hold back your questions until I have finished. Then I shall do my best to explain everything."

Curious men pressed forward to listen. Schumann, standing close to Beccione, threw a glance of triumph at Roberts. Puzzled, the American tried to read Kessler's expression but the German presented only a tall silhouette against the setting sun.

"My first news for you is that the Germans have not turned back as I had hoped, even though they know we have captured the battery. This you might already have guessed from the continued Allied air activity. As this is having some effect on the Germans, their main force is not now expected to reach the valley before noon tomorrow.

"I am afraid this delay in the Germans' plans does not help the Allies, however. Although they responded quickly once they had confirmed the German counteroffensive by rushing up troops and armor, they have discovered their route here is more heavily mined than was expected. As a result, they no longer believe they can be here in strength before the late afternoon or early evening. Because it is imperative for the safety of the town that they occupy it first, I suggested they send forward on forest tracks an advance company of artillerymen who could take over this battery and hold back the Germans until the minefields are cleared and their main force can break through."

Men could be heard translating his words. Magda's low voice expressed their general puzzlement as she leaned towards Beccione. "What does he mean—he suggested to them? How could he do that?"

Beccione motioned her to keep quiet. Kessler continued. "This idea has not proved practical. The Allied task force does not have enough skilled men to operate German artillery. Instead they propose sending forward a small, mobile force of infantry. By bringing no armor with them, these men can also use forest tracks and so be the first in Valderosa. However, as they have to be briefed and the woods are vast, it is felt they cannot safely leave until daybreak."

Men were beginning to show impatience as well as curiosity. Confident he knew the reason, Schumann held up a hand. "What time are these men expected here?"

"Barring mishaps, the present estimate is 10.00 hours."

"So if we leave an hour before they arrive, as we must for safety, we have little more than twelve hours left?"

"That is correct."

Schumann turned towards the restless crowd. "Then I think the men are puzzled why we are now wasting so much time. Like all of them, I believed our reward for capturing this battery and allowing the Allies to take it over was a share in the cathedral treasures you assured us were buried here. As you felt certain the town would be destroyed otherwise, it seemed a reasonable reward for saving hundreds and perhaps thousands of lives. Yet now that we hold the hill, you seem totally uninterested in the treasure."

The loud shouts of agreement told Schumann he had gauged exactly the mood of the rebels. Beccione wished he could see Kessler's expression but the red sun behind the German was still too dazzling. The shouts died down as Kessler's voice turned cold. "Did you not hear what I said earlier, Captain Schumann? I asked that questions should be withheld until I had finished my address."

"I heard what you said but we have a right to know what you are doing about the treasure. That is why my men are here. Why haven't you made enquiries about where it is hidden?"

The shouts that ensued were even louder and more impatient than before. As Roberts turned in an effort to control the men, Kessler's contempt suddenly slashed out like a razor. "What do you all put first, human life or money? Because that is the choice that is facing you at this moment."

The shouts died away as if a switch had been thrown. Icy with challenge, Kessler stared down at Schumann, then at the hushed rebels. "All along it has been my intention to persuade the mayor and the bishops to reward you for the risks you have taken. It is still my intention when the opportunity presents itself. But what is happening at this moment reduces reward into insignificance."

A total silence had now fallen. Men at the back of the crowd were pushing forward in an attempt to hear the German more clearly. "Many of you may think that, because the Allies are making certain they will win the race by sending ahead this small force, the town will be saved. Nothing is further from the truth. With the Germans still pressing forward in spite of the loss of this battery and in spite of the Allied air attacks, it is obvious Valderosa is a vital part of their counteroffensive strategy. Then is it likely they will be deterred by a couple of Allied battalions? They will throw their entire might on the town and it will *still* be annihilated."

"Do the Allies realize this?" Roberts asked.

For the first time Kessler allowed his hatred of all things military to enter his voice. "Of course they do. I have pleaded with them. But what is one small mountain town to soldiers? To them it represents a strongpoint and nothing more. If it can be held until the main Allied force arrives, the operation will be considered a success even if every building and every vineyard is laid to waste."

A twangy Australian voice broke in. "Couldn't the townsfolk evacuate until it's over, skipper?"

The tall impassioned man on the jeep swung a contemptuous arm east and west. "Evacuate to where? Who around here can feed a couple of thousand people? Old women and children will suffer and many will die. And what will those who survive return to? How will they live without homes and food?"

Schumann's handsome face wore a long-held suspicion. "So what are you proposing we do?"

A born orator, Kessler waited until every sound had died. "I am proposing that we stand here and fight until the main Allied force arrives. Only in that way am I confident we can save the town."

The hush that followed his words was like a missed heart beat. Then there came an outcry that sent nesting birds clattering into the evening sky. Men shouted their astonishment, their alarm or their contempt according to their characters and temperaments. Hoots, whistles, catcalls and stamping feet added to the din and sense of outrage.

The consternation was as great among Kessler's lieutenants. Schumann was shouting something at Roberts; Johnson was arguing furiously with Williams. Magda looked as if she could not believe her ears. "He can't mean it! He can't!"

Beccione was eyeing the tall black figure in fascination. "He means it all right. All the way to hell and back."

"Then his mind has gone. He's mad."

Kessler made no attempt to quell the outcry. He waited until it had exhausted itself before holding up his hand. "Needless to say, in case one side or the other should decide the game is not worth playing, both have been informed of my decision."

In the outrage of his earlier declaration, his disclosure of

the links he maintained with the two armies went almost unnoticed. Johnson expressed the astonishment of all. "Then
you're suggesting we open fire on the Allies as well as the
Germans?"

"Yes. There is no other way. If we allowed the Allies to
enter the town with such a small force, the Germans would
turn artillery on them no matter what we did and the town
would still be destroyed."

Schumann's laugh was full of derision. "In other words,
you want us to draw everyone's fire?"

Kessler's voice did not falter. "For a few hours, yes. But
only until the Allied main force arrives."

Schumann turned towards the aghast rebels. "In case you
did not hear that I will repeat it. We are expected to fight
two armies. One hundred of us. But not for long. Only for a
few hours."

The younger German's sarcasm brought another massive
outburst of catcalls and whistling. The ground shook under
the stamping of feet. Kessler called for silence three times
and each time he was rejected. When he turned and climbed
into the rear of the jeep Beccione believed he was admitting
defeat and about to withdraw. Instead he spun around and in
a single movement uncoupled the .50 Browning and swung it
on the whistling men. In the sudden silence that fell, the click
of the breech block could be heard right across the clearing.
Kessler's threat provided an added chill as he lowered the
machine gun and aimed it at Schumann's chest. "If you inter-
rupt me once more, Captain Schumann, I shall kill you." The
black gun barrel paused a moment on the stiffened German,
then lifted again and traversed the entire company. "Just as I
shall kill any other man who has not the courtesy to hear me
out."

A nervous cough was the only reply. Although Kessler now
rose to his full height, the Browning remained pointed at the
hushed men.

"You are all behaving like hysterical women. Have you
forgotten why the Germans sited the battery on this hill? Its
specific purpose was to hold back an Allied force at least as
large as the one the Germans are sending. And yet it was
manned by a company of artillerymen hardly more numerous
than yourselves." The German threw his scorn like acid into
the faces of the rebels. "Your hysteria can only mean you believe yourselves inferior in courage and skill to those men.

You, who I have often heard claiming to be the best fighting men in the war."

Furious at this unexpected counter to his revolt, Schumann opened his mouth to protest but the Browning lowered again and frustrated him.

"In your hysteria you have given yourselves no time to consider the strength of this position. This hill might dominate the southern valley, but it dominates the northern one even more. Moreover, the northern valley has a narrower exit. Now consider the crushing firepower the Germans have crammed up here. Unless our gunnery fell far below its normal standards, we could destroy every vehicle that tried to break out. The same applies to infantrymen. The valley floor on either side offers them no cover except for the river course to the south. And even if a few survivors were to reach the hill, consider its near impregnability with its steep north and south faces."

From their appearance, some men were almost bursting blood vessels in their desire to protest and demonstrate, but the menace of the machine gun kept them silent. At the far side of the clearing a peasant truck had driven in and halted but only Kessler from his vantage point had noticed it. The rest of the assembly were too occupied with his words and the restraint he was imposing on them.

"I know you will be thinking that our firepower will be weakened by having to fight on two fronts. This will not be the case. Expecting a long siege, the Germans have provided the battery with a massive surplus of guns and ammunition. If you are wondering how we can redistribute the guns, the answer is we move them in the same way the Germans brought them here. All are on mobile carriages: we simply fold back the outriggers and attach them to the SdKfz's the Germans have left us. If the Allies launch any air attacks, again we do what the Germans have done: wherever possible we site the guns in the mouths of caves. Those same caves will give us personal protection, as will the monks' cells which are very strongly built. In addition there is the powerful 20mm shield which is an integral part of the gun battery. If you add to all that the dense woods that will offer excellent camouflage, you will realize that this is an ideal place to defend."

Schumann, growing more and more incensed, held up a hand. "Have you finished yet?"

"No, Captain Schumann, I have not. You and the rest of

my lieutenants can interview me when this meeting is over. Until then you will keep silent." The tall German glanced back at the muttering men. "However, I will allow the others of you a few questions. Only keep them brief because we have much work to do tonight."

Believing the restraint lifted, men began shouting their protests again. When the machine gun silenced them, a couple of dozen hands shot up. Kessler chose one on the third row. "Yes, Razzoni."

"What about La Capella, Padrone?"

"As you know perfectly well, Razzoni, I have taken care of La Capella. If the Allies should enter it during our absence, no trace of us will be found." The German pointed at another raised hand. "Yes. What is your question?"

The speaker had a strong German accent. "If we were to stay, how would we get away after the Allies have occupied the town?"

Kessler nodded. "I have a plan for that which I believe has an excellent chance of success. Remember, if we drive back the Germans we shall have saved the Allies many lives." Before the man could question him again, Kessler pointed at another raised hand. "Yes, Rossi."

The baby-faced Italian spoke in his own language. Kessler dryly translated the question. "Rossi asks why we should fight for this small town at all. I find it an odd question coming from an Italian, but no matter. The answer is very simple. It is in mortal danger and we are in a position to save it."

The renewed bedlam of shouts and catcalls died as once again the machine gun traversed the assembly. "Do you have a question, Toschack?"

"Yeah, I have, skipper. Do you want it straight?"

"Yes. Only make it brief."

"Aren't you askin' too much of us? As things are, if we're not killed or captured, we've a chance of a fresh start somewhere after the war because nobody knows we've joined your outfit. But if your plan for our escape fails, we're as good as dead. There's another thing. Some of us don't mind helping these peasants—they're good people. But if we go for bust now, that's the end of it for them as well as us. Do you think one small town's worth that?"

Kessler waited until the sullen murmurs of agreement died away. "Yes, I do. And I will explain why. If the Allies and the Germans are allowed to fight over this town, it will become another San Pietro. Children will wander among its ruins maimed, blinded or with their minds destroyed by the horrors they have witnessed. Indeed the slaughter of the innocents has already begun." As puzzled men stared at one another, Kessler waved the truck forward. "Let me show you an example of what will happen tomorrow unless we are men enough to prevent it. You all heard those two landmines exploding this afternoon. Now you will see the consequences."

The crowd parted and Jean Pierre drove the old truck into its midst and halted. A priest and four middle-aged Italians wearing black were seated beside two small pine coffins. As men jostled to look, Kessler's voice rose again. "Because so much is at stake, these two bereaved families have agreed to exhibit their loss to you. Those coffins contain the remains of two small boys whose only crime was to miss school today and to play where they have played so often before, in the entrance of the southern valley. Only this time the men of war had preceded them and sown their seeds of death."

The mood of the rebels had changed dramatically by the time they were all back in their places. Among the low fierce arguments that were heard, a lone voice suddenly cried out: "But why us, Padrone? Why us?"

The torment in the cry released all the complex emotions that boiled inside the tall German. His passion seemed to make the still evening air tremble. "Why? Now I will tell you all why. You must save this town because the protection of civilians is the very basis of your existence. It is the reason I created you and the reason you cannot betray yourselves now."

In the slanting sunlight the faces of the rebels were a study in amazement. Someone shouted "He's crazy" and half a dozen other men laughed. But the majority stood transfixed as the German's impassioned voice held and dominated them.

"Everything I am telling you is true, as my lieutenants will affirm. Every move we have made has had its purpose. When you attacked convoys, you helped to weaken battles that were bringing suffering and death to civilians. When you brought back booty, the money it raised helped to feed war victims. When you stole explosives, you were helping to bring the war to a swifter conclusion. You have thought yourselves the criminals and murderers of this war but you have been wrong. The criminals are the soldiers who have left nothing but misery in their wake. You have been the guardians of the people, the defenders of civilization, the crusaders in a war against war. So in God's name how can you betray yourselves on this hilltop tonight?"

The lone voice sounded again in the astonished hush that followed. "But why haven't you told us this before, Padrone?"

"How could I tell you before? Look at the way some of you are behaving now. Men behave according to their belief in themselves: the armies had taken from you all your self-respect. If I had spoken to you before I would have lost you. But now, standing alongside the maimed bodies of those children, I believe you are seeing the vision that I saw when I formed this unit."

When no answer came, the German's tone changed. With the sun almost down, Beccione could see the glitter in his black eyes.

"And there is far more at stake than even this town, my friends. Until now our existence has been kept a secret by all countries because they fear its effect on a world weary of war. But if you stand fast tomorrow, they cannot hide the truth any longer. Knowing the importance of Valderosa, there will be war correspondents accompanying the Allied task force. Think of the story we can give them! A pack of criminals trying to save a town against two armies that must for a time unite against us. Armies which, if they are successful, will then become enemies again and tear the town asunder like wild dogs fighting over a rabbit. Could anything bring to the world more graphically the insanity of war? I tell you, if you are men enough to grasp it, tomorrow you can achieve immortality."

To Beccione, mesmerized by the scene, Kessler's silhouette seemed to be growing taller—an almost supernatural presence whose passion and eloquence was turning dross into gold.

"I believe with all my heart that tomorrow our small band can write a page in history as glorious as anything the world has seen. And who knows the lesson we might teach the world? I truly believe you are the finest and most versatile soldiers of the war. Who then is better qualified to fight against war itself? Now you must make your choice. To use your skills to save the innocents or to crawl away like curs to everlasting shame."

The sigh that escaped from the massed men sounded like wind through tall grass. A man coughed with emotion, another gave a cheer that found an echo at the far side of the assembly. Running like fires through tinder, the cheers suddenly burst into a roar of acclaim that could be heard in Valderosa itself. His voice hoarse, Beccione turned to Magda. "He's done it! My God, he's done it! It's a miracle."

For a long moment Kessler stood staring at the rapturous company. Then he bent forward and motioned Roberts towards him. "Take all my officers back to the command post. Make certain Schumann speaks to no one on the way. I shall be with you shortly."

43

A large moth was fluttering around the pressure lamp as Schumann's athletic figure crossed the floor of the command post. "He has deceived us all. You do realize that?"

Roberts, a few paces ahead of him, dropped down on an ammunition crate beside the radio table. His expression was wry. "I'd say that was a fair comment."

The German's accusing stare moved to the other officers. Nickolai and Tito gazed back impassively. Etienne was looking more excited at the prospects of battle than disturbed by the possibility of deception. The rest were showing varying degrees of disquietude. Schumann turned back to Roberts. "Then how can you agree to stay? You have a wife and children in England. So has Williams. Don't you want to see them again?"

Frowning, Roberts pulled out his pipe and pouch. "What sort of a question is that?"

"A very relevant question. We have all known Kessler has a death wish. But now he is asking the rest of us to share it with him."

Beccione broke in angrily. "Why don't you can it, Schumann? We'll make our own goddamned minds up."

Magda, who had followed the American into the hut, turned to him in concern. "But he's right, Joe. This time Kessler has gone too far?"

"Too far?" Schumann asked. "His hatred of soldiers has become an obsession. His mind has gone."

For a moment no one answered him. Then Roberts, who was packing tobacco into his pipe, raised his head. "I'm not

disagreeing with you altogether, Schumann. Although I've no
cause to like the army, I've never been able to see eighteen-
year-old conscripts as enemies of mankind. The trouble is, I
can see Kessler's point of view as well. Little Johnnie with a
gun obeying orders is just as destructive as Big Brother with a
gun. And so if I have to choose between little Johnnie and
old women and kids—and that's often the situation out
here—then I've no problems with my conscience."

"Haven't we all done the same? Haven't we all appeased
this obsession of his?"

The Englishman struck a match and applied it to his pipe.
"I'm not saying we haven't. But perhaps we've had different
reasons."

"What if we have? Like your little Johnnie and your Big
Brother, the results have been the same. But this time he has
made it impossible for us to go along with him. First he
tricked us into coming here. Now he is demanding we make
a grand gesture to the world by committing suicide."

The shadow of the moth flickered across the faces of the
rebels as they gazed at the German. Johnson voiced their
thoughts. "He's right about the treasure. That must have been
hogwash. And I bet Kessler guessed the Germans would get
here first."

"He didn't guess," Schumann said contemptuously. "He
knew."

Beccione frowned. "How could he know?"

Before the German could answer a sound at the entrance
made everyone turn. As Kessler entered the hut, Schumann
attacked without preamble. "Why did you make fools of us
out there? Why didn't you tell us earlier what you intended
doing?"

Kessler's brusqueness hinted he was in no mood for pen-
itence. "I had no choice. You might have resisted me and it
was imperative the men stayed."

"You are right I would have resisted you. And there are
others here who would have done the same. We have endured
your sentimentality and your obsessions as long as they did
not warp your judgment. But today they have destroyed it."

Kessler's deep-set eyes fixed on the German. "No, Helmut.
You have endured my sentimentality and my obsessions because you have made a handsome profit from them. But everything has its price and today I am presenting the bill."

"By asking us to commit suicide? To hell with your bill.
You have lied from the beginning to the end about this oper-

ation. You said there was treasure here but you have made
no effort to find it. You said the Allies would be here first but
secretly you knew they would not. You have forfeited every
man's loyalty by this deceit."

Johnson's concurrence was clearly painful to him. "I hate
saying it, Kessler, but for once he's right. You've sold us right
down the line."

There was a murmur of agreement from Williams. Kessler
turned to Roberts. "How else could I get you all here?"

"You might have tried trusting us," the Englishman said
quietly.

"You think the men would have come if they had known
the truth?"

"I didn't say the men. I meant us, your officers."

Schumann gave a laugh of triumph. "You see. Even your
most loyal supporters agree with me. And so will the men
when I have spoken to them. They are not going to stay and
fight once they have got their hands on the treasure."

As Kessler started, the German laughed again. "Yes,
Franz, the treasure. Before the meeting I sent Weiss and
Mogelli down to interrogate the priests. The men are hardly
going to spend the night preparing for their deaths once they
know where the treasure is hidden."

Kessler's sharp intake of breath could be heard right across
the hut. "You have dared to do that? If those two use violence—if they lay a hand on anyone—I will have them shot
the moment they return."

Schumann walked towards the entrance, then turned.
"You're a hypocrite, Franz. We must not harm one hair on a
civilian's head, but you can lie to your men and expect them
to die for you. You knew there were three minefields down
that road to hold up the Allies but you still brought us here.
You had planned all along that we should fight for the town.
The men have a right to know this."

With all eyes on the two Germans, no one noticed Beccione give a violent start. As Schumann turned for the entrance again, Kessler snatched a Luger pistol from his holster.
"You are telling the men nothing, Helmut. Stay where you
are!"

For a moment Schumann's old fear of the German made
him hesitate. Then he smiled mockingly. "Are you going to
shoot me, Franz? You forget—I know you too well. You are
incapable of killing a man in cold blood."

"But I'm not, you sonofabitch." The snarl came from Beccione who had snatched up a German carbine. "How did you know there were three minefields along that road?"

Although caught by surprise, Schumann recovered immediately. "As I remember it, Franz told us at our briefing."

Kessler shook his head when Beccione glanced at him. "I had no way of knowing their number. Once I warned the Allies about the Germans' plans I could not send men to investigate because I knew the Allies would have engineers there."

Schumann shrugged. "Then I assumed it. It is a pattern the Germans often use. I have seen it done many times before."

Beccione took a step forward. "You're lying, Schumann. When you heard we were going to Valderosa, you went ahead of us to take a look at the terrain. That was when you found those minefields. You ordered Weiss to give us a route that suited you and then you sat back and waited."

Magda gasped in sudden recognition. "Of course. It was you who laid that ambush."

Kessler motioned Schumann away from the entrance. Lifting an eyebrow, the German obeyed. As he drew nearer Magda, he suddenly pounced like a striking cat. Seizing her around the waist, he swung her in front of him and put the muzzle of his pistol against her temple. "Drop your guns! Drop them and kick them away or I'll kill her. I mean it."

For a moment every man in the hut was paralyzed. Then, as Kessler nodded at them, guns began clattering down to the flagstones.

Beccione was the last to obey. Dragging the girl back towards the entrance, Schumann turned his pistol on the American. "What shall I do, *Liebschen*? Kill him now or leave him for the soldiers tomorrow?"

His taunt was a mistake: it galvanized Magda into retaliation. Letting her knees sag, she forced Schumann momentarily to adjust his grip. As he did, she drove her elbow back into his body with all her strength. Iron-hard as he was, the German only staggered but the girl had gained a second to grab his arm and jerk it over her shoulder. Schumann gave a gasp of pain and dropped the pistol. Before she could kick it away, she received a savage blow to the head.

Beccione, who had been expecting the girl to put up a fight, dived forward the moment she struck Schumann and tried to grab the fallen pistol. But the German was nearer. Snatching it up, he evaded the American's dive and again aimed the pistol at him. Beccione was helpless on the floor: there was nothing he could do to save himself. As two explosions came, deafening in the confines of the hut, Magda gave a cry of despair.

Gun outstretched, Schumann was standing over Beccione as if frozen in triumph. Then suddenly his legs gave way and he crumpled like a man whose bones had melted. Swinging around, Magda saw that Kessler held a smoking pistol in his hand.

Kessler at once slid the pistol into his holster and knelt over the dying German. Blood was oozing from his mouth, and his handsome face was turning ashen. Recognizing Kessler, he tried twice to speak and failed. Then he made a massive effort and his hoarse whisper carried across the hut. "You have not won, Franz. . . . None of you have won. I shall see you all tomorrow."

His head fell back and less then thirty seconds later he was dead. Kessler, although pale, was showing no remorse as he turned to Etienne. "Jean Pierre has gone back to tell the partisans of our decision. Take four men with you, find Jean Pierre and then arrest Weiss and Mogelli. If they have harmed anyone, execute them on the spot. If not, bring them back here to me."

The Frenchman nodded and left the hut, and Kessler turned towards his hushed officers. "We have little more than fourteen hours before the first of the soldiers are due. So there is not a minute to waste. Organize your men into work parties and start moving the guns."

44

That night the hill resembled a volcano to the anxious inhabitants of Valderosa. Headlights ceaselessly probed the sky and powerful lights shone through the trees as the 88mm guns were hitched either to jeeps or German SdKzs and dragged to their new sites. The numerous 20mm cannons were also resituated to give the hill anti-aircraft cover on all sides.

At the same time other rebels were sent down the hill to the entrances of each valley. Their task was to establish markers using conspicuous objects such as large rocks, trees without branches, or piles of petrol cans, all at calculated

ranges from the guns. This would ease the problems of range
finding when enemy vehicles were moving at high speeds.
However, even with bright moonlight to help them, the men
found the task difficult and it was decided to complete it at
daybreak.

While all this intense back-breaking work was in progress,
Kessler and his gunnery specialists were working out the
angle of sight for the north-facing guns. This calculation,
once fed into the 88s, would mean their gunners would only
have to reset the tangent elevation for the differing ranges of
their targets. Unfortunately for Kessler's purposes, there were
no radar-control predictors available—the German controllers
had managed to destroy them before the rebel occupation of
the hill had been completed. This meant his gunners would
have to use more traditional methods.

Meanwhile down in Valderosa fretting women were
watching the intense activity from their gardens or windows
and men were speculating excitedly in bars and taverns. The
partisans were deluged with questions but by this time most
of them were too drunk to care. Convinced by the air activity
that afternoon and now by Kessler's measures that the
Tedeschi were still advancing, a deputation of townsfolk
marched on the mayor to clarify the situation. After futile at-
tempts to contact the battery by telephone—it was found out
later that the Germans had cut the line—the mayor was trying to obtain a truck from the partisans when he saw Jean
Pierre's jeep draw up in front of the *palazzo comunale*.

The Frenchman brought a message that tore Brosio from
the arms of a plump and grateful matron and sent him yelling
orders to his lieutenants. As the alarm spread around the
town, partisans staggered from taverns and brothels, festooned by their clothes, ammunition and weapons. Within
thirty minutes the entire contingent had evacuated the town
and followed Jean Pierre to hastily-selected battle stations.

By this time every citizen in Valderosa knew the worst.
The *Tedeschi* were coming back and their town was a vital
pawn in a gigantic military game. Its one hope of survival lay
in the Padrone and his men who had promised to defend the
town until the main Allied force arrived. In the meantime
those who could find shelter elsewhere were advised to leave.

Few took this advice. With privation everywhere, most
townsfolk preferred to remain with what little they had and
to put their faith in God and the Padrone. They flocked in by
the hundreds to the special masses that were called. In the

great cathedral, tier after tier of candles began to blaze around the empty bier of Santa Rosaria. If ever a miracle were needed, it was needed now. Alongside their sleeping children, parents prayed for the Padrone, his men and their own gallant *giovonotti* until they too fell asleep. Others could find no rest and tossed about in their beds, fearful of what the dawn would bring.

Beccione found Magda at one of the German observation posts on the southeastern rim of the hilltop. The post, a flat outcrop of rock on which a small tent perched, commanded an uninterrupted view of the town and the entrance of the southern valley. The girl was wearing a man's greatcoat with its collar turned up against the night's chill. She sat beside the tent gazing at the town. A white bubble of moon floated overhead and the amethyst sky looked low enough to touch.

Showing relief at his appearance, she moved for him to sit beside her. "Is everything ready?"

He dropped wearily down. "More or less. There are a few more markers to set up when it gets light. And the shells have to be fused and a few other problems sorted out. But Kessler thinks there's time to do the rest in the morning."

"How is he posting the men?"

"Apart from one or two 88mm specialists to help the guys on the north side, most of the Germans will be facing the Allies. The other two squads will take on the German main force. The partisans under Jean Pierre are providing the infantry cover. You probably saw them moving in earlier. They're among the trees halfway up the hillsides."

She nodded, studying him. Like the rest of the men, he had been working since sundown and it showed on his unshaven face. The civilian clothes he was still wearing were torn and dirty. "Where is Kessler now?"

"He's back in the command post with the radio. I guess he's still trying to stop the Allies from sending that advance force. Most of the other guys have been laid off to get some sleep." Taking the cigarette she offered him, he inhaled smoke greedily. "They're sure going to need it in a few hours."

"I never believed they would stay. Not when the effects of Kessler's speech had worn off."

"Neither did I," he confessed. "But he's been keeping the

pressure on them all night and now they're too tired to do anything but sleep."

"Yes, he's very clever. Is it true Jean Pierre has brought Weiss and Mogelli back?"

"Yes. Apparently he caught up with them before they'd roughed anybody up. They're under close arrest in one of the cells until Kessler decides what to do with them."

"I was surprised at the way Roberts and the rest of his officers took all this."

He shrugged. "I don't think they were all that surprised. I think they figured that sooner or later a situation would arise when it would be the civilians or themselves and they knew what Kessler's choice would be."

"Then they're stupid," she said hotly. "A leader who isn't loyal to his men doesn't deserve loyalty himself."

"Who says Kessler's disloyal? He's never hid his preferences."

"That doesn't put any obligation on his men to accept them."

"No, but old habits die hard. Anyway, there's no obligation. Kessler's arranged for a convoy of jeeps to leave here at dawn. Anyone who wants out can get on it."

"Still, he deceived us all. I find that unforgivable."

He glanced at the town. "Even to save a place like that and maybe a couple of thousand people?"

"Yes. We should have been given the chance to make our own decisions."

"Aw, c'mon, kid. If Kessler had told us the truth we'd all still be running."

"Then you admit it's a suicidal gesture?"

He frowned. "I never said that. It's just a tough assignment, that's all."

"Just a tough assignment!" Her sarcasm disguised her despair. "That means only one thing, doesn't it? You're staying too."

He rose and walked to the rim of the ledge. In the moonlight the cathedral looked as if it were washed in milk. Above the sable-black mountains a meteor traced a hairline of light on its way to extinction. He thought of the peace now and the hell tomorrow and, as he took a deep breath, he felt as if all the joy and sorrow of the world were flooding into him in a strange and potent exhilaration.

"Yes," he said simply. "I'm staying."

Her expression was hidden in shadow. "Is it because of that girl?"

For the first time when speaking of Maria he felt certain of his reply. "No. It has nothing to do with her."

"Then what is it?"

He turned towards her. "I don't know."

"I do. It is Kessler. He has made all of you feel that until now your lives have been wasted."

"Is that a bad thing?"

"Yes, because he is playing God. No one but God can say that a man's life has been in vain. Kessler uses men's sense of failure for his own ends."

"How can you say that? Tonight he did the opposite: he told the men they were not the thieves and murderers they believe themselves to be. He let them believe the angels were on their side."

"Tonight, yes, but only for his purpose. He is clever. He understands that no man is as zealous as the sinner who is offered salvation."

His laugh was hard. "What's wrong with salvation?"

"Because it is sentimental claptrap. Your sacrifice is not going to change the world. The world never changes. If you stay and fight, you will simply be giving your life away for one man's obsession."

He glanced down at the lovely, frightened town. "I've known worse obsessions than saving a place like that. And it's ironic, but by keeping the two armies apart we might be saving hundreds or even thousands of young soldiers' lives."

"By killing them yourselves?"

Her sarcasm made him grin wryly. "That's right."

"So now you're concerned about the soldiers too? You'd better not tell your master that. He wants your allegiance only for himself and the civilians."

His mood changed. "Why have you turned against Kessler like this? Because he killed Schumann?"

She had moved out of the shadows while they talked and was only a couple of feet from him. She met his stare for a moment, then bit her lip and turned away. "Think what you like. It doesn't matter."

"But it does matter. The guy's trying to save women and children. And who's to say he's wrong about the wider issues? Maybe some people will stand up and take notice if we fight to save the town."

As he spoke he noticed for the first time that her greatcoat was at least two sizes too big for her. She looked like a waif wearing discarded clothing. When she did not answer him, he swung her around. "Tell me why you've turned against Kessler. I want to know."

She tried to pull away. Then, giving up, she uttered a sharp despairing cry and threw herself into his arms. "You're such a fool, Joe. You're so blind."

Taken by surprise, he tried to lift her face. But she buried it deeper into his jacket. Her muffled voice was fierce with shame and bitterness. "To hell with Kessler and his grand gestures. I want you alive, not some dead hero the world will forget in ten minutes."

He tried to laugh at her fears. "No one's going to die. Have you taken a look at the firepower we've got up here? And we only have to hold the hill for a few hours. On top of that, Kessler has a plan to get us out."

"With one or the other army surrounding the hill and thirsting for our blood? You don't believe that any more than I do."

He frowned. "Kessler's a smart guy. He's done impossible things before."

She pulled away from him, a gesture of finality. "Kessler is going to die and we shall die with him. We *must* die. If we don't become martyrs, his grand gesture won't have its impact."

"For God's sake stop hounding the guy," he muttered. Then he started violently. "*We*? What do you mean by that?"

Her defiant eyes lifted. "You have convinced me. I have also decided that I want to stay and save the world. I want to become a martyr too."

"Like hell you do. You're getting into one of those jeeps and driving away."

Her lips curled at his anger. "What's the matter? Do you feel you must have a monopoly on self-sacrifice?"

Muttering something, he moved away to the rim of the ledge and stared again at the town. When he turned back to her, he was pale. "I can't walk out now, kid. You must see that. But make it easier for me. Please."

Her beautiful face was adamant. "I will go if you go. But if you stay, I shall stay. Nothing will alter that."

"Kid, I must stay. I can't walk out on those guys now."

"Then there is nothing more to discuss, is there?"

There were beads of sweat on his forehead now. "For God's sake, Magda. Don't do this to me."

Her shrug taunted him. "What am I doing that is so startling? No one is going to die—you said that yourself." She glanced at her watch. "We have one hour to daybreak. Are we going to waste it arguing out here?"

Lowering his head in defeat, he followed her into the tent. Under the blankets their bodies felt chilled, but as they embraced they drew warmth from one another. Their love making was fierce and urgent, an effort towards a union that could defy man's power to harm them. Once she gave a sharp cry. "I've only known you mere days, Joe. . . . I want a lifetime to know you better. I want your children."

He hushed her and their bodies bonded together again. When at last the tumult was over and their passion spent, he lay with one arm over her and fell asleep. Her breathing quieted with his own but her eyes did not close. She was listening to the distant crowing of a cock, aware with every tingling nerve that already, in the east, cold luminous fingers were tearing away the protection of the night.

Her eyes, tender in the darkness, moved to the man at her side as he shifted in his sleep. Every minute now was a jewel. In the valleys to the north and to the south, engines were racing as men drove themselves towards their chosen slaughter ground. Listening to the cock crowing, Magda imagined she could hear the thunder of approaching Armageddon as she felt her lover's warm breath on her cheek.

45

Because of a pre-dawn mist that rose from the valley, full light did not come until 05.45 hours that morning. It found Kessler's men back at their task of laying markers on the approach roads and on any other flat stretch of ground that vehicles might use. At the same time Rossi was laying charges on the bridge that spanned the river and other men were hurriedly digging up mines that lay beyond it. These were rushed away and re-buried around the mouth of the northern valley and along the road that led to Valderosa.

By 08.45 it was considered to be too dangerous for the outlaws to remain in the valley any longer and they were ordered back to the battery. When the last man had crossed the bridge, there was an explosion that sent pigeons clattering into the air above the town. The last echoes died away and the bridge was rubble: the steep-sided river bed was now a formidable obstacle to anything but tracked vehicles.

At 09.00 hours Kessler issued an order for his lieutenants to report to his command post. When Beccione arrived he saw a travel-stained jeep standing near the hut with Toschack bending over its engine. The bony Australian was wearing his national uniform complete with bush hat. Curious, Beccione approached him. "Where have you been all night? Out on the town?"

Toschack grinned. "You'll never guess, mate. Not in a million years."

"Try me."

"Roberts and me have been visitin' the Allied main force."

Beccione took a second look at him. "You drunk, Toschack?"

"Naw, it's dinkum. We drove through the woods until we were above 'em. Then we went down and fraternized."

"You fraternized?"

"Yeah. They've got a real scratch outfit there—Yanks, British, Aussies, French—anyone they've been able to lay their hands on. But from the way they've chucked security aside, it looks as if they've got the message it's urgent. They've rigged arc lights up and they're using infantry as well as engineers to dig the mines up. So no one took a blind bit of notice of us when we drifted in among the Yanks."

"But what for?"

Toschack motioned at the command post. "Come and look."

Beccione followed him into the hut. Dazzled by the bright sunlight outside, his eyes took a moment to adjust. Then he saw Kessler's lieutenants were grouped around two men standing before the radio table. One was Kessler himself, the other a stout middle-aged man with iron-grey hair wearing American battle dress. Beccione did a double take when he saw the badge of war correspondent on his shoulder. Toschack grinned.

"You getting the idea now? Roberts found him watchin' the mines being lifted, told him about us, and after that you couldn't hold him back. He didn't even leave a message where he was goin' for fear the other correspondents would muscle in on the story. He's from the *Washington Post* and he says it'll be front page news whether we pull it off or not."

Beccione took a deep breath. "Kessler really means to get his message across to the world, doesn't he?"

"Yeah, but there's more to it than that. According to Roberts he's doing a deal with this guy, Sylvester. He gets the exclusive story and in return he threatens the Allies with exposure if they don't let us go after we've saved the town."

Beccione nodded in admiration. "You have to hand it to Kessler. He's got it all figured. Army chiefs hate to get egg on their faces. And public opinion counts, particularly in the States."

"Then you think it might work?"

"Christ knows but it's clever. Has the main force got much armor with them?"

"Oh yeah, they're loaded. There'll be no stopping 'em once they get here. It's just those bloody minefields blocking the way."

"Did you see any of the advance force before you left? You can't have been far ahead of them."

"Roberts saw them assembling. He said there looked to be around three battalions."

"American or British?"

"About half and half, he thinks. No armor, of course, but they're bringing Bren gun carriers and jeeps."

"How much longer do you guess we've got?"

"Not that long. An hour. Ninety minutes at the most."

Across the hut Kessler had caught sight of Beccione and was motioning him to join them. Beccione grimaced at the bony Australian as he moved forward. "Let's hope the main force hops to it and Kessler's plan works."

Toschack flashed a lopsided grin. "There are only two snags, sport. One, the Jerries might take us. Two, if we ain't alive at the end of the day it doesn't matter a damn whose plan works."

Beccione crossed the room and introduced himself to Neil Sylvester, the war correspondent. "Beccione. You're another Yank, aren't you?"

"That's right."

"Aren't you a long way from home?"

Beccione decided to play it very cautiously. "A mile or two."

The reporter appraised Beccione through shrewd watchful eyes, then nodded at the expressionless Kessler standing alongside him. "How do you feel about this job your boss is asking you to do?"

"It's a job."

"That's no answer."

"What sort of an answer do you want? That I like having to fight two goddamned armies to save a town?"

The correspondent's suspicion that he could be part of a massive hoax showed in his question. "Couldn't there be another reason? Isn't there talk of treasure up here?"

Beccione lifted an eyebrow. "There is?"

"C'mon, Beccione. You must have heard the cathedral artifacts are supposed to be hidden in one of these caves."

Beccione turned to Kessler. "Did you know that, Kessler?"

He saw the German's eyes smile in appreciation. "Of course I have heard the rumor. But we are hardly avaricious enough to fight two armies in the elusive hope of finding it.'"

Sylvester shrugged. "Don't blame me, Kessler. It isn't every day a pack of guys who've killed hundreds of GIs suddenly turn into Snow White."

Kessler smiled and took his arm. "Hardly Snow White. But perhaps before the day is over we might convince you we have not been the Wicked Queen either. Let me take you round the hilltop to see the preparations we have made."

The first sighting of the Allied advance force was made at 09.47. Kessler's immediate move was to send an alert through his signals switchboard for all gun crews and infantry to stand by. Then, accompanied by Jean Pierre and Sylvester, he hurried out to the nearest 88mm post, a site along the southern face of the hill. A fully-manned 88mm gun was positioned in the mouth of a cave, a 20mm cannon stood guard on it fifty yards away. The tops of the nearby trees had been lopped off to give a clear view and field of fire. Zimmermann, acting as the gun position officer for the entire south-facing battery, pointed through the gap. "They are in the woods east of the valley entrance, Padrone. We think they have vehicles with them."

Both Kessler and Jean Pierre lifted their binoculars. The Frenchman gave a grunt. "Yeah, there they are. They must have come along one of the forest tracks."

Kessler passed his high-powered glasses to Sylvester.

Through them the correspondent could see men assembling among the trees that ran down the mountainside. He also caught a glint of sunlight on a windshield.

Kessler was talking rapidly to Zimmerman. "They are almost certain to wait until every company has arrived. So you have fifteen minutes to half an hour to be ready. Although they are sure to have been told of our intention, they will probably try to call our bluff by attempting one direct advance on the town. If we hold them, they will then either attack us or try to get round the back of the town by skirting the mountains. They might even try both ways at once. Whatever they do, we must stop them. It should be possible: we have enough guns and ammunition to saturate all their paths. If we can hold them long enough, I am hoping they might retreat back into the mountains and try to circle round that way. If they do, it is most unlikely they will become a threat again before their main force arrives. So the next hour or two could be critical."

Nodding, Zimmerman drove off to make a final check on his gun crews. Kessler took the binoculars back from Sylvester and stared through them again. The wood looked alive now as more men filtered in along the forest tracks. At the sudden scream of engines and airfoils, all three men turned sharply, thinking for a moment the battery was already under attack. Instead they saw a flight of fire-bombers leaping over the valley a mile east of the hill. Sylvester gave a grimace. "So the Krauts are still advancing too?"

Jean Pierre nodded. "Yeah. We got a report from one of our scouts, Berrati, fifteen minutes ago. Although the bombers have made a hell of a mess of the road, he still thinks they'll be here by noon at the latest."

Turning to Kessler, Sylvester nodded at the wood opposite. "You do realize that the moment you open fire on those guys, you're going to get a clobbering from the air?"

With a battle against superhuman odds about to begin, the German sounded almost jaunty. "Of course. Their aircraft will be standing by, if they are not already airborne. But we are ready for them. All the 20mm cannon are manned and by using our jeeps as well we can promise them a warm reception. When the attack comes, I want you to take shelter in one of the caves."

With the first group of their enemies now in sight, the tension among the outlaws, particularly the Germans of B Squad who would be the first into action, was almost unbearable.

Every artillery piece was already loaded and aimed at its marker; dry-mouthed men poured one last time over their range tables, checking on wind speed, temperature and all the other factors that affected the trajectory and drift of shells. Few could find any errors, but here and there men made minute corrections more to appease their nerves than to increase the accuracy of their guns. Although ample shells had been fused already, gun captains ordered more. The men, already bone-weary after a back-breaking night, swore as they dragged more heavy projectiles from the caves, heaved them into transports, and added them to the mounting piles that stood behind each gun. Other men pulled and fiddled with the netting that was stretched over them, acutely aware their lives might soon depend on the efficacy of the camouflage. With A and C squads unlikely to be called into action for the next two hours, men drifted across the hilltop and gave gratuitous advice to their tense German colleagues.

Similar scenes were taking place around the 20mm cannon sites where gunners and loaders talked in low tones without taking their eyes off the sky. Everyone had a special curse for the god of weather. The early morning mist that had raised hopes of protection against aerial assault was now shredding away and revealing a blue dome of sky.

The unnatural hush prevailed everywhere on the hill. Even the engines of the jeeps that prowled restlessly along the crisscrossing forest tracks sounded muted. The jeeps, which had been brought up the previous evening, were under the joint command of Beccione and Johnson. One of their tasks was to augment the firepower of the 20mm cannons against aircraft. A second was to aid the infantry shield against ground attacks, although this was not expected to become necessary until the German main force arrived. A third task was to help resituate the 20mm guns so that they could be used for ground defense purposes should a heavy threat appear at any point of the perimeter.

The rest of Kessler's officers were given equally responsible roles. Roberts was the gun position officer of a troop of three 88s almost directly opposite the northern valley. Williams served in this capacity for a similar battery to the right of the Englishman. Tito, with Etienne his second in command, had a battery of two guns on the western hill face. Nickolai, because of his fluent German, commanded a battery between Tito and the right flank of the German south-facing guns. Weiss, although not one of Kessler's lieutenants, had been put in charge of one of those batteries. He had been released when Kessler decided that every fighting man in his company would be needed before the day was over. Jean Pierre was in overall command of the infantry shield with Brosio his second in command. These men, all armed with automatic weapons, were positioned among the trees halfway down the hillsides. With Kessler's limited resources in men reduced by the needs of the guns above, the infantry shield consisted mainly of Italian partisans. It was this thin shield of men that the jeep crews had to try to help if a breakthrough appeared likely.

Among the rest of the men, Toschack was acting as Beccione's driver and co-gunner; McAllister was controlling a battery of 20mm cannon; Greyson was one of Roberts's 88mm gunners; Mogelli, pardoned like Weiss, was a loader in the German's battery. Russell, aided by two heavily-armed rebels, had the responsibility of guarding the German prisoners in one of the larger caves. Because of the shortage of manpower, each detachment officer was having to manage with six men per gun and one fuse-setter for the entire battery. The surplus 88s had been taken over to the northern hill crest—going on the supposition that if any gun was put out of action but its crew unharmed, they could switch to the spare 88 and retain the battery's efficiency.

Acutely conscious of his shortage of manpower, Kessler had retained only two men as assistants in his command post, Razzoni and a young German signaler named Klaus. For the same reason Magda's decision to stay had delighted him. Secretly expecting heavy casualties, he had put her in charge of his casualty station, much to the fiery girl's resentment. The hut he had chosen for the wounded was not far from his command post. Magda's assistant was Schiller, the only man Kessler felt he could spare.

10.30 came and went without a move from the woods opposite, although to the watching rebels they appeared alive with men. The unexpected wait affected the rebels in different ways. Some talked loudly, some in whispers. Some smoked cigarette after cigarette, some lay back in the sunlight and gazed at the white flocculi of clouds that had appeared above. Some, like a young German named Waltermann who had a presentiment of death, were finding a bonus in every extra minute of life. To Kessler, painfully aware of how precious time was to Valderosa, the delay was a godsend.

At 10.45 there was a shout from an outpost as increased

activity was noticed across the valley. Knowing that the moment they opened fire retribution would fall on them like fire
from heaven, rebels swallowed to lubricate their throats.
Many regretted their decision of the previous evening but
found they could not desert while their comrades remained
firm. At 10.48 shouts all along the south face of the hill
made their hearts burn and race. Khaki-clad figures were
leaving the woods at last and moving in combat order
towards the river and Valderosa.

GPOs nodded at their detachment officers, who in turn
swung around to their gunners. The first command that was
yelled out—"*Achtung!*"—sounded right across the hilltop.
Hardly a man who heard it did not wince at its implications.
Then came "*Feuer!*" and a loud explosion that signaled the
crossing of the Rubicon. A second later all the German batteries were in action, and a massive resonant heave of sound
reverberated back and forth, ripping the peace of the valley
to shreds. The first phase of the battle for Valderosa had begun.

46

The advancing Americans never heard the first of the shells
that rained down on them. One of the many fearsome aspects
of the 88mm gun, with its high muzzle velocity, was that its
projectiles arrived before the sound. The only warning the
soldiers received was a huge fountain of earth and stones and
hissing steel splinters that tore through their ranks like a giant
flail. Before they had time to throw themselves down, the first
full salvo arrived, sending up a deadly palisade of steel.
Hearts pounding, bodies sweating, men buried their faces in
their arms as the ground shuddered and heaved beneath
them.

Up on the hill the command had been to fire by order,
which meant after the first salvo was fired, each crew worked
at its own pace. With the German gunners still wound up
with tension, the pace became almost frantic. After the initial
round had been aimed at his marker, each gunlayer was making minute corrections to ensure that each shell burst a few
yards ahead of its predecessor.

The result was as terrifying to the prostrate infantrymen as a creeping wave of molten lava. Armed with the AZ23 fuze, the shells wasted little of their explosive power into the ground, hurling their razor-sharp fragments outwards instead. As boulders crashed around them and steel hissed overhead, men bit into the flesh of their arms to suppress their fear.

On a ledge in the woods behind them, the commanding officer, an American named Lazenby, was watching the scene with dismay and mounting anger. He was a big man of forty-five, with a crew cut, heavy jowls and bright aggressive eyes which he turned on the two officers alongside him. "So the sonsofbitches meant it!"

The two men were named Armstrong and Newman. The former was British, the latter American. Armstrong was tall and fair-skinned, Newman stockier and darker of complexion. Although both were young for their rank, they were seasoned men. Neither one had developed a liking for the man put in charge of their battalions. At the moment both were looking shaken at the slaughter being inflicted on their men.

Lazenby's voice sounded through the thunder of the shells. "This comes from playing patsy with a bunch of hoodlums. I wanted to clobber 'em from the beginning, but Hutchinson and his outfit felt they'd be useful to hold the Krauts back in that pass. I don't think he believed they'd fire on us when the chips were down. Now look at that goddamned shambles." Cursing, he turned to his radio operator. "Tell Stanmore to pull 'em back into the woods and wait for further orders. Then put out a call for that air strike. Tell 'em we're pinned down, so they should give the sonsofbitches all they've got."

Newman was showing some dismay. "Do you think that's wise, sir? If they can handle 88s like this, they could be useful when the Germans get here."

"What use is that if they keep us pinned down as well?" Lazenby demanded.

"Does that matter as long as they let the main force take the town?"

"Of course it matters, for Chrissake. That town's our objective. What kind of Charlies are we going to look like if a gang of hoodlums keeps us out?"

The young colonel hid his expression by glancing down at the river bank again. Having received his order to retreat, the field officer in command was wasting no time. Whistles were shrilling and NCOs were waving shaken infantrymen back from the fury of the shells. Spoiling for a fight, Lazenby glowered across at the hill. "Those 88s ain't got a depression of more than 3 degrees. If we can get our guys near enough, we might get beneath 'em."

This time it was Armstrong who showed alarm. "We'd lose fifty percent on the way, sir. And they're certain to have thought of that and dug the legs in."

"So what do we do? Sit on our asses until the main force gets here?" Lazenby demanded. But his tone changed when he again took in the scene below. "All right, we'll wait until the Air Force has clobbered 'em. But after that I'm going after the bastards."

Bent double, infantrymen were running for the trees to escape the screaming shells. Back near the river a young officer, trying to conduct the retreat with dignity, was helping out two NCOs. Suddenly all three men vanished in an eruption of earth and rocks. When the smoke cleared only a smoking crater could be seen. Lazenby uttered a savage curse. "We're going up that hill, you guys. And we're going to stick every sonofabitch left alive."

Although Newman had just lost a friend below, he retained his grasp of the wider aspects of the situation. "They're deadly accurate with those 88s, sir. They could pick off the Kraut tanks the moment they come out of that pass."

Lazenby's face turned ugly with anger. "You're not still asking me to cancel that air strike, are you?"

"No, sir. But wouldn't it be wise to attack only the guns on this side of the hill? That will clear our way to the town and still leave them the capacity to harass the Germans."

Lazenby stared at him. "You think they'll still fight after the kites have attacked them?"

"I don't know. But you were told it was their intention to defend the hill on both sides."

Somewhat bravely, Armstrong backed his American colleague. "I think he's right, sir. Don't you think it's worth a try?"

Lazenby turned his scowl on the Englishman, hesitated, then spun around on his radio operator. "All right. You hear that, Mitchell? Tell them to keep their attack to the south side of the hill." When the NCO nodded and switched on his microphone, Lazenby glanced back aggressively at his younger officers. "Don't get any wrong ideas. This doesn't mean I'm not going after the sonsofbitches. Before I've finished with 'em, they'll wish they'd never been born."

*   *   *

There was no exultation on the hilltop when the Allied infantry was seen to be withdrawing. Everyone knew it was only one move in the deadly game of chess that was being played. While stretcher-bearers picked up the dead and wounded beyond the riverbank, GPOs ordered "rest" to their gunners, a term that indicated further action was expected soon. Men cleared away empty cases and brought up new shells, lookouts scanned the bright morning sky for the dreaded aircraft. The 20mm gunners, aware their turn was near, swiveled their cannon from side to side nervously. In the jeeps, which were posted along the forest tracks behind the 88mm guns, all automatic weapons were cocked and ammunition belts ready. After the thunder of the 88s, the silence had a viscous quality through which the shouts of men sounded unreal.

The second phase of the battle began at 11.12 when a lookout, squinting into the bright morning sun, jumped down from a rocky knoll and began frantically winding the handle of his field telephone. "Jaboes, Padrone! Coming in from the east!"

The scream of engines was heard a few seconds later. The eight aircraft were Boston IIIs of the RAF Desert Air Force which, after the recent invasion of Southern France, had been made responsible for Army close support along the entire Italian Front. Already briefed the previous night, their flight commander had received his scramble order less than twenty minutes ago. With the morning bright and clear, he had decided to make his first pass with the sun behind him in order to blind the enemy gunners. This way he was hoping to identify the sites of the 88s before their defenses went into action.

It was a ploy that could well have succeeded were it not for the precautions Kessler had taken. As it was, the flight commander spotted only the 20mm gunsites that out of necessity had to stand on open ground. Expecting the attack to come from the south and west, the gunners were taken by surprise and no great weight of shot was turned on the first two low-flying aircraft.

The remainder that followed were not so lucky. With their guns now swiveled into position, the rebels put up a blizzard of fire that made the startled pilots break away and dive into the valley for safety.

Highly-experienced in ground support, the flight com-

mander made a snap decision. With the guns camouflaged, he
would have to try to overwhelm them by sheer firepower. Receiving their new orders, the flight regrouped over the mountains into a line-abreast formation. Then, like a troop of
charging cavalry, they wheeled into the valley and made
straight for the southern crest of the hill. At 800 yards range
each aircraft launched two rockets.

The effect was like a short-range broadside from a bat-
tleship: the hillcrest seemed to leap upwards as the heavy
rockets burst within seconds of one another. Across the valley
Lazenby was watching the attack with massive satisfaction.
"That's the goddamned ticket. Let's see how the sonsofbitches
like . . ."

His voice broke off as one of the Bostons, about to soar
over the hillcrest, received a burst of 20mm shells on its star-
board engine. The wing tore clean away with the impact and
the remains spun down and exploded among the trees. A second Boston appeared to be pierced by half a dozen white
lances as it banked sharply over the hill. Shuddering, it tried
to dive for safety over the town but its fuel tanks exploded
and bits of debris fluttered down like confetti.

The six surviving aircraft circled away, followed by ven-
omous whips of tracer. There was dismay in the glances
Armstrong and Newman exchanged. "Six aircraft aren't going to knock them out," the Englishman said. "I counted
twenty guns firing during that attack."

Newman nodded. "They must have a full regiment of AA
guns up there."

The pessimism of the two colonels was justified. The wood
that covered the hill was huge, and although the rocket attack
had been formidable, its chance of doing serious damage to
the 88s had always been slight. In fact not one gun had suffered damage and only two men had been wounded, and they
only slightly by splinters of wood. Kessler's only concern at
that moment was the fires the rockets had started. Two were
burning near to gun sites and the German ordered men over
from the northern hillcrest to extinguish them.

Morale among the rebels had been given a considerable
boost. In the brief lull that followed, Toschack, loading a
new belt into his Browning, grinned at Beccione. "Two down
out of eight. That ain't a bad kick up the arse, cobber."

Beccione grinned back. "Not bad at all."

The Australian nodded at the southern sky where the Bostons, appearing no larger than flies, were circling in a tight pattern. "They look to me as if they've had enough."

"No. They're hard-nosed bastards. They're just working on something. They'll be back."

Beccione was more correct than he knew. The flight commander was in contact with Lazenby and the two men agreed on a new strategem. As the Bostons broke their orbit and went into their line-abreast formation again, whistles shrilled across the valley and infantrymen burst out of the woods and began running hard towards the hill. At the same time mortar smoke shells began bursting ahead of them. Watching from a ledge near his command post, Kessler nodded his approval. The advancing infantry would force the 88s into action and the pilots of the Bostons were hoping that either their gun flashes or smoke would betray their positions.

With no other option open to them, the 88s opened fire again, laying a line of bursting shells across the infantrymen's advance. Driven on by their officers and NCOs, sweating men ran a few yards, dropped among the vines, fired grenades from their rifles, and ran forward again into the smoke they had created. The ploy did little to minimize their casualties: the terrifying 88s were too well sited and accurate. But before their rush had lost its impetus, the Bostons had dived into the valley and the hill was straight ahead of them.

The guns were giving off little if any smoke: German smokeless propellants were highly efficient. But because of the configuration of the hill, parts of its southern face were not in direct sunlight and here and there flashes were visible. Although difficult to fix because of their split-second duration, they did give a rough indication of a gun's position and the Bostons were primed to miss no chances. Like wolves going for the jugular, fiery rockets leapt out from them and smashed into the hillcrest.

Although not all the 88s were attacked, a reduction in their overall efficiency was inevitable as trees were hurled upwards and boulders crashed down the hill. Deafened men could not hear the orders of their officers, gunlayers were blinded by the smoke of fires. The 20mm gunners near the attacked 88s were also half-stunned and their vision obstructed. The least affected of the AA defenses were the mobile jeeps, and they put up a withering fire as the six Bostons flashed overhead at treetop height. One was raked from nose to tail. Dipping a wing, it struck a tree and exploded on impact. The remain-

der, shell-torn and riddled with bullets, took cover behind the
hill and dived away.

Along the hillcrest one 88 had received a direct hit and its
five tons of metal had been riven and hurled aside like a broken toy. One man had been crushed beneath it, a second
killed in the explosion. Three other men were wounded. A
fierce fire was burning near the pile of shells but Nickolai, a
stolid, reassuring figure, waved back the gunners who were
running towards it. Below, heartened by the slackening of the
shell fire, infantrymen were almost halfway across the valley.
They were the immediate danger. All else had to wait.

With the aircraft gone, men settled down to their tasks
again. Those that could see the infantry below depressed their
guns. Those still handicapped by smoke guessed the new
angle and fired blind. Soon the rate of fire from the 88s was
almost as high as before. Where possible, 20mm cannons and
the .50s of the jeeps joined in, their tracers arcing down like
uncoiling string. On the hillside below, Jean Pierre gave the
go-ahead to the partisans and their weapons were adding to
the din. Meanwhile, on Kessler's orders, more men from the
northern hillcrest were joining in the battle against the fires.

Most of the infantry were past the point of no return. With
howling shells falling behind as well as in front of them, they
could only make for the dry riverbed that divided the valley.
Staring through binoculars, Lazenby watched them scram-
bling across the white stones for the shelter of the northern
bank. There, soaked in sweat, gasping for breath, they hugged
the steep bank as if it were the body of their mother.

The guns continued to fire until the last man fell or
reached temporary shelter. When at last they ceased firing the
hush was like an explosion. The gunners breathed fresh air
again and gazed at their handiwork. From the river back to
the woods the ground was pitted by smoking craters and littered with untidy bundles. As soldiers on both sides conversed
in low shocked tones, the measured tolling of a bell could be
heard. Men stared at one another until they realized it was
the cathedral calling the frightened townsfolk of Valderosa to
prayer.

47

The deadlock at Valderosa, broken only by the occasional threatening shell, chatter of automatic fire, or crack of a sniper's bullet, continued until noon. Back in the woods Lazenby had urgently demanded more air support and barely contained his fury when told that all available aircraft were now in action against the advancing Germans. Along the riverbank, while recovering their breath, Allied infantrymen had been given reassuring words by their company officers and NCOs in an attempt to bolster their shaken confidence. Wherever possible wounded men had been treated, the hillside carefully scanned for enemy defenses, and light machine guns set up to cover the next advance. Up the hill all but one of the fires had been extinguished and the gun sites cleared for the next action. Magda and Schiller had treated the wounded men and a new gun crew had been created to man one of the surplus 88s. In effect the hill's defenses were as formidable as ever but there was one vital difference. At least eight hundred Allied soldiers, and possibly more, were now crouched no more than a thousand yards from its lower slopes.

During this time Kessler had been receiving constant reports from Berrati who was expertly shadowing the advance of the German division. Lazenby had been obtaining the same information from the Allied aircraft that had been in action since dawn: information that had driven him into making this recent assault which had cost two hundred men. Ignoring the heavy air attacks, the Germans were still surging forward and would in all likelihood reach the valley within an hour.

Prudence suggested Lazenby should now wait until Kessler was occupied with the Germans, then withdraw his men and wait until his main force arrived. But that would mean leaving the defense of the town entirely to the rebels. A ragbag of thieves and deserters to gain the glory . . . the very thought of it choked Lazenby with bile. He could not storm the hill yet—even his aggressive mind accepted that—but when the

Germans arrived and the sonsofbitches up there were fully occupied, he would try to rush in through the back door, seize the battery, and hold on until the main force arrived. That way he would achieve his objective and eliminate these mongrel bastards at the same time. Although it was a plan that initially startled Armstrong and Newman, with their troops fully committed they could see the logic of it and orders were sent to the field commanders to be ready to attack when the word was given. Without shade, with the sun now high in the sky, men sweated, slapped at flies and cursed the fate that had brought them to Italy. In the meantime Lazenby moved his observation post further west to gain an uninterrupted view of the northern valley—although, because the road entered the main valley at a slight angle, he could see no distance down it.

Nevertheless, the relays of Allied aircraft crossing the valley and the clearly-heard explosions of bombs and cannon fire were giving startling evidence of the rate of the Germans' advance. By 12.30 however the aircraft were withdrawn and an uneasy silence fell. A radio call from Berrati confirmed Kessler's suspicions. For some time the aircraft had found it difficult to plant bombs in the narrowing valley. Now the operation had become unproductive and too dangerous. In the command post, Sylvester (who had refused to stay put in a cave, even during the heavy fighting) turned to Kessler. "So what happens now?"

"If Berrati is right, the German advance guard will be here in fifteen minutes. Perhaps less."

"Do you expect the Allies to turn their bombers against you now that they can't use them against the Germans?"

"Not if they're wise. I have promised to engage the Germans and they already have evidence what our gunnery can achieve."

Sylvester's lined face was betraying his inner conflict. "It's a tragedy you had to kill all those Allied youngsters."

Kessler's curt voice offered no apology. "Who is to blame for that? You heard me pleading with your commanders to the last minute not to send that advance force."

"Yes, I heard. But it's a tragedy just the same. So you think the Allies might hold off their aircraft?"

"No one can be certain. But they will be fools if they do not."

"Maybe. But will professional soldiers play ball with you like that?"

"They have many times before. I don't see why not now."

"Yes, so you say." Sylvester continued to be incredulous of Kessler's history and ambitions, despite what he'd seen. "It's one hell of a story. How do you rate your chances now?"

"Reasonably good provided the Allies do not use their heavy bombers and their main force keeps its ETA. But we shall sustain heavy casualties. That is why I must ask you again to take shelter in one of the deep caves when the attack commences." Although the German gave his dry smile, the concern behind his request was unmistakable. "We must not lose our only mouthpiece to the world."

The tough correspondent gave a noncommittal shrug. "Let's play that when it comes."

The third and critical phase of the battle began at 12.47 when the first German scout car was seen emerging from the mouth of the pass. From its cautious entry it was clear Kessler's threat was not being taken lightly. Kessler, who ten minutes earlier had handed the telephone switchboard over to Klaus, was standing with Sylvester and Roberts when a yell of warning came from an outpost. Studying the valley for a moment, Kessler lowered his binoculars and turned to the tense Englishman.

"Now it is your turn, Peter. Let them get as far as the markers, then open fire. Remember the object is to force them to attack us on this hill. So make your initial attack as destructive as possible."

All the eleven 88s along the northern hillcrest were loaded and ready for action. As a second scout car appeared and halted close by the first one, the tension among the watching rebels became almost palpable. Every man knew that within minutes a storm of rending ferocity would break over them. In addition, there was a real possibility they might also be attacked from the rear and from the air. Suddenly every leaf on the trees, every stone on the ground, took on clear and sharp outlines. In the sunlight the air seemed to fill with golden dust. Men became conscious of their heartbeats and the strong flexing of their muscles. Some felt themselves immortal, others felt certain they would die. A few resolved that if they lived they would never again waste the gift of life.

Straining eyes watched the two scout cars. The first one began moving again slowly towards Valderosa. The second one turned away westward and bumped along a cart track that ran along the foot of the mountains—its task was to inspect the hill. All eyes however were on the first car as it neared the minefield the rebels had laid. A gunner in Roberts's troop coughed and men stared at him as if he had committed an offense.

The first scout car halted yet again. Then it began moving faster as if its driver had decided to put his trust in speed. It had just passed a clump of trees when black smoke belched all around it. The thud of the exploded mine followed three seconds later. When the smoke cleared, the car was seen lying on its side and burning fiercely.

Someone let out a cheer to release his tension. It was followed almost immediately by a dull explosion from the mountain opposite, then a louder explosion on the hilltop. Two more similar dual explosions came a few seconds later. Sylvester turned to Kessler curiously. "You haven't got more guns back in the woods, have you?"

Kessler shook his head. "No. It's enemy fire. They must have sent artillery teams ahead of their main force."

His guess was correct. The divisional commander of the German counteroffensive was a highly-experienced officer named Klugermann who had served in the First World War and subsequently with distinction in the Netherlands and France. Warned about the rebel occupation of the battery by his HQ and aware an Allied force of even greater strength than his own was making for Valderosa, he had tried to counter the harassing Allied fighter-bombers by sending small artillery teams with mobile guns along the forest tracks. Protected by the trees and so able to travel by day as well as night, these teams had reached the valley in time to witness Lazenby's abortive assault. Working frantically, they were now in position with their guns sited along the mountain slopes facing the hill. Some had been ready to go into action a couple of hours earlier. But, Klugermann, fearing that Allied aircraft might be diverted to them, had issued an order that none must reveal its presence until his main force arrived.

As two more heavy explosions came, this time nearer the northern hillcrest, Roberts glanced at Kessler. "What do you think they are?"

"Almost certainly 75mm mountain infantry howitzers," the German told him. "They probably brought the parts up in light transports or on mules and assembled them on the spot."

"Shall we try to knock them out?"

Kessler's voice turned sharp. "On no account. Our task is to stop their main force from reaching Valderosa. For that we shall need every gun that we have."

The first German tank was sighted at 13.02. Even battle-hardened men could not repress a shudder at what it portended. Warned by the fate of the scout car, it halted forty yards from the glowing wreck, lowered its long gun barrel, and fired a shell at the road. Moving forward another thirty yards, it fired again. Roberts, into whose battle zone the tank had now entered, fixed his binoculars on a tree along the roadside. As the tank drew level with it he jerked his arm down. The 88 nearest to him kicked violently and sent its high-velocity shell screaming down. Roberts saw it strike the ground ten or eleven yards from the tank. He shouted his instructions, the gun-layer made a minute correction and the 88 recoiled again. This time it scored a direct hit. The tank slued violently and smoke began pouring from its turret. A few seconds later flames were visible.

There was no time for congratulations among the gunners. As if everything else had been a prelude and the gods of war had been waiting for that one deadly blow, all hell broke loose in the valley. Grey-clad infantrymen, who had been rushed east and west the moment their transports halted, burst out of the woods and began streaming in great waves towards the hill. At the same moment every gun on the mountainside commenced firing. Further to the east other soldiers broke out of the woods and began clearing a way for the tanks that were jostling behind them. Knowing how formidable the defenses of the hill were, Klugermann had decided from the onset that if Kessler kept his threat, he would try to overwhelm the hill and thin out its firepower by a massive frontal attack. At the same time, with Kessler's guns fully occupied, he would use his engineers and tanks to punch a hole through the hastily-laid minefield and make straight for Valderosa. His opening gambit with the scout car and the tank had been only to convince himself that Kessler meant business. With that point emphatically established, Klugermann had decided to waste no more time. He ordered the full-scale attack.

Although the odds were overwhelmingly on his side, there were two factors against him. One was the narrow confines of the pass which gave the 88s a chance to attack his armor before it could deploy and present a more difficult target. The other was Kessler's fanatical determination to keep all soldiers, German or Allied, out of Valderosa. Although the waves of grey-clad soldiers running towards the hill looked large enough to sweep right over it, Kessler's orders were that every 88 within range should zero in on the men and armor that were pouring out towards the town. In the meantime only rebels armed with short-range weapons and the partisans down the hillside were to engage the infantry.

Aware their lives might depend on a quick repulse of the armor, the 88 gunners worked like galley slaves, heaving shells on to loading trays and tossing away empty shell cases while the gun barrels jerked back and forth like the tongues of snakes. With eleven guns firing at their maximum rate, a terrifying deluge of over two hundred shells a minute burst among the tanks and engineers.

To Allied observers across the way the very ground seemed to be boiling as if an enormous geyser had erupted beneath the valley floor. Armstrong's face had a pallor as he turned to Lazenby. "They're giving Jerry a hell of a pounding, sir. They must have half as many guns again on that side of the hill."

Lazenby's grunt gave nothing away. "Yeah."

With no help from his superior officer, Armstrong was forced to stick his neck out. "As they appear to be keeping their word, sir, don't you think we should leave them to it? They seem to be doing a very efficient job."

Lazenby turned towards him aggressively. "What if the Krauts take that hill? You thought of that? They'll occupy the town and they'll pin our main force back in the valley."

"But aren't we going to make it easier for the Germans to take the hill if we attack it from this side?" Newman broke in.

"Not the way I see it. As the Krauts start to soften 'em up, they'll pull out more men from the southern hillcrest. If we time it right, we can have our bayonets up their gunners' asses while they're still in action."

The younger officers exchanged glances. "But even if we take the hill, sir, do you think we can do as good a job as those rebels are doing?"

Newman could hardly have made a more unfortunate remark. Lazenby's thick neck visibly swelled. "Goddamn it, man, they're shit up here. Cowards and deserters. Are you telling me our guys aren't better soldiers?"

Newman held his ground. "No, sir. I'm asking if we can

handle 88s as well. I know we've brought some artillerymen
with us, but those rebels handle 88s better than the Germans
themselves."

Lazenby's face darkened. "What's wrong with you guys?
We were told to take this town and by God that's what we're
going to do. So quit bellyaching and get ready to move when
I give the word."

Klugermann's attempt to storm into Valderosa lasted less
than five minutes. Because of the need for speed, his division
had been given only light tanks and their thin armor was no
match for the deadly 88s. As tank after tank burst into
flames under the hurricane of shells, even the tough German
crews were forced to draw back into the safety of the valley.
The engineers had already retreated, although not before they
left behind a third of their number wounded or killed.

This time, however, the rebels had not escaped without
loss. The German 75s on the mountain slopes opposite them
had been firing unhindered, and with all northern-facing 88s
in action it had been relatively easy to fix their positions.
Three guns, two in Roberts's troop and one in Williams', had
been hit as a consequence. Greyson had been a gun-layer for
one of these stricken guns. Throughout the action his shrill
voice had never stopped complaining, but neither did he
flinch when the 75mm shells had crept along the hillcrest in
search of his 88. The explosion killed two of his crew, half-
stunned him and badly gashed his head; but he had staggered
back, rallied the survivors and somehow kept the gun firing.

Roberts's second gun crew had been less fortunate. A shell
had burst behind its shield and killed all but two men. Williams' gun crew had suffered a similar fate although only one
man had been killed. The effect of all this, with the wounded
having to be taken by jeep to the casualty station where
Magda and Schiller were already overworked, was that two
full gun crews had been lost—a loss that Kessler countered by
ordering two German crews across the hilltop to man surplus
88s.

In the meantime, although the advance on the town had
been halted, there was no respite for Kessler's gunners. In
spite of the frantic fire put out by the rebels' infantry shield,
the first wave of German soldiers was already halfway across
the valley. Moreover, on Klugermann's orders, a dozen tanks
had detoured away from the fire-swept road and headed for

the relatively safe ground beneath the mountain slopes. This armor, well spread out and leading columns of soldiers behind it, was also advancing on the hill.

The threat was apparent to all. Artillery was deadly against infantry in the open, but almost useless against infantry hidden in woods. If the hordes of soldiers once reached the hillside, even its steepness would not save the rebels. Mopping up the sparse defenders on their way, the Germans would be able to climb by the hundreds to the crest where the rebels' guns would be virtually at their mercy.

If the Allied main force did not arrive in time, it had to happen; Kessler had always known that. Time would be either his enemy or his friend. His terse orders were shouted by the GPOs to their gunners. The target now was the infantry. Sweating men swung and depressed the 88s, discovering to their immense relief that the infantry had not advanced too far to be beneath their sights. Officers did not bother to call corrections: every gun-layer knew his task and the range was relatively short. As fast as guns were laid they fired, recoiled and fired again. Great fountains of earth and steel rose ahead of the advancing soldiers and moved in fearful array towards them. Like a field of corn suddenly bending in a gale, men threw themselves to the ground while frantic officers and NCOs called for smoke protection. With no natural cover available, the tanks zigzagged in an effort to throw off the gunners'. aim.

But the 88s sought them out. Shells smashed through their thin armor and crushed their crews to pulp. 20mm fire snaked out from the hill, slowly at first, then racing in spurts of dust towards the prostrate German soldiers. Heavy smoke, caused by the shell fire and the call to the German 75s for smoke protection, began to drift along the valley. Under its cover, whistles shrilled and the grey-clad soldiers retreated.

There was no time for jubilation on the hillcrest. GPOs, who had been trying to pinpoint the sites of the German 75s during the action, called immediately for their gunners to open fire on them. When the 88s fell silent at last, only an occasional enemy shell dropped on the hilltop. Sylvester, who had refused to take cover during the German assault, turned to Roberts. "Do you think you've knocked most of them out?"

Still wearing his old khaki sweater, Roberts was busy lighting his pipe. "A few perhaps. But my guess is that like us they're taking a breather."

Sylvester galnced at the Englishman's gunners. Soaked in sweat, panting hard from their efforts, they had dropped on any seat they could find. Some had lit cigarettes; others were laying back and staring blindly at the smoke-hazed sky. The sound of a jeep made the correspondent turn. Kessler who, regardless of the danger, had been patrolling the hillcrest during the action, called Roberts towards him. "I've just had a report that the Allied main force is making good progress and should be here by 15.00 hours or even sooner. The Germans will know this too, so expect another attack shortly."

Sylvester had stepped within earshot. "If things are getting that tight, what are they waiting for?"

Kessler nodded at the mountain slopes opposite where columns of black smoke were rising from fires caused by the 88s. "They will have realized their troops must have more artillery cover. So they will assemble more guns as fast as possible. When they judge they have enough, they will attack again."

"Can you hold them?" Sylvester asked.

Ignoring the question, Kessler turned back to Roberts. "Nickolai and Weiss say there is general activity along the riverbed. So don't be surprised if we get an attack from there as well."

"But that would be crazy," Sylvester protested. "You're doing their job for them. So why should they attack you now?"

Kessler glanced at him. "How many wars have you covered?"

The question took the American by surprise. "I've done my stint. I was in Spain and China. Why?"

The German's voice was dry. "With all that experience you should have learned more about the military mind." A moment later his jeep roared away, leaving Sylvester staring after him.

In fact Kessler's suspicions were justified. From his own lookout post and from his men spread out along the western riverbed, Lazenby had gathered blow by blow details of the German assault on the hill. When, for an alarming moment, it had appeared that the German infantry might break through the guns, the American had been within a hair's breadth of ordering his men forward again in a desperate bid to win the race to the hilltop. Klugermann's withdrawal, coming just as Lazenby had the radio microphone to his lips, had given him an extra breathing space to complete his plans. At the same time, as aware as Kessler that the next German attack could not be long delayed, he was making every second count.

Since the air attack the armed jeeps had found little to do. After a word with Johnson, Beccione had taken the opportunity to visit Magda. The makeshift casualty station stood in the woods less than two hundred yards from Kessler's command post. Its size suggested it had served as another of the monks' communal houses, perhaps the place where they had eaten together. As Beccione ducked through its low entrance, the sickly smell of antiseptics and blood greeted him; the more serious casualties from the 88s had already been brought in. There were no beds: the wounded were lying on the floor on pallets collected from the German tents. Although one or two men were moaning softly, most appeared to be unconscious. Schiller, a hypodermic needle in his hand, was moving among them. Magda was bandaging the arm of a shaken young German who was sitting on a table. Beccione hurried over to her. "How is it going?"

Intent on her task, she had not noticed his entry. For a moment she showed relief that he was not wounded. Then she gave a shrug of bitterness. "What does Kessler expect us to do? We are not surgeons. We can only try to stop their loss of blood and give them morphia."

Her appearance distressed him. The apron she had put over her battle dress was soaked in blood and her face was drawn and pale. "It's tough, I know. But we're doing all right out there. We've driven back both attacks."

She nodded at the unconscious men. "For them the sooner someone occupies the hill the better. It must be soon or half of them will die."

"The Allied main force can't be far away," he said. "And they'll have all the medical facilities they need."

Her inactive role was clearly depressing her. "You mean they will cure them only to shoot them later?"

Ignoring her comment, he leaned forward and kissed her. "The next hour or two could be really rough. When it starts I want you to take shelter in one of those caves. Anyone can dish out morphia. O.K.?"

Her eyes flashed angrily at his suggestion. Then, as she saw the extent of his concern, her expression softened. "I won't take any unnecessary risks, I promise you."

He had to be content with that: the demands outside were too great. The stench of cordite was everywhere as he made for the command post. He wanted to discuss with Kessler the

best disposition of his jeeps before the next German attack
came, but before he reached the hut there was a massive roar
overhead followed by the hammering of cannon fire. Through
it he heard the resonant explosion of an 88 on the southern
hill crest. It was succeeded almost immediately by another
and then another. The shadow of a second aircraft flashed
right over him. Within seconds the rolling gunfire and the
staccato pounding of the aircraft cannon made the trees
shake like aspens in a wind. Under the air strike he had at
last obtained, Lazenby was launching his third assault on the
hill.

48

The aircraft this time were fighter-bombers from 239
Squadron. Forewarned about the formidable defenses of the
hill, they came in fast and low and from all directions to thin
out the AA fire. As before, their targets were the 88s on the
southern hillcrest. With blackened and still smoking scars visible near the guns, they were able to launch their rockets with
greater accuracy than previously. Worse from the rebels'
point of view were the strafing attacks they launched along
the hillcrest. With bullets and shells hammering down and
ricocheting viciously from the trees, gunners were forced to
fling themselves down for protection, and the 88s rate of fire
was consequently reduced. In the meantime American and
British soldiers had launched themselves from the riverbed
and were making a desperate bid to reach the safety zone that
lay below the dreaded 88s. For the first four hundred yards
their casualties were high, but as men saw their comrades
reach comparative safety and wave them on, they took fresh
heart and kept on running.

During the lull Jean Pierre had moved his men further
down the hillsides and, wherever possible, had set up machine
gun posts. But these were too few in number and the Allied
soldiers were able to flood through the gaps between them.
Recognizing the danger, Jean Pierre had no option but to call
his men back. Bringing with them what automatic weapons

they could, the partisans re-climbed the hill and tried to establish new defensive positions.

From the northern mountain slopes Klugermann was witnessing the action with mixed feelings. He knew that as yet the Allies had only two battalions in the valley, and he believed that even if they occupied the hill, it was extremely unlikely they would be able to use the 88s as efficiently as the rebels. At the same time the hill was the key to the entire affair; the occupation of Valderosa was of little use to the German unless he controlled the heights above it.

With every minute bringing the Allied main force nearer, Klugermann felt the situation slipping rapidly away from him. Yet if he acted quickly, with the rebels now under attack from both the south and the air, he might still be able to turn the situation to his advantage. Accordingly he ordered an immediate, all-out assault on the hill. The time was 14.05 hours.

The 75s, now in greater numbers than before, began the attack with a devastating salvo. Their shells had hardly exploded on the hillcrest when German infantry began pouring out of the woods. Tanks, which had crept unseen among the trees, also broke out on a wide front and began moving at speed across the fields. To observers on the hillcrest, reeling under the barrage of heavy shell fire, the valley suddenly seemed to fill with soldiers and armor—an irresistible tidal wave that looked capable of sweeping the very hill away.

Roberts gave his weary gunners no time to contemplate the odds, his terse voice driving them back into action again. The 88 shells screamed down once more, soldiers were tossed into the air like empty sacks; but this time, because the attack was made on a wider front, the barrage was less concentrated. Moreover, the shell fire from the German 75mms was now being augmented by the darting tanks, whose guns were spitting continuous fire as they searched along the hillcrest. To the frightened inhabitants of Valderosa, the entire hilltop seemed aflame.

Above, the aircraft radio channel was filled with shouts of warning as pilots reported the massive assault by the Germans. Expecting to be diverted against them, they were bewildered when they were ordered sternly to maintain their attack on the southern hillcrest.

Time was beginning to run out for the rebels. The 88s were still firing and soldiers of both armies were still being wiped off the valley floor like flies off a wall, but the number of guns and their rate of fire was being drastically reduced as shells and rockets exploded among them. Although tanks were burning all over the northern battlefield, some had now broken past the 88s' zone of fire and, like an offshore battle fleet, were cruising back and forth along the hill's lower slopes, directing their fire at its slender infantry shield. This breakthrough forced Jean Pierre to switch half his partisans from the southern slopes, which in turn created even greater gaps in his defenses for the Allied soldiers to exploit. As the first of the German infantry reached the hill, Jean Pierre had no choice but to order a general retreat.

The attacks were like irresistible waves, held apart for the moment by the hill but sweeping around it and converging at its western end. As the enemy soldiers came within range, they turned their attention from the rebels and began firing at one another.

During this time the fleet of jeeps had been in nonstop action, helping the 20mm gunners against the fighter-bombers and ferrying the wounded to the casualty station. Their own casualties were heavy, however. Many had been destroyed by the shells and rockets that were now descending on the hill-top like a meteor swarm. The rest were finding it more and more difficult to traverse the shell-cratered tracks. With the trees dry from the summer heat, forest fires were raging everywhere.

Aware that the western side of the hill contained fewer guns, Beccione and Toschack, with two other jeeps, had rushed there when the news reached them that the two attacks were converging. The twin-gun batteries of Tito and Nickolai were both in action when the jeeps arrived. Because of his position Tito, to his massive disgust, was the only battery commander who had not previously been called into action. But the Yugoslav was making up for lost time now. His gunners, firing at a phenomenal rate, were causing fearful casualties on both the Allies and the Germans. Nickolai's gunners, although they had suffered casualties from the air attack, were also taking their toll. But every man knew he was only delaying the inevitable. Sections of the waves of infantry that had swept around the hill had been beneath the trajectories of the 88s for some time: and these men were already fighting their way upwards. The only bright spot for the rebels was the cessation of the air attack as the fighter-bombers ran out of ammunition.

Beccione and Toschack were watching the scene from a

knoll of rock when a jeep halted behind them. Kessler was its sole occupant. With many telephone lines cut by shellfire and with too few radios to keep him in touch with all aspects of the battle, the German—totally disregarding his own safety—had been everywhere during the last desperate half hour. His jeep was dented by shellfire and blood was soaking through the back and right shoulder of his uniform. Ignoring Beccione's question, he clambered onto the knoll. His shout came through the rolling gunfire and heavy explosions. "How are things here?"

Beccione put his mouth to the German's ear. "We won't be able to hold these 88s much longer. Infantry from both sides are already climbing the hill."

Kessler was gazing at the stretch of valley beyond the hill where Allied and German soldiers, prostrate on the ground, were firing at one another. As the gunfire diminished for a moment, his voice, full of aversion, reached Beccione. "Look at them! Although both are dying beneath our guns, they still cannot stop killing one another. There you have it in a microcosm, Beccione. The vile and terrible disease of man."

The next instant the German jumped down from the rock and ran towards Tito's battery. A few seconds later the Yugoslav's guns ceased firing. Appearing out of the trees again, Kessler waved Beccione and Toschack towards him. "Tell Nickolai he must cease firing also."

"What for, for Chrissake?"

Kessler climbed painfully into his jeep. His drawn, implacable face turned to the American. "Do as I tell you. On this side of the hill they cannot harm the town if they fight one another. And it will give us that little extra time."

"But why stop the guns?"

The German showed his contempt for the question. "Have you learned nothing about the nature of man? Hate unites him. If we continue to kill these soldiers, they will unite against us before they turn on one another again."

Toschack gave a start. "He's right."

Once again Beccione found himself fascinated by the German's bitter astuteness. "Have you received any more news about the Allies main force?"

Kessler waved him off and started up his jeep. "Hold out here as long as possible but don't allow yourselves to be cut off from the rear. When the time comes I intend to defend a perimeter at the far side of the hill. The jeeps will be invaluable then, so make certain you bring them."

"We've only got one battery of guns at that side," Beccione said. "Can it hold the Germans out of Valderosa once they've captured the rest of the 88s?"

Kessler's weary face set like a mask of concrete. "It must. But by that time I believe it will not be necessary—for the very reason I have ceased firing on those soldiers below. When the battle reaches its final stage and we are killing every soldier within our reach, their hatred and thirst for revenge will force both commanders to deal with us first."

By 14.50 the hill resembled a scene from hell. Even deep down in their caves, Russell and the German prisoners could feel the massive pounding of the shells. No longer subdued by the 88s, the German gunners had been greatly reinforced during the last hour and were now able to fire at will. Had the rebels commanded enough manpower to operate their surplus guns, the story might have been different; but casualties were draining away their lifeblood. Nickolai, that most amiable of men, had died instantly from a direct hit. MacAllister's gun had been struck by an aircraft rocket and the New Zealander lost a leg in the explosion. With the rest of his gunners either dead or wounded, he had been left too long without attention and died from loss of blood. Mogelli had literally been blown to pieces when the ammunition dump from which he was fetching shells had been hit by a strafing aircraft. The vectors of fate had played a similar trick on Zimmermann. In making his rounds, the German artillery expert had arrived at a spot in the woods at the same time as a howitzer shell. When the smoke cleared there was little to see of the jeep and nothing of the man.

Casualties were high everywhere—among the gunners, the jeep crews, and not least among the partisans. However braggadocio their behavior in the town the previous evening, the Italians had defended the guns with almost suicidal courage. But as more and more Allied and German soldiers began scaling the hillsides, their task became physically impossible. Firing automatic weapons from behind every tree, hurling grenades whenever possible, they began the retreat towards the eastern hillcrest where Kessler intended making his last stand.

Ironically they were aided by the very destruction both sides had inflicted on the hill. Huge fires, raging along both hillcrests, gave them considerable protection on their flanks

for the retreat. In addition, as ammunition dumps blew up,
massive explosions followed by blinding clouds of smoke
checked their pursuers.

The ground Kessler had chosen to defend was a five-
hundred yard stretch of woodland, from a dogleg of monks'
cells to the west to the eastern hillcrest that overlooked Valderosa. In its center was his command post and, nearer the
perimiter, the casualty station. The latter was now full of
wounded, and new casualties were being taken to the command post or laid in monks' cells. An hour earlier German
medical orderlies had been brought up from the prisoners'
cave to help Magda and Schiller. Now Kessler had decided to
release the rest of the captives, feeling their number could
hardly make an appreciable difference to the already over-
whelming odds facing the rebels.

While the last rearguards made their retreat, Jean Pierre
was rushing automatic weapons to the monks' cells. The rest
of his men were deployed between these strongpoints. As the
jeeps came in, they were posted behind the cells to gain cover
and yet be able to dart out and give quick support when
needed. Aware of the massive onslaught that must come
soon, men found what shelter they could behind trees, rocks,
and clumps of bushes.

It was soon apparent that barely sixty per cent of the original party was available for the final battle, and of these more
than half were wounded. Johnson's neck had been badly
gashed by a shell splinter; Jean Pierre was wearing a blood-
soaked bandage around one huge forearm. Weiss, whose
bravery surpassed his morality, had been wounded in the
thigh but insisted on manning the perimeter with the rest of
his men.

None of the rebels cared any longer which army he faced.
Judging from the way soldiers had been bayonetting or shoot-
ing rebels where they lay, it was clearly going to be a fight to
the death. Before the battle had commenced, only the commanders who had been told the full story about the rebels
had felt a desire to punish them for the betrayal of their
flags. But rumors had inevitably spread and now, after the
holocaust of the 88s and the dead who stretched out on both
sides of the valley, it was the rank and file who were thirsting
for revenge.

It was an emotion that ideally suited the needs of both
army commanders. What only Kessler had anticipated, however, was that in their desire for revenge, Allied and German

soldiers had not only begun to ignore one another but had now begun giving each other active assistance. In order to prevent a handful of criminals from saving a town, nationally prescribed enemies had become comrades in arms. Never was the madness of war more vividly illustrated than on that small hill in Italy in 1944.

By 15.15 all the rebels and partisans were inside the perimeter. When the news reached the 75s opposite, their full firepower was directed on the small enclave. High explosives tossed trees into the air; phosphorus bombs flung out their hideous white tentacles. Screams were heard as the fierce burning chemical clung to men's flesh. To escape the holocaust men tried to burrow into the earth, praying as they dug for the arrival of the Allied main force. Even death by execution was preferable to this hell. But no word had been received for the last thirty minutes and observers could see nothing for the black smoke that hung like a pall over the hill.

At 15.23 the crushing barrage lifted. Shocked men, some with ruptured eardrums, lifted their eyes, believing their prayers had been answered. More experienced colleagues shook their heads, cocked their weapons and waited.

There was no preliminary mortar attack: the thick woods would have prematurely exploded the shells. Out of the smoke khaki and grey-clad figures suddenly appeared, running from tree to tree. No one on the perimeter waited for orders: the enemy was too close. Every available weapon opened up and a hail of bullets lashed through the trees. Soldiers stumbled and fell, the rest retreated back into the smoke.

Only the surviving partisans showed elation. The rebels buried their heads in their arms and waited. An uncanny whisper sounded through the crackling of the fires. As men stiffened it grew like a rising wind. A couple of seconds later the ground beneath the prostrate men heaved in anguish as enormous shells came raining down. Desperate to remove this last pocket of resistance, Klugermann had brought his heavy howitzers into action.

The second infantry attack came the moment the barrage lifted. This time it was in greater strength, and a platoon of soldiers broke through on the left of Beccione where a forest track linked the cells together. Beccione nodded and Toschack sent the jeep leaping towards them while the American opened fire with the .50 Browning. Five men fell, the rest broke and ran back. Not daring to turn the jeep on the narrow track, Toschack headed for the next cell while Beccione sprayed the trees. When the jeep braked behind the cell, a hail of bullets ricocheted off its stone walls. Toschack gave a shaky whistle. "If that main force doesn't get here soon, there'll be nothing left of us but dog meat."

Up to this point there had been two things in the rebels' favor. One was the raging fires that gave their enemies only a relatively narrow corridor from which to launch their attacks. The second was that the soldiers lacked heavy weapons—a situation that initially created some degree of parity between them and the rebels. Indeed the .5s of the jeeps were the heaviest automatic weapons either side carried on the hilltop. But by this time over half the jeeps had been disabled and the surviving vehicles left in poor condition. With the Allies and the Germans possessing unlimited resources and the rebels bled white, it seemed certain to all that the third assault would be the last.

It was a view that was apparently shared by the German artillery because this time, no doubt for fear of harming its own soldiers, it did not open fire again when the attack was repulsed. In the unnatural silence that followed, Beccione had a word with Toschack and then ran to the casualty station. As he reached it, Kessler ducked out of the entrance. Haggard, grey-faced, he gave the American an angry stare. "Why have you left your post?"

"I came to see if Magda was all right."

"Magda isn't here. There is no morphia left, so there is nothing more she and Schiller can do. They have both gone to reinforce the perimeter. The German orderlies will take care of the wounded here until help arrives for them."

"What about Sylvester?"

Kessler jerked his head in the direction of the command post. "We have more wounded back there and he is doing what he can for them." He gave Beccione a violent push. "Get back to your post! The next attack must come at any time."

Beccione held his ground. "Isn't there any news yet about the Allied main force?"

The German shook his head. He was carrying a Thompson submachine gun. Blood from his wound was staining his shirt. As he started towards the perimeter, Beccione caught his arm. "Kessler, you have to surrender. After the fight those guys have put up, they deserve a chance to live. And you've got the wounded to think about."

Kessler jerked away. His stride quickened and a drifting bank of smoke half-hid him from sight. Skirting a shell crater, Beccione caught up with him again. "Did you hear what I said? If the main force hasn't arrived, you have to surrender. If you don't, those guys will die for nothing."

The German's laugh was full of scorn. "Do you think they will let us live after what we have done to them? Allies and Germans alike, they will kill us all, even the wounded."

"I don't believe that, Kessler. Not when their officers get charge of them."

"We are not surrendering, Beccione. There is still time for the main force to arrive. So get back to your post."

"You can't quit, can you?" Beccione shouted. "Not even when a blind man could see you've lost. Goddamn it, Kessler, why can't you face it? You've lost."

For a moment the German's deep-set eyes burned in their sockets like coals. Then he turned and strode away. As his gaunt figure disappeared into the smoke, another ammunition dump exploded, hurling flame and uprooted trees into the tortured sky.

49

Beccione found Magda crouched behind a tree, a Sten gun in her hands. Her appearance alarmed him. The sight of so much death and suffering had imprinted itself on her face: her eyes were sunken and bruised and the skin was tight over her cheekbones. She was shivering violently as he bent down close to her. "Come to the jeep," he urged. "There's more cover there."

She followed him past crouching men and dead bodies without resistance, but refused to take cover inside the stone cell. "No, Joe. I'd rather die in the open. Out here with you."

He did not argue and she sat alongside Toschack in the front seat of the jeep. A huge fire on the southern hillcrest was spreading: they could feel its heat on their faces. It tinted red the smoke between the trees from where they knew the final attack must come.

A long minute passed, then whistles began shrilling. Reaching forward Beccione put a hand on Magda's shoulder. A lump came into his throat as she reached back and gripped it.

The attack this time came from the Germans alone. To Lazenby's intense frustration, the huge fires on the southern hillcrest had moved right in front of his men and halted their progress. Whistles shrilled again and grey-clad figures, firing machine carbines and rifles, burst out of the smoke. Seconds later the woods came alive with the clatter of automatic fire and the hoarse cries of men.

Beccione and Toschack were already in action, laying a crossfire before the Germans' advance. Magda joined in with her Sten gun. Soldiers were falling everywhere but for every casualty two more men appeared. With the trees and the smoke often giving cover until the last moment, men found themselves face to face with their enemies. Soon the battle became a surrealistic nightmare of red-stained figures writhing in mortal combat and faces contorted with hatred swimming in and out of the choking smoke.

This time the attack was massive and it was clear that resistance could only prolong the agony a short while longer. Yet only half a dozen of the defenders threw down their arms. The rest fought on, although by this time few remembered the reason. Urged on by a complex of emotions, from the basic instinct of survival to the ecstasy of self-sacrifice, men committed acts of desperate bravery. Greyson, a Mauser pistol in his hand and screaming at the top of his voice, ran straight at a group of German soldiers and killed three before he fell riddled with bullets. Waltermann, the young German who had anticipated his death, stood his ground with great courage until he was killed by a hand grenade. Rossi, badly wounded and with his jeep on fire, stayed at his gun and continued firing until he fell back into the flames. Brosio, an arm half-severed by a shell splinter, crawled back into the fight and fired his Sten single-handed until a bayonet stilled him at last. Jean Pierre, massive and blood-stained like some Norse God, was seen clubbing two soldiers to death after his Thompson machine gun ran out of ammunition. And the architect of the resistance, Kessler, was everywhere that the fighting was fiercest. An almost supernatural figure in the swirling smoke, he seemed to bear a charmed life as again and again he rallied his men.

Screams, curses and prayers sounded through the crash of grenades and the bursts of fire. One by one the jeeps were destroyed and their crews killed. Slowly but inexorably the defenders were driven back towards their command post. If they were to make a last stand there, they had first to cross the open clearing that lay before it.

Beccione, whose jeep was still in action at the southern end of the defense line, recognized the rebels' danger and thumped Toschack's shoulder. "Try to get us back to the side of the clearing. Otherwise they'll have no cover."

The Australian understood and jumped back into the driver's seat. With no hope of survival if he drove forward from the protection of the stone cell, he was forced to back the jeep through the trees in the hope of finding a suitable track. As the huge fire on the hillcrest drew nearer, the two men and the girl could feel its heat scorching their faces. But with the dense smoke now hiding the jeep, Beccione and Magda were able to cease firing and help guide Toschack back. All three were half-suffocated by the time they maneuvered onto a track, but the smoke thinned out as they neared the clearing. Seeing a clump of bushes on its southern perimeter, Toschack backed the jeep into it.

The first of the defenders appeared half a minute later. These were the wounded who could still walk: Kessler had been forced to abandon the rest. They were a pitiful sight—filthy, blood-stained, some supporting comrades more stricken than themselves. The rest stumbled on, the forty yards to the hut an agonizing journey. Mercifully, the dense trees surrounding the clearing prevented mortars being fired at them.

The last had barely disappeared into the command post when the rearguard came into sight. They were pathetically few and some looked almost as far gone as their wounded. Beccione caught a glimpse of Roberts at the far side of the clearing; he was throwing smoke grenades to blind the advancing Germans. Tito's bald head could be seen glinting through the smoke as he sprayed the trees with fire from a captured M.40 carbine. Williams, although he had one arm broken, was using a pistol effectively with the other. Jean Pierre was also back in action. He had torn a Sten gun and ammunition from a dead partisan and was firing with one hand while he hurled hand grenades with the other. Etienne was not far from him. Incredibly, the small Frenchman appeared to be grinning as he also tossed grenades into the smoke.

The last man to appear was Kessler. Backing slowly, he was shepherding his men towards the command post as he fired burst after burst at the invisible enemy. Knowing that the German would be the last to retreat, Beccione warned Toschack and Magda to get ready. The girl tried to smile at him but her pinched face was very pale. She was as aware as the men that the moment they gave their position away they would become a target for every soldier in the woods.

Kessler, who was still in the jeep's line of fire, appeared to be defying every bullet aimed at him. In that brief moment before Beccione believed his death would come, his thoughts turned fanciful. The German was more than mortal, a being of loftier aims and ideals, and one impervious to the destructive urges of man.

At a sharp cry from Magda, his fantasy burst like a bubble. Kessler had stumbled, then sunk to his knees. In seconds Jean Pierre was at his side. As the Frenchman heaved Kessler on his massive shoulders, Beccione braced himself and nodded at Toschack.

The three guns in the jeep fired together, raking the fringe of the smoke-wreathed wood. Realizing what was happening, the remainder of the rearguard turned and ran after Jean Pierre. The crew of the jeep continued to hose their fire the full length of the clearing. When his Browning ran out of ammunition, Beccione yelled at Magda while he desperately threaded in another belt. "Run for the hut! Quickly while there's still time."

She could not hear his words for the hammering of Toscahck's gun, but she guessed their meaning and shook her head. Beccione took a quick look at the command post. Less than a dozen men remained outside and they were diving through its entrance as fast as they could. There were also flashes of automatic fire from the windows: the rebels were wasting no time in making the hut a strongpoint. Grabbing Magda's arm, Beccione tried to force her down from the jeep. "We've done our job. Now get over to the hut."

When she struggled with him he cursed and struck her. She went immediately limp and Beccione pushed her towards Toschack, who by this time had also run out of ammunition. "Get her over there! I'll cover you."

The Australian saw his expression and jumped down at

once. He ran with the girl's limp body towards the hut. Beccione cocked the Browning and began hosing the trees again. The soldiers, identifying the source of the firing this time, started to respond. Bullets snipped twigs from the bushes and hammered into the jeep's engine. A sudden blow on his right shoulder flung Beccione backwards across the seats. He tried to reach the gun again, but in the act toppled sideways and fell into the bushes.

It was an accident that almost certainly saved his life. The Germans opened fire in earnest, and a hail of bullets shattered the jeep's windshield and ricocheted off the gun mountings. Aided by the drifting smoke, the bushes, and the cover the rebels were giving him, Beccione managed to crawl within ten yards of the command post when his strength gave out. He was trying to drag himself forward by his elbows when Jean Pierre ran outside, picked him up like a sack of potatoes, and bundled him into the hut entrance. Beccione could just barely lift his head. "How's Kessler?"

Jean Pierre was looking grief-stricken. "He's badly hurt. Get inside."

50

The command post looked like a butcher's shop with wounded men lying everywhere. The air stank of smoke, blood, sweat, antiseptics and fear. The windows on both sides were fully manned: the rest of the partisans and rebels were slumped down with their backs to the stone walls. Some were assisting the wounded; others looked too far gone to care. Outside bullets were striking the walls and keening away.

Kessler was lying on a blood-stained blanket near the radio with Schiller and Roberts in attendance. As Jean Pierre hurried back to his stricken leader and Beccione tried to follow, Magda ran up to him. Although dazed and in pain from the blow he had given her, she was showing alarm at his appearance. "Where are you hit?"

He tried to push her aside. "It's nothing," he muttered. "Let me get to Kessler."

Shock seemed to have sapped his strength because the girl

was able to force him down on an empty ammunition box. Cutting open his shirt, she probed at the wound beneath. Her face cleared as she reached out for a bandage. "If I can stop this bleeding you should be all right until you see a doctor. Keep still until I've finished."

He tried to rise. "I said leave it. I want to talk to Kessler."

"You can't talk to him. Kessler's unconscious."

"Is he dying?"

"Yes, we think so. He's very badly wounded."

He felt sick as he sank back. She was tying the bandage in position when there was a sudden horrified cry from the window behind them. "*Mein Gott! Flammerwerfien!*"

Someone gave a gasp of fear. Roberts, still sprightly after his exertions, ran to the window. Beccione saw him start, then turn and nod at the grim-faced Jean Pierre who was close on his heels. Helped by Magda, Beccione joined them. He was in time to catch a glimpse of a platoon of soldiers through the drifting smoke. In their midst two men were being helped on with large packs, while ahead of them two other soldiers were carrying long hoses with nozzles.

The smoke closed in before anyone had the presence of mind to open fire. No weapon brought such terror to soldiers as the *Flammerwerfer* and with good reason. Using compressed air or gas as a propellant, its hose could spew out a searing tongue of flame that consumed everything in its path. For a moment Magda's eyes were huge with fear. Then, as she turned from the window, her expression changed. "Keep your voices down. The wounded must not know."

Her courage gripped Beccione by the throat. But her plea was in vain. The German's cry had been heard and fear was written on every face. Sylvester turned on Jean Pierre. "You can't let this happen, Moreau. You've got to surrender."

Cries of agreement came from the exhausted survivors. Returning to Kessler and seeing he was still unconscious, Jean Pierre dropped heavily on an empty crate. Sylvester followed him. "Never mind what Kessler would do. These guys have given everything. You can't let them die now."

Swollen and bloodshot, the Frenchman's eyes lifted to him in dislike. Roberts crossed the floor. "He's right, Jean Pierre. It's over."

He received a fierce scowl. "Franz would never quit. Never."

"He would have no choice. And you must be quick. They could attack at any moment."

The Frenchman's tortured face betrayed his conflict of loyalties. For a moment he seemed about to refuse. Then he turned away, his voice hoarse with contempt and self-hatred. "All right, goddamn it. Have it your way."

Sylvester swung around on Magda. "Have you got anything white?"

The girl fumbled beneath a table and came up with a blood-soaked rag. The correspondent glanced at it, then shrugged. "I guess it's appropriate. Wait here, all of you."

As he made for the entrance, a shrill whistle sounded. "Here they come," Roberts muttered.

Jean Pierre ran with him to the window. They were in time to see a red Very light arcing over the clearing. It was followed by more whistles and shouted orders. Fearing he might be too late, Sylvester ran for the entrance. As he reached it the telephone from the eastern battery began buzzing. Klaus snatched it up, then turned in excitement to Jean Pierre.

"The Allied main force is in the valley, captain. The battery could not see them before because of the smoke. The Germans are withdrawing."

Sylvester, who had heard the announcement from the entrance, ducked outside and saw the clearing had emptied of soldiers. As he listened, whistles could be heard up and down the northern hillside. "I think it's true," he shouted. "They sound as if they're drawing back."

In fact, Klugermann's scouts had reported the Allied advance guard at the entrance of the southern valley fifteen minutes ago; but with his men so close to capturing the hill, the German had gone against his better judgment and allowed the assault to continue. His change of mind had come after the rebels' successful retreat into the command post. With raging fires destroying the 88s and their ammunition and so making their capture pointless, and with Allied armor beginning to stream across the valley, he was now forced to withdraw his infantry in a hurry.

Nor was there any question of a direct confrontation with the Allies once his force was in one piece again. From the onset Klugermann had known his mission was to pose a threat to the enemy, not to fight a battle of attrition. With the element of surprise lost, Klugermann's only option was to retreat back to the Gothic Line where his division would be sorely needed in the battles ahead.

Sylvester's triumphant announcement had brought a wave of cracked cheering from the wounded men. Magda, hardly daring to believe her ears, had buried her face in Beccione's torn shirt. It took Etienne, ever the realist, to bring the situation back to earth. "Why are you all looking so happy? Do you think the Allies are going to bring you candy and ice cream?'"

The reminder killed the rebels' euphoria like a shower of cold water. Williams, propped up against a wall with his broken arm in a makeshift sling, lifted his lugubrious face. "Baba's right. From the way they were bayoneting our guys out there, they'll be as happy to fry us as the Jerries were."

Beccione went to the window where Roberts was gazing out. "Isn't there any sign of them?"

The Englishman shook his head and Beccione's voice dropped. "I don't get it. I thought they'd be straight through that gap once the Krauts withdrew."

Shell and rifle fire could now be heard from the northern side of the hill. Roberts nodded in its direction. "Perhaps they're leaving us until they've chased the Germans out of the valley."

Roberts's guess was the right one. The commander of the Allied main force, a West Point officer named Rawlinson, had been shocked on his arrival to see the number of dead Allied soldiers strewn across the floor of the valley. He had decided right then to inflict the most rigorous punishment possible on the rebels. At the same time, he was an officer who put first things first and, seeing no way the rebels could escape, he had made his initial task the pursuit of the withdrawing Germans. To Lazenby's fury, this advance had involved his own battalions which were in closer contact with Klugermann's men than any of the more recently arrived Allied units. Only a hundred of his soldiers had been left on the hilltop and their orders were merely to contain the rebels until Rawlinson had time to deal with them. However, no one who knew the strict humorless officer had any doubts that when that time came he would make sure the punishment fitted the crime.

With no knowledge of this, the rebels renewed their watch on the woods. As puzzled as anyone, Sylvester joined Jean Pierre who, with the care and gentleness of a woman, was dabbing Kessler's face with a damp sponge. "I'm going into those woods to see what's happening," the reporter announced.

The Frenchman lifted his grieving face and nodded at the

rows of wounded men. "What do you think? Can you talk the Allies into giving them a break?"

The correspondent hesitated. "I can get them medical attention."

Tension and distress made the Frenchman irascible. "I don't just mean medical attention, for Christ's sake. Can you get 'em a pardon?"

Sylvester lowered his voice. "Do you think it's likely? After the clobbering you've given them?"

"They asked for it, didn't they?" Jean Pierre snarled. "Kessler warned them time and time again what would happen if they came."

Over by the window Roberts and Etienne had been listening to this exchange. The Englishman turned and approached Sylvester. "Etienne and I will take a look outside. You stay here until we know what's going on."

When Sylvester protested, Etienne gave his cynical grin and pushed him back. "You can be a hero later, *mon ami.* Right now you're our only hope of staying alive."

As the two men ducked outside Schiller motioned urgently at Jean Pierre. Moving quickly to Kessler's side, Jean Pierre saw the German was stirring and his eyes had opened. He dropped on his knees beside him. "Franz! How are you feeling?"

For a full ten seconds Kessler's eyes were empty of everything but exhaustion and the nearness of death. Then he recognized Jean Pierre and tried to smile. Hiding his emotion, the Frenchman bent over him. "Franz! Can you hear me?"

This time Kessler managed to nod. "Then listen, Franz. You've won. The Allies are here in strength and they've surrounded the town."

Beccione knew that as long as he lived he would remember the German's expression of radiant gratitude. It was as if oil had been poured on the dying fires within him. He raised his head a couple of inches and his hoarse whisper carried to the men gathered around him. "Is there any damage?"

"No, Franz. There was no fighting in the town. Everyone is safe."

The man's bruised eyes closed in relief. When they opened again they fixed on Sylvester. The correspondent took Schiller's place. "What is it, Kessler?"

Although death was at the German's elbow, every man present could feel his will fighting it back until his task was completed. "You have not forgotten your promise?"

The tough American was clearly moved. "After what you and your guys have done? I'll move heaven and earth, Kessler. You can count on that."

"And you will do your best to save my men?"

Sylvester's nod betrayed none of his fears. "Yes. Everything. You have my word."

By this time the German was living on will power alone. With the cords of his neck extended, he was gazing at Sylvester as if assessing his sincerity. Satisfied, he sighed and his head fell back. A moment later a violent spasm of pain made him stiffen. As Schiller leaned over him with a morphia needle, he shook his head and turned his face to Jean Pierre. It was a last farewell to a friend. Thirty seconds later he was dead, his weary face peaceful at last.

No one could bear to look at the Frenchman as he reached out and closed Kessler's eyes. His calloused hand touched the dead man's cheek and lingered there before he turned away. There was barely a dry eye among the other men. Magda was sobbing bitterly, Tito was muttering something in Serbo-Croatian as he crossed himself, and Beccione was gazing down as if he had lost an apostle. At the far end of the hut Roberts appeared and hurried towards the ring of silent mourners. The emotion the Englishman showed when Williams muttered the news was in excess of anything he had revealed during the battle. Recovering quickly, he turned towards Sylvester. "They've got a cordon of men stretched across the hillside but there's no sign they're planning an attack. It seems certain they're keeping us on ice until they've dealt with the Germans."

The distant crash of shellfire and the resonant sound of tank guns added substance to his words. Sylvester nodded and turned towards the entrance, but Beccione's contemptuous voice checked him. "'Forget it, Sylvester. You were right the first time. They're not going to spare us now."

The correspondent's face was lined with distress. "I've got to try, Beccione. You heard me promise Kessler."

"Yeah, and I also heard you promise to get this story published. You shouldn't have made him that promise either. A bunch of deserters saving a town from their own armies? They'll put a blue pencil through every goddamned line." As Beccione watched Schiller cover Kessler's face for the last time, his bitterness exploded. "Anyway, what difference would it make? Guys like Kessler have been dying this way for two thousand years. And what has it changed?"

"They can't kill ideas, Beccione."

"They can't? They can do better—they can screw them up. Even some of *us* didn't understand all Kessler's ambitions. So think what *they*'ll do with them They'll make out he was a sick half-crazed bastard taking his revenge for everything life had dished out to him."

Sylvester nodded heavily. "They'll try. I know that. But don't forget there are a dozen other newspaper guys out there who've seen what's happened. When I tell them the full story and what Kessler told me last night, it's going to be tough even for the Army to screw things up."

Beccione's expression changed. "You're ready to do that— to share your story with the other newsmen?"

The correspondent nodded at the rows of wounded rebels. "Give me a break, Beccione. I'm not all lead and printer's ink."

Toschack opened his mouth to ask a question but Magda was too quick for him. "What exactly did Kessler say to you last night?"

As Sylvester turned towards the girl, men packed closer to listen. "He said that after a lifetime of soul-searching he had reached two bitter conclusions. One was that mankind had a basic flaw that turned men into aggressors and even into killers if the wrong people gained power over them. The second was that pacifism as he had once practiced it was an impotent thing. The only answer to man's aggression was to use that aggression against itself. His vision was a League of Nations Army prepared to do battle anywhere in the world to stamp out war. That is how he used you: as a prototype international brigade. He argued that if the world had created such an army, there would have been no Fascist Italy or Germany. Kessler wasn't unbalanced as I think some of you felt. He was a visionary. That's why, come hell or high water, I'm going to see the world gets this story."

Smoke-blackened, exhausted men were staring at one another, a few still clearly bewildered by the correspondent's words. Eyes turned to the mound on the flagstones now covered by a brown army blanket. In the hush that had fallen, the sudden chiming of the cathedral bell could be heard. Roberts spoke his thoughts aloud. "The town must be feeling safe at last."

At that moment the eastern battery telephone began buzzing again. As Roberts moved to answer it, Etienne ducked into the hut. Panting hard, the small Frenchman was grinning

like a delighted gnome. "Guess what, *mes amis*. The whole
town is coming up the hill."

With their wits dulled by pain and fatigue, men gazed at
him uncomprehendingly. Jean Pierre let out a grow. "What
the hell are you talking about, Baba?"

"I'm talking about the townspeople. They are coming up
the hill. In their hundreds."

Roberts lowered the telephone. "It's true! The battery con-
firms it. They believe they're coming for us."

Magda, the first to understand, lifted her drawn face to
Beccione. "Of course! Why did none of us think of this before?"

Forgetting their watch at the windows, men ran towards
the entrance. Supported by Magda and followed by other
wounded men, Beccione managed to reach the ledge where
he and the girl had spent the previous night.

The sight brought a gasp from them both. Although the
valley was filled with Allied armor and infantry, the hillside
below was alive with civilians. There were tradesmen still in
their aprons, black-shawled women, apprentices, women
pushing carriages, bent old men with sticks, and hordes of
shouting, cheering children. At their head in a horse and cart,
resplendent in his chains of office, was the portly figure of the
mayor.

The sight was bringing tears to Magda's eyes. "At least,
thank God, they appreciate what Kessler has done for them.
Last night I did not think they would." Then she turned to
Beccione. "There is still one thing I do not understand. You
once told me that Kessler killed either with fanaticism or
with remorse. How does that fit in with what Sylvester has
just told us?"

He was watching the crowd surge up the hill. "It's simple
enough. At heart he was a true pacifist, so to kill was blas-
phemy for him. At the same time his experience and intelligence had made him realize that in an imperfect world the
only way to stop a thug is to chop him down. So he put his
head before his heart, even though it twisted the guts out of
him and sometimes drove him to extremes. That's why I believe he was glad to die."

Like a running tide, the crowd made for the hilltop. Halfway along the road a platoon of Allied soldiers were manning
a road block. As the mayor approached, a young officer in
charge ordered him to halt. The mayor hesitated, and a menacing roar rose up from the multitude behind him. The be-

loved Padrone and his men, for whom they had prayed throughout the long night, had saved their children, their lives and their homes. Now it was their turn to save his gallant survivors and no one, not even the Allies who were liberating their country, were going to stand in their way. Puffing out his chest although his face was pale, the mayor ordered his driver forward. A moment later the protesting officer and his men were swept away like a sand bar by an irresistible tide.

Up around the hairpin turns the crowd swept, and streamed through the camp entrance. When they caught sight of the thin line of rebels, a cheer went up that could be heard by the retreating Germans. Men hugged them, women kissed them, children danced and buzzed around them like flies. The emotion that engulfed the hilltop was more intense than the fires that raged there.

Frustrated soldiers from Lazenby's battalions tried to move forward but a solid wall of grim-faced civilians pushed them back. While officers and NCOs argued with one another and waited for orders that never came, carts began rolling into the clearing carrying doctors, medical supplies, food, wine, and most of all civilian clothing. When the townsfolk moved back to Valderosa, they were determined that the rebels should be indistinguishable from themselves.

Magda, wearing a clean dress instead of her blood-stained apron, was helping Beccione into a peasant's smock when Sylvester approached them. It was clear from his expression that he was living out a journalist's dream. "Look at these people! They're prepared to die for you guys. I've never seen anything like this before."

Stretcher after stretcher was being carried out of the command post. Although all were receiving reverent attention, one stretcher could barely be seen for the weeping, black-shawled women who surrounded it. Sylvester's euphoria died as he watched the procession move to an empty cart. "If only Kessler had lived to see this."

Magda shook her head. "No. He died as he wanted to die. He knew that only the dead can influence the living."

The correspondent eyed her with new respect. "I guess you're right at that. From the looks of these people there could soon be a second shrine in that cathedral of theirs."

Magda's mood changed. Until the invasion of the townsfolk the rebels had been resigned to imprisonment and likely execution. Now hope had been resurrected, but with it had come fear that this new vision of freedom might still be snatched away. The girl's unsteady voice betrayed that fear now. "Do you really believe that after all we've done, the Army will let these people spirit us away?"

Sylvester's eyes were on the determined faces of the townsfolk as the array of stretchers began to be loaded carefully into the carts. "What else can they do? They'd have to shoot these people to take you and how can they do that with a dozen reporters watching their every move? When they hear about Kessler's death they'll know you're a spent force. My guess is a report will go to headquarters that you're wiped out and a blind eye will be turned on what happens afterwards."

As he moved away, Magda turned back to Beccione. "Last night I was certain we were going to die. Yet here we are alive and perhaps soon we shall be free." When the GI did not answer, her voice lost its confidence. "What will you do?"

He shrugged. "First find a safe place, I guess. If there is one."

"And then—when the war is over? Will you go back to America?"

"You're looking a long way ahead, aren't you, baby? I don't know. In any case they'll probably make us all stateless persons."

His remark brought a quick glance from her before she turned away. The silence that followed was full of unanswered questions. Sensing it, he waited. When she spoke again her voice was casual, almost indifferent.

"What will you and I do? Stay together for a while?"

"Yeah, why not? I've known worse company."

For a moment she did not move. Then, as he turned towards her, she saw he was smiling. "You bastard," she said.

He stood gazing at her. Her amber hair was clogged with dust and sweat and she stank of cordite fumes. Yet she looked like the most beautiful thing he had ever seen. "You try getting away from me, kid! You just try!"

She murmured something in her own language, kissed him, then put her arm around his waist. On the track that ran behind the command post a cart containing a man and a woman was making towards them. As they waited for it, the laughter of children sounded again and with it came the wild benediction of the bells.

Epilogue

If a reader in his travels should ever stumble across the small mountain town of Valderosa, he will soon discover that Sylvester was right in his prophecy. From the townsfolk he will learn that on every anniversary of the salvation of the town, men, women, and children, led by the clergy, walk in candlelight procession through its narrow streets. And if he enters the Basilica di Santa Rosaria, he will discover a chapel off the eastern apse of more recent construction than the rest of the cathedral.

He will find candles burning inside this chapel no matter what time of the day and night. More than likely a marble sarcophagus, adorned with winged putti, will first meet his eyes. On it is inscribed in Latin the legend: *Sepulchrum inimici qui amicus nobis fuit* (The tomb of an enemy who was our friend). Then, as his eyes lift, they will be held by a beautifully illuminated plaque suspended above the casket. Inscribed on the plaque is this simple homage.

> In memory of Franz Kessler and his followers, who laid down their lives to save this town from the barbarism of war. *Sacrificio salvifiunt peccatores. Requiescant in pace.*

ABOUT THE AUTHOR

FREDERICK E. SMITH joined the R.A.F. in 1939 as a wireless operator/air gunner and commenced service in early 1940, serving in Britain, Africa and finally the Far East. At the end of the war he married and worked for several years in South Africa before returning to England to fulfill his life-long ambition to write. Two years later, his first play was produced and his first novel published. Since then, he has written twenty-four novels, about eighty short stories and two plays. Two novels, *633 Squadron* and *The Devil Doll,* have been made into films and one, *A Killing for the Hawks,* has won the Mark Twain Literary Award.

JOIN THE 633 SQUADRON

The original 633 SQUADRON, written a number of years ago, has become a classic of air literature, translated into many languages. The British author, Frederick E. Smith, had not planned any further books until he was deluged with reader inquiries from all over the world asking for more information about the members of this Yorkshire-based Special Service Unit. He finally was persuaded to continue the series of books about this legendary Mosquire Squadron of the RAF. The results are rousing, action-filled stories which are now being published in the United States for the first time.

633 SQUADRON

The mission was called Vesuvius, and the invasion of Europe depended on it. The squadron's target was a Norwegian fiord where Germans were developing something so secret that even the RAF crews were told nothing about it. But everyone knew this was a dangerous, almost suicidal, mission. Caught between the attacking German aircraft and the grim mountain walls, the 633 Squadron plunged into the howling valley of death.

633 SQUADRON: OPERATION RHINE MAIDEN

Under the young, brilliant, new Commander Ian Moore, the squadron flew a mission to thwart the new German anti-aircraft rocket which posed the most deadly threat to Allied invasion plans. The squadron had to come in on a daylight bombing run to wipe out the rocket factory and strike an underground target buried deep in a Bavarian valley.

633 SQUADRON: OPERATION CRUCIBLE

Autumn 1943. To restore world confidence in the RAF, which had been blamed by a British correspondent for heavy U.S. losses over Europe, the RAF and the 8th Air Force top brass chose the 633 Squadron to perform their most hazardous mission yet—giving ground support to American troops going in on a daring Dieppe-style landing against totally unforseen odds.

633 SQUADRON: OPERATION VALKYRIE

February 1944. The squadron was called on to destroy a large consignment of heavy water being smuggled out of Norway to Germany. To succeed in this mission seemed impossible until Intelligence Officer Frank Adams came up with a bizarre scheme—the only hitch was that it would put the entire squadron in great peril.

633 SQUADRON books are published by Bantam, available wherever paperbacks are sold.